A NIGHTMARE COME TRUE

Through Shadow's eyes, Campbell stared at the magazine, at the surprised face of six-year-old Jesse Hampton, who had gone missing March 12, and whom he had "seen" placed in a grave and destroyed by a shotgun blast in a vision less than a week ago.

His hands were shaking, and he could not make them stop. He wanted to look away from Jesse Hampton's face, but could not relay the command to Shadow. Instead he stared into Jesse's wide eyes and remembered, over and over again, the dark shape towering over the boy, bringing death. And in this memory, the dark shape was himself.

<u>BOOK YOUR PLACE ON OUR WEBSITE</u> AND MAKE THE <u>READING CONNECTION!</u>

We've created a customized website just for our very special readers, where you can get the inside scoop on everything that's going on with Zebra, Pinnacle and Kensington books.

When you come online, you'll have the exciting opportunity to:

- View covers of upcoming books
- Read sample chapters
- Learn about our future publishing schedule (listed by publication month *and author*)
- Find out when your favorite authors will be visiting a city near you
- Search for and order backlist books from our online catalog
- Check out author bios and background information
- Send e-mail to your favorite authors
- Meet the Kensington staff online
- Join us in weekly chats with authors, readers and other guests
- Get writing guidelines
- AND MUCH MORE!

Visit our website at
http://www.pinnaclebooks.com

JACK ELLIS

SEEING EYE

PINNACLE BOOKS
Kensington Publishing Corp.

http://www.pinnaclebooks.com

PINNACLE BOOKS are published by

Kensington Publishing Corp.
850 Third Avenue
New York, NY 10022

First Printing: September, 1995
First Pinnacle Printing: September, 2000
10 9 8 7 6 5 4 3 2

Printed in the United States of America

ONE

Campbell reached for the alarm and calmly turned it off. It was 7:00 A.M., Monday, June 21st. He knew it was 7:00 because his internal clock had woken him five minutes before the alarm. Welcome to another day of night.

He had chosen his clothes the evening before, folding them neatly on the chair by the door. Six months ago he had identified all his clothes with crude, braille-like tags. This morning he chose beige cotton pants and a blue denim shirt. A line of six dots represented the pants, two lines of two dots represented the shirt. Claire had organized the tagging and had spent days helping him memorize the numbers. It was the one truly constructive thing he had done since the accident.

The coding of the clothes was one of a number of simple, efficient grooming methods he had adopted. He kept his hair cut very short; a single sweep with a brush did the job for the day. He kept the toothpaste tube in the same cup with the toothbrush, never the twain to be separated. He owned forty pairs of identical socks, any one a perfect match with any other. If nothing else, blindness had increased his store of common sense.

In the kitchen he poured himself a bowl of Kellog's Corn Flakes and a glass of grapefruit juice. These were simple foods, but most importantly, they required no preparation. He ate sitting at the kitchen table, facing the window. By the heat on his face he knew the morning was sunny. The crazy thing was, the small muscles around his orbital cavities were tensed, trying to narrow his eyes, as if they were unaware that there was nothing there to protect. Old habits.

After eating, he carried his dishes to the sink and ran them under warm water, dried them with the towel hanging over the dish-rack, then put them back in the cupboard. He had long ago simplified the layout of his furniture, discarding a lot of it, opening unobstructed lines of passage between doors and across rooms. One of the few pleasures that remained to him was the fantasy that other people might think, if they did not draw too close to him, that he could see. He often imagined the postman at the bottom of the drive, or a jogger passing on the trails, or even one of his curious neighbors, looking up at the house, through the windows, seeing him as he could never see them. He would be walking purposefully between rooms, head angled as if watching television, moving without hesitation, and they would think, *I thought that guy was supposed to be blind.*

He crossed the kitchen to the hallway. He counted the six long strides and came to a stop as his right hand thumped against the hallway wall. Too fast. He stepped back, touched the wall, and walked into the living room. He sat in the chair by the phone table, then rewound the answering machine. As the messages played, he leaned back as if he were staring at the ceiling. One of the other survival mechanisms he'd developed was to stop his headlong rush to answer the phone whenever it rang. He'd bumped and scraped himself too many times in the early days, and most of it for sales calls. Now, he played his messages every morning, and every few hours thereafter, and returned only those calls that required him to. Those had become fewer and fewer as the months passed.

There was only one message.

"Cam, it's Claire. Just a reminder that I'm coming out tomorrow morning. I'm bringing Russell to meet you. See you then."

He'd forgotten about that. Though she hadn't spoken it, he could hear the admonishment in his sister's voice: *Please don't embarrass me, please don't offend Russell, please don't be your usual self.*

He rewound the tape and turned the answering machine back on. He did not want to see Claire today, did not want to meet her lover, did not want to hear the pity in her voice, nor the anger. With every visit he ended up hating her a little bit more. She was inept at hiding her feelings, or perhaps he had simply become good at detecting them in her voice, in her silences. Whatever it was, he hated to be near her now. Every visit was like a judgment, condemning him. It was as if, even in blindness, she expected him to excel, to succeed. And how easy that had been only a year ago! God, the pleasure he had taken in her pride of him! Now, all he could hear in her voice was disappointment.

If she found him here, waiting for her, her suspicions that he was wasting away, wallowing in self-pity, would be confirmed. He could almost hear her voice now. *You're looking well, Cam,* but, meaning all the while, *you're looking as well as can be expected for the poor, pathetic wretch that you are.*

He miscounted the steps to the hallway and banged into the wall. Even blind, stars danced in his head. He breathed deeply, composed himself, crushed his anger.

Let her come looking for him. He would not be here when she arrived.

When Claire and Russell left Minneapolis a line of harmless, fluffy clouds sat on the northern horizon like a herd of grazing sheep, but by the time they'd reached St. Cloud the sky was dark. Claire drove with the driver's side window open, the wind like thunder in her ears, while Russell dozed in the passenger seat. They stopped in St. Cloud for breakfast, and Russell took the wheel after that.

The countryside was green after the spring rains, almost pretty enough to make the thought of summer seem pleasant. Almost. In another month this landscape would seem arid, a place of grim-faced farmers and dust-caked highway workers.

Despite this being the first official day of summer, the temperature was mild. The long, hot days lay ahead, and Claire was not looking forward to them. Since childhood she had preferred spring and autumn. She had never much liked summer with its suffocating heat; she had thought sunbathers fools long before ozone depletion became a topic of conversation, and had, in recent years, come to think of the air-conditioned environments of her home and office as natural. Sun bunnies were going to be extinct soon anyway.

That Campbell had chosen to live in a cabin on a lake that was, for the most part, a summer resort, was beyond her. He, like her, preferred the cool breezes of spring and the bite of autumn. Secluding himself in the cabin at Battle Lake was some sort of punishment. That was so like Cam since the accident. He had abandoned his old life with a vengeance. Sometimes it was hard to believe they were related, or ever had been.

It was 11:30 when they turned off I-94 at Fergus Falls. Russell pulled into a Mobil station to fill up. Claire took the wheel again after that. She drove through the town, feeling almost like a local, knowing the way by heart. And wasn't that a horrible thought! She left Fergus Falls by the State 210 East exit.

"Couldn't he pick a lake closer to civilization?" Russell asked.

"That's the point."

"Does he ever come into town?"

"If I force him."

"What the hell does he do out here, anyway?"

She often asked the same questions, but hearing Russell ask them made her feel defensive of Cam. Russell was whole and healthy. Tall and thin, almost frail, with a shock of dark hair that hung down nearly to his eyes. He *looked* intellectual, almost effeminate. Big, brown eyes. So unlike Cam. The eyes, of course, the biggest difference of all. Russell could still see. What right had he to question Cam's life?

"What would he do in Minneapolis?"

"He'd be closer to things."

"What things? He's got no friends but me. Everything there would only remind him of what he lost."

"Hey, I didn't mean anything. I'm sorry."

Claire inhaled deeply. "Me, too."

"It must be difficult for him, getting by out here."

"A woman cleans for him once a week and picks up some groceries. His neighbors keep an eye on him for me."

"He must be thrilled about that."

"He doesn't know."

They drove on in silence, the road twisting through the rolling hill country like a drunkard's straight line. When the trees thinned they could see small farms, their fields rising and falling with the hills. How did they cultivate fields like that, Claire wondered. What did they grow there? Cam had told her that the main crop in the area was potatoes, but some of the fields seemed to be sown with taller plants, some with flowers.

As they drove up a low grade the earth seemed to peal away to reveal a dark, metallic core. The lake. The view was breathtaking, but all she could think was, *Cam has never seen this.*

They passed the turnoff for Battle Lake, and Russell twisted his head in surprise. The town was a main strip with a few stores, a gas station, and a small motel.

"You mean to tell me he doesn't even live in the town?"

"On the lake."

"Man!"

"He's going to be difficult," Claire said suddenly.

"That will change when he hears what I have to say."

"Don't count on it. You don't know Cam. He'll look on the dark side. Just be prepared. It may take awhile, but I know he'll come around. Even if it's not today. Okay?"

"I think you're underestimating your brother. Nobody in his right mind would pass up this offer."

"Who said he was in his right mind? Sometimes I don't even know him myself."

"We'll see."

* * *

Campbell heard the car pull in behind the cabin, and swore softly under his breath. The throaty rattle of the muffler and the squeak of the brakes told him it was Claire's Camaro.

The doctors had told him that his other senses would not become more sensitive because of the loss of his sight, but sometimes he wondered. It had been a year since the accident, a year since he'd seen anything. Probably, he was simply paying more attention to what he'd always felt, smelled, and heard.

It was so pathetic, so typically *blind,* for nature to try to compensate. He hated it, because it was just one more indication of his loss. If he'd still had his sight, he wouldn't *need* to listen so carefully.

He angled his head so that the lake breeze blew into his face. He could hear it rushing across the water, the world sighing. He pictured the water rippling, tree branches swaying, his hair stirring. That was another thing he'd become very good at: picturing the real world inside his head, an image to match the information his other senses were giving him. That was the curse of having once been sighted: you knew exactly what you were missing, and were able, in a distorted, perverted way, to mimic the sensation. He wondered, not for the first time, if it would have been better never to have seen at all. What kind of representation of physical reality would his other senses then produce? Certainly not a pathetic imitation of sight. It would be something else, he imagined. A world of sound and smell and touch, a *whole* world, not tainted by the knowledge of the loss of a great part of it.

"I thought we'd find you down here."

Campbell started, shocked by the proximity of the voice. He had been so immersed in his own thoughts that he hadn't paid attention to the sound of Claire's approach. She came to his right side and kissed his cheek. She hadn't even gone inside to find him. She had *expected* him to be down here, as if he came down here all the time.

"Is it that time already?"

"I brought someone for you to meet."

"Hello, Campbell. My name is Russell Graham."

"I told you about Russell."

A warm hand picked up his and shook it, but he did not shake back. "Did you?"

"I told you a *few* times."

"Bad memory, I guess."

"It's nice to finally meet you. Claire has told me a lot about you."

"Did she tell you I was the perfect big brother?"

"Once or twice."

"What do you want?"

There was a pause, and he knew that Russell was looking at Claire for guidance.

"I've got a proposition for you. Mind if we go back up to the cabin?"

"I'm fine here."

Another silence. "I don't pity you, if that's what you're thinking."

"I'm not thinking anything."

"I don't know what Claire told you about me, so I'll take it from the top. I work for Miriam Technologies. Most of our work deals with computer imaging systems, primarily for law enforcement agencies and the military, but we do a lot of basic research and development."

"Never heard of you."

"Cam, please!"

"Over the past three years we've been looking closely at the human optic nerve and visual cortex. One of our projects has involved the linking of the optic nerve with remote sensing devices."

"Eye transplants?"

"That can't be done. Not yet, anyway. And probably not soon enough to make any difference to you. Besides, your optic nerves were severely damaged."

"Claire likes to talk."

"She showed me your records."

"Thanks for respecting my privacy."

Another pause, and this time Russell spoke to Claire. "Let me talk to him alone. Go up to the car."

He listened to Claire climbing the shallow, sandy embankment to the trail.

"You're hard on her."

"I'm hard on everybody."

"She said you had become bitter and depressed."

"Maybe you should go."

"Maybe I shouldn't. I'm going to say what I came to say. Unlike Claire, I don't much care if I hurt your feelings."

Campbell turned his head so that the breeze was again blowing directly into his face. A futile gesture. He knew by the tone of Russell's voice that nothing would deter him.

"I'm in a position to offer you the opportunity to participate in research that might prove beneficial."

"To whom? Me, or you?"

"We've developed a surgical procedure with the potential to restore your sight."

Campbell forced his breathing to remain normal, despite the pounding of his heart.

"Short of guinea pigs?"

"We've performed this procedure five times already, with varying degrees of success. May I tell you something about it?"

"Do I have a choice?"

Russell laughed. "You have no eyes, Cam, and severely damaged optic nerves. There is no surgical technique or existing technology that will ever allow you to see again. There is, however, a way by which we can allow you to see through other eyes."

"Whose?"

"A dog's eyes. Don't laugh. Guide dogs are old hat. We've simply updated the technology. We can link your visual cortex directly to the optic nerves of the dog. The dog will see for you."

"Claire never said you wrote science fiction."

"I told you, we've got five successful subjects so far."

"It's illegal to experiment on humans."

"Clinical trials with human volunteers are an accepted part of medical research. I'm asking you to volunteer."

"There must be thousands of blind guinea pigs who would jump at the chance. Why me?"

"You're Claire's brother."

"And that affords me special status?"

"It does in my book. Does that surprise you? I'm giving you a once-in-a-lifetime opportunity. Claire's your ticket. Take advantage."

"I'm not interested."

"I know you can't help being a burden on Claire. I know you didn't ask to be blinded. I know you probably weren't always this bone-headed. But I'm giving you a chance to change all that."

"Leave me alone."

"Take a week to think about it."

"Are you deaf? Go away!"

"Nice to meet you, Cam."

He listened to Russell retreat up the embankment. Then he heard Claire's light-footed approach.

"It was a four-hour drive out here. You could have at least listened to him."

"I did listen. It's four hours back. Go now and you'll be home before dark."

"Cam . . ."

"I'm not a guinea pig. I wouldn't be good at it. And I hate dogs. Did he tell you about the dogs?"

For a full minute there was silence. He couldn't hear her, but he guessed she was crying. She had become expert at keeping that particular noise from him. When she spoke again, her voice was calm.

"It might rain. Let me take you back up to the cabin."

"You've been the dutiful sister. Thanks for the visit. Now, leave me alone."

This time, she did cry. One sob, quickly stifled. He heard her footsteps receding. Then voices, muffled, talking urgently, angrily. When the Camaro roared to life, he started, unprepared. Claire didn't usually take him at his word. He had half-expected she would wait in the cabin for him. Russell's influence?

Now he was alone. The wind blew hard. He sat with his hands clasped, face turned to the lake. He had long ago stopped hoping for the miracle that might open the darkness around him to reveal a vista of light.

TWO

When Hope got back from Fergus Falls the sky was dark, clouds billowing in from the northwest like smoke from a forest fire. The young German Shepherd bitch in the back cage of the wagon seemed to sense the approaching storm, and lay whining with her head on her fat paws. Her name was Jill, one of the stupider, if not quite the stupidest, dog's name Hope had ever encountered, and she was to be in Hope's care for the next two weeks, a prospect that now seemed daunting after having walked the dog from her owner's home to the car.

She pulled up behind the cabin, got out of the car, and attached Jill's leash before opening the rear door of the cage. Jill immediately strained to reach the kennel, yanking Hope's arm painfully.

"Hold on!"

She closed the car, and grabbed onto the leash with both hands. Jill weighed at least eighty pounds, all of it muscle and bone. If the dog wanted to go somewhere, the dog was going to go somewhere. She had intended walking the other three dogs, all much smaller than Jill, but the prospect of locking Jill into her kennel now struck her as too intimidating to attempt. Perhaps she could calm the dog by walking her first; let her get a sense of her new surroundings.

She dragged Jill away from the kennel, down toward the path that led to the water. As she came around the front of the cabin she noticed the figure sitting on the beach. After a second or two she recognized her blind neighbor, Campbell Knight. Her

initial curiosity turned to surprise, and then to curiosity again.
In the six months that he had lived here, she had never met him,
had only seen him outside his cabin a handful of times.

What was he doing on the beach on a day like today? The
approaching storm looked ominous. The wind had died down,
but that was merely a lull. She glanced with concern toward the
boat moored at her dock, wondered if she should raise it out of
the water. The dog yanking on the leash decided for her, and
she scurried down the trail after the animal, holding tightly with
both hands.

"Slow down!"

On the beach, Jill squatted, looked up at her, and urinated
with gusto. Afterward she raised herself, wagged her tail, and
brushed against Hope's leg.

Campbell Knight had apparently heard her voice, for his head
turned slightly toward her, then away again. She resisted the
urge to introduce herself. He obviously valued his privacy. If
he'd wanted to meet her, he would have knocked at her door.
Still, that didn't mean she couldn't look at him. As a sport, this
entailed far less risk than looking at sighted men, who could
look back without warning.

Nonchalantly, she walked Jill down to the water so that her
angle for viewing her neighbor was improved. She continued
to watch him as she gently turned the wheel that lifted the dock-
ing platform, raising the boat from the water. He was a young
man, perhaps only a few years older than herself. She guessed
his age at 35. Trim, with arms that looked muscular even from
here. His hair was cut very, very short. Almost a brush cut, like
the trims her father had given her brother. Would anybody cut
their hair like that by choice?

Fool!

He would have no mirrors to look at, no way to judge how
well he groomed himself. Short hair was the perfect solution.
She found herself smiling as she watched him, feeling as if she
understood him a little bit better. He was not looking directly
at her, but seemed to be studying the lake. Could he see anything

at all? She remembered the sister saying something about an explosion, and losing his eyes completely.

How horrible!

She saw, then, the pain etched in his face. He was wearing dark glasses that concealed his eyes. His mouth was a straight line. She knew *that* expression well. It was a holding in of emotion, a protective habit to keep the world at arm's length. She knew the expression because it was one she often wore herself, and for the second time since seeing him her heart went out to him. What suffering he must have gone through!

In sudden empathy with his pain, her eyes closed, and for a handful of seconds she thought, *this is his world, all the time.*

Jill yanked hard on her leash. Hope let go of the leather handle with a yelp of pain, and the dog bolted across the pebble-strewn beach toward Campbell Knight.

"Jill!"

Hope lunged after the dog, swearing softly under her breath. Campbell Knight must have heard Jill's approach, for he turned his head sharply and held out a hand to defend himself. Jill pressed her snout into his hand, tail wagging, and Hope heaved a sigh of relief. It would be just what she needed for a dog in her care to attack a blind man!

Campbell Knight continued to hold out his hand, now waving it to shoo Jill away. But Jill was having none of it, and pranced around his chair like a puppy. As Hope approached, the dog barked playfully.

"I'm sorry! She just got loose. She didn't scare you, did she?"

He turned to the sound of her voice, and she could see herself reflected in his glasses. His expression was a taut, cold mask.

"It didn't scare me. Just take it away."

For a moment she wasn't sure what he was talking about, and when she realized the "it" referred to Jill, she gritted her teeth. She forced the anger down quickly. He was blind, and, no matter what he said, the dog had scared him. He had a right to be angry, and she most certainly did not.

"I'm your neighbor on the east side. With the kennel. Hope Matheson."

He looked out over the lake again. *Look,* she realized, wasn't what he was doing. He *faced* the lake.

"You're Campbell Knight, right? I met your sister a few months ago."

"You know Claire?"

"I don't *know,* her, exactly. She asked me to look out for you and to call her if . . ."

"Well you can stop looking. I'm fine. Just take your dog away."

She realized how stupid she'd been the moment she'd spoken. She had made him feel helpless, dependent, needing of care. The way her mother made her feel, the way she hated to be made to feel. And she had just done it to somebody in a far less enviable position than her own. How often had she seen this man through his cabin windows, stalking back and forth as if he could see. Not because he really was so competent, she now realized, but because he *wanted* others to see him that way, wanted to assuage their need to help him, pity him. Her first instinct was to do exactly what he wanted, to leave him alone before she made another blunder and hurt him even more deeply, but her second, more thoughtful urge, restrained her.

"I'm sorry. I shouldn't have said anything. I should tell you that it's going to rain any minute now. Probably pretty hard. Let me give you a hand getting back up to your cabin."

"No."

Don't say another word, she thought. You're only making it worse. She tugged Jill's leash, pulling the dog away from him.

"I'm sorry for disturbing you. Goodbye."

He turned his face to her, it was full of a pain that she could partly understand, and she walked quickly away, pulling Jill after her. Her heart was pounding when she got Jill up the embankment, not just from the exertion, but from the sight of Campbell Knight's face. She had seen in the tautness of his jaw, in the compressed line of his mouth, the same pain and loneliness that she herself fought. Not *exactly* the same kind. His was deeper than her own. His was a near-physical pain, and his loneliness could never be breached the way that hers sometimes could, because he was trapped inside himself, cut off forever from the outside world.

It made her want to cry for him. But she tugged, instead, on Jill's leash, and pulled the dog into the trails that meandered behind her cabin, feeling on some strange level that she had met, for the first time in her life, a kindred spirit, and had somehow, horribly, made him her enemy.

When the first drops of rain splattered against Campbell's cheeks, he stood. The wind suddenly picked up, blasting him with a gust that sounded like a freight train speeding by only inches away. He had felt the storm coming since early afternoon, had felt the temperature quickly dropping, the wind picking up, the sound of the lake changing from smooth lapping to angry chopping, but he had remained seated, waiting, the thought of returning to the empty cabin too depressing to contemplate.

Why had Claire taken him so literally? She knew how angry he got, how quickly he could say things he did not really mean. She should have stayed, even if she sent Russell away.

Another gust of wind shook him. More rain spattered his face, and this time did not immediately let up. He wondered if he should have let Hope Matheson help him. But the dog had frightened him, and he had not been thinking clearly. He had heard the animal rushing toward him over the beach, and the only image his mind had been able to conjure was of a huge wolf, lunging to tear out his throat. He had held out his hand to ward off the attack, and instead had felt the dog's snuffling nose in his palm. By then, he'd been too angry, too flustered to be reasonable.

He should have been more civil.

Or perhaps not. Hope Matheson was merely Claire's spy, wasn't she? She'd said so herself.

Claire, the next time I see you, I'm going to . . .

He inhaled deeply, cutting off the thought, and calmed himself. Sometimes he wondered if the only way emotions could escape the mind were through the eyes, because since he'd lost his he'd felt at the mercy of forces that remained bottled inside him and gained strength until they had the power to bring him to his knees. Perhaps eyes weren't simply the windows to the soul, perhaps they were the only door out of it!

Thunder crashed very close by and he gasped for breath, shocked at the proximity of the blast. If he'd been able to see, the lightning would have terrified him. He'd never been on very good terms with nature. Time to go. Time to compose himself and take control. He was not helpless, no matter what Claire or Hope Matheson thought.

He braced himself against the wind, and turned around. He picked up the lawn chair, folded it, and began to walk toward the embankment. He had taken six steps to get down here, and he took six now. On the seventh step, he felt the first of the flat stones that led up to the trail. Holding the chair tightly, he climbed.

Thunder crashed again and rain lashed down, but he kept himself upright. Nine more steps to take him across the grassy knoll to the main trail. Nine steps, and everything would be fine. The wind howled like a mad dog, and he felt its teeth on the back of his neck. The rain drops were so large they stung his shoulders through his thin shirt. He was immediately soaked to the skin.

What had she said? *If you like, I'll give you a hand getting back to your cabin.* Had he actually refused her?

He was suddenly angry at himself, at his pride, at his stupidity. This was dangerous.

When the hail started, he had taken his first step on the gravel path. He heard it first, sharp crackling in the trees. When the first ball of ice struck him on the shoulder he cried out. The second struck him directly on top of the head, a blow so sharp it made him suddenly dizzy with pain, then the ice chunks were falling in numbers too great to count. They crashed into him, tearing at his face, his shoulders, his arms.

Walk, he thought. Walk!

He knew before he had finished taking that first step that something was wrong. His right heel slid away from him, and suddenly he was careening forward, off-balance. He crashed heavily on his back with a loud cry.

A mud puddle!

For a handful of seconds hail battered his face. He heard one of the lenses in his glasses shatter. He rolled over so that the ice was slamming into his back. The pain was so intense he could hardly breathe. With one hand he found one of the ice balls on the ground. It was about an inch in diameter, rough edged, cold and dry.

He tried to stand, but he was wobbly on his feet. It took him three tries to find his footing, and then, with hands held out, he stumbled on. Eighty-six steps. Eighty-six steps through tree cover, on gravel, to the back porch of the cabin. Eighty-six steps.

He counted each one. Three . . . five . . . fourteen . . . thirty . . . thirty-six . . . fifty-five . . . sixty-eight . . . seventy-four . . .

The hail stopped at seventy-eight and a hush descended. For a few seconds, even the rain and the wind fell away. To Campbell, it felt as if he'd been spun around in a merry-go-round and suddenly let off.

How far had he counted? Seventy-four.

Seventy-five . . . seventy-six . . .

The rain started again, and from behind him he heard the approach of the wind, a low moan slowly rising, pushing at him.

Eighty . . . eighty-three . . .

The trees around him hissed and rustled and water fell in torrents, fresh rain as well as whatever the trees had captured. It was like being inside a waterfall.

Eighty-four . . . eighty-five . . . eighty-six . . .

Campbell stopped, held out his arms. He should be there. His hands found the smooth, slippery trunk of a tree. There were no trees next to the cabin. No trees within fifteen paces of the cabin. Had he miscounted? The sound of the rain and the wind filled his head, making it impossible to think.

He kneeled and felt for the gravel path, but found only mud and grass, wet and slippery between his searching fingers. Somewhere in the last eighty-six steps he had left the trail. He tried to picture his surroundings, but the input from his senses, the howling wind, the pattering rain, his own dizziness, produced an image inside his head that nearly made him sick: a swirling vortex of green and black.

Campbell sat down and crawled forward until he found another tree, then turned so that his back was pressed to the bark. Thunder crashed very close, and his ears rang. Rain lashed his face, each drop feeling like a tear.

The boy sat in the corner of the cage and did not move, did not lift his head, did not even make a sound as Eleanor entered the cellar and turned her flashlight on him. His name was Jesse Hampton, he was six years old if you could trust the news reports, and he had been her one true love for almost a month now.

Max padded down the stairs behind her, tail wagging, and sat at the side of the cage.

"He looks so sad, doesn't he, Max? What's wrong, little Jesse?"

When she addressed him, the boy lifted his face from his knees to look at her. His eyes were swollen from crying, his mouth turned down in a grimace.

"Boys who don't act nicely, don't get their dinners," she said.

"I want to go home."

"Now, now. We've talked about this."

He lowered his face again, refusing to look at her, and she felt a stab of anger at him. The little monkey! After all she had done for him! Feeding him and taking care of him all this time!

She opened the cage and brought the tray of food in with her. Jesse looked up again, his eyes frightened now.

"Are you going to eat this food, or should I give it to Max?"

Be reasonable. That always did the trick. Don't shout, don't get angry.

But he did not lift his head, did not respond.

"Oh, Jesse."

She swung the flashlight as hard as she could, because there was no point in inflicting punishment unless it was *real* punishment with *real* pain, and it slammed into the top of his head with a thud that reminded her of barrels full of diesel fuel dropping from a truck. Jesse cried out, lifted his hands to cover his head. In the beam of the flashlight she saw the blood seeping out from his nest of blond hair between his fingers.

She swung again, bringing the flashlight down on his fingers, feeling an almost physical satisfaction at the sound of crunching bone. This time, Jesse Hampton screamed at the top of his lungs.

"Oh, my poor, poor Jesse."

Eleanor fell to her knees beside the weeping boy. She held out her arms without touching him, and he looked up at her through teary eyes. He was shaking, blubbering.

"I'm so sorry, Jesse. I didn't want to hurt you, but you were being a bad, bad boy. I love you, Jesse. I love you with all my heart. Come here."

Even in his pain and confusion, he knew when comfort was offered, and he needed it badly. He threw himself into her arms and she cradled him, pressing his hot, wet face to her neck. He continued to sob, gripping her like a little animal, small hands tugging at her shirt, holding her, tears pouring into the creases of her flesh. The tears of love, of need.

She held him, stroked him, caring not even a little bit that her fingers became sticky with his blood. This was love.

Behind her, Max whined. She turned to look at him. He stared at her through the bars of the cage, his eyes golden disks. Love there, too, she realized. Love for her. It almost made her weep.

It was good, so good, to be loved.

THREE

Campbell was not sure how long he had sat there on the soggy ground with his back pressed into the slick trunk of the tree, but he knew that the storm drew closer, that the rain fell harder, that the wind howled like a ghoul in a graveyard. Of mercies, there were but one; the hail had stopped. Every part of his body, even the backs of his hands, stung and throbbed. He remembered how as a small boy he'd once accompanied his mother to a dollar day sale at some giant department store, had waited in the crowd with her until opening time, had rushed with her through the doors like water through a burst dam, and had immediately tripped over his own feet. For a terrifying five seconds he'd been swept away by the rush of bodies, pummelled by knees and shins and shoes, until finally he was yanked to his feet by his mother who dragged him onward without a nod of concern. He felt like that now. Trampled. Then, as now, he was not sure if the pain was physical, or merely injured pride.

Nature had always terrified him; as a boy he'd cowered in his room as thunderstorms approached, covered his ears as they unleashed their fury. It was so huge, so impersonal, nature. It cared nothing for the people who lived within its domain, just marched on. To be trapped outside in this storm, blind, was worse than any nightmare he'd entertained as a boy. The wind was huge and angry, the rain never ending. God *had* promised never to flood the earth again, hadn't he? That was the covenant, wasn't it? Funny how you could start taking religion seriously at times like this.

Most people, Campbell realized, entertained such bleak possibilities at around 3:00 in the morning, while alone in bed, staring into the darkness of their bedrooms. Life seemed more **fantastic at times** like that; Hell seemed nearer. But his own darkness was never ending. There was no dawn coming to ease his fears, no comforting daylight to make his night terrors seem silly. Since the accident, he'd been trapped in a world of perpetual darkness, where night was day, day was night, and his terrors had free reign. Now, in this storm, with trees swaying and rustling around him like restless giants, he was at the mercy of his imagination.

He drew his knees up to his chest, wrapped his arms around his shins, and pressed his face into his thighs. Most sighted people could close their eyes at moments of terror, shutting out the world, entering an inner world where they could not be harmed. But that option was closed to him. He *lived* in that inner world now, his blindness had forced him to make it *his* world, his reality. To where could he escape? Was there an inner world *beyond* this world of darkness? If so, he had yet to find it, could not imagine what the doorway would be like. Death, perhaps.

A sudden gust of wind sent a spray of cold water into his face and he gasped. The storm was not abating. He was trapped outside, and he did not know where he was. Somewhere close to the cabin. He had walked only a short distance, he knew that. In all likelihood the cabin was only a few paces away; perhaps he'd only miscounted five or six steps, or perhaps he'd left the trail only a yard from the porch. He was close to home. That was what was so horrible about blindness. You could be within arm's reach of your destination and you might as well be a thousand miles away.

For some strange reason he found himself trying to remember the last thing he had ever seen. This was a game he played with himself on occasion, a game he could never win, because he could not remember. The image, whatever it was, had been stolen from him as surely as his sight. Logic told him it must have been the battery, just before it exploded. Perhaps he had been looking at it the moment the casing had shattered. Perhaps he'd even registered the approach of the shrapnel-like fragments that had smashed into his face. It must have been something like that, but he could not remember, could only imagine. He could not even recall the reason he'd been in the shop to begin with. Something silly, probably. He should not have been there.

What he did remember, and remembered clearly, were the voices afterward, the sensation of bodies bending over him, of faces pressing close, of being unable to see them.

"Mr. Knight, you've suffered extreme trauma to both eyes."

"Mr. Knight, I don't think I'm making myself clear. I'm afraid you'll never see again."

"Mr. Knight, you can still live a productive life."

"Mr. Knight, you'll just have to accept what has happened."

And after that, darkness as he had never known it, not only for his eyes, but in his soul as well, deep, impenetrable. There had been a month there, at the beginning, where he had seriously considered suicide. *That* darkness, he had reasoned, could be no worse than this. But he remembered little of that month. Just liquid blackness, a sea of it, and him tossed endlessly like driftwood between shores of confusion and fear. And Claire, of course, at his side every day, talking to him, holding him, urging him to embrace life again. There had been times, in that month, when he hated her more than he hated any other person.

His reverie was interrupted by the sound of approach, and Campbell stiffened, lifting his face from his knees.

"I should never have left you down there!"

It was Hope Matheson. Even as her voice registered, the wet, cold nose of a dog pressed into Campbell's face.

"Stop it, Jill! Are you all right? I saw your chair on the trail. You took the wrong turn."

"Where am I?"

"You're almost at the road, between the cabins. Let me help you up."

He was surprised at the strength of the arm that lifted him, but he used his legs to push himself to his feet. Then one of her arms was around his back, half supporting him, half guiding him. He felt the flush of shame creep into his face, but surely she could not see it through the rain.

"I knew that storm was coming in. You should have let me help you."

"Just take me back to the trail. I can manage."

She grunted, and then she was holding his hand, guiding him. He counted the steps as they moved.

"Here's the trail, but you couldn't have left it here. You must have taken the side trail down by the beach."

"I fell. Just point me toward the cabin."

"Don't be ridiculous. I'm not going to leave you out here again."

"How far is the cabin?"

"Only a few yards. Come on."

"I said . . ."

"Just shut up. Now come *on*."

She almost yanked him off his feet as she tugged him forward, and he felt like a little boy, trampled underfoot, ashamed and frightened. He was so angry he forgot to count the steps. They had walked into the wind for a short way, but now it was at their backs. His sense of direction was totally fouled. When she slowed him, and then helped him up onto the first step of the deck, he was utterly surprised.

"Here we are. Just wait here."

"I don't need any more help."

She let go of his arm, and for one terrifying second he thought he was going to fall down. He heard the latch being worked, the door opening. Then she was holding his arm again, pulling him forward. When they were inside, she closed the door behind her.

"Your dog . . ."

"I tied her up on your porch. That's okay, isn't it? If you like, I could help you get out of those things and . . ."

"Please, I'm fine. Thank you. Just leave me alone."

He heard shuffling feet, and then her hand on his arm again, pulling him forward. Before he could resist she had turned him around and pushed him backward a step.

"Sit."

The seat creaked beneath him as he sank into it.

"You're sitting in a chair by the phone. Do you know where that is?"

"Yes. You've done enough, thank you."

"Get your bearings before you move again."

He took a deep breath. "Just leave me alone."

"All right."

"Go and phone my sister if it will make you feel better."

"Do you want me to?"

"Can I stop you? You're her hired gun, aren't you?"

He heard footsteps, the door opening, wind keening. Then her voice, sounding almost hurt. "You know, it's not a crime to need help."

Before he could answer, the door had closed. He heard more footsteps on the porch, then the deck. Then, silence.

Shivering, cold, ashamed, he covered his face with his hands. It seemed like a long time before he felt composed enough to reach for the phone.

Claire drove with both hands on the wheel. Battle Lake was still twenty minutes away. This time, the sky was completely clear, the sun blazing down. The interstate shimmered with rising heat. The kind of day she hated with a passion.

Campbell's call had come as a complete surprise, but Russell, when she told him about it, acted as if he'd expected it from the start. Campbell had sounded small and frightened, and it had made her want to be with him, to hold him and to protect him. It had reminded her of the first days following the accident. There had been a hopelessness in his voice over the phone, a deep pain, fear. Something had happened.

"What changed your mind?" she had asked, knowing she should not push him, but curious.

"I just want to find out more about what your mad scientist boyfriend is up to."

Still, she had pressed some more, and he had broken a little. The woman next door, he admitted, had helped him back to his cabin after Claire and Russell had gone. That surprised her. Campbell was not the type to accept help, especially for a little thing like getting back to the cabin.

What was the woman's name who lived next door? Claire vaguely remembered her. She'd talked to her when Cam first moved in. Charity. No, one of those three. Charity, Faith . . . Hope. Hope, that was it. Hope Matheson. The dog lady. That had to be whom Campbell was talking about. On the other side was a retired Air Force man who lived alone, and who spent his days fishing and drinking beer.

She wondered, now, if Cam had been hiding something. As she passed through Fergus Falls, and drove along the state highway to Battle Lake, she became convinced of it. Something had happened to Campbell, something traumatic. Nothing else could explain how he had sounded, how reluctant he had been to talk about it.

At the cabin, all her fears were confirmed. The place was a disaster. It looked, in fact, as if it had been tossed by a burglar in a very great hurry. Campbell was sitting in the living room, suitcase between his legs.

"Let's go," he said.

"What happened here? Hasn't Mrs. MacIntosh been in to clean?"

"I told her to go to hell."

"Jesus, Cam, it's like a hurricane blew through here!"

"Let's just go."

In the kitchen, she found dishes piled in the sink, food left out on the counter. This was not like Cam at all. How had he managed to survive in this mess for even a single day?

She led him out to the car, got him seated and strapped in, then told him to sit still.

"Where are you going?"

"I'll be right back."

"She phoned you, didn't she?"

"Nobody phoned me but you."

"Go and thank her for me," he said bitterly.

Before he could protest further she walked away, ignoring his calls for her attention. Hope Matheson's cabin was a short walk away along an open, sunny trail. As Claire approached, she heard the muffled barking of dogs. When she left the trail she saw a figure by a long, low cement shed, carrying a hose. The woman turned, saw her, and dropped the hose.

Claire approached, smiling. "Hi! I don't know if you remember me. I'm Claire Knight, Campbell's sister?"

Hope Matheson brushed the front of her overalls with her hands, then held one out to Claire. "I remember."

Claire shook the offered hand, and was surprised at the strength in the other woman's grip. Her own pale fingers, tipped with manicured nails, looked alien in Hope Matheson's tanned, strong hand.

"Campbell said you helped him up to the cabin earlier in the week."

Hope looked surprised. "He told you?"

"Well, not exactly. Can we talk for a minute?"

"Oh, sure. Come on in. I was about to break for lunch."

Inside, while Hope washed her hands in the kitchen, Claire sat in the living room. This cabin, like Campbell's, was small, austere. The kitchen led directly into the living room, and the back section was divided into two bedrooms with a bathroom between. Unlike Campbell's cabin, Hope Matheson had decorated hers to meet the needs of a normal human being. There were paintings on the walls, blown-up photographs of dogs, a collection of decorative spoons in a wooden rack shaped like a thistle. The furniture was plain, but serviceable. It was certainly not the kind of home she could have lived in herself, but it seemed right for Hope Matheson.

Hope returned to the living room and sat in the sofa across from Claire. The last time Claire had met her, she had guessed Hope's age in the late thirties, but now she estimated slightly lower. Early thirties. Perhaps even her own age. Sun and outdoor work, or perhaps even worry, had given her face some lines, but she was not unattractive. Her hair was long and blonde, tied in a braided ponytail, Claire guessed simply to keep it out of harm's way. Her eyes were dark blue, like a clear sky at night, alert.

"Campbell thought you might have phoned me," Claire said carefully.

Hope Matheson blushed, and the color that entered her cheeks took another three years off her age. "Did he?"

Claire laughed softly. "Actually, he was *worried* that you might have."

"He virtually ordered me not to."

"And you didn't."

"I respected his wishes."

"He didn't tell me much. Only that you helped him back to his cabin."

Claire could see that she had put the other woman in a dilemma. Campbell had obviously impressed upon her that he did not want his troubles shared. Finally, Hope shrugged.

"It was raining. He needed help with his chair. I helped."

"That's it?"

"He can tell you more, if he wants to."

It took Claire a few seconds to realize what she was seeing in Hope Matheson, and when she did she fought to control her shock. This woman *liked* Campbell. Perhaps even *more* than liked. And suddenly the lines on her face took on a completely new meaning to Claire. Not worry, not sun, not hard outdoor work, but pain. Pain, she guessed, that might even be on a level with Campbell's.

Why do *you* live out here, she wondered. What is it that has made you isolate yourself from the world?

"Sometimes Campbell can be very difficult," Claire said.

Hope Matheson laughed at that. "That's putting it mildly."

"I wish you could have known him before the accident. He was a completely different person."

Hope made no effort to hide her interest. "What was he like?"

"Well, for one thing, he was very active. He owned his own business, you know. A car dealership. He started working there when he was fresh out of college, parking cars on the lot. Moved up to sales a year later, and two years after that he was general manager. When things got rocky for the company, he bought in. Two years later, he was sole owner, and business was booming. He loved what he did, and he was good at it."

"Was he married?"

"He could never find the right kind of woman. Well, I suppose he thought he had. He was engaged when the accident happened, but afterward, she left him."

"That's cruel."

"You can't blame her. Looking after a blind man was probably not what she had in mind for the rest of her life."

"Campbell can look after himself," Hope said.

"I think he felt that he was a great burden to me, and to some of his friends. I think that's why he moved here, to prove to himself that he could be self-sufficient."

"I've never seen his friends out here."

"No," she agreed.

Hope shook her head, and Claire could not tell if it was anger or sadness. "I don't blame him for moving out here. I don't know how I would react if that happened to me."

Claire inhaled deeply. "I hate to ask this, I know it's a great imposition. I'm taking Campbell into the city for a few days. His cabin is a bit of a mess, and he's frightened the regular cleaning lady away, I'm afraid."

"No problem. Do you have a key?"

Claire pulled it from her purse and handed it to the other woman. "I really appreciate this. Campbell will, too."

"I doubt *that,*" Hope said. "What's in the city for him?"

Claire stroked her chin, wondering if she should say more, then shrugged. "Possible surgery. For his eyes."

"Could he see again?"

"Not like you or I, but it is possible."

"That would be wonderful."

"Yes, it would." She stood. "Thanks for everything, Hope. Thanks for what you did for Campbell."

"It was nothing."

"Oh yes, it was," Claire said.

She walked back along the trail, thoughts focused on Hope Matheson. There was something about the other woman that had impressed her deeply, but she was not sure what it was. On the one hand she seemed very much like Cam. Running from something painful, beaten but not cowed. On the other hand she seemed utterly together, in control of her life. Most impressive of all, Hope Matheson had seen something in Campbell that other people had been unable to see since the accident: something good, something worthwhile, something worth liking.

Hope Matheson might be exactly the thing her brother needed. Especially if the surgery proved unfeasible.

As she slid into her seat, Campbell turned to her with an angry glare.

"Did she tell you how much fun she had helping the blind man."

"Grow up, Campbell."

He turned away from her, face to the sun. Claire started the car and pulled out onto the road.

"She's nice," she said.

"She's a pain in the ass. Her *and* her damned dogs."

They lapsed into silence until she turned off the gravel road and onto State 210. The blacktop hummed under the wheels.

"She didn't phone you?" Cam said.

"No, she didn't. I just wanted to thank her for giving you a hand."

"She didn't say anything?"

"She said I should ask you if I wanted to know more."

He made a grunting sound and crossed his arms.

Claire smiled. "She likes you."

"Then she's a bigger fool than I thought."

FOUR

Russell's voice came from Campbell's left. "Campbell, you're on the sixth floor, east wing of the building, in one of our board rooms. It's about fifteen feet square, carpeted, with a round table in the middle of the room, surrounded by six chairs. There are three people in the room with you. Claire, myself, and Doctor Ladeceur."

Campbell was at once grateful and surprised at the information Russell had offered. Grateful, because this shuffle along the corridors and through the doors of the Miriam Technologies building had ruined his sense of direction and place, and now he was able to form a picture in his mind and place himself squarely within it. He felt better in moments. He was surprised because he had been sure they'd only risen three floors in the elevator.

"Mister Knight, I am Nina Ladeceur. It's nice to finally meet you."

The voice had come from Campbell's right, probably two seats away. He turned in that direction and gave a slight, acknowledging nod. He had not missed the meaning of Nina Ladeceur's words, *nice to 'finally' meet you.* They had obviously discussed his participation for some time. It was not as impromptu as he had been led to believe. Claire was wrong; he was more than just a potential candidate for the surgery.

"What has Russell told you about us?"

"He told me about the surgery, the dog. That's about it."

Nina Ladeceur made a sound that might have been a truncated laugh, or a cough. Campbell could smell her perfume; pungent, musky. By her voice, he guessed she was in her late fifties. By her perfume, he guessed she tried to look much younger.

"If you undergo the procedure, you will be the sixth to do so," she said. "Our results have been generally good. The procedure links your visual cortex with the optic nerve, and thus the entire seeing mechanism, of the partner dog. This requires surgical alteration of the dog, as well as the human subject. The technology comes in the linking, of course, in the cortical implants on your end, and the optic nerve bus on the dog's end."

"He explained that already."

Nina Ladeceur continued as if she had not heard him. "Naturally, the quality of vision will not equal what you had before. Dog eyes are different than human eyes. They distinguish little color, and their visual acuity is low, but they detect movement very well, and their ability to see in poor lighting is good. From your point of view, it would be like trading in a large screen color television for a twelve-inch black and white."

"I don't have a television at the moment. Even a twelve-inch black and white would be an improvement."

Again, Russell laughed, and Campbell found himself liking his sister's lover. Nina Ladeceur found nothing to laugh at.

"Naturally, we've made efforts to enhance the quality of the image experienced by the human partner. This, again, is where Miriam Technologies makes its input. On the dog's side, there is no change in perception via the surgery. He experiences vision as he always has experienced vision. On the human side, it's a very different story. It's not simply that your quality of vision will have altered, but the very nature of your perception. Remember, the dog walks beside you, and about four feet lower. It takes some getting used to. Some of our subjects have never been able to adjust."

Campbell said nothing, trying to imagine what it would be like to see the world from four feet lower, and in black and white. But *seeing* was the key word there. Seeing from any perspective, in any degree of quality, would be miraculous. Campbell broke away from his thoughts when he realized that the table was silent. He had the disconcerting notion that the others had left him alone, and that he had been too self-absorbed to notice. He turned his head toward Claire, then toward where he had placed Russell.

Nina Ladeceur spoke again, this time from a point directly behind him. "Do you like dogs, Mister Knight?"

"We get along," he said, and had a sudden flash of Hope Matheson's beast lunging across the beach toward him.

"Then perhaps it is time to make the acquaintance of your prospective partner."

The place was ripe with a hospital's patina of fear, antiseptic, and blood. But this was animal fear, animal blood. He sensed that it was a very large room, cool. He smelled a background of dung and urine, also byproducts of fear. He heard the chirruping of monkeys; a strange wailing that had to be cats; dogs yelping.

"It sounds like a zoo."

"Our research involves many kinds of animals," Nina Ladeceur said.

Russell held his arm, and led him through the large room, into a smaller corridor, and finally through a door that led outside. The sun was warm on his face, but a breeze kept the temperature down. Its touch on his face and arms was welcome.

When they stopped again, Russell released his arm, and Campbell, free for the first time in what felt like hours, swayed like a tall plant. Again, he had the disconcerting impression that the others had deserted him, but this time he did not look around himself. They were here somewhere. He was the main attraction, after all.

"I'm going to put something in your hand," Russell said.

He felt the warmth of Russell's skin, and then the cool hardness of a leather strap.

"That's his harness. He's attached to it. Don't yank too hard."

Campbell kneeled so that the harness handle was directly in front of him, then held out his free hand. A cold snout pressed into his palm, sniffing.

"Hello, boy," he said softly.

The dog moved closer, pushing at the harness. Campbell released it and let the dog come to him, holding out his hands to touch its head and back. It wasn't a large dog, perhaps a labrador. Its back was very broad, muscular, its head almost triangular, bony. The harness was attached to its torso, but seemed to be of a strange sort. If he held it, standing upright the dog would be kept a pace or two behind him. He ran his hand over its head again, fingers stopping when they encountered a hard, cool ridge behind the dog's ear.

"That's the port for the linkup cable," Nina Ladeceur said. "It's not uncomfortable for him. He doesn't even know it's there."

"His name is Shadow," Russell said from behind Campbell. "He's a black lab, three years old. He doesn't bite."

Campbell stood. "Can I take him for a walk?"

More silence, then Nina Ladeceur's voice, speaking softly, so softly that Campbell could not hear the words.

"Sure," Russell said, and again Campbell felt the other man's hands on his arms, turning him. "You're in Shadow's walkway now. It's about fifty feet long, eight feet wide, grassed. There's a chain link fence on either side, and at the end."

Campbell held the harness and began to walk, slowly. The dog kept pace with him, so closely that he hardly felt the weight of the animal on the end of the harness. He did not need to tug, did not need to guide. When he slowed, Shadow slowed. When he walked faster, Shadow walked faster. After twenty paces he stopped, sure he was near the end of the walking area, and turned around. Shadow turned with him.

Campbell kneeled again, pulled the dog toward him, reached out with his hands. The dog's face came close, he could feel its warm breath. He petted its head, its sides, running his hand down its back. When Shadow's tongue lapped at his face he did not pull away.

"So, you want to be my eyes, eh boy? Those are pretty big shoes to fill."

He could hear the dog's tail wagging, swishing through the air. When he stood, Shadow took his place behind him. He started to walk. Shadow followed.

For the first time in a long time, he began to hope.

On Sunday afternoon, after feeding and walking the four dogs in the kennel, Hope drove into Fergus Falls to have dinner with her mother. This was not the usual course of events for Sunday; though they lived fairly close, she and her mother did not get along well, and Hope visited as little as she could. On this day, her mother had called and virtually pleaded with her to come for dinner. She was lonely, she was thinking of Hope's father, she needed somebody to talk to. Hope had reluctantly given in.

Since she'd been sixteen, when her father had died, her mother had tried to control her life. The manipulation had been obvious and crude, but manageable. She'd set up dates for Hope with the sons of her friends, she'd arranged for Hope to teach Sunday school despite Hope's reluctance, had forced her to act in school plays despite her innate shyness. Hope had always known that eventually it would end, and that she would get on with her own life, and so she had put up with it.

But it had not ended. It had only grown worse. When Hope finished high school, and had wanted to attend university to get her veterinary degree, her mother had refused. Her father had set up a fund for both his children, to be used when they reached college age to advance their education, but Hope's arguments had had no effect on her mother. Her decision was final. Animals were not an occupation for a young lady; if Hope wanted to go to university, then she would study religion, or literature, as she herself had done. A woman thus educated could find many pleasing and rewarding occupations in life. The fund had gone unused. And Hope, who had never worked or saved money, had refused to attend the university of her mother's choice.

At nineteen, after one more year of living under her mother's thumb, Hope had found a job with the Humane Society, and immediately moved out. At first, she had rented a small house in Fergus Falls, but two years later she had purchased the cabin on Battle Lake. It was her brother Michael who finally pointed out to her that mother had no right to control the fund that their father had set up. It was in each of their names, and could be used for whatever purpose they liked. To her mother's horror, Hope had used the money to pay off the mortgage on the cabin, and to build the small kennel at the rear of the property. Since then, she had lived frugally, self-sufficiently, depending on neither her mother nor any job to sustain her. The kennel brought in enough to keep her going, and the small amount left from her trust provided an annual stipend that smoothed the rough spots. It was not what she had always dreamed of, but it was not what her mother wanted, and that was enough to make it worthwhile.

When she arrived at her mother's home it was close to 5:00 in the evening. When her mother answered the door she was wearing a summer dress, makeup, high heels. Hope looked at her, confused, while her mother returned the gaze in horror.

"Couldn't you dress up just a little?"

"It's just dinner, isn't it?"

"But I invited someone over."

"Who?"

"Just come in."

"Mother, who did you invite?"

"Just a friend."

"Somebody I know?"

"Does it matter?"

"It matters."

Her mother shook her head, hardly able to control her anger. Her red lips pursed, and her powdered brow furrowed.

"I don't know what to do with you, Hope. I've tried to do so much for you, to steer you on the course to a proper life for a young woman, and all you've done is fight me every step of the way."

"It's Warren, isn't it. You invited Warren."

Her mother lifted her chin. "It's my house, I can invite whomever I choose."

"Oh God, Mother."

"It was silly of you to let him get away from you."

"I didn't . . ." She forced the words back, determined not to get into *that* argument again. "I'm going home."

"Don't you dare! He'll be here any minute. Don't you understand? He's alone again, Hope. He's coming back here. He's available."

"I'm not."

"Don't be ridiculous!"

"I have my own life. I'm happy with it. I certainly don't need him. Especially him."

"You're being vindictive."

"I'm not going to discuss it. I'm going."

"Well, it's too late now! He's here."

Hope turned, horrified, as the pickup truck pulled up in front of the house. Her hands started to shake as Warren climbed out of the truck and walked up to the house, head bent down, hands stuffed into the pockets of casual slacks that looked to have cost around two hundred dollars. His dark hair gleamed. He looked smooth, polished, pampered. He smiled sheepishly as he approached.

"Hello, Mrs. Matheson," and then, much more softly, "Hello, Hope."

"Hope was just saying how much she was looking forward to seeing you again," her mother said.

Hope looked up, furious, but her mother had already turned to go inside the house. Warren looked at her, his brown eyes questioning, mocking. And it *was* mocking, she saw. The line of his mouth, the twinkle in his eyes, the cockiness of his pos-

ture *all* mocked her. He had been sure she would be here, sure
that he would be welcomed.

"You're looking well," she said, trying to make her voice
firm, then followed her mother into the house.

Dinner was the disaster she had expected. She and Warren
were seated across from each other, her mother at the end of
the table. Mother deferred to Warren in everything, according
him the status of Man of the House. He cut the meat, he served
the wine, and his eyes never left Hope. She returned his look
as long as she could, and when that didn't seem to deter him,
she looked down at her plate as she ate.

"It was such a pity about your wife," her mother said. "What
was her name?"

"Gloria," Warren said, still looking at Hope. "Not such a
pity, though. It made me realize that she wasn't right for me.
The kind of woman I need is a special kind of woman. I know
that now."

Her mother smiled, looking directly at Hope. Hope chewed
her meat mechanically, swallowed.

"How long are you here?" her mother asked.

"As long as I want to be," he said. "I run the business now,
you know. Almost, anyway. But it can get along without me for
awhile. I might even make my home out here. There's a lot out
here I like. Home security is big business, you know. I've made
a lot of money."

Hope worked her way through dessert, fielding the questions
that were directed at her as best she could, putting as much ice
into her look as she could muster. She refused the offer of coffee, and stood with a smile as Warren took his first sip.

"I have to go," she said. "The dogs need to be walked."

"Surely you can stay a little longer," her mother said.

"No. Sorry. Enjoy your stay, Warren."

She left the house quickly, but was only halfway down the
path to her station wagon when Warren came after her. He
passed her and leaned on the car, smiling, tongue working at
something in his teeth.

"You really aren't in that big a hurry, are you, Hope?"

"Yes, I am."

"After I came all this way to see you?"

"I'm sorry you wasted your time."

"You can't tell me you're not glad to see me. We had something good together."

She looked at him steadily for a good five seconds, then shook her head. "We had an empty relationship based on a lie," she said calmly.

"Come off it. You know what we had. Your mother says you're still alone. Why be like this?"

When he reached for her, she was so shocked that at first she did not react. His arms swept her up, pulled her toward him, and then his mouth was on hers, hot and tasting of coffee. She let it go on for a few seconds, utterly surprised by something she had not expected. He had been right about one thing. Their physical relationship *had* been good, satisfying anyway, and she had feared that seeing him would rekindle some of the desire she once had felt. Now, as his lips touched hers, she felt only revulsion and anger. It was something she savored, and so she let the kiss go on for a few seconds longer than it should have.

When he pulled away, she could see in his eyes that he understood how she felt. He wiped his mouth and stepped away from the car.

"I'm the only person whose going to look at you like that, Hope. You know that."

She opened the door and turned to him. "If you touch me again, I'll break your neck," she said.

He looked startled, and stepped back. Hope got into the car. As she pulled away, she saw her mother standing in the living room window, shaking her head.

She had just driven out of town on 210, past the Otter Tail Wetlands Conservatory, when the tears came. They filled her eyes, turning the headlights on the road into blazing stars, blinding her. She pulled the car off the road, sending gravel and dust up in a plume.

Blinded by her tears. Blinded, as surely as Campbell Knight had been blinded, she thought.

She waited for her tears to dry, wiped her eyes. She thought of Campbell Knight, bringing his face to mind. For the second time that night, she felt something inside of her that surprised her. This time, it was the very reaction that Warren Daniels had been hoping for.

Heart pounding, she pulled the car back onto the road and continued driving.

FIVE

It was unnerving having Campbell live with her again; it reminded Claire of the first months after the accident, when he had spent all his time in her apartment, seated at the living room window in the mornings while the sun warmed his face, turned to the television in the evenings as if he could see it. There was, however, one big difference. Then, Campbell had slipped into a morass of despair and anger that filled every room with an almost palpable darkness. She had hated coming home in those days; hated sitting with him in the evenings; hated what had happened to him; hated *him* for letting it happen to him. Now, though much of his anger remained, his presence seemed to imbue the apartment with boundless energy and excitement.

He had tried hard, she knew, to remain cynical about the surgery, about Miriam Technologies, about the whole possibility that he might see again, but the sheer wonder of the prospect was too much for him. In the mornings, when she left for work, he was stalking back and forth between the sofa and the wall unit in the living room, hand pressed beneath his chin, a human pinball in constant motion. In the evenings, when she came home he was waiting in the kitchen for her, staring at the door, face lit up as if he were a child and she had brought him some wonderful present.

Everything moved too quickly for Claire. She hadn't realized that Russell and Nina had chosen Campbell as their next subject long before they even met him. After that, it was just rubber stamping. Russell said that Campbell's injuries were perfect;

they could do no more harm to him should things turn out badly. As well, Campbell had a fire inside him that would help him overcome the obstacles he would soon face.

The first of those was the news that the surgery could not be performed in Minneapolis, not in Minnesota, not even in the United States. Miriam Technologies was working well outside the framework of accepted medical practice, even for clinical trials. Campbell would have to travel to Switzerland, to the Af-foltern Clinic outside Zurich, for the implant of the cortical interface, and would return to the United States for the link-up with the dog. It was an obstacle because, since the accident, Campbell hated to travel. Claire had thought this might be the complication that would change Campbell's mind, and she was shocked when he agreed so readily.

"Will I be going alone?" he had asked.

"Claire has agreed to go with you," Russell had told him.

Yes, she had. She'd arranged to take two weeks off work, time enough to travel to Zurich with Campbell, stay with him through the surgery and the two days recovery, and even to participate, if she were allowed, in the initial stages of his link-up with Shadow.

Four days after Campbell's interview with Russell and Nina, on Sunday, June 27th, she and Campbell boarded a Swiss Air Boeing 747. Campbell sat quietly beside her. He had taken the window seat so that he could have something to lean against. He put one hand in hers and pressed his face to the window, breathing slowly, deeply. As usual he wore the dark wraparound glasses that covered the horrible wounds of his eyes.

During the flight his mood darkened, and she did not know why. He did not speak, did not touch his food, did not drink. He only stared out the window at the clouds, as if he could actually see them, as if they contained secrets vital to his well-being. When the plane finally landed in Zurich, Campbell gripped her hand tightly as they walked into the terminal. Outside customs they were met by a chauffeur who spoke perfect, precise English, and who drove them from the airport to the clinic. It was a two-hour drive, bypassing Zurich entirely, along roads blasted through rocky passes, over hills as green as Christmas holly, through valleys full of swirling mist. Claire thought the country beautiful, but said nothing to Campbell who sat silently, still holding her hand. When they arrived at the Affoltern Clinic, a sprawling, ranch-style compound that looked more like a Nevada motel than a center for experimental surgery, it was raining heavily. On the short walk from the car up to the entrance, Campbell hunched his shoulders and made a frightened, childlike sound, but once inside he straightened up and inhaled deeply.

"We're here," she said to him.

He nodded, but did not smile. A tall, bearded man in a gray suit was waiting for them. He approached, smiling, and shook Claire's hand.

"I am Doctor Schattdorf. You must be Claire. And this, I presume, is Campbell."

He shook Campbell's hand, smiling into his face. Campbell's mouth had formed a tight line, but now his lower lip trembled a little. He's scared, Claire realized, and wanted to reach out and hold him. But Schattdorf was already leading Campbell away.

"Please make yourself comfortable, Miss Knight. You'll be shown to your quarters immediately. I will introduce your brother to the rest of the medical team."

And that was that. Campbell was gone, led down a long, bright corridor, through glass doors, and away. Claire found herself following a short, stocky woman in a nurse's uniform, who led her in the opposite direction from Campbell, and two minutes later was ensconced in the room that would serve as her quarters for the remainder of her stay.

Alone, she opened the window and looked out over a field that disappeared into mist and rising hills. Rain was still falling. She closed the curtains, inexplicably depressed, and lay down on the bed. It was hard and uncomfortable, but after the flight she was exhausted. That exhaustion seemed suddenly far more acute than it had only minutes ago. She did not even have time to get undressed before sleep overcame her.

It was two days before Claire saw Campbell again, and by that time she was nearly out of her mind with boredom and worry. She had spent all her time in her room, or in the lobby, or in the common room that patients and staff alike used for watching television. The television shows were all in Italian or French or German, and she understood none of them. The staff repeatedly suggested she take walks to calm herself; there were many trails around the clinic, pleasant and easy. But she refused. She wanted to be nearby, in case Campbell needed her.

Early Tuesday morning, when one of the nurses finally told her that she could see Campbell for a few minutes before the operation, she nearly broke down. She was led into a small room in which a gurney sat alone. Campbell lay on top of the gurney, covered in a sheet, hooked up to an IV tube that slithered up a metal rail to a clear plastic bag above his head. Claire held her breath for a moment, transported back to the days following the accident, when he had looked just this way.

She found his hand and said, "It's me."

He squeezed back hard, head turning slightly. "I wondered where the hell you'd gotten to."

"They wouldn't let me see you."

"Just as well. They were sticking things into every opening in my body. Bloody Swiss vampires."

"You look fine."

"No thanks to them."

They had shaved off most of his hair, and on his scalp they had drawn a blue grid. The blue lines disappeared beneath the bandage covering his eyes. Claire bit her lip.

"It will all be over soon," she said.

Campbell nodded. He did not let go of her hand.

"I'm scared," he said, after a minute of silence.

She was not sure he had spoken to her, or that he was even

aware that she was still here. He seemed to have nodded off, and she realized they must have given him something to relax him. But she squeezed his hand to let him know she was still with him.

Five minutes later two nurses, masked, wearing protective glasses, wheeled Campbell away from her.

Alone, Claire said what she had wanted to say only minutes earlier. "I'm scared, too."

Hope finally got around to cleaning Campbell Knight's cabin on Wednesday, almost a full week after he'd left with his sister. She'd put it off mostly because she did not want to seem too eager to explore her neighbor's home. She knew she could delay no longer. She had promised she would clean the place, and the likelihood now loomed that Campbell would return any day and find the cabin in disarray, and at that point he'd likely be more angry that she hadn't done what she'd said, rather than impressed that she had no desire to invade his privacy.

The morning was cool and sunny when she walked across the trail that led to Campbell's cabin. She noticed, dismayed, that the grass was getting longer. Usually somebody came in to cut it for him. Perhaps Claire had put everything on hold until Campbell returned. If she had time, she'd cut it herself.

The cabin was a disaster. Claire had been right about that. When she'd helped Campbell after his misadventure in the rain, it had seemed to her that he kept a neat house. Now, the living room was strewn with papers, and furniture had been pushed over. The kitchen sink had at least a week's worth of dishes piled inside and beside it, all stinking now. Flies buzzed between rooms, seeming at home wherever they lighted. When she walked, she had to pick her way carefully through the mess. What must it have been like for him, blind?

He was angry, she realized. This is my fault. This was the result of a temper tantrum. She had humiliated him by helping him back here, treating him like a child, and so he had acted like one.

With a sigh, she got to work in the living room, and once started realized it wasn't as bad as she had thought. It took her less than twenty minutes to get the living room straightened, and afterward she began to perceive the simple organization of the place. Lots of open spaces, lots of unobstructed straight lines. She reconstructed it as best she could, straightening furniture, putting all the papers into a bag for Claire to sort out later. Some of them were bills, some simply fliers, but some looked personal, perhaps even important. She resisted the urge to read any of them.

The kitchen took longer. The dishes had dried with food caked to them, and she needed four sinks full of hot water to soak and clean them. She emptied the fridge, throwing out cartons of milk that were sour, dried cheese only partly wrapped, rotten smelling wieners, and soggy apples. She found a mop in one corner and used it to wipe the floors.

I should do this for him more often, she thought. I live right next door. I'll talk to Claire.

Afterward, she found a can of Black Flag beneath the sink and sprayed every room. When she opened the bedroom door, she realized she had more work to do. Papers and photographs littered the floor. Despite her success at resisting to look at his papers in the living room, she found herself studying each photograph before she put it back in the empty box she found behind the door. Most were of people whom Hope had never seen, some children, some grandparents. She recognized a very young Claire, perhaps sixteen or seventeen, in an evening gown with a corsage at her wrist. The young Claire was slim and elegant, showing the promise of the Claire whom Hope had already met.

If I had looked like that, I'd have gone to my prom, she thought.

But the pictures that most intrigued her were of Campbell. Like Claire, there were some of him as a young man, even as a boy. How different he looked! How full of life and happiness!

All smiles! Some of the more recent photographs showed him with a woman, holding hands, hugging, kissing. These made her uncomfortable, and she put them quickly away. The fiancée, she guessed.

How could you have deserted him after his injury? How could you have been so heartless?

At the foot of the bed, in a brown paper bag, she found a book and two cassette tapes sealed in shrink wrap. The book was titled, *Braille Made Easy,* with accompanying tapes. Inside, she found a receipt dated almost eight months ago. Campbell hadn't even opened the book, hadn't tried to learn.

You resist your blindness, she thought. You refuse to accept it, and so you get stuck in the darkness.

By noon, she was finished. Probably not the way Campbell wanted it, but better than it had been. She left the bag of papers behind the bedroom door for Claire to sort through.

She sat on his sofa and looked through his living room window at the lake, only a hundred yards away. The water gleamed in the midday sun. Campbell had never seen this view.

Why had he come out here? What purpose was served by living so far away from Claire, from the civilized amenities that helped the blind? It was as if he were hiding.

She closed her eyes, trying to imagine what it was like for him. Darkness, all the time. No relief. With her eyes still closed she stood, trying to picture the layout of the room. She took two steps forward, hands at her sides. This is what it was like for Campbell. She felt dizzy, and her heart pounded. Darkness.

She made half a turn and started walking toward where she imagined the doorway to the living room would be, but after four steps slammed into the wall. Stars danced behind her eyes and she lifted a hand to rub her nose. Fool. No one should do this who didn't have to!

Poor Campbell. Out here all alone. Bitter, angry. She suddenly understood his predicament. Trapped inside himself, with nowhere to run. Everyone had a hell inside of them, isn't that what they said? Campbell had found his, and he had made it worse. To live every day with his anger, his bitterness. . . . Just the thought of it made her queasy.

It was with relief that she finally opened the door and stepped into the porch. The sunlight stung her eyes, but she welcomed it.

I can see, she thought.

Campbell Knight might sell his soul for even a few seconds of that kind of pain.

On Wednesday afternoon, Eleanor Dueck clipped a handful of roses from the garden at the side of the house, wrapped the prickly stems in a sheet of newspaper, then loaded Max into the pickup truck and drove into Hollyfield. The sky was clear of clouds, but the day was cool. Dust rose from the shoulders of the road as she drove, lifted by the stiff north-westerly breeze.

Hollyfield was quiet. As she drove through town hers was the only vehicle on the road, though there were many parked at the side of the road, in front of the hotel, and in the Gerber's Foods lot. As she passed the police station she waved to Bill Kelly who was just coming out of the building. He raised a hand to her and she grinned, stepping a little on the gas to give him something to think about, but in the rearview mirror she saw that he had already climbed into his car and was turning back into town.

"Couldn't get yourself arrested around here if you tried," she said to Max.

The black lab turned to her, tongue lolling, head cocked as if waiting for her to say something else. She scratched him behind the ears.

"You love me boy, don't you? Sure you do. Love your Ma."

Max licked her hand then turned his face out the window again. In the breeze, his loose jowls inflated and fluttered and made a noise like raw liver being slapped on a cutting board. His saliva, driven by the wind, splattered the seat of the car, white strings dribbling back over his snout and forehead.

At the Hollyfield cemetery, two miles out of town, she parked the car in the gravel lot and let Max out. He ran immediately into the maple trees bordering the parking lot, and reappeared moments later as Eleanor walked along the path into the cemetery. She carried the bundle of roses in both hands, half smiling as the breeze tried to steal her breath.

Luke's grave was a short walk into the field, a small, plain headstone, humble and quiet amidst the larger, more ornate ones surrounding it. Eleanor kneeled and ran her fingers over the cold granite, tracing the letters slowly.

Luke Dueck
1981-1986
A soul well loved

She placed the roses by the headstone, then closed her eyes and said a short prayer. Max sat a few paces away, watching her with keen, earnest eyes, long black tail whipping through the grass like Death's scythe itself.

Her son had been five years old when he died, his heart and body racked with the pain of mortal illness, and yet still bursting with love for her, needing her. She had so much love to give, and needed so much love in return, she had wondered what would happen to her. Loveless, unneeded, she would have died.

But there had been Max, of course. And Ruth Burns, whose love and need had been a torch that burned in Eleanor's heart long after the girl's bright soul had left this world. And now there was little Jesse Hampton, who needed her more than ever, who pronounced his love for her with every beat of his brave heart.

The world was full of love, if you only knew where to find it.

She cried a little for Luke, remembering him, his smiles, his cries, his pain, and then she stood and brushed the dust and grass from her overalls, and started back to the parking lot. Max ran ahead, urinating on headstones, stopping and waiting for her, tail wagging slowly. At the car, he hopped in through her door and immediately stuck his head through the window and lolled his tongue. Eleanor started the truck, but did not put it in gear. She reached out and touched Max's flank, then lifted her hand to his head, stroking gently. The dog continued to stare out the window, oblivious, waiting for the wind.

She slammed her hand hard on top of his head, knocking his snout into the top of the glass with a sharp clack of teeth. He yelped and pulled his head back into the truck, turned to her with a snort of pain. He lowered himself to the seat and rubbed his face with one paw, still whining.

Eleanor's heart throbbed, and she reached out for him, touching him gently. "Poor, poor Max. It's okay, boy. It's okay. Mama loves you. Mama loves you so much."

The dog whined again, and she put her arms around him, hugged him, pressed her face into his mane. He lapped at her neck, loving her, and warmth spread through her body.

"Good boy. Good boy."

She let him go, put the truck in gear, and started driving. By the time she got back to the house it was after 2:00, well past Jesse's lunchtime. The thought of the boy gave her a lump in her throat. He would be overjoyed to see her when she went down with the tray. He might even call her Mama, and hug her and kiss her, while she stroked his hair and murmured sweetness to him.

She quickly prepared a grilled cheese sandwich, put it on a tray with a glass of chocolate milk, and took the tray outside. Max followed her to the cellar door, then down into the darkness. She turned on a light at the bottom of the stairs, enough so that she could see the cage at the end of the narrow stone corridor that had once led to the coal room. Inside his cage, Jesse Hampton lay on a mattress, knees pulled up to his chest, hands clasped below his chin as if praying. His face was mottled from crying. His eyes seemed even more swollen than last time.

She gently rapped on the bars of the cage. "Lunch time, Jesse."

The boy did not stir. Even when Eleanor reached through the bars and stroked the side of his face.

"Jesse, it's Mama."

She held a finger beneath his nose, felt the soft feather touch of his exhalation. Worried now, she opened the cage and went inside to him. She lifted him into her arms, shaking him a little. Still, he did not stir, remaining stiff and unresponsive.

"Oh, Jesse, you poor, poor boy. I have so much love for you. So much. And I know you love me, too. You do, Jesse, don't you? You know you do."

As she stroked his hair, she paused. His skull, in places felt soft, almost spongy to the touch. His hair was still matted with blood where she had accidentally hit him with the flashlight, but he had seemed to recover from that. As she pressed her finger against one of the soft spots the boy's breath sputtered.

She held him tightly. "Poor Jesse," she whispered into his hair.

He did not respond. He did not love her back.

After a minute, she lowered him to the mattress again. He had not even opened his eyes since she had come down, had not smiled for her, reached for her, hugged her.

Max lay down on the floor outside the cage and watched the boy, tail wagging slowly, whining.

"He's a sick little boy," she said to Max. "He's lost all his love."

Max looked up at her, and his tail stopped wagging. It was as if he knew, Eleanor thought, as if he understood.

When there's no love, there's nothing.

Nothing at all.

SIX

Claire sighed with relief when the wheels of the plane touched down at Minneapolis International Airport.

It was Friday, July 2nd, 4:30 in the afternoon. It had been six days since they'd boarded the flight for Zurich, but to Claire it felt like months. The flight there, with stops in New York, London, and Paris, had lasted almost 17 hours, and the flight back, skipping the stop in Paris, had lasted a good 15 hours. The time at the Affoltern Clinic had been an interminable wait, with little to occupy her mind; after the operation she had seen Campbell once a day, for five minutes at a time, but during those visits he had been mostly unconscious, forehead and eyes bandaged so that it very well could have been somebody else. By the time she set foot on American soil she was exhausted, body numb from jet lag, mind empty. It was all she could do to concentrate on leading Campbell through the gate, then through customs.

Campbell had been quiet for most of the flight back, talking little, squeezing her hand once in a while as if he thought she needed reassuring. He'd been right about that. Once the plane had started its descent, he'd become more animated, as if he sensed the end of his ordeal were approaching, and had not, until now, wanted to delay that event by his own excitement or expectation.

Russell met them at the airport. Claire let herself lean against him, let herself be hugged, but Russell's attention was perfunctory. He was really interested in Campbell.

"You're looking good, Campbell."

"When can we hook me up to the dog?"

Russell released a short, explosive laugh. "Not today, that's for sure. You need rest."

"I feel fine! I want to get started."

Claire put herself between Russell and Campbell, her own exhaustion fading in the shadow of what she knew was to come. "What happens next?" she asked.

"First, you both get some rest. We've got quarters set up for Campbell at the lab. We won't even think of doing anything until he's had a good 12 hours of sleep."

Campbell swore softly, and Claire squeezed his hand. "That sounds like heaven," she said.

The afternoon was sunny, hot, and humid, the streets crowded with rush hour traffic, but Claire was so glad to be home she did not care. Russell drove to her apartment, and left Campbell in the car as he walked her up to the door.

"He looks so tired," she said.

"So do you. He's fine. It went perfectly. We got all the reports from the clinic."

She leaned against him, then turned her face up for a kiss. After they parted, Russell sighed.

"It pains me to say this, but we'll have to stop here. Get some sleep. I'll see you tomorrow."

"Can I be there? I mean, when it starts?"

"I'll talk to Nina. It's going to be tough for him at first. Call me tomorrow, okay?"

She watched them drive away, Campbell rigid in his seat as he always was while being driven anywhere, facing straight ahead. Heading toward a new life, she hoped. New sight. Light.

Alone, her exhaustion returned with a vengeance, and she dragged herself to the elevator, then upstairs to the welcome darkness of sleep.

"How long did I sleep?" Campbell asked.

"Sixteen hours," Russell said.

"You drugged me!"

"That's right. How do you feel?"

"Great. Fine. Excellent. When can we start?"

"Soon. How was breakfast?"

"Just fine. Where's Shadow?"

"Be patient. Just relax. Dr. Ladeceur will be here soon. I'm going to leave you alone for a minute. Please, don't move."

Campbell listened to Russell's footsteps move across a hard floor, then fade suddenly as if he'd turned a corner or passed through a door. It felt as if he'd been up for hours, but he guessed it was no more than forty minutes since he'd woken. Since that time he'd showered, eaten, and been taken in a wheelchair, protesting every inch of the way, from the room he'd slept in to another room he guessed was one of the labs he'd visited on his first visit. The place smelled sterile, and it sounded big. Cool air circulated from all directions, much cooler than typical air conditioning. There must be electronic equipment nearby.

More footsteps, two sets of them, and then, like a hot current in the cool air, the smell of perfume. A hand lightly touched his shoulder.

"Good morning, Mr. Knight. It's Dr. Ladeceur."

"Good morning."

"We're all set," Russell said. "Are you ready for a hard day's work?"

"Yes."

"Good. Just relax. You're going to remain in that chair for most of the day, so get used to it. If you need to stretch your legs, let us know. Right now, we're going to test the integrity of the implant and the coupling circuitry."

"Okay."

The wheelchair turned gently and began to move. Campbell guessed he was rolled fifteen feet, then turned.

"Just relax, Campbell," Russell said. "You're going to feel my hand on your face. I'm going to unwrap the dressing."

Almost immediately, he felt a gentle touch on his left cheek. Russell's fingers moved up to his left orbital cavity, to the ear, behind the ear. As the dressing was unwound his skin felt chilled.

"How does that feel?"

"Good."

"It looks excellent. Very good. If you want, you can touch the interface, Campbell. It's just behind the left ear. Be gentle."

Campbell lifted his hand and ran fingers behind his ear. Despite being warned he was shocked; it was like finding a growth he had been unaware of, a tumor suddenly born. He had expected the device, whatever it was, to be above the skin, and was surprised to find it just below the surface, a smooth protuberance, perhaps half an inch in diameter. It moved slightly to the touch.

"Give it time, you won't even notice it. The coupler rests on top. The implant picks up the impulses through the skin. It might tickle at first, but again, you won't notice it after awhile. The impulses are relayed to the cortical implant via the embedded circuitry."

"So now I can tell them Cam is short for Camera."

Russell chuckled. "If you like. Are you ready to begin?"

"Hell, yes."

The device on Campbell's face felt like a pair of eyeglasses, only slightly heavier. The ear pieces were larger than normal, and pressed tightly against the implants beneath his skin. Two wires ran from the glasses, behind the wheelchair, where they presumably connected with the testing equipment.

"Ready, Cam?"

"Yes."

"When we activate the linkup you might experience a few moments of dizziness. Perhaps even a flash of light. Don't let it bother you. It will pass. In a few moments the test patterns should register, and we'll take it from there. Activating, now."

Campbell felt a tickling sensation behind his ears, as if a mild electric current were being applied, but it was not uncom-

fortable. What *was* uncomfortable was the sudden throb of pain
in his forehead, and then the wave of dizziness that came after
it. He gripped the arms of the wheelchair tightly and the dizziness passed. What followed was even more disconcerting, just
as Russell had warned: a flash of light. It was not exactly like
seeing a flash of light, but as if a bolt of lightning had somehow
entered his head and were sizzling across the inside of his skull.
It made him grit his teeth, neck straining.

"Relax, Cam."

Hands pressed reassuringly on his shoulders and he allowed
himself to sink into the chair. He inhaled deeply, let the breath
out, took another.

"Has it passed yet?"

"Yes," Campbell said, and heard his voice waver.

"Good. Hold your breath. This might come as a surprise.
We're going to activate a test grid. Ready?"

Campbell held his breath and nodded. This time, there was
no flash of light. Instead, in the darkness inside his head, a grid
of white lines appeared, like the outline of a chess board. The
lines seemed to glow, as if they were made of light itself. To
Campbell, it still wasn't like *seeing;* it was as if he had visualized the image inside his head, in the same place he attempted
to visualize everything else. The difference was, this image was
static, precise, unwavering. Real, not imaginary.

"My God."

"What do you see?"

"White lines. A grid. Like a checkerboard."

"Is there a frame?"

"No frame. Just the lines."

"How's clarity?"

"Razor sharp."

"This isn't vision yet, Cam. This is mere stimulation of the
cortical implant."

"It's incredible."

"Depth?"

"It looks like it's floating against a black backdrop. Did I say *looks?* Jesus. Well, it's floating, anyway. In front of me. I have the impression of depth, yes."

"Campbell," Nina Ladeceur said, "we're going to place a marker on the grid and we'd like you to state its position."

"Okay."

A white point of light appeared within one of the grid boxes, and Campbell's heart raced as if he were a hunter who had glimpsed an elusive deer in the forest.

"I see it."

"Position?"

"Just left of center. Four down, four to the right."

"Now?"

"Top right corner."

"Now?"

"Bottom left."

The test continued smoothly, the white point moving from square to square, until it returned to the center position. After that, they repeated the test. Then again, until, head throbbing, Campbell refused a fourth replay.

"When do I get hooked up to Shadow?"

Russell slapped his shoulder. "Later. A few more tests."

Like the grid test, all the others involved white lines and white dots, and seemed to be designed to determine, as far as Campbell could tell, his own willingness to undergo such torture. There were bars of varying shades of gray, black at one end white at the other, which he described over and over again to Russell and Nina. There were points of light that expanded to reveal that they were made of other points of light which in turn expanded to reveal universes of other points of light until Campbell began to forget that he was sitting in a chair and imagined, dizzily, that he was floating in space, a forgotten satellite. There were other dots that entered the field from the edges, top or bottom, left or right, while Russell or Nina had him call out the moment they became visible or disappeared. After a while, bright dots filled his head, and he could not differentiate between the real and the imagined.

Only one of the tests was at all entertaining, and it seemed to be of the shortest duration. Two lines, one horizontal one vertical, intersected each other and divided his view into quadrants. A white point appeared in one of the quadrants and began to move. His task was to turn his head so that the white point moved back to the point of intersection. This was more difficult than it seemed, and so it became a challenge, and thus enjoyable. The first time it took him almost five minutes to get the point back to center. It was as if he were chasing a slippery blob of oil through an even more slippery medium, with mental hands themselves coated in oil. After five tries, he chased the point with greater facility, returning it to the intersection of lines in seconds, balancing it there like a drop of water on the head of a pin. After that, the test was over. He could not convince Russell to run it again.

It was early in the afternoon, after a light lunch of fruit and cheese, when Russell admitted that the tests had ended. Campbell, sitting in the wheelchair in darkness again, only the memory of the grids and lines and points of light now left to him, listened to Russell and Nina talk quietly in some far corner of the room. Finally, Russell approached and touched Campbell's shoulder.

"I think we're ready to give Shadow a try. Are you up for that?"

Campbell only nodded, not trusting himself to speak.

"Again, you may experience dizziness, a flash of light, mild discomfort. It will pass."

Nina Ladeceur spoke almost disinterestedly, as if she were concentrating on something else. Campbell had heard Russell return with Shadow, the dog's claws clicking lightly across the floor, each step sending goose bumps marching across his shoulders. When he touched the dog, petted him, cradled that angular head in his lap, he felt an almost electric charge. He and the dog were going to be close; very close.

"Don't expect much at first," Russell said. "It takes time to accommodate the connection.

"Where's Claire."

"I asked her not to be here. You can see her later if you like."

He nodded, impatient to begin. On the arms of the wheel-chair, gripping the metal rails, his hands sweated. If he let go even for an instant, he feared, he would float away and become lost in the world of white points and intersecting lines. Shadow was on his belly in a cage beside the chair. Campbell could hear the dog's breathing, could smell his fur and breath.

"Shadow is ready," Nina said quietly.

"Here we go," Russell said. "Linking, now."

There was no dizziness, just a sharp prod of pain above his nose, somewhere inside his skull. He jerked his head involuntarily, but the pain was gone before he could draw another breath. Lightning flashed in his head, receded, faded like a passing storm. He was tempted to count the seconds to the thunder. A gray mist rolled in to replace the darkness.

"We're linked," Russell said.

"I don't see anything."

"Describe what's there."

"It's light, I guess. Mist."

"Then we're definitely connected."

"But there's nothing *there*."

"Just sit still, Campbell. We'll run some diagnostics."

Russell and Nina shuffled about, and then he heard Shadow growl softly. Inside his head, it seemed as if a cloud moved across the evenly illuminated mist.

"I saw something."

"Describe it?"

"A sense of movement, something big."

"Now?"

Part of the mist flared brightly, and Campbell moved his head to get away. "Bright light!"

"Did you have a feel for which eye?"

"Right, I think."

"Now?"

"Left. Now the right again. Left."

"Excellent."

"You were shining something in each of my eyes," Campbell said, hardly able to contain his excitement. "That's it, isn't it?"

"Not *your* eyes, Campbell. Shadow's eyes."

Campbell's heart was beating hard now, and a swell of nausea rose in him. Of course. Shadow's eyes.

"Are you telling me this is as good as it gets? Just light? Mist?"

"Give it time," Russell said carefully. "You've been blind for a year, Campbell, and this is a new form of seeing for your brain."

Campbell forced himself to breathe deeply.

"Relax," Russell said. "Describe what you're seeing."

"Damned mist."

"Now?"

A shadow impinged on the wall of mist, blocking off half of it. "Right eye dark. Now the left. Both misty again. You covered his eyes."

"Right. Believe it or not, this is excellent. You have to trust me, Campbell, it takes time."

"How much time?"

"Sometimes hours, sometimes days. Worst case so far has been three weeks."

Campbell heard himself groan softly.

"You aren't going to be the worst case, Campbell. Definition will improve in the next 24 hours."

"What do I do until then?"

"You remain linked to Shadow, 24 hours a day, to allow your visual cortex to accommodate the connection. And you get some more rest. You're still exhausted. That's having an effect."

Russell and Nina walked away, talking quietly between themselves. Alone, Campbell searched the mist that, had he been sighted, he would have described as floating before his eyes. It was formless, vague, infinite, and he could not penetrate it. It was as if one, great milky cataract had been lowered over his inner eye. He could not even make himself perform the routine operation of visualizing his surroundings. The mist permeated his inner world, filling every crack.

He reached down and petted Shadow through the mesh of the cage. The dogs snout pressed at his fingers, cold and wet.

"Maybe you're as blind as I am," he said softly. "That would be funny, wouldn't it?"

He heard Shadow's tail wag a couple of times, whacking the sides of the cage, and then a soft whine. With a sigh, Campbell leaned back in the wheelchair. The mist hung before his eyes, agonizingly opaque, and for the first time in a year he wished for darkness.

"Russell said everything went perfectly," Claire said.

"He's got a strange way of looking at things."

"He says you're impatient."

Campbell laughed halfheartedly. He was back in his room, lying in bed. Shadow lay beside the bed in his cage. Between them snaked the cable that linked them. The formless mist still filled Campbell's head, making it difficult to think, to talk.

"Russell says I can be here tomorrow."

"It won't be very exciting, trust me."

"Don't get discouraged, Campbell. It's only the first day."

"They said I'd see again."

"And you will."

Campbell said nothing. The nurse who was attending him had made him swallow a pill just before Claire arrived, and he was beginning to feel the effects of it now, warmth spreading up his back to his shoulders, into his neck.

"They're drugging me," he said. "It's a conspiracy."

Of course, Claire took that seriously. "It's just to help you sleep, Cam. It is. Don't excite yourself."

"I was joking," he made himself say.

For the first time since being linked to Shadow, the mist in his head was fading, as if a curtain were slowly being drawn across it.

"It's getting dark," he said, and heard his words slur.

"I'll be back tomorrow," Claire said.

She kissed his cheek, and it felt to him like warm water being poured on his face. Then the mist was gone, and he was smothered in darkness, familiar, comforting. Why had he ever wanted to see again? This darkness, this womb, was far preferable.

Campbell woke suddenly, terrified. If it had been a dream, he could not remember it. For a few seconds he did not know where he was, did not recognize the echoing quality of his own breathing. He tried to sit up, but found himself unable to move.

He was at Miriam Technologies. Yes. In that room. Probably strapped down to the bed so that he could not inadvertently disconnect himself from Shadow.

He focused his hearing, searching for the dog. The animal's breathing was deep, slow, coming from his left. Shadow was asleep. Somewhere else in the room he could hear an electrical hum, the sound of paper slowly shuffling. He listened to that sound for a long time, but could not determine its source. In the end, he decided it must be an EKG monitor, hooked up to either himself or to Shadow, with the audio turned down, making a paper record. That was all. It sounded very loud.

For a seeing person, this was the equivalent of waking at 3:00 in the morning and trying to determine the source of shadows on the ceiling. For Campbell, however, there was no shutting his eyes to escape, no blocking his ears. Only one thing to do, another survival mechanism he had developed over the year of darkness.

He hummed.

With every exhalation of breath he released a small groan, as if he were in pain. The sound did not block out the others, but it did focus his attention on his body, on his inner world. Sleep came to him again, pulling him into a deeper darkness.

The dream came suddenly, so suddenly that he was aware that he was dreaming. Unlike his other dreams of the past year, this one was primarily visual, and crystal clear, as distinct and razor sharp as the grid imagery he'd been forced to endure earlier in the day. He was in near darkness. Perhaps a cupboard, or a small storage shed, or a cellar. He was looking through a doorway, or perhaps even a gate. Something barred, like a prison cell. He was looking into the room beyond the bars, and was certain that he himself was not the prisoner. Beyond the bars, on the dark floor, lay a boy.

Campbell stared at the boy, wondering who he was. As if in answer, the boy struggled to a sitting position and stared back at him. His face was mottled, bruised, his eyes swollen shut. He tried to smile, but only half his mouth seemed to work, the other side hanging down as if he suffered a debilitating nerve disorder, or had recently experienced a stroke. He held out a small hand toward the bars. Campbell wanted to reach for it, to touch him, to bring him comfort. It occurred to him then that this dream was silent. He had not heard a thing.

Suddenly the view shifted. Not instantly, as in most dream transitions, but a deliberate changing of position, as if he'd turned his head. He was now looking into a long tunnel, a tunnel at the end of which a faint light glowed. Into that light a figure stepped and began to move toward him.

Campbell was suddenly frightened. This was more real than any dream he'd ever had in his life. He seemed to have no control, no will in the dream. He could only watch as the figure advanced on him, huge and dark, like death itself stalking this long, strange corridor. The figure was suddenly above him, but he could see nothing but its silhouette. It opened the door to the cell and went inside with the boy, picked him up and cradled him in its arms. The boy squirmed, and the figure of death put him down again.

Death towered over the boy, and though Campbell could see very little in the darkness of the dream, he sensed a potential for terrible violence. The scene before him seemed ready to explode.

The figure reached down to the boy, this time with something in its hand, and hit him across the head. The boy did not stir. The huge hand came down again, clubbing the boy, mashing the dirty blond hair into bloody soup. Clubbing. Clubbing.

Campbell woke, panting for breath, soaked in sweat, straining against the straps that held him down. The dream imagery clung to him, hovering beyond the misty darkness in his mind. Through his terror he heard a door opening, footsteps. Then a voice, whispering to him, calming him.

"It's okay, you were dreaming. Lie still. Swallow this. Chew it. That's it. Relax. Breathe deeply. We'll disconnect Shadow for now. Shush. Lie still."

He felt the glasses being lifted from his face, and then the mist receded as if a wind had blown through his mind. He almost cried out with relief. His mouth burned with the bitter chemical taste of whatever pill she had given him, but he was too exhausted to ask for water. It took only seconds for his inner darkness to reach up and take him to safety.

SEVEN

"Are you awake?"

Campbell turned to the voice. "Yes."

"How was your sleep?"

He recognized her voice. She was the one who had rescued him from his dream. Hearing her, the terror of the nightmare returned, then slowly passed.

"After you unhooked me from Shadow, it was fine."

"Do you feel rested?"

"Sure, I guess so. What's the agenda for today?"

"I'm just here to get you dressed and ready. Lie still for a minute." Cool fingers with long nails touched his chest, pulling off the EKG pads. Her breath touched his face, warm, laced with the aroma of coffee. A trace of unfamiliar perfume, probably some cheap drugstore variety, but pleasant nonetheless, lingered around her. She must be young, he thought, younger than her voice. With a cold, moist tissue, she wiped the skin where the pads had rested, expert and firm. "There are clothes on the chair on the other side of the bed. Can you dress yourself?"

"How private is this room?"

"I'll close the door."

"Is there a bathroom?"

"If you get dressed, I'll take you." She crossed the room and turned off the EKG monitor. "I'll wait outside the door. Tell me when you're ready."

He waited for the sound of the door closing before sitting

up and swinging his feet off the bed. The clothes were where she said they would be, and he was surprised to find that although they were his own, they were not the clothes he had arrived in. Claire must have provided them. No, not even that. They'd simply taken them from his suitcase. He found his shoes beneath the chair, slipped them on, and called out that he was ready.

She entered the room immediately, picked up his left arm, and led him to the door.

"If you guide me, I'll count the steps and then you won't have to take me again."

"I don't mind taking you."

"I'd rather be able to do it myself."

"That won't be necessary."

He started to protest again, but already the argument had lost him his count, and he gave in to her firm pull as she took him through the doorway, and then left. She led him through another door, and then brought him to a halt so abruptly that he nearly lost his footing. She's trying to disorient me, he thought. It was a ridiculous suspicion, but he could not shake it.

"It's right in front of you. Do you need help?"

In as firm a voice as he could muster, he said, "No."

"Call me when you're ready, and I'll take you back."

He waited until the door had closed, then shook his head and swore softly under his breath. What was she trying to do? Humiliate him? She was treating him like a child! Or perhaps she simply had no experience with the blind. Either way, she was the wrong person for the job.

When he had finished he did not call out for her, but held out his hands and found the doorway of the small cubicle. He opened it and stepped confidently through.

"I'm finished," he said.

"You should have called me."

"I'm not helpless. In fact, if you would just guide me back I won't need your help again for getting here."

"I don't think that would be a good idea."

She pulled him sharply forward, into the room, and to the bed. He was so angry he could not even speak to her, but sat silently, fuming.

"I'm going to hook you up to Shadow," she said.

"Hadn't we better wait for somebody who knows what they're doing?"

"I know what I'm doing."

He recoiled as the glasses were slipped over his eyes and around his ears, but she held him firm. She connected the wire-harness to his shoulder and left arm. A surge of irrational fear swept through Campbell.

"I don't want to be hooked up to him again," he said.

"There may be a flash of light and dizziness."

"Wait . . ."

Light flared in Campbell's head. The rudimentary map of the room and the hallway he'd been unconsciously building fled before the mist that rose behind his eye sockets. He was lost again.

"There," she said. "Hold his harness. Good. Now just wait here. I'll be back in a minute to take you to the lab. They're waiting for you."

As she left the room, Campbell shook, half from fury, half from despair. Shadow, pressed into his left leg, whined once, softly. Mist roiled inside Campbell's head.

Had she said a minute?

How much time had passed?

An hour, surely. An hour at least.

He could not sit here any longer. Another minute would drive him insane.

He stood carefully, holding tightly to Shadow's harness. The dog shifted position, moving behind his leg. The mist inside his head darkened for a moment, then flared again. Campbell concentrated on it, looking for degrees of brightness or shadow. Was it as uniform as it had been last night? He could not say with certainty. It seemed to him that there were dark blotches within the mist, like distant shapes dimly perceived. It was as if he were staring at a range of mountains through clouds. Once in a while, one of the dark peaks was revealed to him.

Was this to be the extent of his new sight? Formless tangles of light and shadow? If so, it would be better to return to what he had before. There would be no "seeing" in this, just a reminder of all that he had lost.

Holding out his right hand, he walked slowly past the end of the bed toward where he estimated the door to be. Shadow put no resistance on his harness, walking in the same position, slightly to the left and behind of him. The dog, if nothing else, was well-trained.

When his hand struck the wood of the door, Campbell gave a short, satisfied grunt. He searched for the handle, found it, and opened the door. Cool air, redolent of noxious chemicals and gasses, particularly ozone, rushed across his face. The mist formed a new pattern of light and shadow. The mountain range was closer. What was Shadow looking at? For all Campbell knew, the dog might be studying the floor. He could not trust the mist to tell him anything about his environment.

"Hello?"

There was no answer to his call. He could hear a uniform, distant humming, as if of air conditioning. No voices, no footsteps.

"I'm ready!"

Still, no answer.

For the first time, he began to consider the possibility that something had happened, something that necessitated the evacuation of the building. A fire, perhaps. Or leakage of a toxic chemical. Would they simply forget about him?

He stepped into the hallway and Shadow obediently followed. Again, the pattern of light and shadow within the mist changed. Now, instead of walking toward a distant range of mountains, it was as if Campbell had entered a forest. Bars of light, like the trunks of huge trees, seemed to block his way. He paused, confused, unable to ignore the misty shapes despite his desire to do so. They must mean *something*. But what?

He stopped moving and kneeled beside Shadow, turning to face the dog. Again, the pattern changed. A halo of mist now surrounded an eclipsed moon. But these degrees of light were themselves so similar he might have been imagining them. He reached out with his right hand to touch Shadow's head. A cold snout pressed into his palm.

"Good boy," he said.

With gentle fingers he moved his hand up Shadow's snout. He covered the dog's right eye with his palm; darkness flooded half the mist inside his head. Campbell started. He moved his hand to Shadow's left eye; the darkness in the mist slid to the other side.

There *was* a correlation. Some part, some *small* part of Shadow's vision, was making the connection to Campbell's visual cortex. But not enough. Not nearly enough.

He stood and stepped forward again. Shadow followed. Bars of darkness moved in the mist. What were they? To Campbell it looked as if something were moving directly in front of his face, giants passing him.

He stopped moving again. Shadow stopped. The bars of darkness were immobile now, an impingement along the right edge of the misty wall.

Campbell stopped breathing. He knew what they were.

Of course!

He was seeing from a different angle! He hadn't made the adjustment! Shadow was walking slightly behind him, and to the left. The dog was seeing, partially, the movement of Campbell's legs!

He swung out his left leg. The bar of darkness in the mist, the giant that had been striding past him, lurched.

Campbell laughed, reached down and patted Shadow.

"Good boy. Good boy. Stupid master. Bad Campbell."

Shadow licked at his fingers. Campbell stood straight, concentrating fully now on the mist. Those were his legs. There and there. Most of the rest of the mist was uniformly white, but there were *some* figures in there. What were they?

He moved tentatively forward. Shadow followed.

He ignored the moving bars of his legs, blocking them out of his perception, focusing instead on the remainder of the misty wall. Again, the distant mountain range. What was it?

As he stared into the mist a new bar of darkness appeared, solidified. Its lines were straight, even. It grew as he moved. Campbell put his right hand out and kept walking, until the darkness expanded to fill the mist. Its shape was so distinct, so sharply defined, it filled him with wonder to see it.

See it. That's exactly what he was doing! Not seeing as he had before. No. Not that. But the mist was clearing. Definitely clearing!

His hand struck wood. He reached down and found a doorknob. The shape was a door! He turned the handle and pushed. Light filled the darkness, making it even brighter than the surrounding mist.

"Hello?"

Campbell stepped forward. Shadow followed.

A door, yes, but a door into what? For all he knew it might be a storage cupboard, or a fire exit.

"Is anyone there?"

The mist flickered. More dark shapes moved, looming closer, over him, confusing him. His arms were suddenly in the grip of other hands.

"Campbell! You did it!"

That was Russell. Then another shape came into the mist, again towering over him. No. Over *Shadow,* not over himself. He felt a gentle touch on his left hand, smelled the nurse's familiar perfume.

"I'm sorry, Campbell," she said. "They made me leave you there. It was part of the test. I couldn't let you count the steps. They didn't want you navigating that way. Are you all right?"

"I'm fine."

Hands guided him, pushing him across the room, into brighter regions of mist, and then he was collapsing into the arms of a chair.

"Tell me what you're seeing," Russell said.

"Not much. Dark shapes in mist. I can't tell what they are."

"But definition is improving?"

"I can't really say."

"Sit and relax for a few minutes. We'll get you something to eat. This is going to be another busy day."

The shapes moved out of the mist, leaving him again floating in a sea of white. He could hear voices, talking softly. Russell, perhaps Nina. The nurse.

Campbell breathed deeply. If he'd had eyes, he would have closed them. Shadow, apparently, did not feel the same way.

When a hand touched his shoulder he started.

"It's Nina. How are you?"

"Okay. Confused. It's not what I thought it would be."

"Russell is right. It will get better." She had moved in front of him, filling the mist with a central region of darkness. He could smell her perfume, more astringent than the nurse's, more expensive. He wondered what she looked like. "Amy said you had a nightmare."

"It scared the hell out of me. It was so real, but I didn't know where it came from. It wasn't the usual dream stuff."

"Your brain attempting to accommodate the linkup. That sort of thing will pass. Most of our subjects experience strange dreams at the beginning. We'd still like to leave you linked up 24 hours a day, for a while."

"It's your show."

"It is, and we're going to put you through your paces today. I hope you're ready for some hard work. Food will be up shortly for both you and Shadow. In the meantime, your sister is here, if you'd like to talk to her."

"I'd like that."

"I'll have her brought up."

Her darkness slid from the mist. Beside him, Shadow sank

down to his belly. Campbell breathed deeply, relaxing himself. Soon, the mist faded, receded as if cleared by a wind, turned to darkness. Shadow had closed his eyes, he guessed. It was calming, comforting. Campbell found himself drifting off, slipping into Shadow's darkness.

How long he drifted, he did not know. He knew only that the darkness embraced him, and again he wondered why he had ever wanted to see again. He could live in darkness. The darkness belonged to him.

When the sound of footsteps came, he knew that he was dreaming. The darkness turned instantly to light. No mist this time, but a grainy, black and white picture, like an old television set.

I *am* dreaming he thought. A deep-sleep dream.

A shape loomed over him. A woman in a light blouse. Her hair was different from the last time he had seen it, shorter, darker. Her face was more drawn than he remembered, and there were lines around her eyes and mouth that had not been there a year ago. But it was definitely Claire.

Campbell sat rigidly. It *can't* be a dream. The sounds were not dream sounds. He was awake. His heart was pounding. He could *hear* it pounding.

"It's Claire, Campbell. I won't stay long. Your breakfast is just coming. They told me you had a hard night. But please, Campbell, please don't give up. Nobody said it was going to be easy. Please, for me, don't give up. Just do what they want you to do."

Even in grainy black and white he could see that her eyes were wet. She was staring at a point somewhere above his head. But of course, he was seeing through Shadow's eyes. She was looking at *him,* not at Shadow.

"Claire!"

"What's wrong."

"I can see you. Get Nina. I can see you!"

* * *

It was a gray, drizzling Sunday morning. Eleanor, watching the rain through the kitchen window, felt that her mood was perfectly matched to the weather. Max, lying on the floor next to the kitchen table, seemed to share her gloom. He had been restless all night, twitching and whining in the grips of some dog nightmare, as if he knew what today was to hold. Life could be so cruel at times, giving love, and then taking love away.

Eleanor, having finished her breakfast, now leaned back with a mug of coffee, surveying the bleak world beyond the kitchen window. And bleak it was. Bleak, and terrible.

Jesse Hampton had been her one true love for only two months, and now his love was gone. Such a short, short time, for love to blossom, grow, and die. It hardly seemed possible. Ruth Burns's love had lasted for nearly a year, a year of paradise, needing, loving, until her flame had sputtered and her love had died. And Luke, sweet Luke, her own flesh and blood, had loved her for five glorious years.

Love lasts forever, of course. Everybody knew that. Sometimes, though, the flesh was too weak to hold it.

With Jesse Hampton it was different. His love had been difficult to grow, hard to nurture. It was as if, she sometimes thought, the boy just didn't have much love in him at all. That would explain why it had left him so quickly. He was an empty shell of a boy, loveless, unloved. And what did that make him?

Evil, she thought, and shuddered.

It made him evil.

That would explain a lot about Jesse Hampton. Six years old, and evil already. Some children never had much of a chance. Some children were born with dead hearts, and would never amount to much. Some, like Luke, were born overflowing with love. And others were born with just a seed inside them, a seed that could flower either good or bad, depending on the gardener. She'd tried to make Jesse's love bloom, but evil had already taken root. She had thought that her love for him might save him, but she had been wrong. She had underestimated the power of darkness. Darkness could smother love, kill it, choke it like weeds choked a rose.

She knew now, she had known since last night, that Jesse's love was gone. And once love is gone, it is gone forever. It can never return to the place that drove it out. And because there was no longer any love in Jesse, there was nothing in this world for him. Not anymore.

She finished her coffee and sighed. Max watched her with alert eyes as she washed the dishes, then followed her, reluctantly, it seemed to her, outside to the cellar entrance. Rain glistened on the dog's black coat, tears from God. As the cellar door opened the dog barked, then growled.

"What's wrong with you, Max?"

He went down on his belly, staring up at her. The growl was lost somewhere inside of him.

"Are you losing your love, Max? Is that what's happening to you?"

She could not believe that. Not Max. As his tail wagged, she knew it was not true. Max was full of love, like all dogs. Dogs, unlike children, were born with a life's supply of love inside of them. She reached down and scratched his head, then turned and went into the cellar.

Max followed her down the stairs; the stone steps glistened with seeping rain-water. She turned on the light outside Jesse Hampton's cage. The boy shuddered in his sleep, but did not open his eyes. Such a sad, sad case.

Max stayed outside the cage as she went in with the boy. The dog lay on the damp floor, snout pushed through the bars. Eleanor sat down beside Jesse, cradled his head in her lap. He did not open his eyes. His scalp was matted with blood and dirt. He had not touched his food or water. He felt as hot as the hood of her pickup after an hour in the sun. Without love, his body was burning up. She stroked his hair, kissed his face.

"Poor Jesse. Poor, poor Jesse. There's nothing here for you now. Just pain and suffering."

Max whined softly, then growled. She stared at him, furious

at his interruption. He whined again, wagged his tail. Something wrong with him. Something bad. Like all dogs, born with love. But in soil that can support love, evil too can grow.

"I have to go, Jesse, but I'll be back soon. I have to go to church. I have to talk to God."

As if he had heard, the boy's breath sputtered, and for a moment Eleanor thought that God might have already intervened, taking him. But he breathed again, small chest expanding spasmodically, sucking air.

"I have to talk to God," she said again. "It's time to go to heaven, son. There's nothing here for you, but in heaven there will be love. I have to ask God if he's ready for you."

She put his head gently down, then left the cage and locked it. She climbed the steps to gray daylight, then paused.

"Max! Up!"

From the darkness below, she thought she heard a growl. Then Max came trotting up, tongue lolling, tail wagging. She watched the dog run back to the house, shook her head, wondering. Then she closed the cellar door, locking Jesse Hampton in darkness with his loveless misery.

EIGHT

An hour after Campbell announced that the mist had cleared and that he could see, he wished he had kept his big mouth shut. The tests he had suffered the day before were nothing compared to what followed, and what followed, seemed to him, to be endless. If there was a hell, a real hell, he came to believe that it would involve tests. Tests of infinite, diabolical variety. Tests, just like Nina Ladeceur's battery of tests, that would have no apparent reason or design. In such a hell, Campbell reasoned, Nina Ladeceur might rule, while the damned would be an infinite classroom of Campbells and Shadows, writhing in an eternity of pokes, prods, white lines, and floating dots.

Can you see this, Campbell? This? This? THIS?

When the tests ended, at 8:00 in the evening, Amy came to him. She was a completely different person than she had been this morning; courteous, helpful. She asked Campbell if he wanted to be wheeled back to his room or if he wanted to walk. He chose to walk, and did so with Shadow at one side, Amy on the other.

"Nina said you did very well today," Amy said.

"Did she?" He was too exhausted to care.

The corridor seemed to move as he walked, but he had no trouble navigating. Given time, Shadow's strange black and white vision would seem perfectly normal.

In his room, he lay down on the bed while Amy put Shadow in his cage. She did not unhook him from the dog. She helped him undress, as if he were an invalid, then got him under the sheets. Campbell half expected her to give him a kiss goodnight, and was half disappointed when she did not.

She turned on the EKG monitor, and at the door turned to look at him. "I'll be just outside. Call if you need anything."

"When do I get to go home?"

She laughed softly. "You're asking the wrong person."

She turned out the light, and Campbell gasped. Immediately, the light came on again.

"Is something wrong?"

"No, I . . . it's just . . . I haven't had to turn out a light for a long time."

"Would you prefer I left it on?"

"No, turn it off. It's fine."

"Good night."

Darkness again. Campbell felt as if he'd come back to an old friend. At the side of the bed, Shadow breathed deeply, settled. The dog's eyes were not closed, Campbell could sense that. As Shadow adapted to the dark, the darkness of the room filled with vague shapes. Campbell reached over the side of the bed and stroked the dog's head.

"Good night, boy," he whispered.

Shadow licked his fingers. To Campbell, his hand, perceived by Shadow, was a patch of darkness within the darkness of the room. The EKG monitor hummed, feeding out its paper record. Campbell groaned softly, concentrating on his inner world, his body, but soon discovered that he didn't need to. He was going from light into darkness; a different world. The transition was enough; his mind knew what it was supposed to do. Like riding a bike. You never forget. Sleep came easily.

"Any more nightmares?" Nina Ladeceur asked.

"None that I remember," Campbell said.

"How do you feel today?"

"Good."

"Ready for a hard day's work?"

"Not if it involves more tests."

Nina smiled, but there was no humor in her expression. "I think you'll enjoy what we've got set up for you today."

"When do I get out of here?"

"That depends on your performance."

"You make me feel like a machine."

"Do I?"

"Forget I said that."

Russell, who was standing beside Nina, shook his head. They were standing in the lab where Campbell had spent most of his time since returning from Switzerland. Shadow was sitting at Campbell's feet, slightly to the left and behind him, looking up at Nina and Russell. Nina looked directly at Shadow, and Campbell had the disconcerting feeling that she was staring right inside of him. He had to remind himself that she was looking at the dog, not at him.

"Do you remember how you got up here?" Nina said, still looking at the dog.

"Vaguely," Campbell said, remembering his own surprise that he was on the sixth floor rather than the third.

"If you go back toward your room, but keep going down that corridor, there is a double door. Through that door is another corridor. If you turn right it will take you past a security desk, to the elevators. If you take the elevator to the first floor, the front doors to the building are directly ahead of you."

"I remember."

"We will meet you outside the main doors," Nina said, looking up from Shadow.

Now, Campbell knew, she was looking directly at him. "Alone?"

"Can you manage?"

Campbell said nothing. Then he nodded.

"Good," Nina said, then checked her watch. "Begin."

* * *

Shadow had been trained to respond to eight commands, and through two days of testing with the dog, Campbell knew them in and out. Left. Right. Scan. Look. Front. Up. Down. Sleep. He took one step forward to bring Shadow to his feet.

"Shadow, scan."

Shadow turned his head slowly to the left, then to the right, giving Campbell a 180-degree view of the room. Nina and Russell were already at the other side of the room, taking a back exit. Campbell gave a tug on Shadow's harness and stepped forward.

Shadow's training made it so that his eyes were generally pointed forward. This was his home position. From that position, Campbell could see his own legs, from the middle of his calves up to the middle of his thigh, and the room in front of him.

No Amy to help him now. No guiding hand. But no mist, either. Compared to yesterday, when he had navigated from his room to the laboratory with only vague shapes before his eyes, this was simple.

He walked toward the door leading to the corridor, and came to a halt. It wasn't going to be so easy after all. A chair had been placed directly in his path. He approached it cautiously, until he saw his own knees touch it, then reached out and moved the chair to the side. Shadow kept his eyes to the front, steady.

At the door, Campbell paused again.

"Shadow, up."

Shadow looked up at the door, bringing the handle and lock into view. Campbell reached out and watched his own hands seek the lock and handle. As he had expected, the door was locked. He unlatched it, turned the handle, opened it. Easy as pie.

You'll have to do better than that, Nina, he thought smugly.

"Shadow, front."

Again, with Shadow looking forward, he walked into the corridor. He had come to think of the process of walking as analogous to operating a remote control toy. He was seeing himself from behind, after all, and was basing his movements on what he saw. He watched his legs move, watched his own tentative progress down the corridor. In a way, it made him feel outside of himself, distanced somehow.

Is that me up ahead, or somebody else?

Outside his room there was a small desk and a chair, where Amy had spent the night, watching over him. A trace of her perfume lingered, or seemed to, in the air. Perhaps it was his imagination. What was not his imagination was the position of the desk. It had been moved to partially block the corridor.

Campbell chuckled softly, but easily sidestepped the obstruction, pulling Shadow smoothly after him. He wanted to laugh aloud, wanted to shout with joy. He was seeing! He was walking down an unfamiliar corridor, alone!

No, not alone. With Shadow.

But Shadow was part of him now. The dog's name was perfect. You are my shadow, he thought. I'll never go anywhere without you.

He came to the double doors that Nina had warned about, approached so close to them that they towered above him, at least from Shadow's perspective. He pushed against the right door, but it did not budge. He tried the left. It, too, was locked.

He stepped back until he had a view of the whole door. There were no handles, no visible locks.

"Shadow, up."

Nothing at the top of the doors.

"Shadow, down."

At the bottom of the doors were sliding bolts, fitted into the floor. Campbell approached, kneeled, and lifted the bolts.

"Shadow, front."

He pushed through the doors, into the corridor beyond. Turn, right, Nina had said. Campbell stopped, turned.

"Shadow, scan."

Shadow gave him a 180 degree view of the corridor. About five yards away was a desk, and sitting at the desk was a man in a uniform. He was holding a cup of coffee, the cup frozen below his lips. He stared at Campbell in surprise.

"Good morning," Campbell said. "How am I doing?"

"Good morning, Mr. Knight. You're doing great."

Campbell grinned as he walked past the desk. A short way along the corridor he came to the elevators. He pressed the down button and waited for the elevator to arrive. When the door slid open, Campbell stepped forward, into the elevator. He turned around.

"Shadow, up."

He pressed the button for the first floor, then stepped back and leaned against the rear wall of the car. The doors slid closed, and the elevators lurched downward.

Campbell reached down and scratched Shadow behind the ears.

"Shadow, look."

At this command, Shadow looked into Campbell's face. Campbell kneeled down and petted the dog warmly. He watched the pleasure on his own face. Not so bad, he thought. Even with those damned glasses.

"Good boy. They're going to have to do better than that, aren't they?"

The elevator came to a stop. Campbell stood.

"Shadow, front."

He had almost stepped out of the elevator when he paused, and stepped back.

"Shadow, up."

The illuminated numbers above the door showed that he was on the fifth floor. Campbell shook his head, grinning.

"Tricky, Nina," he said.

He waited for the doors to close, and leaned back against the wall again. He allowed Shadow to keep looking at the numbers. The elevator stopped again on the fourth floor. This time there were three women standing in the corridor, watching him.

"Hi," he said.

They smiled back at him. The doors closed. The car lurched as it continued its downward journey.

The dizziness struck Campbell suddenly, between the fourth and third floors. He put all his weight against the wall and groaned softly. The numbers above the door faded into blackness, and Shadow whined. The blackness brightened again, but it was not the elevator that Campbell was seeing.

Trees and grass rushed by at a frightening speed. He saw a road below him. A car rushed toward him, then past, and his eyes swung to watch it recede in the distance. Then he was turning again, looking to his left.

Campbell's heart pounded. He was sitting inside the cab of a small truck, staring up at the figure from his nightmare. He saw large hands on the steering wheel, above them a round, pale face, black eyes. In his terror and confusion he saw nothing else. The figure was nightmarish, vague, a shapeless blob of flesh.

One of the hands left the steering wheel and lashed out at him. He felt nothing, but sensed that he had been struck, and struck hard.

He heard whining. Shadow. His mouth tasted of blood.

A bell rang.

The truck faded away, dissolved into glowing numbers above the elevator door. Shadow whined again. Campbell stood straight, breathing deeply. The illuminated numbers showed he was on the first floor. He tried to calm himself as the doors opened.

"Shadow, front."

His voice was hoarse, hardly intelligible, and he repeated himself. He walked slowly from the elevator, legs feeling weak. People were walking around him, in front of him, behind him. He could hear their footsteps, their breathing, their voices. Some of them looked at him, or at Shadow, smiling. Campbell ignored them and walked straight ahead to the door.

It hadn't been a dream, not this time. His heart was still

racing. Again, he had heard nothing, felt nothing . . . but it had seemed so real, so clear.

He reached the front doors, pushed on them, and stepped outside. Warm air blew in his face, the smell of trees, grass, exhaust. For a moment he was back in the truck, full of terror. Then the sound of cheering came, and he realized that he was looking at a small group of people gathered on the steps. I'm a celebrity, he thought. A God-damned celebrity. I'll have to get an unlisted number. And then he thought: but it's Shadow who's the star, not me. He's the one who can see.

From the group, Nina, Russell, and Claire, came toward him.

"Five and a half minutes," Nina said brusquely. "Any problems?"

Campbell shook his head. Russell kneeled and looked directly into Shadow's face.

"Good boy, Shadow. Good boy." His hand passed something small and brown to the dog.

"What about me?"

"Good boy, Campbell," Russell said.

"You did it Campbell," Claire said, and hugged him fiercely.

Then Russell was looking into Campbell's face with concern. Campbell watched from below, from Shadow's perspective, feeling as if he weren't even there.

"Are you okay, Campbell?"

"I'm fine. Your trick in the elevator almost caught me, that's all."

"Nina's idea. You sure you're okay?"

"Fine. Just one thing. This linkup with Shadow. All I get is what he sees, right? Nothing else?"

Russell frowned. "Just what he sees, right. Why?"

Campbell said nothing.

"Campbell, you have to be straight with us. If something happened, we have to know."

They'll take Shadow away from me, he thought.

"I'm still trying to come to grips with it, that's all. It's amazing. What's next?"

Russell was not entirely convinced, and he looked hard at Campbell for a good five seconds before speaking again. "We're going to spend the rest of the day debriefing you on your short trip, making sure you know how to control Shadow, and that you knew what you were doing and didn't fluke it getting down here. And then, tomorrow, another test."

"Damn it, Russell, not another one!"

"It will be the last one. And the hardest one of all, Campbell. Real life."

NINE

"It's beautiful," Campbell said.

Claire turned to look at him. He was sitting in the back seat with Shadow. The dog was staring out the window at the passing countryside. They were five minutes out of Fergus Falls.

This is the first time he's seen any of this, Claire reminded herself. Three weeks ago, driving up here with Russell, she'd been painfully aware that Campbell had never seen how beautiful Otter Tail County really was. It had made her feel guilty in an odd way she couldn't understand. To live here and never see the gently rolling hills, the glittering summer lakes, was unimaginably sad. Now, she shared Campbell's joy at the view, more than shared it. Her own joy was multiplied a thousand fold, simply because Campbell could see.

"I really picked a spot, didn't I?"

Russell turned to Campbell with a wry smile. "This is as far as you can get from civilization without crossing into Canada."

Campbell laughed, and even that sound intensified the smile on Claire's face. When was the last time he had laughed? Really laughed? So long ago it might as well have been in another life.

"Shadow, front," Campbell said.

Campbell continued to face the window for a disconcerting second or two, then leaned back in his seat. His face, in the rearview mirror, seemed to be smothered by the dark glasses. Claire had a hard time accepting that it was not her brother's eyes that did the actual seeing. He no longer looked like a blind man. Even with the glasses, his expression was one of alertness.

She had to consciously stop herself from looking away. *Those eyes can't see me.*

"What are you looking at, Claire?"

"Nothing."

But Shadow could see her. With a blush she turned her attention to the road. Campbell laughed again.

When Claire turned onto the gravel road that led down to the lake, Campbell tensed, sat straighter.

"Shadow, scan," he said quietly.

As the dog slowly turned his head from left to right then left again, Campbell's head also turned.

"It's off the beaten trail, isn't it?" he said.

Claire pulled in behind his cabin and parked beside the utility shed. Through the trees, the lake was a brilliant stretch of burnished gold, glittering in the morning sun. A handful of small boats moved serenely across the water, and somewhere close by an outboard motor puttered. In the back seat, Campbell did not move.

"My heart is pounding," he said.

"I told you this would be a hard test," Russell said. "You've only been here blind. You only came here *because* you were blind. You're going to have a hard time *not* equating this place with your blindness."

Campbell scowled. "Let me out."

Russell opened the door and slid the seat forward. Campbell pushed Shadow out, then hauled himself after the dog. Before Claire had even unfastened her seat belt he had walked to the front of the car.

"Hold on, Campbell," Russell said.

Claire got out quickly and rushed to her brother's side, but when she tried to take his arm he pulled it away. Russell came up beside her and took her hand.

"Shadow, scan," Campbell said.

After a few seconds he walked confidently along the stone path to the front of the cabin. Claire and Russell followed.

"Place needs a paint job," Campbell said. "Nobody told me."

"Would you have cared if I had?" Claire asked.

"No."

He stepped up onto the deck, walked forward without hesitation, opened the porch door and stepped inside. Standing at the inside door he reached up to an empty plant holder hanging from the ceiling, put his fingers inside, and pulled out a key on a leather tag. Again, without hesitation, he unlocked the door and opened it. Inside, he stopped.

"Shadow, scan."

After a moment, Campbell turned around. Claire was painfully aware that Shadow was staring at her, and she squeezed tightly on Russell's hand.

"I was going to ask you to excuse the mess, but the good fairies have been at work."

"That was me," Claire said. "I mean, I . . . I asked your neighbor to drop in and . . ."

"Hope?"

"Yes. Don't be angry. She wanted to help."

"I'm not angry, Claire."

When he stepped right up to her she was so surprised that she nearly backed away.

"Shadow, up," he said quietly.

The dog looked up at her, but Claire continued to look into her brother's face, into the dark glasses that covered his eyes.

"Thank you," he said. "Thank you for bringing Russell up here, for making me listen, for looking after me for so long, for putting up with me."

He touched her face, gently, and kissed her cheek. Claire choked back tears.

"You, too, Russell," Campbell said, and turned away from her.

But Shadow did not turn away, and she knew that what Campbell continued to see was her.

"You were the perfect candidate for the surgery, Campbell."

"But if you hadn't been seeing Claire . . ."

Russell shrugged. "These things have a way of working out."

"I guess it helps that I'm the luckiest son of a bitch alive."

Claire could hardly believe she had heard those words. Campbell, calling himself lucky? He'd always thought so before the accident, but in the past year that had changed.

"Let's get you settled in," Russell said.

Campbell shook his head, tugged at Shadow and turned around.

"I can do it myself."

He walked along the hallway to the kitchen, commanded Shadow to scan, then turned around again.

"Go back to Minneapolis. I'll be fine."

"We can't just leave you here alone," Claire protested.

"Why not? I live here. I've lived here six months now, blind."

"But . . ."

Russell squeezed her hand again. "Are you sure you're up for it?" he asked.

"It has to happen sometime. It might as well be now. Don't worry, Claire. I can see now. I'll be fine."

"Okay, Campbell," Russell said. "We'll come and get you next week for the follow-up. Make sure you call if you need anything. Me, or Claire."

Then Russell was leading her out of the cabin, back to the car. She opened the driver door, then shook her head.

"I can't drive."

Russell didn't question her. He helped her into the passenger-side, then slid behind the wheel. As they pulled away from the cabin, he squeezed her thigh.

"He'll be fine."

"I feel . . . useless."

"Don't worry about him. That's the last thing he'd want."

But she couldn't help it. She'd been worrying about Campbell every day for a year now. It was the main focus of her life. She doubted she would ever be able to stop.

* * *

Campbell smelled and heard Hope Matheson's cabin before he saw it, or rather, he smelled and heard the dogs.

That was the strangest thing to Campbell about his linkup with Shadow. His other senses, hearing, smell, and touch, had remained as acute as they had ever been. The vision Shadow provided was augmented with audio, olfactory, and tactile data he had never been aware of during his truly sighted days. A month ago his entire universe had consisted of sounds, odors, and touches, and he had reached the point where he could function reasonably well in that dark world. Now, the light had returned. In many ways, it was "super" seeing, all four senses combined in a powerful, new way. It was an awareness, not only of what was directly in front of him, but of the entire world around him.

Walking along the trails between the cabins, he was preternaturally aware of the sound of the wind rushing through the trees, the feel of it across his face. Without looking down, merely by the feel of the ground beneath his feet, he had visualized the topography of the path. The odors of moist earth, rotting bark, even of the nearby lake, all clamored for his attention. The black and white image coming from Shadow was only one small part of the entire scene.

The barking of the dogs became more intense as the cabin came into view, became almost hysterical as he walked up the path to the front porch. He was nearly there when the door opened and a woman stepped out, looking toward the long, low kennel in the rear. She hadn't yet seen him.

So, this was Hope Matheson. The woman standing at the edge of the deck was tall, slim, dressed in jeans and a plaid shirt. Her hair looked blonde, though it might have been light red, tied in a ponytail that hung between her shoulders. He tried to remember her voice, tried to match it to the image he was now seeing. He was surprised to discover that he had never tried to visualize the face that went with the voice, and yet he was still surprised by the woman he now saw.

When she finally turned and saw him, she frowned, and then

her mouth opened in surprise. For a moment, a fraction of a second, it seemed to Campbell that a smile of pleasure turned her mouth.

"Campbell?"

"You must be Hope," he said.

"I didn't know you were back!"

She quickly crossed the deck, then stepped onto the path to meet him.

"I just got in," he said. "I wanted to thank you for cleaning the cabin for me."

"It was nothing."

"I also wanted to apologize for the way I acted when you . . . found me on the trail."

"You were upset."

"Yes, I was."

She was still looking down at Shadow, frowning a little.

"His name is Shadow," Campbell said.

She looked up at him, surprised. *She doesn't know I can see,* Campbell realized.

"He's beautiful."

"To tell you the truth, I've never seen him."

Her mouth opened in horror. "I'm sorry. I didn't mean . . ."

"No, no, I mean . . ." Campbell chuckled. "I see *through* him, so it's hard to actually see him."

She frowned again. "He's your guide dog?"

"Oh, more than that. Did Claire mention anything about why I was going to be gone for so long?"

"She mentioned a possible operation," Hope said carefully.

"Well, it happened," Campbell said.

Hope looked at him, eyes narrow. "Did it . . . I mean . . . can you . . ."

"You're wearing a plaid shirt, jeans, hiking boots. Your hair is in a ponytail. You're looking a little shocked now. Now your mouth is open. You've taken a step backward."

"How?"

"Shadow. I see through his eyes. The ultimate guide dog."

"No!"

"Yes."

She kneeled and looked closely at Shadow. Campbell studied her face. The lines of her cheeks and jaw were strong, straight. Her eyes were wide, pale-colored, surrounded in tiny lines. Either she laughed a lot, or she worried a lot. The same lines framed her mouth. It was hard to tell how old she might be, but he guessed somewhere in her early thirties.

"I've never heard anything like this. I never even knew they could do anything like this."

"If you have some time, I'll tell you all about it."

She stood, looking surprised. "Sure. Come on in, and I'll . . ."

"Actually, I didn't come just to thank you and to apologize. I sent Claire back to Minneapolis, and then I realized I didn't have any food in the house."

"When I cleaned out the refrigerator, I threw most of it out."

"It's okay. But maybe you could help me. If you have a car, you could drive me into Battle Lake, and . . ."

"Just let me lock up. I'll be right with you."

As she walked back to the cabin, she looked over her shoulder, but she did not look at Campbell. She looked directly at Shadow.

He expected he was going to be seeing a lot of that.

The drive into Battle Lake was a tense one for Hope. Her feelings for Campbell Knight had confused her and shocked her as they had developed over the past few weeks. Until today, she had met him only twice, once on the beach, and once when she had found him on the trail. Yet there had been something about him, something that attracted her to him as she had been attracted to no other man. He, she had imagined, of all men, might understand her, as she felt she might understand him.

The night of her dinner with her mother, those feelings had come to a surprising climax. She had felt nothing but contempt for Warren when he had tried to reestablish his claim upon her, but his kiss, in some odd way, *had* ignited the dry core of her inner feelings. But not for Warren himself. When she had stopped the car that night, unable to drive because of the shock she was feeling, it had been Campbell Knight's face that had filled her mind.

As she drove now to Battle Lake, Campbell beside her, Shadow peering out the window, she could not help but suspect that he knew what was in her heart. She had never been good at hiding her feelings. Somehow, it must all show on her face. A month ago that wouldn't have mattered. Campbell had been blind. But now . . .

"Shadow, left."

The dog turned to look at Hope, and her hands tensed on the wheel.

"I really appreciate this, Hope."

"It's my pleasure."

My God, had she actually said that? *My pleasure?* What must he be thinking now? Those words, as surely as if she had planted a kiss on his mouth, must tell him what was in her mind!

But he said nothing. After a few seconds, he said softly, to the dog, "Shadow, front."

When Shadow turned away from her, Hope released her breath and relaxed. It was strange, almost frightening, to have the dog's eyes focused on her, and to know that it was Campbell who was seeing her.

In town, she accompanied Campbell into the grocery store, and helped him choose his supplies. He talked of inconsequential things, about how he hadn't expected Battle Lake to look this way, about how beautiful everything was, and she listened, smiling, nodding, saying little. In fact, she realized, these were not inconsequential things to Campbell. He was seeing again, after a year of blindness. What else could be more important to him?

Once the groceries were loaded into the car, he did not immediately climb in.

"Are you in a hurry?" he asked. "I thought, if you're not, I could take you for a coffee, or something."

Hope, her door already open, hesitated.

"If you need to get back . . ."

"No. Coffee would be nice."

She was surprised when he put his arm through hers, but said nothing. Perhaps he didn't feel fully comfortable with Shadow, perhaps he still needed a little help. But Campbell walked quickly, almost pulling her along. The sidewalk was crowded with strollers, teenagers, families with children. Battle Lake was, in many respects, a summer town. It was in its glory.

Faces turned to them as they walked, staring at Campbell, at Shadow. Campbell paid no attention, but Hope felt embarrassed and angry for him. What right had they to stare at him?

In the ice cream parlor, Campbell sat at a table near the back and asked her if she would mind getting the coffees as he still didn't have experience handling money with Shadow watching. At the table next to theirs, a young boy stared over his mother's shoulder at Campbell. Hope went to the counter and ordered two coffees. Looking back at Campbell, she was horrified to see the young boy stick his tongue out. The boy's mother put a finger to her lips and frowned at him, then turned to look at Campbell. Campbell sat quietly, face impassive, as if he really were blind. But Shadow, sitting on the floor, stared up at the woman and the boy.

When Hope returned to the table, the boy was still making faces, and the woman looked up at Hope with a tolerant smile. Campbell grinned at her as she sat down.

"It has been a long time since I was in a restaurant. Without Claire, that is."

He was looking directly at her, but his view of her, she realized, was from Shadow's perspective. He was actually looking *up,* at her. Could he see up her nose, she wondered. She could not stop herself from blushing.

"What's wrong?"

"Nothing, nothing." Oh, God, this was horrible! She was as

bad as the horrible little boy at the next table! She was treating Campbell like a freak.

"I know it takes a lot of getting used to."

"I'm so sorry."

"Don't be."

He sipped his coffee, still smiling. The dog's stare was unwavering. Unlike a human partner, who might look away momentarily, Shadow's eyes never left her face.

Campbell reached across the table and touched her hand. It was a tentative, blind move, and when he made contact, he covered her hand with his and squeezed gently.

"Listen. It's me who's looking at you, not Shadow. Okay? Look at me, not at him. Don't be uncomfortable. I'm *not* staring at you, I promise."

She blushed again, looked down, then forced herself to look into his face and smile. "I'm sorry. I'm a fool."

But his gentleness and concern had broken the tension, and her smile was honest. When they finished their coffees, she was actually sorry, and wished they could stay longer. When they stood, the boy at the next table looked up at Campbell and stuck his tongue out. This time, the boy's mother did nothing.

Campbell stuck his thumbs in his ears, waggled his fingers, and stuck his tongue out. Both the boy and his mother stared up at Campbell in horror, mouths open wide, caught. Campbell chuckled as he walked to the door, then outside. Hope burst into a laugh as she caught up to him.

"I think you just ruined their day!"

"I'm good at playing blind, aren't I?"

Back in the car, the tension returned. They drove in silence. Words came to Hope's mind, but she could not bring herself to speak them. Campbell, too, seemed subdued. He stared out the passenger window, mouth a straight line, while Shadow stared straight ahead. She wanted to reach out and touch him, squeeze his hand, say the things she had been thinking. Tell him that she wanted to get to know him. Tell him that if he needed anything, anything at all, he should come to her before he went to anybody else. Tell him that . . .

But she said nothing. Because this Campbell was not the Campbell she had met on the beach. This Campbell was not the helpless man she had fantasized about. This Campbell could see. This Campbell could see as well as Warren could see.

Was that what had attracted her to Campbell in the first place? His helplessness? Had he merely awakened a mothering instinct within her, the same instinct her dogs awakened?

When they arrived back at Campbell's cabin, she was more confused than she had been an hour ago. It was as if the wonderful time they'd had in the ice cream parlor had never happened. The air seemed to crackle between them.

She helped carry the groceries into the cabin, helped to put them away, then made her excuses. She had to go. The dogs needed to be fed and walked.

On the porch, Campbell seemed distraught, nervous.

"Listen. I was thinking. I know I haven't been the best of neighbors, but . . . I'd like to thank you for all your help. If you'd like to stay for dinner, I could . . ."

Hope shook her head, far too quickly. "The dogs," she said.

"Some other time, then?"

"Maybe. Yes. Some other time. Goodbye."

She walked quickly back to the car, and when she backed up sent a spray of gravel into the air. On the short drive to her own cabin, her face burned.

What was wrong with her? What had happened to her? He had wanted to get to know her better, and she had acted as if he were the last man on earth she'd like to see!

But she couldn't help it. This Campbell was different from the Campbell she had first met. This Campbell was . . . whole. And whole, like all men, he was predatory. Like Warren. Like all the others who had trampled on her.

This Campbell frightened her.

TEN

Campbell led Shadow down the trail to the stony beach that fronted his property. The evening was comfortably warm, the sky clear. On the shore, he picked his way carefully over sand and rock as he walked.

He wished Hope Matheson were here. It would be nice to be holding her hand. Not for guidance, or support, just to hold. He stopped and turned Shadow to face the shore, but could not pick out her cabin in the trees. She was up there somewhere. Alone.

When he turned to start back, he saw the small group walking along the shore toward him. They were still some distance away, but he could pick out three distinct figures. Like him, they were walking slowly, picking up rocks, throwing them into the water. As he drew closer, he saw that they were teenagers. Two boys and a girl. The boys were tall, lanky, tanned already, wearing cutoffs and loose T-shirts. Their faces, Campbell saw, were similar, bony and beak-nosed, and he wondered if they were brothers. The girl was younger, wearing jeans and a denim shirt, long blonde hair, round face, too much makeup.

"Hi," Campbell said as he approached, and smiled.

They skirted him by a few yards, glancing toward him curiously, then stopped.

"He's blind," one of the boys said.

Campbell kept walking, sensing something in the voice that he did not like.

Footsteps came up behind him.

"Hey, mister!"

He stopped and turned around. The girl was standing with her hands in her pockets, some distance away, smiling. Campbell heard footsteps again, and realized the boys were behind him.

"Nice dog, mister."

They still had not come into Shadow's field of vision. Campbell stood still, head cocked as if listening for them. Let them think he was blind. They were in for a surprise.

One of the boys, the taller of the two, danced in front of Campbell, grinning. As Campbell watched, the boy edged stealthily closer. The boy behind Campbell suddenly coughed loudly, and Campbell turned his head slightly.

The boy in front of him reached out and slapped him hard across the cheek before Campbell could react.

"What's the matter? Didn't see it coming?"

Both boys broke out laughing, both coming into Shadow's field of vision. Campbell had the sudden intuition that to reveal to them that he could see them would be foolish, and dangerous. They were playing with him at the moment, confident in their anonymity. If they thought he could identify them, things might get serious very quickly.

He cocked his head again, as if trying to locate them by hearing alone.

"Leave me alone," he said. "I just want to walk."

The boys snickered, and then became silent. Again, one of them circled behind him, while the other edged closer.

"Leave him alone!" the girl called out.

The boy in front of Campbell ignored her, moving silently closer. The boy was so stealthy that Campbell heard nothing, and felt a stab of fear. Without Shadow, he really would have been at the mercy of these sadistic little monsters.

"Please, just let me go. I haven't done anything to you."

"Nice dog," the boy behind Campbell said.

Campbell turned his head slightly, keeping up the sham of blindness. Suddenly there were hands gripping his arms, holding tightly. Campbell cried out. The boy in front of him stepped closer, lifted his fist, and smashed it into Campbell's face.

Being hit was the strangest sensation of all. His vision, through Shadow, remained absolutely steady, and yet stars danced inside his head. He stumbled backward, yanking Shadow. Only the boy holding his arms stopped him from falling.

Then the boy in front of him was coming at him again, coming directly at Shadow.

"What is this?" the boy said. "You got him plugged in or something?"

"Leave that alone!" For the first time, Campbell's voice carried true fear.

It happened so quickly that it left his head spinning. One second he was staring into the boy's nasty, frowning face, and the next moment he was floating in darkness.

As he cried out, his fingers were pried away from the harness; the hands that had been supporting him were suddenly gone, and he crashed heavily to the stony beach.

Laughter, shouting. Shadow barking.

"Wait! I need my dog! Please!"

But the voices receded along the beach, swallowed by the sound of lapping water and wind.

Darkness had returned to Campbell. And this time, he was utterly lost in it.

As she ate a quick dinner of reheated Kraft Macaroni, Hope wondered why she had turned down Campbell Knight's offer.

Fool. Coward.

He frightened you. Big deal.

Wasn't that you who was complaining about having no relationship? Wasn't that you who listened to Warren tell you no other man would be interested?

That *was* you, wasn't it?

She ate her meal in sullen silence, angry at herself, ashamed. Warren would love to see this. Love it.

She finished half her plate and scraped the rest of the day-old macaroni into the trash. She had a choice here. Simplicity itself. She could spend the evening alone, or she could spend it in the company of a man whom she felt attracted to, and who seemed to be attracted to her.

He *was* attracted to her, wasn't he? He had invited her to eat with him, after all.

Standing at the kitchen sink, Hope closed her eyes and cursed the circumstances that had made her so self-conscious, so doubting, so lacking in confidence. One circumstance, really. Her mother.

Damn you!

Think about what it would be like if she and Campbell really hit it off. *Really* hit it off. She'd take him to visit her mother, introduce him as her lover, her friend. She could imagine her mother's reaction perfectly. The shock, then the contrition. Maybe Warren would be there, too. The look on *his* face would be worth paying to see.

Fool. Indulging in commonplace daydreams while the man who had invited her to spend some time with him sat at home alone.

Hope nodded to herself, firming her resolve. Walk the dogs. Jill, anyway. The others could wait. Then she'd knock on Campbell's door. Too late for dinner, but how about a drink? She imagined his smile of pleasure. Yes. She'd do it.

Outside, the dogs in the kennel started howling as she walked to the end of the building. Only three of them, but they made enough racket for a pack of wild dogs. Two hyperactive Springer Spaniels, and Jill. Jill, who had been boisterous and rebellious the first few days of her stay was now moody and unpredictable. When Hope entered the kennel the German Shepherd regarded her solemnly, without rising to her feet. The two spaniels leaped at the doors of their cages, desperate for release.

"Just you, Jill. Walk time. Come on, girl." She rattled the dog's leash.

Jill rose to her feet, and walked with a distinct lack of enthusiasm to the door. Hope leashed her and took her outside. The spaniels continued to howl and bark until Hope was well along the path toward Campbell Knight's cabin.

Jill paused to urinate twice on the short trail, each time looking up at Hope with sad eyes.

"Come on, girl. It's not that bad. They'll be back soon, and then you'll be going home. You'll see. They haven't forgotten you."

After this inspiring speech, Jill went down on her haunches and dropped a load in the middle of the path, looking up at Hope with a *so, what are you going to do about it,* grin. Hope sighed. She'd forgotten to bring along the scoop. She'd return later and clean up after the dog. That, or she'd step in it sometime during the next couple of days. Never failed. Divine justice at work.

There were lights on at Campbell's place, on the porch, in the kitchen. Hope paused on the pretense of allowing Jill to urinate, and studied the cabin. No sign of him. No movement inside. But he had to be there. Where else could he go?

She resisted the temptation to knock on his door at this moment. Better get Jill back, settled. She pulled on the leash until Jill followed her past Campbell's cabin, on into the trails.

The evening was pleasant, neither warm nor cool. The sunset would be gorgeous. A thin line of clouds rested on the western horizon, above the lake. When had Campbell last seen a sunset? That might be nice. Perhaps he'd like to walk down to the beach and watch. No harm in asking, anyway.

As she passed the cabin adjacent to Campbell's the tree growth thickened, blocking out the view of the lake. The evening shadows became longer, sewing her in a web of dark green vegetation. Mosquitos buzzed around her.

Jill, she noticed, was acting strangely. The dog was walking erect, ears pricked, alert.

"What is it, girl?"

A skunk, perhaps. Or a rabbit. Jill would be hard to control if that were the case.

Ahead, on the trail, something made a noise. An animal noise. Snuffling.

Hope, ready to yank hard on Jill's leash, froze, listening. She stared down the trail.

"Hello!"

The black shape lunged out of the brush at the side of the trail, and Hope gasped. Jill tugged violently on the leash, straining to reach the interloper. It took Hope only a couple of seconds to recognize the dog.

"Shadow!"

Shadow, still in his harness, turned to her, wagged his tail, and walked briskly up to her. Jill strained to reach the other dog, tail slashing back and forth. Shadow paid her no attention, but came directly to Hope. Even when Jill nearly clambered on the other dog's back, Shadow remained oblivious, supercilious.

Where was Campbell? Had Shadow somehow escaped from the cabin? Did Campbell know?

She grasped the harness, then yanked on Jill's leash, pulling the dog to her right side.

"Heel! Heel!"

It took her nearly five minutes to navigate back to Campbell's cabin, Jill lunging around her legs to get at Shadow, Shadow remaining poised and perfectly positioned behind her left leg. She tied Jill to a tree outside the cabin, then knocked on the door. No answer. At her heel, Shadow whined.

Hope opened the door and went inside. Surely Campbell wouldn't mind. It wasn't as if she were intruding. She was simply returning his dog.

"Campbell? It's Hope. I found Shadow outside."

But the cabin was empty. A dish and an empty wineglass sat on the porch table. The groceries had been put away. No sign of Campbell.

Which meant what?

That he was outside somewhere. Without Shadow.

And without Shadow, he was blind.

She took Shadow outside, worried now. Very worried. How could Shadow have gotten loose? If Campbell had fallen, perhaps, the cable might have become disconnected. Or perhaps Campbell had even collapsed, unconscious, and Shadow had freed himself. Either way, Campbell could be lying on the ground somewhere, blind, terrified, waiting for help.

Although Jill whined and barked frantically, she left the German Shepherd tied to the tree, and guided Shadow down the trail toward the beach. That was the direction he had come from.

On the shore, she looked both ways, but saw nothing. The beach was empty as far as she could see.

"Where is he, boy? Where's Campbell."

But Shadow was too well-trained. He waited to be guided, waited for instructions. He was not going to take her to Campbell.

Hope nearly cried out in frustration. Campbell could be anywhere. It might take hours to find him. Anything might happen to him, if it hadn't happened already.

Swallowing her self-consciousness, she took a deep breath and yelled.

"Campbell!"

In the ensuing silence, she listened. Nothing.

She turned the other way. "Campbell!"

Again, she listened.

This time, from the west, a reply. A voice. Faint, but audible.

She pulled Shadow behind her as she ran along the beach. A hundred yards along she found Campbell. He was sitting against the side of a sandy embankment. His face was covered in dirt, his clothes disheveled. Blood caked his upper lip, his chin.

For the first time, Shadow pulled ahead, eager to sniff his master. Campbell's hands found the dog, stroked its face.

"Hope?"

"Yes. What happened?"

"Kids. Attacked me. Took Shadow."

"Are you all right? Your face is covered in blood."

He nodded, but she could see that he was shaking, that he was deeply affected by what had happened. His hands trembled as they snaked along Shadow's harness cable.

"I can't find the coupler," his voice verged on breaking. "Can you . . ."

She kneeled by him, brought the harness close to his hands, used both her own hands to reconnect the cable. Campbell stiffened, and groaned softly.

"Thank God," he said softly.

Hope helped him to his feet, and he leaned on her heavily.

"Are you okay?"

"I think so. Could you help me back? I feel dizzy."

Without another word she put her arm through his and led him along the beach toward the path to his own cabin.

"You can't let them get away with it," Hope said.

Campbell winced as she wiped his nose, and Hope winced in sympathy. The table was already covered with soiled napkins. Campbell's nose was swollen, red.

"They were just kids, raising hell."

"Not this way. This was assault. You have to go to the police. If they get away with it, they'll do it again. Maybe not to you, but to some other blind person. I mean, a *real* blind person."

"You know any other member of the white cane brigade who lives around here?"

"Campbell, I'm serious. You have to do it for yourself. You can't be a victim all the time."

She had not intended to sound so furious, but the tone of her voice finally reached him. Both Campbell and Shadow stared at her.

"I'm not a victim."

"Okay, then. I'll drive you into town. We'll report it."

Campbell took a deep breath, let it out in a sigh. He nodded slowly.

The drive into Battle Lake was even more silent than their earlier trip. Campbell seemed lost in thought, brooding. Halfway there, he spoke without even looking at her.

"They didn't even care. They thought I couldn't see. That's what made it fun for them. It was a big joke. They left me blind."

He shook his head, disbelieving.

Hold that anger, she thought. Keep it burning, Campbell.

At the police station in Battle Lake, she followed him inside. The small station was home to a single deputy sheriff, a middle-aged man named Hugh Cronin, who had held the position for nearly twenty years. He was leaning across the counter when Campbell and Hope came in, leafing through a gun catalog.

Campbell stood back from the counter and said, "Shadow, up."

Shadow immediately looked up at Hugh Cronin, who looked down at the dog with a frown.

"What can I do for you folks?" He addressed Hope.

Campbell said, "I'd like to report an assault."

Hugh Cronin looked at Campbell's face, raised his eyebrows. "On you?"

"That's right."

"When did it happen?"

"Earlier tonight. A couple of hours ago. South shore."

Hugh Cronin looked back and forth between Hope and Campbell.

"What happened?"

"I was walking on the beach. Three teenagers attacked me. Two boys and a girl. They punched me up, took off with my dog."

Hugh Cronin sighed, looked at Hope, frowned. "Were you alone at the time?"

"Just me and the dog."

Cronin cleared his throat. "You're Campbell Knight, right? Living at the old Peterson cabin?"

"That's right."

"Pardon me for saying so, but you're blind, aren't you? In fact, you lost both your eyes, didn't you?"

"I did, yes."

"How can you be sure it was two boys and a girl?"

"I saw them."

Cronin stared at Campbell for a few seconds, then turned to Hope with a confused smile.

"I'll tell you what I'll do. I'll ask around, see if anybody saw anything. If we can get a witness, maybe we'll be able to identify the boys."

"I said, I saw them."

Cronin stared at Campbell, sucked at his lips, glanced at Hope. "Maybe you can tell me how you managed that, being blind."

Campbell grinned humorlessly. "You're leaning across the counter toward me. Your hat is beside your left elbow. There's some sort of stain on the right side of your shirt collar. Your badge is slightly askew. Now your eyes are a little wider than they were a second ago, and your mouth is hanging open. Now you're standing up straight."

"That's enough."

"You just lifted your left hand to your chin. Don't look at Miss Matheson, look at me. I'm the one who got assaulted. I told you, I saw them. I recently underwent surgery that restored part of my sight. I can identify the boys, and the girl."

"You don't have sight to restore, Mr. Knight. You don't have any eyes.

"There's a calendar on the wall behind you. It's still on June. It's a photograph of a horse behind a fence. The 27th is circled, but I can't read the note that's written there."

Cronin turned around and stared at the calendar, then turned back to Campbell. "Well, I'll be damned."

"Not until after I've laid my complaint."

ELEVEN

When Campbell woke, Shadow was already up. The dog was alert, anyway. Lying in bed, Campbell surveyed the room. The bed was darkness to his right, like a cliff face jutting into a gray sky. The floor stretched away like the plain of a moon crater. The walls and doors were distant craggy mountains, holding at bay a world of vacuum and darkness.

He did not know how long Shadow had been awake, or even what time it was. His internal clock was off. Judging by the light in the room, it was past dawn, anyway. Campbell sat up and swung his legs off the bed.

"Shadow, front."

As if he'd been waiting all his life for just this command, Shadow stood abruptly. The view shifted to the dresser. Campbell felt a moment of fear when he saw himself reflected in the mirror. He reared tall and white, a solitary cloud shaped like a man. His face was bisected by the glasses, the dark bulbs glistening like the eyes of some deep-water fish straining for glimmers of light.

He had remained linked to Shadow through the night, as Russell and Nina had suggested. There had been no further dreams. Not that he could remember, anyway.

He had accommodated the linkup. That's what they'd say, anyway.

He unhooked himself from the dog, plunging into darkness. For a few seconds he was utterly lost, floating in blackness. It astonished him how helpless he felt, how quickly the ability to function without sight had faded, withering like a plant without water. It seemed impossible that he had lived like this for a whole year, more, that he had actually *functioned*.

He felt around for the chair by the bed, found his clothes, and dressed as quickly as he could. When he put the glasses back on and hooked up the cable to Shadow's harness, he let out a low sigh of relief. In the dresser mirror he looked presentable. He ran a hand through his hair, pushing it back. Good enough. He smiled. His reflection looked grimmer than he had intended.

In the kitchen, he suffered through another five minutes of darkness while Shadow fed. Staring into the dog's bowl was too disconcerting. Better this momentary plunge into a tunnel. That's all it was. He sat by the dog, listening to the sounds of food being bolted, water being lapped. He would develop a routine soon enough. A large part of his life would now revolve around the maintenance of Shadow. Feeding, walking. As any sighted person might care for contact lenses. When Shadow had finished, the dog slapped a wet tongue across his hand, and Campbell hooked himself up again. Some contact lenses.

His stomach was growling, but Shadow, he knew, needed out. He could eat later.

He had stepped off the deck and onto the path when Hope called to him.

"Good morning!"

"Shadow, right."

He grinned as she approached. She was wearing jeans, a thin sweater, hands stuffed into her pockets.

"I was just about to take the dogs out for a walk, and I thought, afterward, if you wanted, we could run into Battle Lake for breakfast."

There was a nervousness in her voice, a tentativeness, that surprised him. Was she intimidated by him? He wondered if he had been even nastier than he had thought that day she had found him on the beach.

"That sounds good," he said. "I have to take Shadow for a spin, too. Why not meet back here in half an hour, say?"

She nodded, half frowning, as if she wanted to say something but didn't know how to put it.

"Are you going to be all right?" she finally got out.

"Sure. Fine. See you in a bit. Shadow, front."

On the beach, he walked toward the town on the far shore, picking his way slowly across the rock strewn sand. He stopped once or twice to allow Shadow to do his business, then brought the dog to a stop overlooking the lake. Morning mist rippled across the water like a fading heat mirage. The water glistened like hot blacktop. A giant parking lot. Water and mist. How long since he had seen anything like this? It seemed like decades. Even sighted, he hadn't gone out of his way to see a view like this in many years. So precious. He wanted to drink it in and remember its every nuance.

A sound down the beach caught Shadow's attention, and Campbell's view suddenly shifted. He was looking along the shore. A figure walked toward him through stray tongues of mist like a giant strolling through clouds. Campbell did not shift his position. He recognized the person who was approaching him. It was one of the teenaged boys who had assaulted him last night.

The boy was moving furtively, picking his way carefully over the rocky sand, looking down at his feet as if afraid he might trip.

Campbell turned toward him as nonchalantly as he could, as *blindly* as he could, and started walking.

"Shadow, front," he said softly.

The boy, twenty yards away, stopped, stared. Campbell moved toward him, angled his head slightly toward the lake as if he were listening rather than watching. The *Stevie Wonder* shuffle. The little punk still thought he was blind.

The boy moved forward again, paused, reached down and picked up a rock as big as his fist. Campbell was close enough now that he could see the sneer on the boy's mouth, the hate in his eyes.

The boy came closer, lifting his feet slowly like a man wary of trampling delicate flowers.

Campbell, within ten yards now, stopped. He angled his head as if listening.

"Hello? Is anybody there?"

The boy frowned, and then smiled. He stepped toward Campbell, hand now raised with the rock. Shadow growled softly, and the boy stopped. Campbell turned his head again, frowning, as if he had lost the sound he had been straining so hard to hear.

"Who's there?"

Again, the smile. A grin, all teeth. The Cheshire Cat. All caution gone. Safe to move in on the blind man.

Campbell turned his face toward the lake as the boy came closer. The idiot didn't even bother to pick his feet up properly. Even without Shadow watching his approach, Campbell would have known he was being stalked.

The boy stopped an arm's length away, staring at Campbell. "Hey, asshole."

Campbell turned, careful not to look directly at the source of the voice.

"Who is it? Can I help you?"

The grin became impossibly wider. "Somebody you got into trouble," the boy said.

Campbell made his mouth open in surprise. "You!"

He took a tentative step backward. The boy's eyes flashed triumphantly.

"You ain't identifying nobody!"

It seemed to Campbell to be almost in slow motion that the boy stepped toward him, arm raised, rock held in fist. At the last instant, Campbell turned directly to face his attacker, and for a fraction of a second saw doubt in the boy's eyes.

He punched hard, bringing his fist up in an uppercut that caught the boy below the chin. The connection was solid, and beneath his fist he felt teeth crash together and give. The boy's eyes filled with confusion. He dropped to the sand hard, rock spilling out of his fist.

Campbell kneeled by him and grabbed his collar, pulling him up hard. The boy groaned. Blood dribbled from his mouth. He looked dazed, frightened.

"Next time you come near me, I'll break your neck, you little shit. Understand?"

The boy groaned, squeezing his eyes tightly shut.

Campbell shook him hard. "Understand?"

"Yes, yes!"

"Get the hell out of here."

The boy scrambled away and got to his feet, backed slowly away, rubbing his chin, spitting blood. Ten yards away he stopped, turning to stare hatefully at Campbell.

Campbell stepped purposefully toward him. "I said get out of here!"

The boy's eyes widened another notch, and he turned and ran. Campbell stood quietly, feeling strangely calm, and watched his attacker's retreat.

"Good, Shadow," he said softly. "Good boy."

He grinned as he turned and walked back along the beach.

God's answer to Eleanor's prayer had been swift and sure. There was a place in heaven for Jesse Hampton. The angels were waiting breathlessly for the boy to arrive. Little baby Jesus himself had prepared a place for Jesse! In heaven, there was love enough to heal the deepest scars on the boy's soul. Any time, God had said. Send him along any time.

Eleanor sipped her coffee, gazing dreamily out the kitchen window. The morning sky was blue, bright enough to highlight the grime on the glass. Five years of dust and rain, dust and rain, dust and rain, dried into a gauzy cake like the bottom of a barroom spittoon. Those windows, she thought, could make the brightest of days look cloudy.

Max lapped at the water in his bowl, then waddled over to her like a dog twice as old. He lay down at her feet and let out his breath in a soft hiss that sounded as wet as the last gasp of a steam radiator. But there was love in those bones. He rested his wet snout on her feet, eyes peacefully closed. She moved her feet and stroked the side of his face with her toes. His tail thumped slowly against the floor and he looked up at her. The dog loved her unconditionally, a baby's love, as love should be.

"We'll take Jesse to heaven today," she said. "We'll take care of him today."

Still, she took another sip of her coffee, then glanced toward the coffeepot to make sure there was more. Despite God's invitation, she was reluctant to send the boy along. It was the goodbyes that she hated. The last looks. The finality of it all. She kept imagining Jesse's face looking up at her, the hurt in his eyes. It didn't matter that he was headed for heaven; he likely wouldn't want to go. That was the hardest. But sometimes love had to be tough, you had to do the right thing no matter how hard it was. That was the nature of love. It desired the best for the beloved, no matter how much that might hurt. Second best just wasn't good enough, not as far as true love was concerned.

At her feet, Max whined softly, slipping into dream. She nudged him awake with her toe.

"Let's go, Max. No sense dawdling. The Lord is awaiting us."

Max rose unsteadily to his feet, stretching languorously, looking more like a dinosaur than a dog. Eleanor turned off the coffeepot, poured out the dusty remains in her mug. She stood at the sink and stared out the window, past the ash windbreak to the long, rolling expanse of land beyond. Her husband, Frank, had farmed that land, had cared for the soil and raised life within it. Now, she leased the land to neighboring farmers, and kept only a small plot next to the house for her own needs. That was another measure of her love, her love for the land. She knew in her heart that the land needed to be tended, and knew also that she was not capable of it. That was an indication of how true and deep her love for this land was. She had allowed others to tend it for her. That was tough love, all over again. Doing what was best for the beloved, ignoring personal desires and needs.

But the land was hers. It always would be. Her love made it hers. And now it thrived, blooming with life. As Jesse Hampton would bloom in heaven. Once she gave him up.

Tough love was never easy.

Max followed her outside, then down into the cellar. The dog stood outside Jesse's cage as she went in to comfort the boy. He lay on his mattress, knees pressed into his stomach, arms pulled into his chest, a baby all over again. She sat down next to him and stroked his hair. His head, she thought, felt slightly swollen. The soft places on his skull seemed to have distended, bulging outward.

Jesse groaned softly as she leaned down to him. He smelled of urine and sweat. Eleanor batted away a fly that buzzed around the boy's ear.

"It's time to go, Jesse," she said.

He astonished her then by opening his eyes. Just a little. A slit of blue, like a glimmer of clear summer sky in the mottled cloud that was his face.

"Home?" His voice was low and hoarse, like the whisperings of an obscene telephone caller.

"Yes," she whispered. "Home. Your true home."

His eyes closed. He looked at peace.

Lifting him, she was astonished at how light he had become; he seemed almost weightless, a bag of feathers. His ribs felt like piano keys through the thin fabric of his shirt, his legs and arms like twisted branches torn from a dried and rotting tree. So unexpected was his insubstantiality that she stood too quickly and stumbled. Jesse's head crashed against the door as she fought for balance, but he hardly reacted to the impact. Just a soft groan, an exhalation of air, a sigh.

A small voice inside Eleanor cried out accusingly, *you did this to him,* but she silenced it immediately, recognizing the misplaced guilt. No, not she. Jesse himself was responsible for his condition. This was what the denial of love wrought. It shriveled the flesh, decimated the soul. Jesse himself had done this, denying himself her love, and denying her his.

Max at her heels, she carried Jesse out of the cellar. As sunlight struck his face he groaned again, eyes opening, blinking, filling with tears. For just a moment a smile played across his lips, like a brief shaft of sunlight spearing through dark clouds, and then it was gone.

She lifted him into the bed of the pickup. The moment her hands left him he curled up again like a hedgehog confronted by a fox. She covered him with a tarpaulin.

Max hopped into the cab ahead of her. She glanced through the rear window at the lump beneath the canvas. It was still.

"It will all be over soon," she said to Max.

The dog whined, staring at her, head slightly cocked, as if waiting for something. She leaned over and opened the passenger window for him, and he stuck his head out.

She drove slowly along the rutted access road that ran beside the leased field, until the path turned into the hundred-acre woodlot she had reserved for her own use. Towering Norway pine caught the sun and sent it down in glittering shards. Shadows capered in front of the truck. Two hundred yards into the trees she stopped, caught her breath, swore softly. Somebody was walking along the trail toward her. As the figure approached, she recognized her neighbor, Len Tate. He raised a dusty hand, grinned.

As he came up to the truck he held a hand out to Max, who sniffed him and wagged his tail.

"Hi, Max. Morning, Eleanor," he said. "Billy ran off into your trees here, but I can't find him."

Billy was Len's dog, an old Springer Spaniel. Eleanor nodded. "I'll look for him," she said.

"Where you headed?"

"Thought I'd let Max chase some rabbits, get us some dinner," she said. She wanted to tell him to get off her property, to mind his own business, to keep his dog under control, but she knew that would be wrong.

Len nodded, leaning into the truck. He looked into the back, at the lump beneath the tarpaulin. Eleanor held her breath. Jesse didn't move.

"Well, if you see Billy, send him on home." Len shook his head. "On second thought, why don't you shoot him. Teach him a lesson."

"I'll do that."

He drummed on the roof of the cab and walked on with a brief wave. Eleanor waved back, drove slowly forward. In the rear view mirror she saw the shape beneath the canvas stir, and her heart pounded. So close.

She followed the trail to its end, to a broad clearing bordered by new growth. Max bounded out of the car and made immediately for the narrow, concealed trail at the east side of the clearing. Eleanor scooped Jesse out of the back of the truck and slung him over her shoulder. Prom the cab she pulled the shovel and the shotgun, dragged both, trailing on the ground, behind her.

A hundred yards out of the clearing, the trail opened into another open area. Here, the intertwined branches of the surrounding trees made a roof overhead, the trunks enclosing walls, the spaces between opening on shards of blue sky like stained glass. Max was sitting quietly, tongue lolling, waiting for her. She placed Jesse gently on the ground, resting his head on a mound of soft grass.

The other graves were disappearing. Grass and moss grew quickly here, hiding all her past work. This saddened her. These small mounds were the only visible signs of her love.

She planted the shovel and scooped out a lump of soft earth, tossed it aside. Then another. Another.

It took fifteen minutes to dig the shallow trench. When she placed Jesse into it his eyes blinked, and for the first time that morning he seemed to see her.

"Home," he whispered.

"Heaven," Eleanor said, fighting back tears.

Jesse closed his eyes. Max whined. Eleanor raised the shotgun.

Something was wrong.

Last night, when Hope had found Campbell on the beach, bleeding, he had seemed lost. Something had gone out of him, some strength, some spirit. The attack had hammered home to him how helpless he really was, at least in some situations. Reporting the incident to the deputy in Battle Lake had restored his self-confidence, as she had known it would, but when she had dropped him off at his cabin afterward she could tell that he had been deeply affected by the attack. He had said goodnight quietly, and when he had closed the door on her he seemed almost cowed, as if a great weight had been placed on his shoulders.

This morning, when she had invited him to breakfast, he seemed, to her, restored. At least to some degree. He was going for a walk with Shadow, down to the beach, and she had understood that he wanted to go alone, that he had to prove to himself that he could do it. She had watched him walk down the path, shoulders straight, and she had wanted to go with him. Only the knowledge that he would hate that, scorn her pity, had stopped her.

When she had met him at his cabin afterward he had seemed excited, almost manic. He had been pacing back and forth on the deck, Shadow by his side, waiting for her. She had understood immediately that something had happened to him while walking Shadow, but he would not tell her what it was. But this was a Campbell she had not seen before. All traces of self-doubt were gone. He looked like a man who had confronted and defeated his deepest fear, finding it to be nothing more than a shadow.

On the drive into Battle Lake he had remained mostly silent, both he and Shadow staring straight ahead, but even then she had sensed excitement in him, an eagerness.

Only when they had sat down at their table in the Lakeside Cafe did he tell her what had happened.

"He was down on the beach," he had said, smiling.

"Who was?"

"One of the teenagers from last night. The one who hit me."

Hope had stared at him, coffee cup suspended before her mouth.

"What happened?"

"He tried to attack me again." Now, the smile turned into a grin, but it was a grin of satisfaction, and there was no humor in it.

"Did he . . ."

"No, it's okay, Hope. I tricked him. I let him get close, and when he tried to hit me, I sucker punched him."

"Campbell . . ."

"You should have seen his face! He went down like a ton of bricks."

"Are you all right?"

"I'm fine. I'm great. I haven't felt this good in . . . a hell of a long time. Hope, you should have seen his face."

When their food came, he dug into his steak and eggs like a man who had not eaten in days. The victor. The victory meal. He had vanquished his foes, and he was feasting.

She watched him, silent, wanting to share his victory, but unable. This was a part of him that she had not seen before, and a part she did not like. He had enjoyed the confrontation, had taken pleasure in the boy's defeat.

They were halfway through their meal when Campbell stiffened, and she knew something was wrong. He was staring at her, hands flat on the table. On the floor beside him, Shadow whined. Campbell's teeth were clenched, his face pale.

"Is something wrong?"

His head turned, as if he were watching something pass by. Sweat popped out on his forehead.

"Campbell, is there something I can do?"

It was as if an electric current suddenly shot through his

body. His hands lashed out, knocking his coffee cup from the table. It crashed to the floor and shattered in a spray of black liquid. Diners at other tables turned to watch.

"Campbell . . ."

He shot to his feet, knocking his knees on the table. Hope's coffee cup tipped over, sending hot liquid onto her hand. She cried out and leaned away.

And then it was over. Campbell slumped into his chair, hands curled into fists on the table. He was shaking. Sweat poured off his face.

"Campbell, do you need help?"

The waitress had observed the incident from behind the counter, and now she approached with a mop and towel. Campbell must have sensed her proximity, for he said nothing until she had finished and gone away.

Hope reached out and grabbed his hand, and his returning grip was so fierce she nearly cried out.

"She killed him," he said hoarsely. "My God, Hope, she killed him!"

TWELVE

"Killed who?" Hope asked. And then, grimacing, "Campbell, my hand."

Campbell released her. He had been gripping her hand so tightly that his own fingers were numb. Hope massaged her wrist, frowning.

"Campbell, what did you mean? Who was killed?"

"I don't know. I saw it."

"When?"

"Just now."

The elation he had felt since confronting the boy on the beach had left him, and in its wake a terrible anxiety had moved in. What he was seeing through Shadow's eyes seemed unreal, hallucinatory. He half expected his vision to cloud, to shift, to take him somewhere else, as if he were in the middle of a nightmare. Hope looked extremely concerned, like Claire sometimes looked. That furrowed brow, like a mother worried about a child.

The waitress returned with two more cups of coffee and placed them on the table.

"Everything okay?"

"Yes," Campbell said quickly. "Sorry about that."

"No problem. Enjoy."

When she left, he said, "I have to get out of here."

"Let me just pay the bill and we'll go."

"I'll meet you outside. I have to go. Now."

Hope reached out and touched his hand. "I want to hear about this. You'll tell me everything?"

Campbell nodded, then stood. He moved slowly for the door, navigating between the tables. Faces turned to look at him, at Shadow, and he felt a blush creep into his face. Even sighted, he was a freak. More so now than ever before.

When he stepped out of the restaurant he inhaled deeply. The cool morning breeze turned the sweat on his face and arms to icy rivulets, and he shivered. He leaned against the outside wall, Shadow at his side, and forced himself to breath deeply. The feeling of panic slowly faded.

This vision had been just like the others, only more intense, more violent. Worse, by far. He had been looking at his own hands cut the food on his plate, absorbed in the process of eating, when his sight had faded. It was as if a lens had slowly closed over his inner eye, a ring of darkness tightening on his mind. But it had not been an empty darkness. The restaurant had been replaced by another view. He was staring at a boy, the same boy from his earlier vision, but this time in a narrow pit. The boy's eyes were open, looking up at the dark figure who towered over him. It had seemed to Campbell that this figure was female, but only vaguely, formless. She was holding a shotgun, pointing down at the boy. In the vision, Campbell had watched as she'd braced the gun against her shoulder, and squeezed the trigger, while the boy's eyes had slowly closed and . . .

"Campbell?"

Campbell started, banging his head against the wall.

"Sorry," Hope said. "You're really rattled, aren't you?"

Campbell nodded, saying nothing. He felt nauseated now, slightly dizzy. When Hope put a hand on his free arm he did not resist her, but allowed her to guide him back to the car. Inside, he opened the window and let the breeze blow across his face.

"Tell me what happened."

"Shadow, left," he said.

Shadow turned to look at Hope, and Campbell turned away from the window.

"It wasn't a hallucination. It was too real for that. I saw a boy. There was a woman with him. She killed him."

"You imagined it?" She looked neither credulous nor skeptical, only concerned.

"I don't think so. It happened before. When I was linked up to Shadow for the first time. I had a dream. I thought it was a dream at the time. I was in a prison, or a cage, and I was looking at a little boy on the floor. He seemed to be sick, but he looked at me and smiled. I remember that. Then a dark figure came into the picture and started hitting him, and that's when I woke up."

"This was the same boy?"

"I think so. The next time it happened, I was awake. It was during one of the tests at Miriam. I was in an elevator, and suddenly it was like the elevator disappeared, and I was in this car or truck, staring at a woman sitting beside me. It was her, the figure from the earlier dream. It scared the hell out of me."

"Did you tell anybody?"

"They said it was just my mind accommodating the linkup with Shadow."

"Maybe that's all it is."

"It seemed so real. I saw her kill the boy. He was in a lot worse shape than the first time I saw him. He looked beaten. It was as if I was really seeing it out of Shadow's eyes. As if he wasn't in the restaurant with us, but was watching this boy get killed."

"It sounds horrible."

"It was."

"How are you feeling now?"

"A little shaken."

She reached to him and squeezed his hand. "It's going to be okay. I'll take you back to the cabin."

As Hope drove, Campbell turned to the window and breathed deeply of the rushing air. He allowed Shadow to continue looking at Hope, and studied her face as she drove. She obviously had not fully accepted the idea that Shadow's eyes were his eyes, for she did not seem uncomfortable at all under the scrutiny. Once she even turned to the dog and petted him gently. Campbell felt a sudden knot in his stomach when that happened.

"Shadow, front," he said at last, turning from Hope to a view of the road through the windshield.

The memory of the boy in the pit lingered in his mind. There had been trees all around him, and shadows everywhere. For a few seconds, in the vision, it had seemed as if the boy were looking directly at him, smiling.

Campbell swallowed hard, feeling some of the panic return. He had wanted to reach out to the boy, to pick him up and hold him. It was as if he had really been there, as if the boy had actually been looking at him.

When the woman had raised the shotgun and pulled the trigger, he had nearly leaped out of his chair. Only the clenching of his teeth had stopped a scream from erupting into the restaurant. Then he had been looking down into the pit again, at the boy, at the blood, at the savage rupturing of flesh and bone . . .

"We're here," Hope said.

Her voice was like a splash of cold water, pulling him back from his reverie. He shuddered.

Hope parked the car behind Campbell's cabin. He sat quietly in the seat, turned to the window, as if unaware that the car had stopped. She wondered if he had heard her. He seemed lost in thought, dreaming.

"Campbell, we're here."

Campbell nodded. He undid his seat belt, opened the door, and got out. Without waiting for her he walked to the front of the cabin. She followed, surprised at how quickly he moved.

Campbell took keys from his pocket and pushed them toward the lock. The key would not fit, and he fumbled with another, swearing under his breath.

"Let me."

"No!"

He held the keys in front of Shadow. He fingered through them until he found the right one, then stood and tried again to insert it in the lock. This time, it went in smoothly and the door opened.

Campbell turned to her, smiling. But it was an empty smile, a mere twisting of his lips, and she did not like to look at it.

"Thanks for breakfast," he said.

"Do you want me to come in? I could keep you company for a while."

He seemed to consider this for a few seconds, then shook his head. "I've got some things I want to do. Thanks anyway."

"I'll come by later, if you like, to see how you're doing."

"If you want."

Then he turned, went in, and closed the door behind him. Hope shook her head. She felt abandoned, and inexplicably hurt. She walked slowly back to the car, trying to understand what she was feeling. Had she *really* wanted to keep Campbell company? Did she have the right to feel offended because he wanted to be alone?

But it wasn't that. It was more complicated than that.

She had reached out to Campbell, and he had turned away from her.

Her pride had been hurt. Nothing more.

In the car, she sat quietly for a few seconds, staring at the cabin. She saw him moving in the kitchen. Pacing.

If he wanted to be alone, let him be alone. It was up to him.

She started the car and drove the hundred yards to her own cabin. The dogs started barking the moment she pulled in behind the kennel, but she ignored them and went right inside. She made herself a pot of tea, then stood looking out the kitchen window. The dogs had fallen silent. She sipped her tea and looked toward Campbell's cabin. Although she tried not to, she found herself wondering what he was doing over there, all alone.

She wondered how long she should wait before knocking on his door again.

* * *

As Eleanor drove, her eyes brimmed with tears that slid down her cheeks and gathered at the corners of her mouth. She licked them away as more flowed, until, half blinded, she pulled the truck to the side of the road until her sobbing subsided. Beside her, Max watched her uneasily, tail thumping against the inside of the door. Sunlight shone hotly on her arms and lap.

Jesse was gone.

Her true love had left her.

In the moment before she had sent him on his way to heaven, she had seen in his eyes the love he held for her. There could be no denying it! She had seen it! She had *felt* it as it poured from his lifeless body into hers.

Love. Pure and true. Like an electric current.

Oh, the poor, poor soul! To have kept so much love inside him!

That was the great tragedy of Jesse Hampton's life. He *had* loved her, loved her with everything he had, but he hadn't known it! Only in death, only as he rushed to be with baby Jesus and his choir of angels, had he understood, had he released his love.

"Oh, Jesse," she whispered, and tears sprang anew to her eyes.

It was always like this, saying goodbye. That's what love did to you. That was the price you paid for loving. The pain of parting. And deep pain it was, seeming to reach to the very center of her.

Had it been this bad with Luke?

She could not remember, not clearly, but she knew that it must have been. Luke was her one and only true blood child, and that was a bond that could tear the heart to pieces when broken.

But she had put such hope in Jesse. She had invested in him all the love she had. It was natural that she should grieve so deeply. He was her child, her love, and he was gone!

It took her a few minutes to calm herself, to dry her tears, and even then, her eyes filled every few minutes as she drove.

She drove through Hollyfield, through Richer, through Cambridge. She drove for nearly three hours through a string of small towns, past glittering lakes, cultivated fields, bristling woodland. She had no destination in mind. She needed to drive. Needed to put Jesse behind her, and to find a new love.

It was late afternoon, as she was looping back toward home, when she drove into the town of Godfrey, just off highway 210. The sky was still clear, cloudless. God was smiling on this day. Another angel had come home. She drove slowly down the main street, then doubled back when she reached the other end of town.

Godfrey was small, smaller than Hollyfield even, with a population less than five thousand. In the middle of town she found a small park, adjacent to an outdoor swimming pool. The park was treed, well-tended, with a playground on one side, picnic tables on the other, and a stone path in the middle winding through a grove of trees and beautiful flowered gardens.

Eleanor parked the truck, put Max on his leash, and walked into the park. She found a bench near the playground and sat down. Max lay on the grass, in the shade, and closed his eyes.

The park was not crowded. The tables near Eleanor were empty; the few by the street occupied by solitary men or women, some reading newspapers, some drinking sodas. In the playground, a handful of children played together, unattended.

Eleanor watched them, heart racing. The children all looked to be about the same age, between eight and eleven she guessed. Three boys, two girls. The boys played together, running from swings, to sandbox, to monkey bars, laughing and shouting. The girls played alone, one in the sandbox, the other on the swings.

A girl this time, Eleanor thought. A girl to love and to hold and to cherish. A girl who knew how to return the love that was given her.

A girl like the one in the sandbox, who even now was looking curiously toward Eleanor.

Eleanor reached down and unhooked Max's leash. The dog sat up and looked at her.

"Go on, then," she urged. "Go *on.*"

Max trotted away toward the playground. Eleanor stood, as if surprised, and ran after him. The girl in the sandbox stood also, and held out her hand to the approaching dog. Max, tail wagging, moved directly to her.

Eleanor held back a little as the girl petted Max.

Eight, she guessed. No older than that. Long blonde hair. Sharp features, though. Narrow nose. Blue eyes, intelligent, observant.

She scratched Max's head, looking still toward Eleanor. Eleanor smiled as she approached.

"Thank you so much for catching my dog," she said.

The girl frowned, but did not stop petting Max.

"You let him go," she said.

"He got away from me."

"I saw you let him go," the girl said.

Eleanor blushed. "Did I? Maybe I did. I knew you were looking at him. I thought you might like to pet him."

The girl put her arms around Max's neck and hugged him. The dog licked her face and she giggled.

"What's his name?"

"Uh . . . Billy."

"That's a strange name for a dog."

"Do you like him?"

"He's nice."

Eleanor put the leash back on Max. Her hand brushed the girl's arm, and a jolt of pleasure ran through her. She could hardly look at the girl without blushing.

"What's your name?"

The girl looked up at her for a moment, pursed her lips, then said, "Teresa. I have to go now."

"Wait, if you . . ."

But Teresa was off and running, moving across the grass toward the picnic tables by the street. Eleanor held her breath, afraid the girl might be with somebody, afraid that she and Max might have been seen. But Teresa paused at the street, then crossed, and started walking. Eleanor sighed, relieved.

She walked Max back to the truck.

Teresa. A beautiful name.

She was the one. Full of love. Full of need.

Teresa.

Not today. Perhaps tomorrow. Or, perhaps the next day.

Teresa.

Her next true love. God had blessed her.

God had taken Jesse into his arms, but He would not leave her heart empty. Not for long.

THIRTEEN

When Campbell arrived at Hope's cabin his mood was considerably better than it had been when Hope had dropped him off this morning. Good enough to almost forget the vision that had incapacitated him for half a day. He knocked jauntily on the door. A chorus of barks from the back of the cabin answered the knock, and moments later the door opened.

"Campbell."

"Hi, Hope. I wanted to apologize for earlier. I was a bit . . . crazy."

"There's nothing to be sorry about."

"Yes there is. I've been crazy for a year now. It's about time I stopped."

"Do you want to come in?"

"Actually, I came to ask you out."

"Out?"

"We could go for dinner. Drinks."

"I, uh . . ."

Even with Shadow's black and white vision he could see the blush creep into her face.

"It wouldn't have to be a date or anything. Just dinner."

"A date would be fine," she said.

Campbell felt a grin spread across his face, and even though he sensed it must look somewhat triumphant to her, he couldn't get it off.

"I won't come in. I'm going to go back and get changed. Would you pick me up when you're ready? That's presumptuous, isn't it? Asking a woman out and then telling her she has to drive. It won't take me long."

She nodded, half frowning. "Are you dressing up?"

"I don't think so. Unless you're in the mood for that. I was thinking Chinese, or pizza, something like that."

The expression of relief on her face was almost comical. "I know a little Italian place in Fergus, casual, and their pasta is wonderful."

"Sounds great."

He turned Shadow around and walked back along the path.

He had asked her out on a date!

Hope didn't know whether to be terrified or excited, but in fact had no choice in the matter. Trepidation made her hands shake as she searched through her closet for something to wear.

Two weeks ago, after that awful dinner with her mother and Warren, she had stopped the car at the side of the road, trembling at the power of the feelings inside of her. Feelings, even then, focused on Campbell. Now, it was like a fantasy. As if some benevolent God had heard her cry of anguish, of loneliness, and had cast a spell over Campbell.

So, why was her stomach knotted with dread? Why were her palms sweating?

She stood in bra and panties before her dresser mirror and appraised herself with harsh eyes. She jammed her fist beneath her chin and shook her head. Weren't you supposed to feel more attractive when somebody asked you out? So, why didn't she?

He's seeing you through the eyes of a dog, she thought cruelly.

More upset now at her own self-doubt than at any perceived flaw in her appearance, she sat down on the bed and covered her face. This was not like her. Not at all. She knew what she was, she had always known. She took few pains with her personal appearance. She never had. Warren had known that, and Campbell probably knew it too by now. She couldn't start changing herself, or worry about things she had never worried about before. She was what she was. If Campbell wanted that, fine. If not . . .

She inhaled deeply, held the breath a few seconds, then let it out slowly.

She chose coffee-colored cotton slacks and a cream blouse and dressed quickly. She debated a few seconds over heels or flats, chose the middle ground with black pumps. The cut of the blouse made her neck look long and bare, so she put on the gold chain and locket she had received on her sixteenth birthday. It was the last present her father had given her; he had died four months later. She touched the cool metal gently, took a deep breath.

Better. Presentable.

"Knock him dead," she said to the mirror.

Despite her best efforts, her reflection looked somewhat doubtful about that possibility.

Primavera was one of two Italian restaurants in Fergus Falls, and had been in business almost twelve years according to Hope, an amazing feat since the majority of the population was of Nordic descent. Vikings and Scots abounded, but apparently they had a taste for pasta.

As restaurants went, it had the comfortable upscale feel of a business that had served its customers well and did not need to impress by ostentatious decor. The hostess, a tall, slim, dark-skinned girl named Natalie, knew Hope by name, and guided them to what appeared to be her regular table. Her dark eyes appraised Campbell coldly, but when she left he thought he detected a smidgin of approval in the curve of her lips.

Within a minute a bottle of red wine had been delivered by their waiter. "Compliments of Mister DeMarco," he said, and poured each of them a glass.

Hope smiled warmly, blushing, and looked toward the

kitchen. Campbell watched her nod her thanks at whomever she saw over there.

"I guess they like you here."

"I guess so," she said.

"Do you come here often?"

"Every couple of weeks. If I'm in town."

Campbell raised his glass. "Here's to first dates."

Hope touched her glass to his, smiling. He found himself grinning back.

"Did I tell you already that you look great?"

"Thank you," Hope said, a blush creeping into her face.

She really was not accustomed to men telling her how attractive she was, Campbell realized. He felt boyishly pleased that he had affected her that way. And she *did* look great. In jeans and plaid shirt, her everyday wear, she had the look of an outdoors woman, healthy, basic. Now, in dress slacks and blouse, the healthy glow had turned to elegant sheen. This was a look that Julia would have killed for. It looked almost practiced, the result of a long haul before the mirror with natural colors. But he knew it wasn't. This was Hope, unpolished.

Hope ordered for both of them, and they slowly worked their way through the bottle of wine. It didn't feel like a first date to Campbell. It felt, in fact, as if he had known Hope for some time, that they'd had a long-standing relationship. He felt completely at ease with her, and by the way she smiled, laughed, and leaned across the table toward him as they talked, he knew she felt the same way.

The realization must have come to them at the same time, for both of them lapsed into silence, gazing at each other across the table. The only thing that saved the silence from becoming uncomfortable was the arrival of their food.

Campbell dug in immediately. Within moments, the enjoyment of the food had replaced the momentary discomfort, and they were again smiling and talking.

For Campbell, it was the first time he had been out with a woman, *really* out, in over a year. And before Julia, it had been two years. Three years in all since he'd actively dated women. He had thought he would never do so again.

They were halfway through their meals when Hope suddenly stiffened, jaw clenching.

"What's wrong?"

Her eyes had grown wide, staring at something to Campbell's left. "Nothing," she said, voice almost inaudible.

"Shadow, left."

Campbell found himself looking at a man and a woman who were being led by Natalie to a table across the room. The man stopped, and looked toward them.

"Do you know him?"

"Unfortunately, yes."

The man was wearing a dark suit and tie, hair short and slick, and had the look of regular health club exercise and money.

"Old boyfriend?"

"Yes," Hope said hoarsely.

"Bad breakup?"

"Yes."

Campbell instinctively reached across the table and found her hand. Her fingers were cold, but gripped him hard.

"It's okay," he said. "You're with me tonight."

"Thanks."

"What's his name?"

"Warren Daniels. Oh, God, here he comes. I don't think I can handle this."

"Take it easy."

Warren Daniels was indeed crossing the room toward their table, grinning. He came to a stop beside Shadow and put a hand on Hope's shoulders.

"Hello, Hope," he said.

"Warren," she said, without looking at him.

She looked as if she wanted to squirm under his touch, but somehow maintained her composure. Even without Hope's evident discomfort, Campbell would have taken a quick dislike to Warren Daniels. His expression was smug, almost practiced.

Everything about him proclaimed him the possessor of all he surveyed. Even Hope. His smile was so condescending, in fact, that Campbell wished he had the nerve to stand up and wipe it from his face.

"Out on the town, are we?"

"Just dinner," Hope said, voice a little smaller than it had been.

"I don't think I've met your friend."

"Campbell Knight," Campbell said, holding out a hand. "You must be the Warren Daniels that Hope's been telling me so much about."

He tried to make his own smile as smug as Warren's looked, but doubted he even came close. Still, he had some effect. Warren's smile slipped a notch, and a look of surprise came into his eyes.

By the way the other man had looked at him, with ill concealed dislike, even disdain, Campbell knew that Daniels had assumed he was blind. After a moment's appraisal, he turned his attention back to Hope.

"I tried calling you, left a whole bunch of messages on your machine, but you never called back."

"I've been busy."

"I can see that."

Campbell stood, still smiling, and turned his head toward where he knew Warren's table was. "It looks as if your date is getting a bit lonely," he said.

Daniels glanced quickly over his shoulder, then back with a small frown. He looked down at Shadow, then up at Campbell, obviously a little confused.

"You seem familiar, Mr. Knight. Have we met?"

"I don't think so."

Daniels reached into his jacket and pulled out a business card. He held it in front of Campbell. Campbell guided his hand to the card, took it, and angled it so that Shadow could see the face.

"Daniels Security Systems. We used your company for awhile."

"Oh?"

"Knight Motors. If I remember, we ended the contract after a short trial."

Daniels was taken aback, and looked back and forth between Hope and Campbell. Then, to Hope, he said, "I didn't know they allowed dogs in here."

The barb hurt Hope. Campbell could see that immediately. Could hear it in the way her breathing changed.

"Warren . . ."

"It seems they let all kinds of animals in here," Campbell said, still smiling.

Daniels turned to him, mouth compressed, furious. Campbell continued to smile, then sat down.

"Maybe you'd like to join Janice and me for dinner," Warren said tightly. "It's a shame to take up two tables."

"I'm afraid we're almost finished, and we've got other plans," Campbell said. "But it was nice meeting you."

He then turned decisively away from Warren Daniels, smiled at Hope, and reached across the table to take her hand again. After a second or two, Warren moved away. Hope's hand trembled.

"I'm sorry," she said. "I had no idea he'd be here."

"Maybe he knew *you* would be here."

Her eyes widened as she considered that possibility, then she shook her head. "If you hadn't been here, I don't know what I'd have done."

"You'd have handled him quite nicely, I think."

She squeezed his hand. "Thank you."

They finished their meals quickly, and by mutual consent, left the restaurant without an after dinner drink. As they left, Natalie gave Campbell a smile that could only mean approval.

The drive back to the cabins was quiet. At Campbell's cabin, Hope held his arm as they walked to the front door.

"Would you come in for a drink?" he asked.

"I shouldn't."

"I hate to end the night."

"Some other time."

"All right."

Then he reached out, put his arms around her shoulders, and kissed her. For the first couple of seconds she was rigid, and then she suddenly leaned into him, mouth softening on his. Then she pushed away from him, and ran around the side of the cabin.

"Hope!"

In the darkness he could hear her sob. Then the slam of her car door, the roar of the engine. He listened as she drove the short distance to her own cabin. He heard her cabin door close.

"Hope," he said again, softly this time, for himself.

Then he went inside.

FOURTEEN

Hope rolled over in bed, pressed her face into the pillow, and answered the phone.

"Hello."

"Did I wake you?"

"No, Mother, I was up."

She wrapped an arm around her eyes to shield them from the morning sunshine. Outside, birds chirped. Leaves rustled.

The memory of last night's date with Campbell pounced on her like a tiger on a gazelle, as if it had been waiting for the moment when she was least prepared. Her lips tingled at the memory of his kiss. She felt suddenly warm between the legs. She also remembered how she had pushed him away, how she had fled.

"Oh God."

"Is something wrong, Hope?"

"Just thinking. Is there something you wanted?"

Poor Campbell. He had looked so shocked, so hurt. Even had she wanted to, she would not have been able to explain her actions to him. She had acted instinctively, and instinct had made her run.

"Can't a mother phone her daughter just to talk?"

Some mothers, perhaps, but not this one. Her mother never phoned her *just to talk*. There was always a reason. An invitation to dinner. A request for information. *Never* just to talk.

Hope sat up in bed, suddenly more awake than she had been. "What is it?"

Her mother sighed. "I was just eating breakfast, and I had a call from Warren."

Hope closed her eyes. "What did he want?"

"You know, whatever has happened between you and Warren, he and I are still on friendly terms. We always have been."

A blood bond with the enemy, Hope thought, rubbing her eyes.

"Mother, what did he want?"

"He's concerned about you."

"I'm fine."

"Warren says he was out for dinner last night and he saw you with a man."

"Did he say anything else?"

"He's just worried, you know. You shouldn't hold that against him. Many women would love to have a man so concerned about their welfare."

Hope took a deep breath, swung her legs out of bed.

"I have to feed the dogs. If there's nothing else . . ."

"Who was he?"

"A friend."

"But *who.*"

"That's my business."

"Your brother never talks to me that way."

"He never talks to you at all."

"Warren said he was blind."

She was not ready for this. Not yet. Not this morning. "Partially."

"He said he didn't like the way he treated you. What's his name?"

"Campbell. And he treated me perfectly."

"Warren said he knew him from Minneapolis. He said you should be careful."

"Warren should mind his own damned business."

"I don't know why you've suddenly turned against Warren. He's always had your best interests at heart."

"He *left* me, mother!"

"You wouldn't go with him. There's a difference."

"I have to go."

"How *could* you. How could you possibly choose a blind man over Warren? It doesn't make any sense at all. Warren has so much to offer. He's virtually throwing himself at your feet. I don't understand you. A *blind* man, Hope?"

"Campbell Knight has more to offer than Warren Daniels ever had."

"Why is it that every time I try to offer you advice, you throw it back in my face?"

"Because you're not offering advice. You're trying to control my life."

"Don't be ridiculous."

"Listen to me, then. I dislike Warren intensely. I want nothing to do with him ever again. I resent his interference with my life, and I resent your taking his side over mine. Is that clear enough? Any more advice?"

"You're impossible!"

"That's what dad always liked about me. I have to go."

She hung up the phone and took a deep breath. Her hands were shaking. Talking to her mother, being *talked to* by her mother, always had that effect. She clasped her hands between her thighs and continued to breathe deeply until her anger and frustration had subsided.

She wasn't even being honest with herself. She'd told her mother that Campbell had much more to offer than Warren, and yet, last night, she'd run from Campbell like a rabbit fleeing a fox. How would she ever know what Campbell's intentions were, or what he *really* had to offer, or even if she *wanted* him to offer it to her, if she ran away every time he tried to get closer to her?

Angry at herself, she showered quickly, dressed, and prepared breakfast. Her thoughts revolved around Campbell Knight, and her own feelings about their developing friendship. Even thinking about him, she noted over coffee, made her stomach flutter, made her hands tremble.

After cleaning the dishes, she took Jill from the kennel. Jill was the only remaining dog in her care. Her owners were coming to pick her up tomorrow morning. This really wasn't a lucrative business. It was going to feel strange, being dogless.

Her heart thumped as she walked Jill along the trail toward Campbell's cabin. The morning was comfortably warm, blue skied, lightly breezed. Somewhere across the lake she could hear a boat's motor, but she could not see the craft. A morning fisherman, she guessed. There wasn't too much water skiing going on yet.

At Campbell's cabin she tied Jill up and knocked on the door. When he answered, Shadow looked up at her.

Her voice faltered as she spoke. "I just wanted to . . . explain about last night . . . when I left, it was . . ."

"You don't have to explain yourself to me."

"I want to. It's important. I was going to walk Jill. I thought you might like to come along."

"Sure."

He came out, closed the door behind him. Impulsively, as if to prove to herself that she could do it, that the idea of it did not terrify her, Hope leaned into him and kissed him on the mouth. Her heart now beat like the wings of a sparrow trapped between two hands. She felt almost dizzy, and for a horrible moment she thought that Campbell was offended, that he was going to pull away from her. But, instead, his arms went around her, and he held her tightly. His returning kiss was warm, but not as fervent as last night's. It was as if he were holding back, afraid of startling her again.

When they parted, Hope was short of breath, and smiled nervously.

"I thought about that all last night," he said.

"Me, too."

Campbell continued to hold her, looking into her eyes as if he could really see her. His smile was genuine, concerned, something more.

"What are you frightened about?" he said softly.

Hope looked down, inhaled deeply, then looked back at his face.

"I'll tell you while we walk, if you'd like."

"Not if it makes you uncomfortable."

"I want to. Come on."

Eleanor parked the truck in a side street across from the park. At 9:00 A.M., Godfrey was as quiet as a graveyard at midnight. When she had left Hollyfield, dawn had been nothing more than a mild glow to the east, like golden speckles applied by a commercial airbrush artist trying to imbue country morning with a sentimental hue it normally lacked. Now, the sky was clear and blue, without a cloud in sight, made to look somehow liquid by that same airbrush.

Eleanor opened the flask of coffee she had brought with her and poured herself a cup. As steam rose into her face she settled into the seat, lowering herself slightly. She did not want to look like an obvious observer to anyone who happened to look.

"Down, Max," she said.

Max looked at her, a little confused, as if waiting for her to let him out and run. She petted his broad, angular head, then slipped her fingers through his collar and forced him down to his belly. He whined, tongue lolling.

"Hold your horses. You'll get out soon."

Head resting on his paws, he regarded her with love and confusion. Mostly love. That deep, unconditional animal love. The kind she longed to find elsewhere, but never had.

"You'll always love me, won't you, Max?"

His dark eyes drank her in. She stroked his head. His tail wagged.

Eleanor sipped her coffee and looked toward the park. The playground was empty. Most of the town looked empty. Since she'd arrived, in fact, only one or two cars had moved slowly along main street, looking like they were lost.

She drank some more coffee. Told herself to be patient. It was early yet.

By the time she was into her third cup of coffee, the town had come to life. It was a miraculous sight, actually. Cars and trucks seemed to materialize out of thin air. Pedestrians strolled along the streets as if they had been hiding behind trees all along. One by one, stores along the main street began to open, and this opening ritual itself was a wonder to behold. Front doors would open, proprietors would step out onto the pavement, look up at the sky as if searching for clouds, then unfurl an awning, or pull out a small table of sale goods, and then return inside. Within moments, pedestrians would approach, enter, then emerge again smiling.

It was a scene out of a country musical. The only thing lacking was the music. A parade. Seventy-six trombones.

The most popular establishments were the restaurants, and Eleanor watched these with envy. Her stomach was growling. She hadn't thought to bring anything to eat.

She glowered and continued to watch the park. This is what she had come for. She could not allow herself to become distracted.

There were children in the park now. One or two, playing on the swings.

But not the child she was looking for.

Still, the activity brought the butterflies to life in her stomach. It wouldn't be long.

She thought about pouring another cup of coffee, but resisted the temptation. Her bladder was already a dull ache. Another cup of coffee and she would not be able to ignore its insistent demand.

Teresa, she thought. Teresa.

She'd checked it in her book of names at home, but its genealogy was not entirely clear. It might be related to one of two Greek islands, the smaller of which was called Thera. Or it might be of Spanish origin. There had been both Spanish and French saints who possessed the name. The French nun, who had been Saint Therese of Lisieux, was Eleanor's favorite. She had been known as "the little flower."

She liked that. The little flower.

A little flower, waiting to be picked, brought home to the garden.

She opened her window to let air into the truck, leaned across Max to open his. A light breeze moved through the cab, smelling of fresh baked bread and diesel exhaust. Eleanor crossed her arms and sank lower in the seat.

It was another hour before Teresa came to the park. Eleanor, who had been half dozing by that point, sat suddenly rigid. Max immediately sensed the change in her and sat to attention.

"Thank you, God," Eleanor whispered.

She was far enough away from the park that her truck would not appear obvious, but close enough that she could see the girl clearly. She was dressed this morning in jeans and a T-shirt, long hair tied in a ponytail.

It made Eleanor's heart ache just to look at her. She thought of the girl's thin, warm arms. The feel of her head cradled gently, lovingly. Those soft hands gripping in their need.

Not like Jesse at all. Not at all.

Enthralled, she watched the girl play. Teresa ran from swings, to slide, to sandbox, and back again. She tended to avoid the other children, of whom there were now five or six, and played alone. Once or twice she helped one of the smaller children, a little boy, on the swings.

So in need of love, Eleanor realized. Hungry and longing for it. The day Eleanor had found her might have been an answer to both their prayers.

Max whined and scratched at his door.

"Not now, Max."

He whined again, more insistently. Eleanor looked at him savagely. His tail wagged once. He whined again. Her own bladder throbbed. In the park, Teresa was alone in the sandbox, sitting on the edge, leaning over her knees, her back to Eleanor.

It would be safe.

She got out of the truck, went around to Max's side, let him
out and put him on the leash. From the box she pulled a small
plastic bag and a child's plastic shovel.

Max pulled her immediately toward the park, but she yanked
back hard, pulling him the other way.

"No, Max!"

They walked fifty feet away from the truck. Max stopped at
every tree to urinate. On the way back he squatted and defecated. Eleanor picked up the excrement with the shovel and put
it in the plastic bag.

When she returned to the truck, Teresa was gone.

Eleanor leaned across the wheel, heart racing. The other children were still in the playground, but there was no sign of Teresa.

"Look what you made me do!" she said to Max. "She's
gone!"

The dog's tail wagged as he looked at her. Eleanor slapped
him so hard that his head rocked and he yelped. He dropped to
the seat, pawing at his snout, snuffling wetly.

"Bad dog!"

She got out of the truck, locked Max inside, and ran across
the street to the park. Once in the park, she walked slowly, hands
in her pockets, sticking to the paved trail. She could not afford
to draw attention to herself. Not now.

Teresa was not in the playground. Eleanor passed it quickly,
scanning the park for any signs of the girl. She had been gone
from the truck less than a minute! Surely the girl could not have
gone far.

She passed the wading pool, then the picnic area. She walked
along the pavement that paralleled the main street. On this side,
she was conspicuous. On the other side, strolling past the shops,
one or two pedestrians turned to look at her.

Eleanor felt a sudden stab of fury for Teresa. This was *her*
fault. If Teresa were with her right now, she'd show the girl what
it meant to . . .

Across the street, Teresa came out of the drugstore. In her

hands she held a package of cigarettes. Eleanor stared at her, horrified. But the girl did not open the package, did not cross the street to the park. Instead, she began walking along the street, slowly, pausing at every store front, looking through the windows.

Eleanor crossed the street and followed her. The cigarettes were for her parents. That's what it must be.

How could she have ever doubted Teresa? Saint Teresa. Her little flower.

Staying far behind, Eleanor followed Teresa home. The girl lived in a two-story, stuccoed house, half a block off the main street. A late-model truck was parked in the driveway. The backyard contained a swing set and monkey bars. Three children's bikes leaned against the side of the house, including a tricycle.

That was good.

She would not be depriving anybody of their only child.

Jesse Hampton had been an only child, and Eleanor had experienced many nights of guilt as the news coverage had focused on his parents' tragedy. Jesse's mother was not able to bear anymore children.

He's in heaven now, she thought. All is well.

She walked past the house, crossed the street, walked slowly back.

Teresa burst from the house as Eleanor approached. A man came out after the girl, tall and lean, face tanned. He laughed, chased the girl into the backyard.

You leave her alone, Eleanor thought.

From the backyard came squeals of delight, more laughter.

Face burning, Eleanor walked quickly past, toward the main street, her truck.

She wanted to take Teresa now. This morning.

But that would not be a good idea.

She needed to watch more. Needed to choose the right time. The safe time.

Patience, she told herself.

Smiling to herself, she crossed the street into the park, then walked briskly toward her truck where Max, needing all her love, waited for her.

I know where you live, little flower.

I know where your garden is.

"The way it looked between Warren and I last night, isn't exactly the way it used to be between us," Hope said.

"Were you in love?"

They had walked perhaps a hundred yards along the beach, and now Jill was running free, splashing through the water, leaping over rocks. Shadow watched the other dog intently, and Campbell watched with him.

"We were going to be married. That was only two years ago. We'd been together two years before that. In the end, he wanted to move to Minneapolis and I wanted to stay in Battle Lake. I guess I was scared to leave. I felt attached to this place. I had just bought the cabin, and I couldn't give it up. He left, anyway. And met somebody else. And got married."

The words poured out of her mouth as if she'd been preparing them for hours, days.

"Ouch."

"It's okay now. It makes me angry more than it hurts. Not that I blame him for what he did. He had his plans, I had mine, and it took us two years to realize our plans didn't involve each other. It was only when he came back that it got nasty. That was partly my mother's fault. She really likes him, thinks he's the best thing that ever happened to me, told him so and told him I was still available."

"Ouch again. Mothers. You don't want to get back together with him? Forget I asked that."

Her hand touched his, and suddenly her fingers were holding him tightly and she was leaning into him. He put his right arm around her shoulders. Shadow continued to look out over the lake, and Campbell fought the urge to have the dog turn and look at Hope.

"I just wanted you to know that last night was hard for me. I like you, Campbell. In fact . . ." her voice trailed off, and a breath caught in her throat. "When you kissed me, all I could think about was Warren. That came out wrong. Not like *that*. All I could think about was how . . ."

"You don't have to say any more."

"When he left me, my life fell apart. All those dreams, all those plans."

"Hope . . ."

"Shut up, Campbell. Let me talk. I've never had much luck with men. I guess I haven't really tried. You know, there was only one other before Warren. It has taken me two years to feel good again, about myself, about the future. Then I met you. Then Warren came back. Now . . ."

She lapsed into silence again. Out on the lake, a handful of gulls swooped down at the water like planes dive-bombing a boat, their caws like distant cries for help.

"Shadow, right."

Shadow turned to Hope. One of her arms was hugged around her legs. Her chin rested on her knees, and she stared out at the lake as if the answers to all her questions were somewhere in the water. She turned to him with a sad smile.

"When you kissed me last night, I thought, here we go again. I'm falling for him. He's going to leave. I'm going to get hurt. I'm sorry I ran."

"Things have changed for me over the past year or two. And now, with Shadow, they're changing again. You're part of that change. But I . . . Did you say you were falling for me?"

Hope laughed. "I thought it was obvious."

"Not to a blind man."

"I thought even that."

"That's . . . cool."

"Thanks for being so sensitive."

"No, I mean, it's great, because I . . . I guess I'm falling for you, too."

Hope continued to stare at him. The sadness left her smile

and a strange shy look crept in. After a few seconds she looked away, still smiling. Campbell inhaled deeply.

"Can I kiss you again?"

Hope turned to him, smile gone, and Campbell thought, what if she says no? But she said nothing at all. She leaned toward him, then her lips were touching his. Her mouth opened slightly and her tongue touched his lips. Then her hand was behind his neck, holding him tightly, pulling him toward her. It was like watching one of those kisses from an old movie. Their faces filled his field of vision. Shadow, apparently, was enthralled.

When Hope parted, she was breathing like she'd run a hundred yards. She took a deep breath, let it out slowly. She looked directly at Shadow.

"If he makes you uncomfortable, I'll unhook him."

"No." She reached out and petted the dog. A frown now creased her forehead, as if she were searching for words.

"What is it?"

Her teeth tugged at her lower lip. "When was the . . . the last time you made love? Don't answer that. I can't believe I asked you that."

"To myself or to somebody else?" he said before she could make additional protests.

The frown disappeared, she grinned. "You know what I mean."

"A long time, Hope."

"Me, too."

They lapsed into a silence so long and uncomfortable that Campbell wondered if it would ever be broken.

"That's going to be hanging in front of us until we do something about it. We're going to be wondering if we ever will, what it will be like. We're going to be wondering if the other person even wants to. It's going to put a big strain on us."

"I suppose it will."

"I want to," she said, and looked away.

"I do, too."

Hope looked at him, lips pursed as if to whistle, thoughtful.

"When?"

"Whenever you want."

"This moment seems right, doesn't it?" she said. "I mean, it's romantic, isn't it?" She did not sound at all certain.

Campbell's heart was pounding. "Yes. I think so."

They walked quickly back along the beach, holding hands. Campbell held onto her so tightly he thought he must be hurting her, but she did not say anything, made no move to pull away.

As they were climbing off the beach toward Hope's cabin, he said, "What if it doesn't work. I mean, what if things aren't right that way between us?"

She stopped and looked at him. "Then we'll know, and we won't spend all that time thinking about it, I guess. Are you sure you want to?"

"It seems kind of . . . calculated," he admitted.

She kissed him again, tongue darting between his lips, body pressed to his. The pounding of his heart nearly made him dizzy.

"It will work," Hope said breathlessly.

She put Jill back in the kennel, and they went together to Campbell's house. Once in his living room, when they kissed, Campbell's knees felt weak. They sank to the floor together. Her hands touched him everywhere, and the sounds they made were muffled by the joining of their mouths.

"What about Shadow?" Campbell said.

Hope looked at him, kissed him, ran a hand down his stomach, between his legs.

"Leave him connected," she said, then pulled him down to the floor.

It worked between them.

It worked brilliantly.

FIFTEEN

Teresa sat on the edge of the world and pushed her feet into the moist sand. She was the god of the sandbox. She could kick out and raise mountain ranges, stamp down and create seas, move her hands and level prairies.

Of course, the sandbox was only a few feet in diameter, substantially smaller than the world the real God had to work with, but the principle was the same. If there were microscopic people living in the sandbox, and nobody could say there *really* weren't, then they would think she was a God.

But what kind of God?

She stopped moving her feet as she considered this.

Gods weren't supposed to go trampling through the worlds in their care, were they? Not good gods, anyway. She had a sudden picture of a kid in the world of the sandbox, sitting in a backyard just like this one, looking up and seeing a gigantic foot rushing down to obliterate her.

And for what?

For fun!

Teresa sighed and decided she'd had enough of playing God for one morning.

Her imagination was too good, too active, and too morbid. That's what her teachers said, anyway. That's what her father said.

He said she spent too much time alone, too much time fantasizing, too much time reading, too much time drawing.

He wanted her to: a) play more with other children, b) get

involved in after school activities, c) play with Barbie dolls, d) giggle, skip, and laugh.

He had even sent her to a psychiatrist last year, presumably because when given his list she'd chosen: e) none of the above. She had enjoyed the way Doctor Phillips had asked questions, piecing together, after long months, a picture of Teresa. She had decided after only a couple of weeks of the sessions that she, too, wanted to be a psychiatrist. She wanted to explore other people's minds.

Even so, Doctor Phillips had come up with an explanation that didn't sound right to Teresa. Doctor Phillips said that it was the death of Teresa's mother four years ago that had left Teresa to rely on her imagination, on herself. Dad hadn't been so sure. He'd told Doctor Phillips that Teresa had been moody, self-sufficient, and imaginative from the start. Doctor Phillips said she doubted that very much but that she'd have to see Teresa a lot more to determine if that was true. Dad said he'd lived with Teresa all his damned life and if anybody knew what she'd been like it was him, but he'd think about it.

Teresa missed the sessions. She had liked Doctor Phillips. She had enjoyed the questions. She had felt, over the period of the sessions, that she had come to know herself even better than she had before.

It was all a game, anyway.

She knew there weren't real people in the sandbox. She knew she wasn't a god. Just like she knew that the world around her didn't exist only inside her mind, although that idea held a strange fascination for her. She'd spent nights considering the possibilities, the horrors. If *everything* were just a figment of her imagination, then that would mean that she was responsible for all of it, all the horrible things that happened, as well as all the good things that happened. She might be a devil, or a god, and who could say which one? It would mean that *she* had thought up the idea of stars and planets and cars and dogs and insects and . . . *everything*. On the face of it, such an idea seemed utterly ridiculous. What did she know about *any* of those things? Hardly enough to even know they existed, never mind to create them. Still, the idea was a fascinating one. Mostly because it was impossible to disprove it. After all, she and everybody else in the planet were trapped inside their own heads, and always had been. In the end, you had to accept the existence of others, and of the world around you on faith.

She'd been surprised to learn, after confiding in her father, that she was not the first to consider such awful things. In fact, there was a name for it.

Solipsism.

Solipsism. Even the name for it had a strange, unreal sound that wanted to slide off the tongue without ever really anchoring there. And her father had one more warning for her.

"It's not wise to think too long and hard on these subjects. They're mental traps, Teresa. Once you climb in, it's very hard to get out."

So, she'd allowed her faith to take over. Okay, *okay* already! The world was real. People were real. She, personally, was not responsible for all the good, or even all the evil in the universe.

Still, it was fun to think about it sometimes. It made her skin tingle, made the hairs on the back of her neck stand on end. She wished she'd talked to Doctor Phillips about it. Doctor Phillips would probably know more about solipsism than dad did.

She moved away from the sandbox and fell down to the grass. It was cool beneath her arms. She stared up at the blue sky. A solitary bird circled overhead, like a buzzard waiting to swoop down and pick at her bones.

She stared up at the bird. Maybe if she thought hard enough, the bird would come down. That would be proof, wouldn't it? That she controlled the universe?

She closed her eyes and concentrated.

Hope rolled to her side and looked at Campbell. He was sleeping, on his side, left arm hanging over the edge of the bed. A thin black cable ran from the glasses over his eyes, down his left arm, over the edge of the bed and down to Shadow who slept on the floor. Campbell's breathing was deep, slow. His pale shoulders rose and fell with each breath.

She kissed his shoulder, touched his hip with her hand. His skin was warm and dry.

Hope closed her eyes, fighting back a surge of emotion.

She had just made love to this man. He had touched her and kissed her and entered her in ways she had thought she might never experience again. In some ways, she had never been made love to more passionately. It was as if Campbell had wanted to possess her wholly, had wanted to cover her body with his, had wanted to make her part of him.

Thinking about it, she felt a flash of warmth between her legs.

In some ways, she had never been made love to more strangely. Campbell pressing down on her, half his face concealed by his dark glasses, making him look like some underworld killer or a robot. Shadow had sat close to them, watching, and that had been the strangest of all: to be watched, by an animal, watched intently, as if Shadow were drinking in every detail.

But Shadow was Campbell's window on the world. It was really Campbell who was watching her make love. To himself. And that realization itself had been the most disconcerting of all, because it made her perceive, for some strange reason, the man on top of her with dark glasses as *not Campbell*. Campbell was watching her make love with this man, his proxy.

Instead of frightening her, or turning her off, these speculations had fueled her desire. It was voyeuristic, without actually being voyeuristic. It was exhibitionist, without actually being exhibitionist. She was a part of it, and yet not a part of it.

Her climax had been so fierce, so prolonged, she had collapsed afterward, breathless, soaked in sweat, unable to speak for minutes.

They had retired to the bedroom then, neither knowing if

they were going to continue making love, or to sleep. Sleep had won out for both of them.

Hope now wished it hadn't. She was wet, aching. She wanted his touch, his kiss, his mouth on her breasts, his thick hardness between her legs.

Impulsively, she reached across his hip and took his penis in her hand. She squeezed it, stroked it. She put her mouth to the side of his neck, moved her tongue slowly in small circles on his salty skin.

Campbell groaned. His penis thickened in her hand, lengthened, hardened. But he did not wake. He groaned again, shifted his weight. Inhaled deeply.

"Hope," he said softly, dreaming.

Hope released him, shocked by the sound of her name on his lips. She stared at him, astounded. In sleep, aroused, he had spoken her name.

She got quietly out of bed and, naked, left the room. Her heart was pounding, and a strange feeling of joy burned inside her. Even as she felt it, was exhilarated by it, she wondered how simply hearing her name on his lips had made her feel this way.

In the living room she sat in Campbell's easy chair and looked out the window. Through the trees she could see the lake. She closed her eyes and lowered her face.

"Oh God, Campbell," she said softly.

What had happened to all the barriers she had put up to protect herself? In the space of two weeks they had crumbled. Campbell Knight had breached her defenses, and now he was inside. Inside her heart.

It was what she wanted, it was what she dreaded. She felt terrifyingly vulnerable, and yet buoyed, elevated, rejuvenated.

I'm in love, she thought, and laughed softly.

I've fallen in love!

She started to laugh harder and covered her mouth so that she would not wake Campbell.

In love.

The thought terrified her as it brought her happiness. She

could be hurt again. She had opened herself to that pain. What if Campbell . . . she tried to imagine him leaving, as Warren had left her, but she could not do it.

It was different this time.

It was the real thing, this time.

Let it be, she thought. Please.

The phone rang and she went to it and answered it before she had realized what she was doing.

"Hello?"

"Hope? Is that you?"

Hope recognized Claire's voice, and remembered in that instant that she was in Campbell's cabin, not her own.

"Claire," she said.

"Did I punch your number instead of Campbell's?"

"No," she said hesitantly.

There was a long pause from the other end. "Is Campbell there?"

"He's sleeping. I'll get him."

"Don't wake him." Claire's voice had become thoughtful, almost playful. "So, you and Campbell are . . ."

"We were just . . . we were . . . I'll get him for you." She could hardly speak. Her face burned with embarrassment.

"I'm teasing you. I just wanted to find out how he was doing. Have there been anymore nightmares?"

Hope sighed, relieved to have something else to talk about. "He hasn't said anything. I don't think so. I haven't talked to him about it since the other day, and he hasn't brought it up."

"Probably nothing to worry about."

"Probably not."

"Well, I better go. Tell him I called."

"I will."

"And Hope?"

"Yes?"

"I'm happy for you. And for him. Really. I think it's great. Bye."

When she hung up, Hope's face was burning. She forced

herself to breathe deeply, calmly. Claire had been bound to find out sooner or later. Better sooner. It was done.

She went back to the bedroom, lay down on the bed beside Campbell. He was still sleeping. As she touched his hip, he groaned and shuddered.

On the floor beside him, Shadow made a snuffling sound.

Campbell moved his head to the left. Shadow moved his head to the left.

Campbell shifted his weight and rolled away from her. On the floor, Shadow shifted his weight and rolled to the other side.

Then they both lapsed into silence.

Hope stared at the pair of them, waiting for more. Whatever strange dream had made them behave as one had ended, apparently.

She still had a lot to learn about Campbell, about his relationship with Shadow. She was certain of only one thing. They came as a pair. Package deal. She had better get used to that quickly.

She leaned over and kissed Campbell's shoulder. No words came to his lips this time.

"I love you, Campbell Knight," Hope said softly.

Campbell continued to sleep.

The bird did not come down. In fact, it flew away, out of sight.

Teresa sighed.

Have faith.

She thought about summer. It was only early July, and the rest of the holiday stretched ahead of her like some interminable straight country road. Every day was like the day before, varying only in the weather. On sunny days she spent her hours outside, walking back and forth between the park and home, sometimes stopping in at the library where she would browse through the stacks of adult books, or at the drugstore where she would sit on the floor by the magazine rack and flip through the women's magazines. When it rained she spent her days in the house, reading, drawing, writing. She was writing an illustrated story about a girl who discovers the doorway to another universe under her bed. It wasn't terribly original, having been done in one form or another in a number of the science fiction and fantasy novels she had read (and come to think of it, none of them had been particularly original either), except that *her* other universe was actually Hell, which probably made it at least *fairly* original in the world of literature penned by eight-year-olds. She had almost a hundred pages of hand-written manuscript completed already, and the story had hardly begun. She had come to think that it might one day be a novel. A big one.

She got up off the grass and went to the back door. She pressed her face against the screen. She smelled cigarette smoke and coffee. Her aunt Elizabeth was inside, purportedly looking after her while dad was at work, but actually watching television. Soap operas all morning, talk shows all afternoon. That suited Teresa fine, since it kept Elizabeth out of her hair. Not that Elizabeth was nasty, or even unkind . . . just boring.

"I'm going to the park," Teresa called out.

Elizabeth came to the door, arms crossed over her breasts. They were big breasts, and her dad sometimes looked at them instead of at Elizabeth's face when he was talking to her. Elizabeth's face was round and pretty. She had been mom's younger sister. She was also the only one of the sisters that had never gotten married and had stayed in Godfrey.

"You've been there already this morning."

"I'm going back."

"On the way, pick me up another pack of cigarettes, will you?"

"I got you a pack this morning."

"It's for later. Please?"

Elizabeth was also a chain smoker, which had only *one* good point: nobody seemed to like it. This struck Teresa as a benefit that far outweighed the long list of drawbacks.

Teresa nodded and took the five-dollar bill from her aunt's hand. The long red nails looked neater than they had this morning. Elizabeth had been doing repairs while watching television. Dad liked those nails, too, Teresa thought.

"Be careful. Don't go anywhere but the park."

"Right," Teresa said.

She walked slowly, scuffing her feet along the sidewalk, looking down. She played God again for a hundred yards or so, imagining that the dust and gravel beneath her feet were cities. Her runners wrought terrific devastation. Each step a gazillion megatons. Kaboom!

She had turned into the lane behind Main Street when she saw the dog. He was walking slowly, sniffing at the ground. He seemed familiar. Big, husky, black.

"Hey, boy," she called out.

The dog stopped, turned his head to look at her. His tail wagged slowly. Teresa went down on one knee, hand held out.

"Come on, boy," she said, and patted her thigh.

She loved dogs. Dad said they were too much work, but she was trying to convince him to get one. She could take care of a dog. Mostly dad didn't want one because Elizabeth hated dogs. Elizabeth said she might have to think twice about coming over during the days if there was a dog in the house. Otherwise, dad would have given in by now, Teresa knew. Dad would do almost anything to keep her occupied.

The black lab walked toward her, head low, tail wagging.

"Good boy," she said, patting his head.

It was Billy, the dog she had seen in the park the other day. The dog with the woman who had looked like a farmer, tall and dry and dusty. She was sure of it.

"Hi, Billy," she said.

Billy sat down. He looked up at her with black eyes that were trying to tell her something. She didn't know what, but she knew the dog was trying to communicate. Something important. Was he lost?

She heard a scuff behind her, turned quickly, relaxed when she saw it was the tall, dusty woman. The woman was smiling.

"Ah, little flower, you found my dog."

In his dream, Campbell was in a back alley, walking slowly. He seemed to be looking carefully at fenceposts, garbage cans, trees. It was a sunny day in the dream, but the shadows were short, as if it were noon.

He knew he was dreaming, and he knew what kind of dream it was. It felt real. He wanted to wake up. Wake up quickly, before he saw anything else.

He saw the girl when she entered the alley. She walked toward him, grinning. She was perhaps eight years old, perhaps a little younger. Long hair tied in a ponytail. Slender, very pretty. An angel, he thought.

She went down on one knee and beckoned him.

Get out of here, he wanted to say to her. Leave.

Instead, he found himself approaching her, until he was right beside her. She reached out to him.

Please, he tried to say to her, go! Run! Something horrible is going to happen!

The girl frowned slightly, as if she knew he was trying to tell her something, but she did not move.

When the dark shape came up behind her, Campbell tried to scream. His heart pounded in his chest like a runaway diesel engine.

It's a dream! It's only a dream!

The girl turned, looking up at the figure that had come up behind her. She did not seem frightened at all.

Then the shape reached out to her. Something was in its hand. Something pale and soft. The hand wrapped around the angel's face, lifted her off the ground.

In Campbell's dream, all he could see were the angel's feet, kicking, kicking, slowing, finally stopping.

Campbell exploded into consciousness with a scream, sitting

up straight in bed. The dream imagery faded from his mind. He was looking at himself, sitting up in bed. Hope was sitting beside him, staring at him in horror.

"Campbell, are you all right?"

"It happened again," he said, and heard his voice emerge as a dry croak. He lowered his head, covered his mouth with a hand. "My God," he whispered.

"Was it the same thing?" Hope asked.

"She got another one," he said.

"Another one?"

"Another child. A girl this time."

By the bed, Shadow whined. Campbell reached over and petted the dog. Shadow licked his fingers, whined again.

"Leave me out of your dreams, boy," he said.

Campbell's heart had slowed. Sweat cooled on his shoulders. He shivered.

"You really are frightened by these dreams, aren't you?"

"They seem so real."

"Maybe you should phone Claire. Maybe there's something they can do. You shouldn't keep this to yourself. What if these dreams actually mean something?"

"Like what?"

"I don't know. Something."

Something, Campbell thought. It *can't* be real. It can't. "God, I hope not," he said. "They're scary enough already."

SIXTEEN

Hope moved over as Campbell sat down on the sofa beside her. His hand touched hers, and he squeezed. She smiled at him thankfully. Claire and Russell had driven out from Minneapolis early in the morning, and had arrived just before 11:00 A.M. Hope felt uncomfortable, scrutinized, an outsider. She also felt empty, and a little sad. Jill had been picked up by her owners earlier in the morning. The silence felt like a death. Not for the first time, she wondered if she should buy a dog of her own.

"You're looking easy with Shadow," Russell said to Campbell.

"Feel like I've had him for years."

"Explain to me again about the dreams."

"They don't feel like dreams. That's the point. I know what my dreams are like, and these don't fit the pattern. If these were just dreams, I wouldn't have called you. Besides, two of them happened when I was awake."

"Two? You only mentioned one."

"There was another one back at Miriam, when I was trying to get downstairs. That last test. I was in the elevator, and suddenly I was in a truck, rolling down the road. It was like I was there, watching."

"The one in the restaurant, where you said you saw a boy killed, were there any indications leading up to the event that something was out of the ordinary?"

"Not a thing. One second I was sitting there talking to Hope, and the next I was watching this kid being put in a hole in the ground and blasted with a shotgun."

Hope felt his hand tense in hers as he spoke. Russell watched Campbell carefully.

"How long did it last?"

"It seemed to me only about five seconds."

"Hope, did you notice anything?"

Hope thought back. Hard to believe it was only two days ago.

"He seemed to go rigid. Not much else. His face turned white and he looked as if he were clamping his teeth. He stood up too fast and knocked over a cup of coffee. Then he sat down and started to shake. I remember that Shadow whined. About five seconds in all. Not much more than that."

"Had you been thinking about your dreams?"

"What do you want me to do, Russell? Write it down for you? It wasn't a dream."

"Sorry. I'm not trying to push you. The way you're talking, though, you're leading me to believe that you suspect it has something to do with the linkup to Shadow."

"Could it?"

"Not a chance."

"It started after the linkup."

Russell shook his head, smiling. "Campbell, it's impossible. You're linked to Shadow's optic nerve, that's all. You see what he sees. It's like a camera. He doesn't even *perceive* things for you, you do that yourself. All you're getting from Shadow are the lenses on his eyes. No dreams, no impressions, no memories. Nothing but what he sees."

"It never happened before."

"Which supports our contention that the dreams . . . the visions . . . episodes . . . whatever you want to call them, are simply the byproduct of your brain accommodating the linkup."

"But why these particular images? Why so violent? Yesterday, I dreamed she got another kid. A girl this time. It's really creepy, Russell. I can't believe it's coming out of my own head."

"You'd be surprised what comes out of normal human minds, Campbell. All I can tell you is, it's not coming from Shadow."

Campbell sighed and lowered his head, strictly a symbolic gesture since Shadow continued to look directly at Russell and Claire. Hope could feel the tension in Campbell. Nothing Russell had said had eased his fears, or her own.

"Has this happened before?" Hope asked.

"Not to this degree. I rechecked the records of the other subjects. Three of them *did* report strange or enhanced dreams for a period of a week or two after the linkup. We've always put it down to the strangeness of accommodation. I'm sure that's what's going on here."

"Can you do something to stop it?"

Russell started to say something, closed his mouth.

"Dreams or not, they really frighten him. They frighten me, too."

"I'm reluctant to suggest drugs."

"I don't want drugs," Campbell said, looking up again. "I just want to know that they're going to stop."

"I'm giving you my opinion. They'll stop soon. Give it time."

"Okay, then."

"While I'm out here, I'm going to check the hardware, make sure everything is working. I brought some equipment." He tapped a metal case at his feet. "It won't take long. Do you mind?"

"No. Here?"

"A bedroom would be better."

Campbell got up and led Russell to his bedroom, and Hope found herself alone with Claire, feeling uncomfortable. She wondered how Claire saw her. The opportunistic neighbor who had pounced on her debilitated brother? Nothing in Claire's expression indicated that, but even thinking it made Hope question her own motives.

"I want to thank you for taking an interest in Campbell," Claire said.

"You make it sound like I'm doing it because I have to."

"I just mean, it has been so long since I've seen Campbell . . . take to someone. It's nice."

"I like him. Your brother is a nice man."

"You're worried about him."

"He was frightened the other day at the restaurant, and yesterday. I didn't like to see it."

"Russell knows what he's doing. I trust him."

Hope nodded. "He seems nice, too."

"He is." Claire grinned.

"How long have you been seeing him?"

"Six months. He learned about Campbell through me. I knew a little bit about his work, but I never knew that it could make such a difference to Campbell."

Something flashed across Claire's eyes, and she looked away. She's lying, Hope suddenly realized. Claire knew all along what Russell could mean to Campbell. Had Claire known of Russell's work *before* becoming involved with him? Had she done so with the purpose of helping her brother?

Claire looked at her, a slight flush on her cheeks, and Hope knew that her speculations had been close to the mark. Claire began to look uncomfortable.

"Okay, so I knew what it could mean to Campbell," Claire said softly, looking over Hope's shoulder at the bedroom door.

She did it for Campbell, Hope realized. Spent six months of her life with a man for her brother.

"Don't look so horrified."

"I'm not horrified. I'm . . . impressed."

"You're lying. You don't approve."

"I haven't thought about it long enough to know if I approve or not, but I *am* impressed. You must love Campbell very much."

Claire looked away again, as if ashamed to be seen by Hope. "The accident changed him. It made him smaller, somehow. Diminished him, I guess, is what I'm saying. The way he was before, and the way he was afterward, it was like two completely different people. I couldn't bear it."

"You don't have to explain to me, Claire. I understand."

Claire looked doubtful, but she nodded. In the silence that ensued, Hope looked down at her hands.

"Does Campbell know?"

"No. And he never will."

Hope looked into Claire's eyes, eyes suddenly hard, commanding. She nodded. She would not tell Campbell. Ever.

When the bedroom door opened, Hope started. It was as if she and Claire had been in another world.

Russell emerged, smiling, and Campbell and Shadow followed.

"Everything is fine," Russell said.

"Had my oil changed," Campbell said, grinning.

Hope put her arm around Campbell's waist, held him tightly.

"I don't think there's much we can do about your dreams, Campbell. But if it happens again, we'll bring you in, if you'd like. Keep you under observation. Its up to you."

"I'll let you know. Thanks for coming out. I really appreciate it. You too, Claire."

Claire kissed Campbell on the cheek, then took Russell's hand. Hope followed them out onto the porch, still holding onto Campbell. Claire waved as they drove away. The Camaro spun its wheels and threw gravel.

"Much ado about nothing," Campbell said softly.

Hope squeezed him. "Now you know. Don't you feel better?"

"Until next time, sure."

"You've got quite a sister, do you know that?"

"She's okay."

"She sure is."

Hope pulled the car up to the curb, parked it, but left the motor running. She turned a worried face to Campbell. "Are you sure you want to go through with this?"

"Reassure me just one more time that I'm going to survive the night."

"I'm not sure I can do that."

"At least that I'll go quickly."

"Slow and painful deaths are more the order of the day around here."

"Give me a bone here, please! Will you at least promise that Shadow and I will receive a decent funeral?"

"Adjacent plots?"

"Flowers every week, too."

"Roses?"

"Carnations will do."

"I think I can manage that."

"Milkbone for Shadow."

"Done."

"He likes the crunchy kind."

"Deal."

"If your mother is this dangerous, why are you taking me to see her?"

"Four reasons." Hope lifted up a hand to count them off. "One, it's a free meal. Two, she phoned to invite us, and I don't get invited often enough to feel right about refusing. Three, the longer we leave this, the more difficult it will be. Four, she'll keep on pestering me until she meets you. Five, Warren already told her about you."

"You said four reasons. That's five."

"Really? Then, it's even more imperative that we get this out of the way."

Campbell slid closer to Hope. He put a hand on her thigh. Through her jeans her flesh felt taut.

"You're nervous."

He was close enough to smell her skin. No perfume, just a clean, soapy odor that made his nose tingle.

"My mother has that effect on me."

"Not me."

He leaned toward her, kissed her. At first her lips were tense and stiff against his mouth, but after a second or two she moaned and her lips softened, opened. Her tongue darted out. Campbell sucked on it gently. Her moan became throaty, deep. He broke reluctantly away.

"Don't be nervous."

"You don't know my mother."

"I know one thing. Nothing she can say or do will change the way I feel about you. Okay?"

"Okay."

They got out of the car. Campbell realized with horror that he had the beginning of an erection. This was going to make a great first impression. Well, at least he'd be going in head first. Shadow stood at his side. Campbell was looking at a row of houses that struck him, in the cloudy dusk, as dilapidated and dreary. Hope took his arm.

"Is that a banana in your pocket, or are you really looking forward to meeting my mother?"

"Hussy. Which one is the lion's den?"

"Right this way. Dinner is at seven. Did I mention that you were the main course?"

They walked along the pavement a short distance, then turned onto a narrow path. Hope took the lead. Campbell followed. Shadow's eyes were firmly focused on Hope's behind. Her buttocks looked firm, round, tight. Maybe this was a mistake. If so, it was turning into a bigger mistake with every passing second.

What had gotten into him? He and Hope had made love only an hour ago, a final laugh in the face of their upcoming ordeal with her mother. Perhaps I'm more worried about this than I'm admitting to myself, he thought. Sublimating everything into sexual impulses. It was one thing for Hope to say that she and her mother did not get along, but it was quite another for her mother to actively dislike the man Hope was seeing. Even Hope might be influenced by that sort of thing. So, whatever Hope said on the face of it, it was important that he make a good impression.

At the door of the house, Hope took his hand, squeezed. She knocked on the door.

"Would you like a blindfold?" she whispered.

"Just unhook me."

The door opened. Light blazed into their faces. Campbell found himself looking up at a woman in her early fifties, thin, angular, wearing a dark dress. The smile became rigid on his face. He and Hope had dressed very casually.

"Mom, this is Campbell Knight."

Shadow whined. *She's looking at my crotch! She saw us down there at the car! She knows everything!*

"Hope has told me so much about you," Mrs. Matheson said, taking Campbell's hand. "And this must be Shadow!"

She bent to pet the dog and Campbell found himself staring right into her face. She made kissing noises at him. Campbell consciously stopped himself from pulling away.

"Isn't he cute! Hope says you see through his eyes. Its amazing what they can do these days. I wasn't sure how you did things, so I put a chair for Shadow next to yours. Is that okay?"

"That's fine," Campbell said.

Mrs. Matheson went into the house.

"This isn't so bad," he whispered to Hope.

"Wait until you taste her cooking," she whispered back, but the tension in her voice was unmistakable.

Eleanor scraped the fried eggs from the pan onto the plate with the bacon and hash browns. The egg yolks had broken, mixing with the whites, forming one great milky vortex, but Teresa wouldn't mind. The girl had been downstairs for nearly ten hours. She must be hungry by now. She wouldn't care what the eggs looked like.

Max sat behind her, watching attentively.

"This isn't for you. You'll get yours soon enough."

She carried the tray to the back door, balanced it on one hand as she took the flashlight from its hook, then opened the door and went outside. The night was cool and cloudy, but not completely dark. The moon was full, and it burned through the clouds like a spotlight obscured by mist. The patch of brightness hovered over the windbreak to the east. The way the clouds moved across it made it seem alive.

She opened the cellar door, held the tray with one hand again, and shone the flashlight down the stairs. The circle of light flashed across rough wood and dark stone. She went down, watching her feet on the steps. The flashlight jiggled as she moved, making the cellar shadows stretch and shrink, as if the walls were alive, breathing. Max followed her down, claws clicking on the steps.

At the bottom, Eleanor turned on the light that illuminated the narrow passage. The ceiling here was low, and she stooped as she walked along, holding the tray out ahead of her. It had taken her a good month to do the work in the cellar. At one time it had been a single, large room, dirty, infested with rats, a forgotten part of the house. Now it served a purpose.

The light from the passage did not fully illuminate the cell at the end, and as she approached it, Eleanor turned on the flashlight again. She kept the beam low, to the floor, not wanting to startle Teresa.

It was hard to keep her excitement in check. She had been thinking of the girl all day long, wanting to come down to see her, to hold her, to comfort her, but knowing it would be better to let the girl sit in darkness for a while longer. When she came down, she wanted the girl to be eager to see her, frightened. Those first few minutes would be precious, a bond would form. For Teresa, it would be like coming out of the womb. Eleanor would be her mother. Even Jesse Hampton had loved her in those first minutes, so happy to see another human face.

The circle of light slid into the cell, found the mattress against the far wall. Teresa was not on it. Eleanor froze, staring at the empty mattress. Her heart pounded and her mouth went instantly dry.

She swung the flashlight in an arc, sending the circle of light flashing across bars, to the ceiling. Shadows twirled and leaped, reaching across the floor and walls like the fingers of a giant hand. She glimpsed a dark lump in one corner of the cell and turned the light on it.

Teresa was sitting on the floor, legs crossed, elbows resting on knees, chin on fists. Eleanor almost cried out with relief. The girl stared at her, alert, frowning.

"Who are you? What do you want? Why did you bring me here?"

The rapid-fire questions caught Eleanor off guard.

"I'm, uh, Ellie," she said.

She stared at the girl, still trying to recover from the shock of finding the empty mattress. Max went up to the bars and stuck his nose through, sniffed.

"Max, sit."

Teresa looked at Max, then back to her. "You lied. His name isn't Billy."

Again, caught off guard, she tried to smile. "I brought you something to eat."

"Are you a pervert or something?"

This wasn't going the way Eleanor had imagined, or expected. Teresa was not frightened. Teresa did not need to be comforted, cuddled, loved. Teresa, in fact, was downright belligerent.

Frowning, Eleanor opened the cell door and went in with the tray. She put it down by the mattress, then turned the flashlight on the girl. Teresa squinted against the light, but did not cover her eyes. She had not moved from her cross-legged position in the corner.

"I think you should take me home before you get in more trouble than you're already in."

"I can't do that."

"Somebody saw you, you know."

Eleanor felt a hollowness blossom in her stomach. The girl was trying to frighten her, that was all. Nobody had seen her.

"I don't think so," she said.

Teresa snorted, as if this was an impossibility. She uncrossed her legs, stood, brushed off her pants, and walked over to the mattress. Taken aback by the girl's brashness, Eleanor backed up a step. Teresa picked up the tray and inspected the plate of food.

"These eggs are all mixed up. I like mine sunny side up."

"I'm . . . sorry," Eleanor said.

"How long are you going to keep me here?"

"I don't know."

"What do you want?"

"I . . ."

"You don't know," Teresa said, mocking her.

Teresa sat down on the mattress. She picked up the fork and began to eat. She ate quickly, finishing the eggs, then starting on the bacon. Her eyes never left Eleanor, and Eleanor began to feel uncomfortable under the scrutiny.

It wasn't supposed to be like this.

Part of her wanted to reach for the girl, stroke her soft hair, touch her cheek. Another part of her wanted to strike her, strike hard, smash her into submission.

But it was too early for that. That would come. If it had to.

Teresa stopped chewing, stared at her as if seeing her for the first time. The girl laughed softly.

"Am I supposed to be your little girl? Is that it? Are you supposed to be my mommy? Do you want to hug me and hold me and make me feel all better?"

Horrified, Eleanor backed away, out the door. She closed it and locked it.

"I think you're sick," Teresa said, biting a piece of bacon. "I think you're a pervert. What kind of stupid God made you? Not me, that's for sure."

"Max, upstairs. Let's go."

Still reeling, she ushered the dog along the passage. At the end, she turned off the light, plunging the cellar into darkness.

"Bye, Max," Teresa called out.

Eleanor climbed the stairs. She felt nauseated, almost dizzy, confused.

At the top of the stairs, before she closed the door, she looked down into the darkness. For just a moment she thought she had heard something. She listened carefully. The sound came again. It sounded like crying. Soft, muffled.

Not so tough, after all.

She closed the door, locked it, and went back into the house.

SEVENTEEN

Highway 210 glistened like a river in the moonlight. Hope felt so good she had to struggle to keep the car under 50 miles per hour.

"Tell me again what she said when I went to the bathroom," Campbell said.

Hope grinned. "She said, 'Of all the men you've had the chance to see, you had to choose a blind one.' "

"And me thinking I was making a good impression!"

"I was impressed."

"You don't count. Not tonight, anyway. I was trying to sweep your mother off her feet."

"If she'd actually approved of you, I don't know what I would have done."

"I get the feeling that part of my appeal is that your mother doesn't like me."

"Makes me sound kind of juvenile, doesn't it?"

Hope turned to look at him. He was staring straight ahead, but Shadow was looking right at her.

"Watch the road," he said.

"What do you think you're looking at?"

"Did you know that in the moonlight your skin glows? It looks like milk. Very nice."

"Did you know that in the moonlight your fur looks like fresh asphalt? Makes me want to pet you."

"I'll purr."

"That's my job."

"Bark, then."

"Cats and dogs sleeping together. Never thought I'd see the day. You won't bite?"

Hope put a hand on his thigh. Through the fabric of his jeans his flesh felt hot, firm. She kept her eyes on the road. Her heart pounded hard, a steady thumping like heavy footsteps. *Intruder inside me,* she thought. *I wish it were Cam. Right now. Right here.* The sexual tension that had been growing between them since this morning had turned into a palpable force, like a Star Trek energy field, binding them together.

She moved her hand higher on his thigh. He shifted his weight. Her fingers brushed across a hard lump in his lap. Campbell made a coughing sound.

"A stick shift," Hope said thoughtfully. "And me thinking all this time that this was an automatic."

"Careful. We're coming up on a curve. Don't want to rev the engine."

The road curved to the right and, a few hundred yards ahead, disappeared behind a dark wall of trees. Hope kept one hand on the wheel, one hand on Campbell.

"Should I gear down for this?"

"Uh."

Light speared out of the darkness. Two headlights, coming right at them. A car, or a truck, with its brights on. Light more intense than a sunrise, so brilliant that even Shadow turned to look.

"Hell," Campbell muttered.

Hope flashed her brights at the oncoming vehicle. The trees at the side of the road seemed to lean in toward them as the brights went down. The oncoming car did not turn down its lights. Hope squinted into the glare.

"Jerk!"

She flashed her brights again. Still, the oncoming vehicle made no move to turn his down. Hope squinted against the oncoming light. The road, the trees, even the top of the steering wheel disappeared into the glare.

The pickup roared past, and darkness engulfed Hope's eyes. She turned up her brights, illuminating the empty road.

"I *hate* that!"

"Okay, okay, okay, okay," Campbell said breathlessly. "You can gear down now. Please. Easy, now."

She was still holding onto him. Gripping him, more accurately. Fingers digging into the stiff flesh between his legs.

"Oops. Sorry."

"No damage. A couple of bruises, maybe."

"I'll take care of those soon."

Hope gently squeezed him, then put her hand back on the wheel.

Campbell exhaled loudly.

Hope turned her head slightly to look at him. Shadow was staring straight ahead. Campbell appeared relaxed, almost sleepy.

Not *too* sleepy, I hope.

She caught the thought, then grinned. What was happening to her? It felt as if she'd sexually awakened only this morning! And she wanted to stay awake for as long as possible. She had wanted him badly enough earlier in the evening, when they'd arrived at her mother's, and through the course of the evening the feeling had grown. During dinner she'd even played footsie with him under the table! Like a teenaged girl! Pushing her bare toes up his legs, between his thighs!

He'd showed admirable restraint, squeezing his legs together, trapping her foot, at the same time engaging her mother in small talk as if nothing were happening.

She grinned, thinking about it.

"Are you tired?" she asked.

Campbell laughed softly. "Would you let me be?"

"Don't be silly. Stay at my cabin tonight."

"Oh, yes, you were going to show me your etchings, weren't you?"

"Sure, yeah, that's right."

"I hear you have a great collection."

When she finally came to the turn-off for Battle Lake's south allotments, Hope wanted to cheer. She drove past Campbell's cabin, pulled in behind the empty kennel at her own. The breeze coming off the lake was cool. Goose bumps rose on her arms and shoulders. She shivered as she took Campbell's hand and pulled him toward the door.

"Easy, now!"

"Heel!"

She fumbled with her key at the door, took two tries to fit it into the lock, and almost screamed when it seemed as if it would not go. It slid in. She turned it. The door opened. She pulled Campbell and Shadow in after her, then leaned on the door to close it. She had left the kitchen light on, and now that hazy, yellow nimbus reached out to embrace them in its warmth.

"Where, exactly, do you keep this etching collection?"

Hope put her hands behind Campbell's neck and pulled his face toward hers. She put her mouth over his. His lips opened and his tongue darted out to touch her. She sucked on it eagerly, then took his upper lip into her mouth, pulling it gently with her teeth.

His hands tugged her shirt free of her jeans, and were suddenly inside, pressed against her skin. She moaned softly as he moved his hands up, cupping her breasts through the fabric of her bra. His thumbs slid under the bra, pushing it up. He was good at this! No hesitation at all.

When his palms cupped her naked breasts, all the breath left her, and she clung to him as if she might faint. His fingers squeezed her nipples. They became instantly erect. So much for playing hard to get.

Still kissing him, she unclasped his pants, unzipped them, gave them a tug. They slid down to his knees without protest. She pushed her forefingers past the elastic at the top of his briefs, pulled them away from his skin, down. She took his shaft in her hand, ran her fingers up and down its length, over smooth skin, marveling at the soft veins that rolled and pulsed beneath her fingers.

Campbell's mouth went to her ear, tugged gently at the lobe with his teeth.

"Best etching collection I've ever seen," he whispered.

"It gets better," she said.

She undid her own jeans, shuffling her legs until they slipped down around her ankles. Campbell's fingers caressed her through her panties. She moaned, feeling her own heat, the wetness that made the panties cling to her. His fingers slid up through a leg hole, tugged the silky fabric aside. Instinctively she spread her legs a little.

"Oh, God, Campbell."

Campbell cried out as if in pain. His hands became claws and dug painfully into her behind.

"Campbell? What's wrong?"

"It's happening again," he said, teeth gritted.

"Oh, God!"

She supported him with hands on his shoulders and pushed him toward the easy chair in the living room. When his legs bumped into the base of the chair he sat down hard, breath expelling in a gasp.

"Don't panic, Campbell."

"I'm not. It's still happening."

Shadow, standing rigidly beside the chair, whined. Hope kneeled between Campbell's legs and clasped his hands. She noted, dispassionately, that his penis was still hard, poking at her sternum through the fabric of her shirt. It meant nothing, now.

"Okay, Campbell. I'm with you. Tell me what's happening."

"The same as before. Darkness. A long tunnel. Something like that."

"Is that all?"

"No, wait. Stairs. Dark stairs. I'm going down. It's a cellar of some kind. A root cellar. A basement, maybe. But it's so narrow. I'm walking along a tunnel. It's so dark. I don't know why it's so dark. Wait. Light. For a second. Faint. Somebody's behind me, with a flashlight. Oh, God, Hope."

The fear and pain in his voice made her flesh crawl.

"What is it, Campbell?"

"It's her. The girl I saw before. She's lying on the floor. No wait. It's a mattress. She's lying on a mattress. Sleeping, I think She doesn't know she's being watched. She doesn't know."

"Who's watching her Campbell?"

"I can't see. It's just a big, dark shape right now. She's still sleeping. She doesn't know. She's an angel, Hope. She looks like an angel. This is going on too long. It has never gone on this long before."

His hands were cold in her own, sweaty, trembling.

"Campbell, I'm going to unhook you from Shadow. If it's coming from him, that should end it, right?"

"I . . . don't . . ."

Hope did not wait for him to finish. She released his hands and fumbled with the cable that snaked over the side of the chair toward the dog. She found the coupler, held it in both hands, twisted. The cables came apart.

Campbell slumped, sighed, shuddered.

"It's gone. Everything is black."

"Then it's definitely coming from Shadow," Hope said.

She was more surprised than she should have been. I didn't believe him, she thought, and flushed. She was glad it was dark, and then realized it wouldn't have made any difference.

She leaned over Campbell, found his mouth with hers, kissed him. For a moment he did not respond, and then his mouth opened. His hands moved up her shoulders, found her neck, and held onto her tightly.

"Are you okay?" she whispered.

"Yes, it's finished."

"If you want, we can . . ."

"I want to see the rest of those etchings," he said hoarsely.

His erection throbbed against her breasts.

"Are you sure?"

He took one of her hands in his and guided it to his penis. His flesh burned against her fingers.

"I'm sure."

Hope kissed him hungrily. Moved her mouth to his chin. Kissed his throat, sliding her tongue along smooth, salty skin.

"Do you want me to hook you up again?"

"No. It's better this way. Everything feels more intense in the dark."

"Really."

"Uh huh."

"Then this ought to feel pretty good," she said.

Teresa sat up and put her back against the wall. It was a wooden wall, rough, but dry. Drier than the floor, anyway, which felt slimy and damp when she touched it. She was alone again. No need to pretend she was asleep any longer. The farmer woman had gone.

When the flashlight had first swept through the darkness she had curled up on the mattress and closed her eyes, had tried to make her breathing sound deep and slow, as if she were fast asleep. It must have worked. The woman had stood at the door of the cell for a few minutes, watching her, and had finally gone away.

Teresa had thought about sitting up and shouting at her, but some gut instinct told her not to. She didn't know much about the woman, other than that she was capable of kidnapping, and she didn't want to find out how far she was willing to go. Not yet, anyway.

She crossed her legs and stared into the darkness. It wasn't complete darkness. Not like the darkness inside the Monterey gold mine she and dad had visited a few years back. That darkness had been so deep that Teresa had to keep talking to convince herself she wasn't dead, kept saying things like, "Dad, when we get out of here, can we get some ice cream," or "Hey, dad, do you remember that movie about those guys in the desert who crash their plane and then they have to make another one out of the broken parts," talking and talking and hardly aware of the questions she was asking, needing only to hear her voice, her dad's answers. This was a milky sort of darkness, full of varying shades of gray.

Just to the right of the door, beyond the bars, were two squares that might be windows. The windows were covered, though. Probably by newspapers. That she could see them at all was strange, because she felt that it must be night. If it *was* night outside, then there must be lights just beyond the windows. Or else the moon was out. A full moon.

Enough light in here, anyway, so that her eyes could adjust to it, given time.

She did not know exactly how long she had been down here. The woman had done something to her in the back lane, had pressed something to her face. Teresa remembered a horrible smell that made her eyes water, her lungs burn. Remembered feeling as if she were a tiny bubble shooting through a long hose, finally expelled into dark, dark water. When she had woken up, she had been lying on the mattress, in this darkness.

She was afraid. No point denying that. She was scared. But she was not panicked. She knew that, too. It was all right to be afraid. Dad said that sometimes. Only fools didn't get scared. She had a right to be scared. It was smart.

She tried to piece together what had happened to her.

She had been abducted.

Abducted.

The word wanted to come to her tongue, but she wouldn't let it. She didn't want to feel it in her mouth. Saying it would make it that much worse. Thinking it was bad enough.

But she had to think about it. She had to figure out what had happened, and what still might happen.

My name is Teresa Dawson. I am eight years old. I live at 220 Third Street, Godfrey, Minnesota. I have been abducted.

I have been abducted.

She thought of other kids who had been abducted. Not that she knew any, personally. But she'd heard the stories. Boys and girls who disappeared in the middle of the day while walking to the store. Never heard from again. Bodies never found. Mostly. Sometimes bodies were found. Decomposed. Mutilated. She remembered seeing posters in the supermarket and the drugstore. Pictures of faces. Have you seen Michael?

She did not want to think about these things in the darkness, but she knew that she should.

I've been gone at least a day, she thought. Half a day. Morning till night. It might have taken a while for Elizabeth to realize she was gone. Elizabeth would think she went to the park. Sometimes she stayed at the park all day long. It would be awhile before Elizabeth started to worry.

By the time Dad got home, though, things would be cooking. Dad would know right away she was missing. Dad would call the police. The police would start looking for her. Pretty soon her picture would be on the bulletin board in the drugstore and the supermarket. Have you seen Teresa?

What did the woman want with her?

Was she *really* a pervert?

The words "sexual mutilation" popped into her head. She'd heard about that on a television show one night, hadn't paid much attention, but now she couldn't stop thinking about it. What, exactly, could it mean?

She heard a noise in the darkness. A snuffling noise, as if somebody had tried to block a sneeze.

She was not alone!

She'd been sitting here, thinking she was alone, when all the time the woman had been . . .

She heard clicking noises. A whine.

The dog.

Max.

She stood up, stepped gingerly off the mattress, and walked toward where the door should be, hands held out in front of her. She touched the steel bars, stopped, kneeled down. She pushed her hands through the bars.

"Max? Here boy? C'mere boy."

Breathing. More clicking. Must be his claws on the floor.

Warm fur filled her hands. A wet nose poked through the bars. Teresa put her face close so that he could sniff her. He licked her face.

It felt so good to have something to hold, something alive, something that didn't want to hurt her, or scare her. She almost started to cry.

"Good boy," she whispered to the dog.

She scratched him behind his ears. She couldn't see him. Not clearly, anyway. Just a black lump in the darkness.

She sat down and leaned against the bars. The dog lay down, too, paws and snout poking through the bars.

He likes me, she thought.

"Did she abduct you, too?"

Max licked her fingers.

Had the woman forgotten the dog down here, or was this intentional? Maybe it was a trick to soften her, bring her defenses down. She considered this, then rejected it. She didn't care if it was.

She lay down on the cold, damp, stone floor, her face close to the dog's. His breath was warm across her forehead. She closed her eyes.

"What is she going to do with us?"

The dog whined, as if he wanted to answer but couldn't find the words.

EIGHTEEN

Hope opened her eyes to sunlight. Golden shafts leaned through the bedroom window and warmed her right leg, the only part of her exposed. The waking was sudden, an instantaneous leap from the fuzzy comfort of sleep to hard consciousness.

Campbell slept on beside her.

She stared at the back of his head, half disbelieving despite her clear memory of last night. Under the blankets his warmth was a dry heat on her belly and breasts and thighs. She wrestled with disbelief, with amazement, with joy. He was here with her! Campbell's breathing was slow and deep, shoulders rising and falling. She half expected him to roll toward her, awakened by the pounding of her heart.

She slid backward out of bed, pulling away from Campbell in increments. When she stood at last, naked by the bed, he continued to sleep, oblivious.

She dressed quickly, pulling on jeans, an old Minnesota Vikings sweatshirt, a pair of beaten running shoes. As she walked past the bed to leave the room a dark shape moved on the floor and her heart leapt to her throat. Shadow's tail wagged once as he lifted his head from his paws. The dog studied her face, as if waiting for her to do something.

Over the past few days Hope had come to accept that Shadow's eyes were Campbell's eyes, that whatever Shadow saw, Campbell saw, and she stiffened now under the dog's gaze, despite knowing that Campbell had unhooked Shadow shortly after slipping into bed.

Was it possible that part of Campbell was expressed through Shadow's eyes? Looking at the dog, she could hardly doubt it. Whether true or not, or even possible, she realized with a shock that a large part of her perception of Campbell was Shadow. In thinking about Campbell, looking at him, talking to him, she was always aware of the dog. They were one, whole only together.

She glanced toward the bed. Campbell had removed his glasses. His eyes appeared to be closed, the eyelids somewhat sunken. The skin around the corners of his eyes was wrinkled, as if he were smiling to himself, but she knew that was not the case. His flesh was scarred, healed now into odd lines, hollows, and puckers. Campbell had no eyes.

Although it was one of the only times she had seen him without his glasses, she felt no revulsion. She had known what the glasses hid. Instead, she felt a strange, warming compassion. She resisted the urge to kneel by him, to kiss his face where he must hurt the most.

Uneasy at her thoughts, she backed away. Shadow lowered his snout to his paws, eyes still following her. Only when Hope was out of the room, the bedroom door closed behind her, did she breathe more easily. Her chest hurt as if she had been squeezed.

Although her stomach growled for breakfast, she decided to wait. She put on a thin nylon jacket and left the cabin. The morning, though sunny, was cool, the air moist and crisp. Mist clung to the ground. Hope walked through it, hands stuffed into her jeans' pockets for warmth, and worked her way along the trails, down to the beach.

Across the bowl of the lake the mist had settled. The town of Battle Lake was invisible, the far shore only a dark smudge like a bloody bone protruding from silvery pale flesh.

Hope walked slowly along the beach, looking down at her feet more often than she looked at the surreal morning landscape. She thought about Campbell Knight, about herself.

No point denying it. They were involved. They were, as a matter of fact, an item.

It was not just the sex. The sex had simply been the seal on the proclamation of their relationship. Their involvement had happened in increments that were hard, now, to delineate. It had started, she knew, the first time she had seen him on the beach. Hard to believe that that was only a few weeks ago!

She recalled clearly how Jill had dragged her down to the water, how the dog had leapt free and run straight for Campbell, as if he had been a shot fired from a gun.

Dogs, from the start, had been integral to their relationship, she realized.

First Jill. Now Shadow.

She understood, guiltily, that what had initially attracted her to Campbell was his helplessness. Knowing herself, she could not doubt it. Campbell Knight was one of the few men she had ever met who might need her more than she would need him. She had allowed his helplessness to draw her to him. He would need her, he would love her, he would . . . depend on her.

She groaned thinking about it, lashed out with her foot to kick at a piece of dry driftwood. It skittered across the rocky beach until it lodged between two pale boulders.

Had she really been that childish? That insecure?

It didn't matter, anyway. For better or worse, Campbell could now see.

We are, more or less, equals, she thought.

If Campbell had been sighted when she first met him, would she have been drawn to him?

She could not answer the question, but suspected that if she could she would be shamed. She knew, instinctively, that she would have pulled away from him, fleeing any chance at involvement.

Too late now, though. She'd been duped by his initial helplessness, had been captured by his . . . what? Spell?

That, she realized, was what frightened her most of all.

He did not need her, not in the way she had anticipated. He was independent, self-sufficient. Whatever it was that he was drawn to in her, it was not her sight.

Then, what? And to what was she drawn in him?

She did not know the answer to that, and suspected that no lovers did. That was the mystery. That's what made it all so . . . awful. Awful in the original sense. Tremendous, awe inspiring. No wonder the poets were so captivated by it. Love.

She walked a little more, then turned around and started back.

She had hoped for unnatural, unattainable security in a relationship. Campbell, blind, had offered that possibility. But now, even with Campbell, the risks were clearly evident.

She might get hurt. She might get hurt, she realized with sudden fear, far more deeply than she had been hurt by Warren Daniels. Because already, after only a few weeks, she had invested more hope, more *of* Hope, in this relationship than she had ever dared invest in her relationship with Warren.

When she got back to the cabin she had resolved nothing, had not achieved the calm she had expected a morning walk would provide. Instead, she was as unsure, as terrified as the moment she had awoken.

Campbell was waiting for her in the kitchen when she came through the door, and she looked away from him, guilty and afraid. He came toward her, Shadow at his side, and put his arms around her. She started to say something, started to voice her fear, to demand of him that he commit himself to her, when his lips touched hers, and his embrace tightened.

Hope's thoughts, her fears, her insecurities were swept away. She clung to him, pressing her face into his neck.

And then, as if he had read her mind, as if he had known of the morning fears that had tormented her, he whispered, "I won't hurt you, Hope. Never. I promise."

She pulled away, looked up into his dark glasses, so that she saw her own face. She was surprised to see that she was smiling.

"You better not, Campbell Knight."

Then she put her head back to his chest.

Teresa's dreams, whatever they were, must have been terrifying, for when she woke it was with a suddenness that startled her, as if ice water had been poured over her face. It took only a few seconds, staring into the darkness around her, to recollect her situation, and for a while she rocked back and forth, hugging herself, eyes squeezed shut.

When she opened her eyes again she realized that the patch of light where the window hung in the darkness was a different shade of pale than it had been last night, brighter, crisper. It was morning beyond the window. Probably a clear morning, with blue skies, sunshine everywhere. Her dad would be waking now, stretching in bed. He would know, now, that she was missing. Probably he hadn't slept at all. He would have been too worried.

Thinking about him, she wanted to cry. She imagined him frantically phoning all the neighbors, her friends, trying to find her. She had a clear image of Aunt Elizabeth, telling her father that the last time she had seen Teresa was when she ran down to the store. Her dad would ask, *what for?* Elizabeth would look down at her hands. *Cigarettes, for me.* And then her dad would just stare at Elizabeth, stare and not say anything, perhaps even with a trembling lip, and Elizabeth would start to cry, and then she'd mumble, *I'll never smoke again, never, never, until Teresa is back home.*

Well, maybe not.

It wasn't exactly Elizabeth's fault. Dad would see that. Sometimes dad sent her down to the store for one thing or another. How was anybody to know that a crazy farmer lady would be sneaking around, looking for stray kids? Besides, I should have known better. It was a trap, and the dog was the bait. It's my own fault.

Still, dad would be upset. More than upset. First mom, and then me. He's losing everybody. He wasn't strong enough to handle that. This is probably easier on me than it is on him. At least I know what's going on.

She stared at the glowing window through the bars and wondered when the farmer lady would return. Perhaps she would bring the dog with her. Max.

She had dreamed about Max last night. Dreamed that some-how Max had come down to see her, and had sat outside the bars, staring in at her, trying to tell her something.

Or had it been real?

Suddenly she was not sure.

The memory was sharp, clear. She remembered thinking that Max didn't like the farmer lady either, remembered thinking that both of them were prisoners. He had licked her hand, and she had stroked the bony, broad diamond of his head.

It *had* been real.

She was relieved to believe so. It meant she had a friend, an ally. Just a dog, sure, but anyone, *anything* was better than noth-ing.

She thought about her dad again, and suddenly squeezed her eyes tightly shut.

I promise, dad, I'll get out of here, I won't go crazy, and I'll get back home.

She had to. For dad. She just *had* to.

She couldn't let herself go crazy. She couldn't let herself fall to pieces or start crying or acting like a little kid.

She had to stay smart. She had to stay alert. She had to keep her eyes open for any opportunity to get away.

Breathing slowly, deeply, strangely calmed by her new re-solve, she crossed her legs, hugged her knees tightly, and stared at the gray square of the window.

And waited.

And waited.

Eleanor waited as long as she could, biting down on her ex-citement, her eagerness to see the girl, knowing that the longer she waited the better it was going to be. She sat at the kitchen table, mug of coffee cradled in her hands, watching the clock on the wall, following the hands as they crept slowly, impossibly slowly, toward 10:00 A.M. On the floor by her feet, Max dozed, snoring softly. He seemed no worse for wear for his night in the cellar. Teresa's breakfast was already prepared. The neatly organized tray sat on the counter next to the back door.

Eleanor sipped her coffee, fighting her impatience.

The longer she waited, the better it would be.

She'd learned that with Jesse Hampton, poor, sweet Jesse. If she went down early with his breakfast and woke him up, he would sometimes stay confused for hours, hardly talking, withdrawing even more deeply into himself. But if she waited, waited until he was already awake, waited until the pangs of hunger were poking at his belly, he would be crying, calling for her when she came down. At those times, she could almost feel the *need* emanating from him. She would hold him, stroke his soft hair, easing his night fears, before feeding him.

Last night, Teresa had been somewhat recalcitrant. The girl's anger had startled her. She should have expected it. The child had not had time to adapt to her surroundings, or to experience her fear. Naturally, anger had been her first emotion.

This morning, hungry, confused, she would be tractable. Max's company overnight might have softened her a little. Perhaps even more than a little.

Eleanor imagined Teresa weeping, shaking, needing to be held. She imagined the girl throwing herself into her arms, burrowing her soft, sweet face into her neck. She imagined the feel of the small body nestled in her arms, needing, loving.

It was too much. She couldn't wait another minute.

She picked up the tray by the door and went outside. Max padded after her, and when she opened the door to the cellar, the dog lunged in ahead of her, disappearing into the darkness.

She turned on the light and went down, holding the tray carefully in front of her. At the bottom of the stairs, she turned on the flashlight and shined it along the narrow corridor that led to the cage.

Teresa was standing, arms crossed, waiting. Eleanor's heart pounded as she drew closer. The light from the flashlight swallowed the girl, surrounded her, giving her an angel's glowing aura.

"Good morning," Eleanor said.

Teresa smiled. She stared directly into Eleanor's face, as if unperturbed by the light in her eyes.

"Hello," Teresa said.

Eleanor put the tray on the floor. "Are you hungry?"

"Yes."

"Will you be good if I come inside with you?"

"Yes."

There was something strange about the girl's voice, something Eleanor could not put her finger on. The tones were sweet, innocent, but beyond them she sensed a calculating mind. She frowned as she pushed the key into the lock and turned it.

"Did you sleep well?"

"I had funny dreams," Teresa said.

She did not look at Eleanor as she spoke, but seemed to be looking around herself, very deliberately. Eleanor stepped into the cage and closed the door quickly behind her.

"Where's Max?"

"He's back there somewhere."

Teresa walked to the bars, held them, looking carefully into the dark area immediately surrounding the cage. Max pushed his nose between the bars, and the girl reached out and touched his nose.

"If you're good, perhaps I'll let him stay down here with you again."

Teresa turned to her, smiling. "I'd like that."

Something is wrong, Eleanor thought. The girl was too friendly, too open, too eager to please.

"Sit down, I'll feed you."

The girl sat down on the mattress, crossed her legs, looked up sweetly. Eleanor kneeled beside her and put the tray between them. She poured milk into the cereal, then scooped up a spoonful and held it toward Teresa.

"I can feed myself, thanks," Teresa said, and took the spoon.

Eleanor leaned away, watching the girl intently. Teresa put the spoon in her mouth, started chewing the cereal. She ate methodically, finishing one spoonful, scooping up another, all the time looking around herself with wide, observant eyes.

"What are you looking for?"

Teresa became still and looked directly at her.

"Nothing."

"There's no way to get out of here, you know."

"I don't want to get out."

Teresa put another spoonful of cereal in her mouth, began to chew, eyes now locked onto Eleanor s. The girl's gaze was hard, judgmental, without even an ounce of love. The pounding of Eleanor's heart had become a steady, shallow beating.

Had she made a mistake with the girl? Was this child to be even harder to love than Jesse Hampton had been?

Her hand moved with a will of its own, it seemed, and lashed out at Teresa. The flashlight slammed into the side of the girl's head. A spoonful of cereal went flying. Teresa's legs kicked out as she fell over, knocking the tray off the mattress. A glass of juice spilled onto Eleanor's foot, and the saucer with toast clattered to the floor.

Teresa curled into a ball on the mattress, shaking, covering her head with her arms. Sorrow filled Eleanor's heart, and she leaned over the girl, reaching out with loving arms.

"I'm sorry, Teresa. I'm so sorry. I didn't want to do that. Honestly I didn't. But you . . ."

As her arms encircled Teresa, the girl stiffened and pulled away. Eleanor tried to hold on, but Teresa's small arms came between them and pushed hard.

"Leave me alone!"

"I didn't want to hurt you! You made me do it!"

Teresa was crouched now, back pressed to the wall, arms hugging her knees. The girl's eyes were wide, watchful.

"Don't hit me again," Teresa said.

The words hit Eleanor like fists. Each one was softly spoken, calculated, free of all emotion. All, perhaps, but hate.

Eleanor backed away. Eyes on the girl, she cleaned up the

spilled food, and took the tray from the cell. Still watching Teresa, she locked the door.

"No more food until you behave," she said.

Teresa said nothing. Eleanor stared down at her feet as she walked back along the corridor. It had all gone wrong. It wasn't supposed to be like this at all. This was a loveless child. An empty child.

Max padded up the stairs ahead of her, but stopped at the top to look down at her. His tail was wagging slowly.

"Go on, Max. Go away."

The dog growled softly, tail suddenly still. Eleanor glared at him.

"Max!"

Max turned and trotted away without a backward glance. Sick, empty, Eleanor went back to the house. She was washing the dishes in the sink when she realized that the butter knife she had taken down on the tray was missing. She stiffened, staring into the water.

She could not remember if she had actually put one on the tray. If she had, then it was still downstairs, in the cellar. With Teresa.

But she could not make herself go back to face the girl.

Campbell listened to the sound of the shower running. Images of Hope's, naked, glistening body filled his head. He imagined her hands slowly caressing her breasts, smoothly lathering soap between her legs. He had a clear memory of the feel of her, the tactile reality of her body, his fingers and tongue sliding into every moist crevice, eliciting from her soft whimpering sounds, sudden muscle spasms. Just bringing it to mind was enough to make him groan.

The sound he had made caught Shadow's attention, and Campbell suddenly found himself looking into his own face. He was shocked to see the dreamy expression on his features.

"Shadow, front," he said quickly.

Shadow turned away, and Campbell once again found himself observing Hope's living room. He tried to ignore the sound of the shower coming from somewhere behind him. Not healthy, that.

In the center of his field of vision sat Hope's television. Although it was not the center of Shadow's attention, it suddenly became the center of Campbell's. He had seen the set a few times, but had never really considered what it meant. And what it meant was . . . a part of his old life.

He stiffened as a memory of the last time he had watched television came to him. It had been the night before his accident. He had been with Julia. They had just returned to her apartment from one of those silly damned agent/client parties her firm kept putting on. She had spent the night schmoozing as he had stood back, watching, distant. They were relaxing, curled up on her sofa. He remembered it had been CNN. News of the space shuttle, something like that. He hadn't really been paying attention. Julia's hands had been all over him. The last time. After the accident, she would not touch him again.

Campbell stood and stepped up to the television. He reached out hesitantly to touch the controls. He had never missed television, and until now would not have considered it one of the things he would have liked to regain, but he found that his hands were suddenly sweaty, as if he were doing something he should not be doing.

He pulled the on/off switch and stepped back. The screen slowly brightened. Campbell sat down on the sofa.

"Shadow, front," he said softly.

He was not sure what he had hoped to feel, could not decide if he had been hoping for some final reassurance that he had regained everything he had lost, but the only thing he felt as he watched the television screen was disappointment. The image was, of course, black and white. But it was also somewhat decayed from what his own eyes might have seen. In the real world Shadow saw shades of gray, a whole range of shadows and depths that Campbell had come to accept as quite normal. In fact, his mind tended to *colorize* the image, so that if he was not particularly concentrating on it, he could not distinguish it from what his own vision had been like. This was the accommodation Russell and Nina had promised him.

But now, staring at the television, he was struck by its artificiality, its unreality. The screen image was so unlike the real world as to be utterly removed from it. The sounds Campbell heard told him he was watching a news broadcast of some kind, but the image he was seeing, a dim, harsh rendering of brilliant lines and empty shadows, looked like something out of a nightmare. He could see a man's face, or what he assumed to be a man's face, hovering in a grayish cloud. The man's voice was talking about President Clinton's health care plan. Behind the face, the shadows swirled, and Campbell assumed background graphics were being manipulated.

"Shadow, right," he said softly.

When Shadow turned away from the screen, Campbell breathed deeply, relieved. How could anyone sit and watch that thing for any length of time? It would require concentration. He felt a headache already, throbbing behind his forehead.

When a woman's voice replaced the man's, Campbell turned Shadow back to the screen. The image he was getting from Shadow made her look exactly like the man had looked, but it was her voice that captured him, cut through the half-life image, transfixed him. And then the image changed again, and even her words started to fade for him, as the new face on the screen, even in its decayed, horrifying television state, stabbed into his mind.

". . . largest search in Minnesota history . . . missing since yesterday . . . no clues . . . continue to search . . . the girl's father."

"What are you watching?"

When Hope came up behind him and put her arms around him, he jumped, almost cried out.

"What's wrong?"

Campbell could only point at the screen.

"Again," said the announcer, voice-over on the photograph that had so affected Campbell, "missing since yesterday, eight-year-old Teresa Dawson. Police continue to search, but with little hope of success."

"Campbell, you're shaking."

"It's her," he said, gagging on words that felt like rocks in his mouth.

"Who?"

"The girl. From the visions. She's real."

NINETEEN

The tractor took up half the road and all of the shoulder. A plume of dust rose from the big wheels and billowed across the station wagon like fog. The driver of the tractor stared stubbornly ahead. Like we're going to go away if he ignores us, Hope thought. Jerk.

"Pass him," Campbell said impatiently.

"I'm trying," Hope told him.

She edged into the left lane. The road was clear, curving behind a peninsula of trees two hundred yards away. She pressed her foot to the accelerator and the wagon slowly picked up speed. Campbell drummed his thighs with white knuckles. The wagon was adjacent to the tractor when a car rounded the curve ahead.

"Shit!"

Hope jammed her foot down on the accelerator, but the wagon continued its smooth, painfully slow acceleration. Even if she decelerated now, there wouldn't be enough time to get back into her own lane. The oncoming car rushed toward them. Hope gritted her teeth and watched from the corner of her eye as the front wheel of the tractor slipped behind her rear bumper, then turned sharply in front of it. The oncoming car roared past, missing a head-on collision, it seemed to Hope, by scant inches. The teenage driver and his teenage passengers laughed hysterically. The tractor swayed on the road, slipped farther onto the shoulder. The plume of dust suddenly filled Hope's rearview mirror, consuming the vehicle. In a moment it reappeared, its driver looking as stoic as ever.

"Jesus," she whispered, mouth dry.

"What is it?"

She glanced at Campbell. He was looking straight ahead, but Shadow was staring out the passenger window. He hadn't even been aware of their near disaster. All he had seen was the tractor.

"Just nerves, I guess."

"You should feel what I'm feeling. I couldn't believe it when I saw her face."

"You can't be sure it was the same girl, Campbell."

"Shadow, left," Campbell said. Once the dog was looking directly at her, he said, "I've never been more sure of anything in my life."

Hope turned away from man and dog and returned her attention to the road. It didn't matter how crazy it sounded, Campbell believed it. The girl in his visions was the girl he had seen on television. She wasn't even the same child he'd envisioned earlier. That had been a boy. The girl had made her appearance only a couple of days ago.

Before Teresa Dawson had disappeared, according to the television report, anyway.

Which meant what, exactly? That Campbell was psychic, and having visions of children soon to be abducted?

Under normal circumstances, she would have discounted such a possibility without consideration. She had never much believed in the supernatural, and certainly had never given credence to stories of psychics or fortune-tellers. Her attitude stemmed from her father's skepticism about such things. But it was also due, in large part, to her mother's wholesale acceptance of the same things. Her father had viewed his wife's beliefs with mild, loving amusement, poking fun but never ridiculing. After her father had died, she had been at such odds with her mother, she would have willingly amputated all her limbs rather than accept her mother's views on anything.

Was that the foundation of her skepticism? A simple aversion for her mother?

A sudden rattling of the car brought her from her reverie. The speedometer hovered close to 80. Campbell, face pressed to the passenger window, hadn't even noticed. Hope pulled back slightly on the accelerator and watched the needle drop to 55.

Campbell's visions were different. She knew that. She had already accepted them on some level. Not, perhaps, psychic in nature, but she could not deny that they affected him deeply. And like Campbell, she had come to accept that on some level the visions were related to Shadow, to the operation that had given Campbell the dog's sight.

Right, she thought. The dog is psychic.

She turned resolutely away from her thoughts and concentrated on driving. They had to find out more about what was going on before they could act.

It was another ten minutes before they arrived at Fergus Falls. As Hope drove through the streets toward downtown, Shadow watched cars and pedestrians pass by. Once, as a dog darted across the road, he looked as if he might leap across the car. As he watched, his head moved slowly from left to right. Campbell, though he was facing forward, mimicked the dog's movements, and looked as if he were reading. They are connected, Hope realized, at some level neither of them quite understands. She shuddered slightly. Perhaps there *was* something to Campbell's visions.

She drove directly to the library and parked by the front door.

"I'll drop you here. I'll look around and see if I can pick up a Minneapolis newspaper."

Both Shadow and Campbell looked directly at her, and for a moment she thought he was going to object. But he nodded and leaned toward her. His kiss was soft, gentle, yet insistent. She responded, putting her arms around him. When he pulled away she was flushed and breathless.

"Hurry back," he said.

She nodded mutely. Campbell opened the door and ushered

Shadow out, then closed the door and waved. She watched as
he walked up to the door of the library, Shadow half a pace
behind him. Inseparable, she thought. He and the dog will always be closer than he and I ever can be. She half expected to
feel bitter, but instead she smiled. Campbell and Shadow were
one, and she accepted them as one.

After they had gone inside the building, she put the car in
gear and drove along to First Street. She tried the pharmacy
downtown, but the day's supply of the *Minneapolis Star/Tribune*
was already sold out. The cashier suggested she might try the
B. Dalton's in the mall. Hope drove up the hill toward I-94 and
Fergus Falls' major mall. Already it was busy, the parking lot
bustling with cars. She walked across the lot, the sun warm on
her back, a breeze blowing through her hair.

Such a normal day to be dispatched on the most bizarre errand of her life. It made the very normalcy seem unreal, the
strangeness of her errand even more pronounced.

She shuddered as she entered the air-conditioned mall, goose
bumps rising on her arms and shoulders. It felt strange to be
walking alone. She had grown accustomed to Campbell's and
Shadow's presence. She felt naked and alone without them, vulnerable somehow.

At the B. Dalton's she found a *Star/Trib,* a *Fergus Falls Ban-
ner,* as well as a couple of regional newspapers. As the clerk
punched the newspapers through the register, Hope studied the
front page of the *Star/Trib.* The disappearance of Teresa
Dawson was headline news. "GIRL, 8, DISAPPEARS," the
headline said. "State and Local Police Continue to Search."
Below the sub-head was a photograph of Teresa Dawson. Long
blonde hair tied in a braid; gleaming, thoughtful eyes; a nice
smile. Beyond the smile, deep within the girl, Hope sensed sadness. Well-hidden, but unmistakably there.

This is no ordinary child, she thought, and could not say
why.

Could Campbell really be seeing this child in his visions?

And if so, what did it mean? Was there a chance he might be able to find her?

She was torn between wanting it to be true, and dreading the possibility. If there was a chance that Campbell could help, then he must. He absolutely must. But if it were true, if Campbell were actually having visions . . . she thought of her mother and shook her head. *I am not my mother.*

With the papers folded beneath her arm she walked back through the mall. She had almost reached the exit when a man emerged from a shoe store and walked directly toward her. Hope hesitated only a moment, but it was enough.

A grinning Warren Daniels blocked her path to the door. "I thought that was you!"

"Warren."

"What are you doing at this end of town?"

"I have to go."

She tried to step past him, but he moved to block her way. "What's the rush? Can't we even chat when we run into each other?"

Hope made herself smile, bit down on the defensive, childish gibberish that suddenly wanted to erupt from her mouth. If only Campbell were here! If only Campbell could step between her and Warren. She was squeezing the newspapers so tightly beneath her arm that her ribs were aching. She let up a bit.

"Maybe some other time. There's somebody waiting for me."

"The blind man?"

Her smile tightened a notch. "Goodbye, Warren."

He did not step aside. "Nice trick he played the other night. Almost had me convinced that he could see."

"He *can* see."

"In his dreams."

"Warren, I have to go."

This time she stepped widely past him. He put out a hand and grabbed her arm. The newspapers spilled to the floor. Swearing softly, she bent to pick them up, but he was on the floor beside her, scooping up the *Star/Tribune* before she could put her hands on it.

"Come on, let's go for a coffee. Just to talk."

Hope stood, staring at him incredulously. "I told you, I'm in a hurry."

"Just one coffee."

"Give me the paper."

"Coffee first, then the paper. Just one, I promise. Just to talk. You owe me that, at least."

Hope exhaled, shoulders slumping, and stepped toward him. He smiled and put out a hand to touch her shoulder. As his hand touched her she jabbed him hard with her elbow, just below his ribs, and pulled the paper out of his other hand. He buckled over with a small, surprised cry, and Hope stepped back.

"Stay away from me!" she said, raising her voice almost to a shout. "I told you what would happen if you touched me again."

Warren straightened up, furious. His eyes were glazed, his cheeks puffed, skin reddening.

"I mean it, Warren! Stay away from me! No coffee! No talking! I don't *owe* you anything!"

He managed to catch his breath. He looked as if he might come at her again, but she did not back away. Instead she took a small step toward him.

"Get it through your skull! We're through! We were through a long time ago!"

She was shouting now. Clerks from nearby stores came to their doors to watch. Warren blushed and tried to stand tall.

"You turned into a queen bitch, do you know that? Your buddy doesn't need you. He's already got a guide dog."

Hope actually managed to smile. "And I don't need you. I've already got an asshole."

She turned away as the redness seeped back into Warren's face like blood into a wound.

* * *

The woman at the information desk looked up from some papers as Campbell walked toward her. She was in her early fifties, Campbell guessed, not unattractive. She half-frowned, looking at Shadow. Campbell stopped in front of her.

"Can I help you?" She continued to look at Shadow, who stared up at her unblinking.

"I'm looking for some newspapers. Minneapolis, or Fergus Falls, or anything nearby. Today's or yesterday's."

She looked up at Campbell now, the half-frown melting into a look of mild confusion. "We don't have today's papers yet, and yesterday's aren't filed yet. We generally run a couple of days behind on the periodicals."

Campbell rubbed his chin, trying to think. Teresa Dawson had been missing since yesterday, but before Teresa he'd had visions of another child. A boy. Lying in a grave. Dark shape hovering over him, pointing a shotgun. Exploding flesh and bone.

"Are you okay? Would you like to sit down?"

Campbell came out of his reverie with a start, realizing he was leaning over the information desk, gripping the edge so hard his fingers were numb. He straightened, stepping back so that Shadow could get a better view.

"I'm fine."

"What, exactly, are you looking for?"

"I'm not sure, to tell you the truth. Information about missing children. I couldn't give you exact titles, but have there been magazine articles in the past, say, six months? Something with pictures, preferably."

She was frowning again. "Do you mean, in braille? I'm afraid our braille selection is rather limited. We have a few books I could bring out to you, but no periodicals."

"No, not braille. Just . . . normal is fine."

She looked down at Shadow again, then back up at Campbell, the confused look again. Campbell did not feel like explaining the truth, but he took pity on her.

"I'm not completely blind," he said. "I can read, but I need the dog for getting around."

"Ah." Her eyes lit up, and she nodded, smiling again. "All right, then, I'll take a look for you, if you'd like to take a seat. The last six months. Missing children. It will take a few minutes."

Campbell walked to a row of tables beside the reference shelves and sat down. Shadow sat down beside him.

The library was, for the most part, empty. A woman with a baby in a back carrier strolled down the aisles of fiction, running a finger over the spines of the books. The baby on her back waved a rattle, drooling quietly. In a reading area to Campbell's right, at the back of the building, an older man wearing a dirty overcoat sat in a chair overlooking a rock garden, a magazine open on his lap. His chin rested on his chest, and he appeared to be snoring.

Although Shadow continued to observe his surroundings, Campbell distanced himself from the imagery, mentally unfocusing, and turned inward. This morning, when he had seen Teresa Dawson's face on television, he had been absolutely certain that she was the girl from his visions, but now, only an hour later, his conviction had weakened. The power of his intellect, however scant that actually was, had turned itself to the problem and had come up unconvinced. How could he possibly have had visions of Teresa Dawson? He had never met Teresa Dawson, had never seen her picture before this morning. And yet, he could not deny he'd experienced the visions. They'd been a major part of his life since the operation, the primary, unpredicted side effect.

No, this was not the time to start doubting. He had recognized the television image of Teresa Dawson because he'd seen her in his visions. What remained to be learned was *why* he had seen her, and *how* he had seen her, and *what* it meant.

He reached down and absently scratched Shadow behind the ears.

"I found these," the woman from the information desk said, and placed a small pile of magazines in front of Campbell.

"Thank you."

"Would you like me to search for books on the subject?"

"No, the magazines are fine. Thanks for your help."

When she had gone back to her desk, Campbell pulled the neighboring chair closer. He patted the vinyl cushion with his hand. Shadow hesitated only a second, then hopped up onto the chair. Campbell did not bother to check on how the woman at the information desk reacted to this.

"Shadow, down," he said softly.

Shadow looked down at the pile of magazines. The selection was smaller than Campbell had anticipated, only seven magazines. The top one was a *Newsweek* from May. The front cover was a selection of photographs of children, fifteen of them in total. The subtitle of the issue was "MISSING: How Safe are America's Children?" The faces of the children on the cover were happy, smiling, unconcerned. Snapshots taken shortly before each child had disappeared. Campbell studied their faces, feeling queasy.

These children had disappeared from the face of the earth. One day they had been living normal lives, going to school, playing with friends, and the next they had been torn away from their homes. The parents of those children, some of whom were pictured inside the magazine, all had a haunted quality to them. Not grief, exactly. Something worse. Something interminable. Their eyes were sunken, their faces pale, as if each of them had been consigned to his or her own private hell.

There is no end to their suffering, Campbell realized. Their children had been taken from them. But they knew not where, or to what fate. They could not even grieve.

Inside, there were more pictures of missing children, but none of the faces were familiar to Campbell. None had come to him in his visions.

He did not read the accompanying text. The images were enough. The faces of the parents told the entire story. Campbell ached for them, but like them, could not grieve. This loss was the kind of loss that could destroy lives, he realized. The people responsible, the monsters who abducted these children, were inhuman. He could think of no punishment severe enough to inflict upon them, no pain that would satisfy the retribution required.

Campbell's hands were shaking when he closed the *Newsweek*. He knew the fate of one of these children. One of them. One unnamed, missing boy.

He pressed his hands flat on the table and made himself breathe deeply a few times before opening the next magazine. Shadow stared down, unperturbed.

The next magazine was the April issue of *Minneapolis,* again featuring a story on missing children, this time focussing more closely on the state of Minnesota. The cover was a photograph of one boy. Not the boy from Campbell's visions, but a face he vaguely recognized.

"Have You Seen Michael?" the subhead asked.

The story inside detailed the Swanson family's search for their son, their refusal to accept that he was dead, their dedication to the task of finding him. They had mortgaged their home to hire private detectives. They had appeared on talk shows, on national news broadcasts. Naomie Swanson, the mother, said simply, "I can feel Michael. I know he's alive. As long as he's alive, I'll keep looking." They had looked for almost two years now, and though they had built a clear picture of the process of their son's abduction, had even managed to construct a detailed composite of the man they believed responsible, they had drawn no closer to the boy.

Campbell read the story almost against his will, compelled by each sentence to read more, horrified yet enthralled. Unlike the faces of the parents in the *Newsweek* piece, the Swansons appeared grimly determined, their pain hidden behind a veil of almost maniacal urgency. Only at the end of the piece were other missing children mentioned, a single page filled with the photographs of children who had gone missing in the past two years.

Campbell studied each face carefully, feeling guilty, almost ashamed, for reasons he could not pinpoint. It felt almost as if he were invading the privacy of the families involved, as if he were a voyeur to their emotional torture. As if, and this was the strangest of all, he were, somehow, partly responsible.

One of the photographs, near the center of the page, was black and white. A boy. Not smiling. Just staring out of the page, as if caught by the camera doing something he should not be doing. Blond hair combed off his forehead. Small mouth, pursed now. Eyes wide, in that surprised, "caught," look.

Campbell stared, unable to look away.

The caption beneath the photograph read: Jesse Hampton, age six, disappeared March 12.

"Did you find what you were looking for?"

She came up beside Shadow. The dog looked up at her voice, and Campbell found himself staring into the librarian's smiling face.

"I . . ." his voice choked in his throat, as if he'd swallowed sand.

"I dug out some more, if you'd like to see them."

Campbell shook his head. "No."

"All right, then. If you need anything else, let me know."

Campbell nodded. She turned and walked away. Shadow watched her until she was back at her desk, then looked down at the magazines again. Campbell stared into the surprised face of six-year-old Jesse Hampton, who had gone missing on March 12, and whom he had seen placed in a grave and destroyed by a blast from a shotgun less than a week ago.

His hands were shaking, and he could not make them stop. He wanted to look away from Jesse Hampton's face, but could not relay the command to Shadow. Instead he stared into Jesse's wide eyes and remembered, over and over again, the dark shape towering over the boy, bringing death. And in this memory, the dark shape was himself.

TWENTY

Hope parked the car in front of the library. She got out and folded the newspapers under her arms. She couldn't remember the last time she'd been here. A couple of years, at least. That seemed like an awful long time. For years nearly every book she had read had been borrowed from this place.

She still felt giddy about her confrontation with Warren. The look on his face as she'd walked away! Priceless. And she hadn't needed Campbell to stand up for her. She'd done it herself. A big girl now. Oh, yeah.

A group of young children were playing in a park across the street from the library, watched over by a couple of mothers with strollers. She couldn't help thinking of Teresa Dawson, the smiling face on the cover of the *Star/Tribune*. One of the children across the street was a girl about Teresa's age. The girl clambered over an arch of colored steel bars, agile as a monkey, laughing. Teresa Dawson might have been doing the same thing only a couple of days ago. And now? Now she's somewhere dark, Campbell had said. With a monster watching over her.

Hope walked up the path to the library door, shivering despite the warm sun on her back and arms. For some reason, she felt like she was somehow a part of Teresa Dawson's disappearance. It was crazy, but she couldn't shake the feeling. It was like guilt.

When she entered the air-conditioned library she shivered again, hesitated just inside the door. The place was virtually empty. A woman at the information desk looked up at her, and Hope felt herself stiffen. There was a reason she had stopped

coming here. The woman, Mary Cunningham, was a good friend
of Hope's mother. Every time Hope had borrowed books, she
felt as if Mary Cunningham had reached for the phone to call
her mother the moment she stepped out the door. She could easily
imagine her mother keeping some kind of record, analyzing her
in light of her reading habits. It hadn't seemed worth it.

Mary Cunningham frowned, then smiled, and waved her over.
Only moments ago she had felt buoyant, triumphant, and now
she felt herself shrivel. She looked around helplessly and saw
Campbell sitting at a reading table with Shadow. Both man and
dog were looking down at a small pile of magazines on the table.
Just go to him, she thought. Ignore Mary Cunningham. But the
older woman waved again and started to stand up. Hope took a
deep breath, smiled, and walked over to the information desk.

"Hope! We haven't seen you in here in ages!"

Hope made herself smile pleasantly. "Hello, Mary. I'm just
meeting someone."

Mary Cunningham glanced quickly around, eyes lingering
momentarily on Campbell and Shadow.

"Oh?"

"I see him over there. I'd better not keep him waiting."

"I talked to your mother last week," Mary said conversation-
ally, but with a sly tone underlying the words. "She says that
Warren is back in town."

"I saw him," Hope said.

Mary's eyebrows rose a fraction of an inch. "And how's he
doing?"

"Okay, I guess. I didn't really talk to him." She felt the flush
creeping into her face, nearly choked on the words. "I'd better
go."

Mary Cunningham could not quite hide her astonishment at
the brusqueness with which she'd been treated, but Hope turned
adamantly away and walked over to Campbell and Shadow. The
dog heard her approach and looked up at her, and at the same
time Campbell's shoulders straightened.

"Thank God you're here," he said, twisting in his chair toward her.

"What's wrong?"

"Everything. Look."

He pushed the mound of magazines toward her as she sat down next to him. His finger stabbed at the middle of the open page, at a photograph of a young boy.

"That's him. The first one I saw. Before Teresa."

Hope felt suddenly chilled. She wanted to hug herself, but didn't want Mary Cunningham to see anything out of the ordinary. She stared down at the photograph of the boy. Jesse Hampton, age six.

"This picture isn't very clear," she said softly.

"It's him. I saw him. I saw him killed, Hope."

She remembered the horror on Campbell's face. She continued to look at the photograph, saying nothing.

"Did you get the papers?"

She pushed them across the table toward him. He straightened the *Star/Tribune,* and muttered something to Shadow. The dog looked down at the table.

"It's her, Hope. It's her. No doubt. I know it. Where did it happen?"

Hope leaned over him, quickly scanned the text beneath the photograph. "Godfrey."

"Where is that?"

"East of Fergus. Maybe a couple of hours drive."

"I want to go there."

"I don't know if that's a good idea."

He turned to face her, tugging hard on Shadow's harness so that the dog, too, was staring at her.

"I saw Jesse Hampton killed. Teresa Dawson is still alive. I know it. I have to do something."

"What *can* you do?"

"I can go to Godfrey and look around."

"To what end?"

"To make sure. I saw it in one of the visions. I mean, if it's not the same place, then . . . At least I'll know, and I can forget about all of this."

Hope inhaled deeply. She knew he was right. She, too, felt as if she had to do something. Campbell's suggestion was the only one that even made a small amount of sense. It would be an hour's drive, maybe two along the narrow country roads. But Campbell was wrong about one thing. It wasn't going to make a difference if he recognized Godfrey or not. Neither one of them was going to forget this.

She waited as Campbell rose from the chair and ushered Shadow to the floor, then walked beside him to the main doors. At the information desk, Mary Cunningham reached for the phone.

Hope started the engine and rolled down her window. The breeze reached through the car like a long cool finger. Campbell was pressed into the passenger door, and Shadow sat between the two of them like a chaperon, watching Hope intently for any signs of libido.

"What are you looking so smug about?" Campbell asked her, without turning toward her.

"I ran into Warren in the mall."

Campbell's head turned slightly. His arms tensed. Jealous? She felt a warming in her stomach at the possibility. She wondered if this was the first time she had made a man jealous. The second, probably, if you counted Warren. Which she didn't.

"With the car?"

"I only wish. He sort of accosted me as I was leaving."

Now Campbell was turned fully toward her, and she could see herself reflected in his dark glasses. "In what way?"

"Verbally. You know. He wanted me to go for coffee with him. I said no. He persisted. That sort of thing."

"So, you ran into him with the car afterward?"

"I just *handled* him, that's all. You should have seen his face."

"I can imagine."

He smiled, just a little.

Hope put both hands on the wheel, but did not pull out into the street.

"Are we waiting for something?"

"I'm still not sure about this. Going to Godfrey."

"I need to do this, Hope. I have to know."

Me too, she thought. Not that she doubted anything Campbell had said so far. And, yet . . . what proof did she have? He claimed to have seen a couple of children in dream-like visions. Now he claimed those children were real. There was no way for her to confirm or deny his assertions. She had to take him on faith. Faith. Her imaginary sister.

"How many times have you seen Teresa Dawson?"

Campbell turned his head slightly away, but Shadow continued to look directly at her.

"Three times, maybe four times. I dreamt of her once. I *think* it was a dream, anyway."

"Have you ever been to Godfrey?"

"I didn't even know it existed until this morning."

"So, describe it to me."

"What?"

"I think it would be a good idea if you were to tell me everything you remember about Godfrey before we get there. If you tell me afterward, I'll never know if you simply . . ."

"Made it up?"

"I wasn't going to say that. But you could assimilate it unconsciously. You could make yourself believe that what you were seeing was simply a confirmation of your visions. If you tell me, before we go, we'll have a baseline to determine how accurate your visions really are."

"Or how truthful I am."

She said nothing. Campbell continued to look out the window. Shadow studied her intently. This disparity in their angles of view made her uneasy. It made her think that Campbell was trying to deceive her in some way, trying to make her believe he wasn't watching her.

He took a deep breath and turned toward her.

"Okay. You're right. Let me think." He lowered his head and put a hand to his forehead. "The first time I saw her it was . . ." a frown creased his forehead and his lips thinned to a bloodless line. "Let me think. A park. I was in a park. Like a town square kind of park. I could see streets on every side. Storefronts. There was an outdoor swimming pool. The park was divided by a stone pathway. A nice flower garden, too. Trees all over the place. Picnic tables on one side of the path, benches, and a kids' area on the other. That's where Teresa was. Swings, climbing bars, a sandbox, slide. She was playing there."

The tension on his face had drained away as he had spoken, until now he looked hypnotized. After a second or two of silence he looked up.

"That's all I remember."

"What about the other times?"

He frowned again. "One was when . . . she was taken. It was in an alley of some kind. There were trash containers. It looked like big buildings on one side, and residential backyards on the other. Maybe an alley in back of the main street. There was a truck. A pickup truck, parked down a ways." He paused now, looking directly at her. "I was in a truck once before. In one of the first visions. At Miriam."

Hope felt a chill. It was creepy listening to Campbell. His words seemed to weave a wall around the pair of them, the *three* of them, blocking out the world.

"What color was it?"

He frowned again. "I don't know. The image is . . . not color."

"Was this a vision, or did you *see* it, like through Shadow's eyes?"

"I'm not sure I could tell the difference. There was no color."

"What make was the truck?"

"Jesus! I don't know!"

"Sorry."

"That's all I remember."

"The third time," she prompted.

"That was different. That was afterwards. It was dark. Teresa was in the cage."

The cage.

Hope turned away, suppressing a shudder. She took a deep breath, then let it out slowly.

"That should be good enough."

Campbell looked straight ahead, turning Shadow with his hand. "Okay," he said.

Hope checked for traffic, then pulled out into the street. She left her window open as they drove through town, but once they were on 210, heading east, she closed it to a slit. The rushing wind was a hoarse whistle next to her ear. Comforting.

Campbell sat silently, face pressed to the glass, as Shadow looked straight ahead at the road. After they passed Battle Lake, then the turnoff for their cabins, Shadow lowered himself to the seat, put his snout on his paws, and closed his eyes. Campbell gave no indication that he had noticed. His forehead bobbed against the window.

Asleep, Hope thought, and felt strangely relieved. It was like being alone, and for the first time since waking she relaxed. She concentrated on the road, kept the speedometer needle hovering just under 50. She was in no hurry to get to Godfrey.

She drove through a succession of small towns, towns she had not visited in a very long time. It had been years, longer even than her hiatus from the library, since she had traveled *east* of Battle Lake. Clitheral, Vinning, Hollyfield, Henning.

The sun rose, and heat waves shimmered on the blacktop in the distance. It reminded Hope of her childhood, driving with her father on summer days to auctions in far corners of the county. She had loved those Saturday mornings away from her mother, alone with her father.

The country east of Battle Lake turned slowly more rugged. Farms became smaller, nestled on the sides of hills. Forest growth expanded, filling open areas. The land itself jutted skyward more forcefully, as if it had recently undergone some calamity. After a while, the trees at the sides of the road seemed to be pressing in on her, enclosing her, and she felt as if she were in a dark tunnel.

"How much farther?"

"I thought you were sleeping!"

"I've been awake for a few minutes."

"You scared me! You should have said something!"

Shadow pushed himself to a sitting position and turned to watch her.

"I just did. How much farther?"

"This is Godfrey coming up."

"Shadow, front."

Hope slowed the car as she approached the exit for the town. Like Battle Lake, Godfrey was a half mile off the highway, nestled in a shallow valley that had probably once been a glacial lake. The land was flat immediately surrounding the town, as if it had been built inside a crater, but darkly treed hills rose like sentinels on all sides.

A sign outside the town proclaimed the population to be 5,236, with the date 1990 underneath the number. It was a typical, isolated lake country town, serving a few local farms, a timber industry, and probably recreational hunters and fishermen.

Hope drove straight into town, past city hall, a small strip mall a modern looking multiplex theater, a police station, the usual collection of small town businesses. She saw the park the moment she turned onto Main Street.

It was exactly as Campbell had described it.

"Son of a bitch," Campbell said softly.

Hope said nothing. She drove around the park. As Campbell had speculated, it served as a town square. Godfrey, in fact, seemed to radiate from the park in all directions.

There were no children in the park. She noticed that immediately. Not a child in sight. They'd been hidden away. Buried, like treasures. Everybody was scared. If it happened to Teresa Dawson, it could happen to anybody's child.

Traffic was thicker than she would have expected. There were state police cars cruising the streets, as well as a number of out-of-state cars, campers, trailers.

They've come to see where Teresa lived, Hope realized, and felt a flash of guilt. Just like us. It's a sideshow.

She parked the car on the south side of the park, adjacent to the children's playground. Campbell and Shadow peered out the window. Campbell's hands were trembling.

"What do we do?" Hope asked him.

"I don't know. I have no idea."

"Do you want to get out and walk around?"

"No!" He twisted to stare at her. "No. I don't want to do that."

"Whatever you want."

"We could talk to the police."

"And tell them what? You had a vision? That it came from your dog? They'll think we're lunatics. They'll suspect us."

"We have to do something."

Hope suddenly thought of Teresa Dawson. In the cage. In the dark. *We have to do something.*

She squeezed Campbell's hand. His skin was cool and dry.

A police car drove slowly by on the street. The faces of the two men inside looked almost savagely angry. Hope could feel their suspicion like cold water on her back.

Campbell stared out the window. His grip on her hand was fierce, almost painful. Shadow's long tail wagged slowly, batting softly against the back of the seat.

"Maybe you should talk to the people at Miriam. They'll have to listen to you now."

"Don't bet on it," Campbell said.

Eleanor opened the fridge and looked inside. Too much to choose from. She didn't feel like thinking, deciding. Hardly felt like eating. But she must. On the middle shelf was a bowl of onion soup, a couple of days old, turned to thick jelly. The sliced onions looked like juicy worms coiled in greasy mud. A white layer of fat sat on top of the jelly.

She took out the bowl and closed the fridge. She took a spoon from the cutlery drawer, then carried the cold soup through to the living room. Max was sitting by the sofa. He raised his head to watch her as she sat down in the easy chair.

She had been watching television most of the morning, since coming up from the cellar. The game shows and talk shows had been peppered with news updates. The hunt was on for Teresa Dawson.

Eleanor used the remote to flip to Channel 5. The midday news was about to start. As the opening music drummed into the room she dug the spoon into the jellied soup and lifted a lump to her mouth. The turgid jelly was heavy on her tongue. She held it in her mouth until it softened, melted, slid down her throat. It was better heated, but she couldn't be bothered. The hardened fat was like icing.

The main story was Teresa Dawson. This was a Minneapolis station, but the missing child was big news. Strange how that was always the way. Jesse Hampton's disappearance had even made the national news. CNN had done a piece on the search, the final failure.

Eleanor stopped eating as a harried-looking man was interviewed. This was Grant Dawson, Teresa's father. He was unshaven, and dark circles weighted his eyes. The reporter on the scene asked him how he was coping. He started to say something, then choked on the words. Tears dribbled down his cheeks.

Oh, that was good. That was excellent acting. He deserved an award for that.

He didn't love Teresa. That much was obvious. Anybody watching him could see that he was simply acting for the cameras. He was probably glad that Teresa was gone.

If only he knew. She's now in a place where she can be truly loved. A place where love is everything.

They replayed an earlier interview with Grant Dawson. He

looked less harried, and the bags under his eyes were not so dark. This was last night. He still had hope.

"Please return Teresa," he said to the camera. "I beg you, just let her go. Whoever you are. She's only eight years old. Please, don't harm her. She's all I have left."

The update on the ongoing search was encouraging. Police had no clues, no suspects. Teresa had walked down to the store and had not returned. Nobody had seen her.

When a photograph of Teresa came on screen, Eleanor stopped eating again, spoon hovering before her mouth. The picture, the voice said, was only a month old.

Angel.

Beautiful.

The girl's eyes seemed to reach out of the screen, to call her. Her face almost glowed with serenity, with love.

Eleanor frowned and put the spoon down.

Where was that love now? Where had the angel gone?

The girl downstairs was . . . different.

The story about Teresa Dawson's disappearance changed into something about a murder in Minneapolis, and Eleanor turned off the television. She stared at the blank screen. Faint ripples of ghostly light played behind the dark surface. Max stood up and whined.

Give the girl a chance, she thought.

She couldn't give up so quickly. The transition from her old life to her new life was probably affecting Teresa. The angel would come back soon enough. Given time. Love.

She carried the half-empty soup bowl back to the kitchen and put it into the sink. From the fridge she took the tray with Teresa's lunch already prepared. A peanut butter and cheese sandwich, a glass of milk, and an apple. No utensils.

She frowned, thinking of the missing knife. Only a butter knife.

It might have fallen off on the stairs. It might be on the floor of the corridor. Teresa might not have it.

Still.

She took the flashlight from its peg and opened the back door. Max scurried out and hurried to the stump of an oak tree at the foot of the garden path. He lifted his leg and urinated, then sauntered to the cellar door. Eleanor shook her head.

The girl liked Max. That much was obvious. She had *some* love in her, if only for the dog.

At the door she looked down and watched Max wag his tail. Suddenly angry, she kicked him hard in the ribs. He whined and stumbled away. He went down on his belly and watched her, tail wagging.

She opened the door. Max stood and came forward. She resisted the urge to kick him again, and let him go down ahead of her. As she walked down after him, she realized that she was nervous. Skittish as a teenaged girl on her first date.

The girl was having a strange effect on her.

She shined the flashlight along the corridor. The light seemed to draw the walls closer. She looked carefully for the knife on the floor as she walked, but did not see it. In the alcove at the end of the tunnel, shadows leaped and scurried. She glimpsed Max, tail wagging.

Damn dog.

When she reached the cage she swung the flashlight around. The beam rippled across the bars, sending long spiky shadows flying to the ceiling and across the walls. Max was sitting by the wall, snout poking through the bars. Teresa was a shadowy lump on the floor next to the dog. Her hands were pale birds, pecking the dog's face.

Still no sign of the knife.

"I brought you lunch."

Teresa looked up at her. Her face was a pink smudge, framed by hair needing a brushing. There was no fear in the girl's eyes. No love, either.

"Thank you," Teresa said.

The child's equanimity was disturbing. Eleanor frowned as she opened the cage door and went inside. She put the tray down on the floor by the mattress.

"Did I leave the butter knife here this morning?"

Teresa still had not moved away from Max. She shook her head.

"Are you sure?"

Eleanor shined the light around the cage. The dark, mottled floor revealed no sign of the knife. She let the circle of light rest on the porta-potty in the corner. Its lid was up. Teresa looked over at it, then up at Eleanor.

"I didn't see a knife."

Eleanor turned the beam on the girl. Teresa did not flinch, but kept her eyes wide, as if the light did not bother her. Eleanor's stomach knotted. After a few seconds, Teresa turned back to Max. She leaned closed to him and kissed his snout. Max licked her face. Eleanor felt suddenly sick.

Was she jealous of the dog?

She stopped herself from rushing across the cage. Part of her wanted to smash the girl, crack the flashlight down on her head, to *make* her love her. But she did not. She did not want Teresa to turn those hard, cold eyes on her again. She was not like Jesse Hampton.

"They've stopped looking for you," she said.

Teresa jerked her head around. "What?"

"It was on the news. Your father and the police. They've stopped looking for you."

I got through to her, Eleanor thought.

"You're lying. They're looking for me right now."

Eleanor shook her head. "They found a body. Near Godfrey. A girl. About your size. Apparently she was badly hurt. They couldn't identify her. But they think it's you. They've stopped looking."

Teresa started to say something, but stopped. Her mouth trembled.

"I'll leave you for now. I'll come down later. If you're good, maybe you can come up. Have a walk outside."

Teresa glanced at her. There were tears on her cheeks. She

sniffled. "That would be nice," she said quietly, voice broken and halting.

Eleanor savored the warmth inside of her, flowering, filling her. Everything was going to be okay. She stepped back, through the door, and closed it.

"Let's go, Max."

"Please. Let Max stay down here with me. I'm lonely."

There seemed to be no guile in the girl's face.

"If you promise to be good."

"I will."

Eleanor turned off the flashlight. In the sudden darkness, she heard the girl sob.

She smiled as she walked back along the corridor to the stairs.

TWENTY-ONE

When the smooth hum of the blacktop changed to the rattle of gravel, Shadow opened his eyes and sat up. Campbell had been half-asleep, hypnotized by the steady drone of the motor and the smoothness of the highway. The sudden light shocked him and he gasped. He brought up a hand to cover his own eyes, realized what he was doing, and laughed softly.

"Sorry," Hope said. "I should have warned you. Almost home."

"It's okay."

Shadow turned to look at Hope. She smiled, but looked tired. More than tired. Maybe a bit frightened.

"It's two o'clock," she said. "If we get out of here by three, we'll be in Minneapolis before dark. Probably not soon enough to see the people at Miriam today, but at least we'll be there for tomorrow."

"We don't have to rush off tonight, do we? We could head out tomorrow morning."

She glanced over at him, frowning. God, she's beautiful. The sun made her skin look very tanned, smooth. She was wearing a denim shirt and jeans. The sleeves of the shirt were rolled up to her mid-forearms. Her arms were deeply tanned, freckled. Two of the shirt buttons were undone and he could see her bra. White, with a lacy trim. The skin of her breasts looked very dark against the white of the bra. Smooth. He imagined putting a hand beneath the bra. He turned his head away, but with Shadow still looking at her his view didn't change.

"Are you sure you want to wait? If this is real . . . I mean, if Teresa Dawson is the girl in your visions, shouldn't we do something *now?* I mean, the sooner we find out exactly what these visions are, what they mean, the sooner we can help."

Campbell took a deep breath. "I guess so."

She turned back to the road, then looked at him again, still frowning. "Am I taking this too seriously for you?"

He turned to face her. "It's not that."

"Then what is it?"

"I'm a little freaked, that's all. You're right. We have to act now. We can't wait."

Hope let out a breath, nodded, and turned back to the road. "Shadow, front."

Shadow faced front as Campbell's cabin came into view. Hope drove up behind his utility shed and stopped.

"I'll give you half an hour to pack, then I'll come and pick you up." She leaned across the seat and kissed his mouth. "Hurry up."

He got out and watched her back up onto the road. She waved, and drove on to her own cabin. Campbell walked around to the front of the cabin, onto the porch. When he opened the door, the air that surrounded him was cool, stale smelling. He sat down by the phone and checked the answering machine. No messages.

He went through to the bedroom and dug a small case out of the closet. He packed quickly, packing mostly underwear and socks, a couple of shirts, and a change of pants. That should be enough. One night. Two at the most, he guessed.

In the kitchen he packed a toiletry case and shoved it into a corner of the suitcase. It closed easily, without having to be squashed, and he carried it through and put it down by the door.

Better feed Shadow before they got on the road. That was something he'd have to pay attention to once they got into Minneapolis. Should he take some food with him? Nah. They'd have some at Miriam, probably, with all those animals.

Back in the kitchen he poured Shadow a bowl of food and

water, then took the dog back to the phone table. He reached down and disconnected Shadow's harness. A brief flare of brightness filled his head, and then darkness. He pressed himself back into the seat, suddenly dizzy, disoriented.

"Eat, Shadow," he said to the dog.

He felt Shadow's warm tongue on his hand, and then heard the dog's paws clicking across the linoleum to the kitchen. He settled himself into the chair, trying to find his bearings. It felt as if a dark sack had been slipped over his head. On top of that, the cabin seemed to be closing in on him, crushing him.

Calm down!

He was disconnected. Floating. Lost. He forced himself to grip the sides of the chair, to breathe deeply, slowly. He focused on the sounds around him. He could hear Shadow eating and drinking. It sounded like some strange mulching machine.

Be calm. It won't be much longer.

He started to count. Slowly, evenly.

He was whispering the words, "Twenty-seven," when Shadow's cold, wet snout pressed into his hands.

Campbell almost cried out with relief. He fumbled for the dog's harness, then the coupler. For a horrible moment he could not find it, fingers probing in smooth fur, and a high whine came from his own mouth. Then his fingers touched hard plastic and he pushed the connecters together.

Light flashed inside his head. Sunrise.

Dizziness.

A feeling of nausea in his belly.

Oh, God, it felt so good.

He was looking up at his own face, sweaty and white.

"Jesus," he said quietly. "Pathetic."

Shadow whined.

"Shadow, front," Campbell commanded.

The dog turned around. Campbell started to rise. The dizziness suddenly engulfed him and he sat down hard. His view of the hallway became dim, then darkened out of existence.

"Shadow?"

He was in darkness again. He must not have connected the cable properly. It had come undone when Shadow had turned around.

"Damn it."

He started to reach for it again.

A pale orb swam into the darkness, and Campbell froze.

A face.

A child's face.

Teresa Dawson's face.

Campbell stared, heart pounding.

He felt the chair beneath his buttocks. The hardness of Shadow's harness in his hand.

But he was no longer sitting by the phone, looking down the hallway toward the kitchen. He was in the strange dark cage of his visions. Teresa Dawson was staring at him. He was close to her. Only inches away.

It *was* Teresa Dawson. No doubt about it. This close, he could see every detail. Could see the shape of her eyes, the curve of her mouth, the plumpness of her cheeks. Although he was suddenly terrified, he made himself be calm. He had to see as much as possible. If this was real, he had to . . .

Oh, it's real, you idiot! This is as real as it gets!

Details. Details. He needed to see details. Something to bring back, something to verify everything he knew.

The face of the girl receded, and he was looking at her whole body. She was standing now, pacing.

Jeans, he saw. Blue jeans. A blouse, long sleeves. Striped. Open collar. Something around her neck. A necklace. A pendant of some kind. Not a heart. . . . A flower? A leaf?

It was too dark to see clearly, but light was coming from somewhere.

Where?

If only he could look around. If only he had some control.

As if his thoughts actually had some effect, his view shifted. In the chair, Campbell gripped his thighs.

Darkness moved in front of him. A pale square hovered in the darkness, somewhere above him, indeterminately distant.

A window?

Must be. But covered by something.

The darkness swirled again, and he was pressed close to Teresa Dawson.

Her mouth was moving. The girl was speaking to him. To *him?* Really?

To *whom,* exactly, was she speaking?

Her eyes were wet. Tears streaked her cheeks.

Campbell wanted to reach for her, touch her, comfort her. We're coming to help you! Everything is going to be okay.

I love you. That's what she had said. I love you. Me?

"Campbell?"

Campbell cried out.

Light speared through the darkness, engulfed it, filled it, eradicated it. Another face filled his view. Hope. She was holding him, leaning close.

"Campbell, is it happening?"

"Finished," he said, and was shocked at the hoarseness of his voice. It felt as if he'd been sleeping for hours.

"The same?"

"I was with her. In the cage, I think. She's okay. It *is* her. It's Teresa Dawson. She was crying."

"But she was okay?"

"I think so. I don't know for how long, though. We have to do something quickly."

"Are you ready to go?"

"All packed."

"Let's go, then."

He followed her outside, locked up the cabin. In the car, he leaned against the window while Shadow stared straight ahead.

I love you.

"Teresa talked to me."

Hope turned to look at him. "To *you?"*

"She was looking at me, anyway."

"You were *there?*"

"It felt like it. I couldn't hear her. I read her lips."

"What did she say?"

"I love you."

Hope blinked. "What?"

"That's what she said."

"To *you.*"

"I guess it couldn't have been to me. To someone. She was definitely with somebody."

"Another child?"

"Nobody I've seen."

"Could you be seeing through the other child's eyes?"

"It doesn't make sense, does it?"

"None of this makes sense, Campbell."

They said nothing more until they were on the highway, the road rolling smoothly beneath the car.

"You should definitely think about that," Hope said, without looking at him. "Your point of view in the visions, I mean."

Shadow turned away from Hope, so that Campbell was staring down the empty highway.

"I'll think about it," he said.

Funny, how the dark wasn't *really* dark.

It was just a different kind of light.

She could see in it now. Could see her own hands when she held them up before her face. Like now.

Count her fingers. One, two . . .

See the silhouette of her hand when she held it up against the square patch of the window. Make a rabbit's head. Floppy ears.

Max whined, so she kneeled down on the cold floor again. She stuck her hand through the bars and stroked his head.

"It's okay, Max."

The dog was warm. His warmth radiated through the bars of the cage, enfolded her. Protected her.

The farmer lady had lied. She had not returned. She had not
allowed Teresa to go along the corridor, up the stairs, outside.
Teresa had eaten the lunch that Ellie . . . she did not think that
was her real name . . . had brought down for her. The sandwich
tasted stale, the milk slightly sour. But she had eaten it anyway.
Forced herself to swallow, to feel the food in her stomach. She
had eaten everything but a few pieces of bread crust. Those she
had pushed through the bars to Max. The dog had taken them
gently from her fingers, soft lips warm against her skin.

How long ago had that been? Two hours? Four hours?
Longer?

She did not know.

The window had grown dimmer, until at one point she had
lost it completely. Then it had returned, glowing faintly.

Night.

Max never left the side of the cage, and whenever Teresa
moved away, even to use the toilet, he whined until she returned.
She loved his smell. He smelled of fur, and strange dog breath.
It made her feel good. It made her not think about what Ellie
had said.

They've stopped looking for you.

That wasn't true. It couldn't be true. Dad would never stop
looking for her. He'd know the girl they found at the side of
the road wasn't her. He'd never stop.

There never was a girl, she thought. Ellie lies. Ellie's a liar.

Time passed. It slipped by like a dream. She sat down on the
floor and leaned her back against the bars. Max pressed his
snout into her side.

Earlier in the day she'd tried to determine how the cage was
constructed. Three of the walls were wood. The wood, she
guessed, was a framework attached to the stone walls of the
cellar. The bars of the cage were embedded into the wood, not
into the stone.

She had paced the cage. Ten paces from left to right, six
paces from back to front. A pantry, probably. Her new home.

At the base of the wood against the back wall she found that the floor had sunk a little. Or the walls had lifted. It didn't matter which. What mattered was that there was a space between the wood and the stone floor. A little bit more than a quarter inch. Enough to slide the knife under the wall.

She'd sharpened it first. It was just a butter knife. When she'd first found it, lying just outside the cell, it had been very dull. She had pressed the blade to her thumb and it felt like a pencil. Safer.

But she had rubbed the edge of the blade against one of the bars. Rubbed and rubbed, alternating sides, until the blade was sharp enough to cause pain when she pressed upon it with any force.

Not much of a weapon. But something to use if the time ever came. If the dark ever went away. But it was only dark. Nothing to be afraid of in the dark. The dark could be anything. The dark could be the inside of her bedroom closet at home. She could be inside her closet right now, sitting on the floor, imagining this.

She could be.

She had done things like this all the time. Imagined she was somewhere else. All she had to do was imagine she was back again. Imagine she was back home. In her closet. All she had to do was reach out and touch the wooden door, reach for the handle, open it, and walk into her bedroom. Dad would be downstairs. He would hug her, kiss her, squeeze her until she almost cried out for not being able to breathe. *Where have you been?* Just in my closet. Upstairs. That's all.

Just reach out. Reach out.

She reached out.

Max's cold nose rubbed her hand and she pulled away with a small cry. Max whined. She lay down on the floor, rolled to her side so she was facing the bars. Max lay down with her, pushed his nose through. She could feel him breathing on her face. Soft, warm, dog breath.

Max stared into her eyes. His dog eyes were black and wet. Like a doll's eyes. She stared at him until he whined softly.

He's trying to tell me something.

But what?

She fingered the charm on her gold chain. A maple leaf. Her mother had given it to her on her fifth birthday. It was the last thing her mother had ever given her. She tried to think of her mother's face, but all she could see was Ellie. Ellie, smiling at her. Ellie, reaching for her.

She closed her eyes tight.

"I love you, Max," she whispered.

Max exhaled softly into her hair.

"Sure, I've heard of her," Russell said, closing the newspaper. "She's the top story everywhere. That's probably where you picked it up."

"Don't patronize me, Russell. I didn't pick up anything. I told you from the start about the visions. All I've done is put a name to the face."

Russell looked from Campbell to Hope, then shook his head. He was trying hard not to appear unreasonably skeptical, Hope realized, but he wasn't succeeding.

"The coffee is ready," Claire said, rising from the sofa. "I'll bring it through."

She looked relieved to get out of the room, Hope thought. She doesn't believe a word we've said.

"Is it possible you just put her name to the face you've been seeing?"

"It's her, Russell. And the boy from before was Jesse Hampton."

Russell shook his head again and looked down at the newspaper. The photograph of Teresa Dawson looked back at him.

"The clothes you described are listed right here in the story. Blue jeans, T-shirt with green stripes."

"I didn't read the article."

Campbell's voice was calm, but Hope heard the hard edge in his words. She reached out to squeeze his hand, and his answering squeeze was so fierce it nearly made her wince. He did not like being disbelieved.

Claire came back from the kitchen with a tray of cups, cream, and sugar. She placed it carefully on the coffee table. Campbell added cream and sugar to two cups and handed one to Hope. He performed the action so smoothly, with such a lack of self-consciousness, that she was startled. She still expected him to have some difficulty with these mundane tasks.

Russell, too, looked surprised, and his eyebrows rose fractionally. He glanced at Claire, then back at Campbell. Campbell didn't seem to notice how impressed everybody was.

"Does it mention a necklace?"

"What necklace?"

"I saw a necklace. A chain, gold or silver, something like that, with a pendant. At first I thought it was a heart, but I don't think so. It might have been a maple leaf. Like a charm."

"It doesn't mention a necklace," Russell said, and sounded rather self-satisfied. "Doesn't that prove my point? It's not the same girl."

"You just finished telling me that I must have picked up my information from the papers and the television. I'm telling you something that isn't mentioned, and now you turn that against me too?"

"I'm just . . ." Russell shook his head, realizing he was on dangerous ground.

Hope sipped her coffee. "I'll tell you something, I believe Campbell."

Russell looked at her sadly. "I'd like to believe him, too."

"I think you're looking at it too scientifically," she said.

"How else should I look at it?"

"Obviously there can't be a rational explanation for this, Russell. He's experiencing visions. He's seeing children who have been abducted. This is something beyond the ordinary."

"And?"

"Well, is it possible that the operation did something to him?

I mean, could you have activated some telepathic or precognitive ability in Campbell's mind?"

"Nothing like that happened with the other subjects. Nobody's mentioned it, anyway. You'd think they would."

"We unplugged Shadow while Campbell was having a vision," she said, still looking steadily at him.

"What happened?" He seemed truly interested.

"It stopped instantly."

Russell took a deep breath. "So, you think that proves the visions are coming from Shadow."

"If not *coming* from him, then facilitated by him. I mean really, Russell, what do you know about dog psychology?"

"You mean *parapsychology*. Enough to know that nothing like you're describing has ever happened before."

Campbell stood. He tugged Shadow and the two of them walked to the living room window. Claire's apartment seemed too small to hold all of them. Campbell stood at the window, Shadow at his side, and observed the night lights of the Twin Cities.

"I know you're upset by this, Campbell," Russell said. "My guess is that you're still accommodating the linkup. Give it time."

"She doesn't have time."

Russell inhaled deeply and sipped his coffee. Claire looked shattered, Hope realized. She looked on the verge of tears. Does she wish him still blind, Hope wondered. Anything but this?

"What do you want me to do?" Russell asked.

"Put me in touch with the others."

"Others?"

"The other five who had the operation. Maybe they're experiencing something similar. If I talk to them, I might understand it better."

"No. No way. I can't do that. I shouldn't even be here talking to you, Campbell. I have a horrible feeling I'm validating your weird theories for you, just by being here. We should be at the lab. Nina should be in on this. If you're experiencing problems, we should be running diagnostics until we find out what's wrong. If we can't fix it, and it *is* a problem related to Shadow, we should set you up with another animal."

Campbell turned. "I don't want another dog. I want to help Teresa Dawson. That's all I'm concerned about."

"Campbell . . ."

"If you won't help me, I'll go to the police."

Russell put down his coffee and stared at Campbell. His face was white. "You wouldn't."

"I'll tell them I'm psychic. I'll tell them what I've seen. Who knows, maybe they'll find something in the visions they've been missing. If it helps to save Teresa Dawson, I'll do it."

"If you draw that kind of attention to Miriam and this project . . . we'll never get the procedure past the stage its at now. That kind of sensational attention . . ."

"Then, help me. Put me in touch with the others. I know what I'm experiencing, Russell. I don't want you to fix it. Not anymore. I just want to understand it, to use it."

Russell looked to Hope. If he'd been hoping for some support, she couldn't offer it. She shrugged. "I'm with him."

"Jesus, Campbell, you don't know what you're asking."

"Maybe not, but I know what I'll do if you won't help me."

Russell sighed. "I can't do what you ask, Campbell. But I'll compromise. I'll contact the others. I'll talk to them. I'll find out if they've experienced something similar to you. If they have . . . then I'll consider putting you in touch with them. If not . . ." He shrugged. "In the meantime, you come into Miriam tomorrow morning, with Shadow, and I'll run some tests."

Campbell turned back to the window. His shoulders were straight, determined. Hope felt strangely proud of him, and her face flushed.

Claire sipped her coffee. Nobody said anything.

TWENTY-TWO

Their room on the sixth floor of the Radisson Downtown overlooked South Seventh Street and Hennepin Avenue. Because it was a corner room, and because the buildings across Hennepin weren't very high, Hope could see the Mississippi River, a black line winding like a scar through the city lights.

"God, it's beautiful," she said. "I can almost understand why Warren would want to live here."

Even just looking out the window she felt the energy of the town. It looked like it had a thousand things you could do at any given moment. Not like Battle Lake, or even Fergus Falls, where your choices were limited to a handful of diversions.

Campbell came up beside her. She felt Shadow brush at her legs and moved aside so he could see out the window.

"Shadow, scan," Campbell said. Then, after a few seconds, "Hmmm."

"That wasn't a very impressed 'Hmmm.' "

"Ever see those films of World War II German planes bombing London? The flashing lights looked unreal from the air. Like Christmas decorations or something. You had to be down on the ground to experience the devastation."

"I've never heard Minneapolis compared to war-torn London."

"Just the lights. Imagine all the lights gone. Imagine this place plunged into absolute darkness."

Hope had a sudden picture of the Twin Cities in darkness, and a shiver ran up her spine like soft, icy fingers.

"Not like home," Campbell said. "It's dark there almost all the time, out on the lake, around the cabins. Nothing to be frightened of. But here . . . the lights keep things hidden. When the lights fade, those things come crawling out."

"People."

"Maybe."

"You're morbid."

"I'm blind. I know what comes out in the dark."

"Are you afraid of the dark?"

He did not even hesitate. "Yes."

She turned to look at him, to see if he was joking. He was facing the window, like Shadow. She could not tell if his lips were smiling.

"Sorry, that was a dumb question," she said.

He turned to her, now most definitely smiling. For the first time since she had met him she wished she could see his eyes. She wanted to be sure the smile wasn't a mask.

"I'm okay. I've got a couple of pretty bright lights in my darkness right now. You and Shadow."

"Sweet talk," Hope said, and heard her voice come out as a whisper.

Whether she liked it or not, Campbell Knight had her wrapped around his little finger. She leaned toward him, put her arms around his waist, and pressed her face into his throat. She kissed him. Then put her mouth around his ear and bit the lobe gently. He groaned. Smiling, she pressed her tongue into the hollow of his throat and licked a hard line down toward his chest. His skin, though salty, had almost a sweet aftertaste.

"Stop that," Campbell said hoarsely.

She moved backwards, pulling him with her toward the bed. He continued to smile as he guided her. Shadow looked up at her, earnest animal. She wagged her tongue at the dog. Campbell grinned and stuck his tongue out at her.

When the backs of her knees bumped the bed she sat down.

"Do you want Shadow connected?"

"The cable gets in the way."

"Let me unhook you."

"Wait. I want to see you."

She grinned at him. He looked as if he might be about to apologize, but before he could say anything she slid back onto the mattress and started to unbutton her shirt. Campbell faced her, mouth drawn taut. He seemed almost nervous. Shadow, sitting by the bed, seemed slightly bored.

Well, what had she expected? The dog was nothing more than a camera, really. He wasn't *supposed* to react.

Her skin was hot beneath the shirt. When she touched herself she shivered. She ran fingers over her breast3s, the fabric of her bra. Her nipples, she realized, were erect. Could Campbell see that?

She hoped so. It wasn't just from the cold. She wanted his hands on her. Wanted his mouth on her.

With a moan, she unfastened her jeans and kicked them off, then kneeled on the bed. She ran her hands down her belly. The skin there was smooth, warm. She slid her fingers into the tops of her panties, touched her own soft pubic curls. She felt hot and slick between her legs. Her panties were clinging.

God, she thought, I want him.

She moved forward on the bed, reached out to him.

"Come here."

She reached for the coupler and unhooked Shadow. The moment he was free, the dog moved to the desk by the wall and lay down. He knew when he wasn't wanted.

She unfastened Campbell's shirt and pulled it free of his arms. The harness that encased his arm looked like something out of a Mad Max movie. It made Campbell look like part machine. Especially the black cable that wound its way from his glasses down to the coupler at his wrist.

She worked at the harness clips and undid them one at a time. Campbell stood there, quiet, head slightly angled, as if he were listening to something far away.

"Take off the glasses," she said.

"Hope . . ."

"I want to see you. Without them."

"It's not . . ."

"I don't care what it looks like. Please."

She reached up and slid the glasses away from his face. He angled his head, pulling away slightly, but allowed her to finish what she had started. She dropped glasses and harness to the floor.

The scar wound across Campbell's face like the shoreline of a continent seen from space. It started at the corner of his left eye, a deep fissure that reached far too deep, sliced across the eye, the top of his nose, and into the other eye. The eyelids, what was left of them, were sealed shut. The scar gouged a chunk out of the right side of his face, and receded toward his ear.

Campbell inhaled deeply, but when he released the breath he shuddered. Hope reached up for him. She lifted her face to his, kissed his mouth.

He responded, holding her tightly. She moved upward, and even as he strained away, she kissed first his left eye, then his right eye.

"You don't have to . . ."

"There's nothing about you that I don't want to know about. To touch."

She pulled him back onto the bed. He moved forward, hands on either side of her, until his face was over hers.

"Turn out the light," he said "Make us equals."

"All right."

She reached for the light switch by the bed and turned it off. The room darkened, but not completely. The lights of the city reached through the window, making Campbell into a silhouette above her.

She kissed his mouth hard. His hands reached beneath the bottom of her bra, pushed it upward, and cupped her breasts. She moaned into his mouth.

Had it ever been like this with Warren? No. Never.

She reached between them, down between his legs. She slid

her fingers into his underwear. The skin of his penis was hot and smooth. She tugged at it gently. The veins beneath the skin rolled slightly under her fingers and the heat between her own legs was suddenly unbearable.

With her hands she slid his underwear over his buttocks and hips. In moments, her own panties were around her ankles. When he touched her, she gasped.

Then, two things happened that made her cry out.

He lunged forward, penetrating her deeply. There was no pain, just a sudden *filling* that made her knees reach for her shoulders and her heals dig into his behind.

And he said something.

As his face moved down beside hers, his mouth touching her neck, he whispered to her, "I love you."

But the sounds coming from her own mouth were derived from so deep inside her that she could not form words, could not answer him. She could only cling to him, move with him, hold him so tightly, that he had to know that she had heard him.

Had to know, that had she been able, she would have whispered the same words back.

As sweat cooled on her belly and breasts and thighs, Hope dreamily watched the ceiling. City lights turned the white plaster into a mosaic of pale reds, blues, and whites. Not enough illumination to read by, but enough to fill the room with shadows. Warm shadows.

Her heart rate and respiration had returned to normal. Her muscles still felt loose, liquid. Her insides felt as if she'd spent an hour on a horse, an experience she remembered clearly from her distant past.

She rolled partially to her side, rested her head on her hand, and looked at Campbell. He was lying stiffly, hands at his sides, as if in a coffin. His chest rose and fell only slightly. Sweat glistened on his torso, mingling with the few hairs on his chest, looking like drops of blood because of the light reflected from the ceiling.

"Are you awake?" she asked him.

He nodded his head, smiled. "Hmmm."

She touched his chest, ran a finger down his belly. His penis was flaccid now, moist and red. He shivered as her finger moved into his pubic hair.

"Are you trying to kill me?"

"Just looking."

I love you.

Had he really said that to her?

Had he really meant it?

She wanted to ask him, wanted to question him in detail, but she could not find the words. She hadn't even responded to his original proclamation! He probably thinks I didn't even hear him.

Or worse, that I did hear, but don't share the feeling.

She lay back down, dropped her hands to her sides, closed her eyes. When she felt his mouth on her shoulder, she started.

"Now who's trying to start something?"

"Just wanted to thank you for coming with me. I know I'm dragging you away from your own life. I really appreciate it, Hope. It means a lot to me."

"Me, too," she said huskily.

She lifted his face and kissed his mouth. The kiss lasted a lot longer than she had intended, and she moaned softly as a warm sensation started between her legs and moved up into her belly.

"I love you," Campbell said.

"I love you, too," she said.

Campbell grinned and lay back down. Hope stared at the ceiling. Her lips were curled in a smile that was almost painful. Her cheeks started to burn.

But it felt so good!

Campbell's hand touched hers. His fingers gently stroked her palm.

"I'm sorry if I'm moving too fast."

"You're not," she said.

"This has never happened to me before. Not like this."

"Same here."

"You've kind of swept me off my feet."

"Easy to do to a blind guy."

"Ho!"

"I was thinking."

"Should I be worried about this?"

"No, I'm serious. About you and Shadow and these visions."

His fingers stopped stroking her hand, and he angled his head so that if he had eyes he would have been looking right at her. He waited, saying nothing.

"Have you tried initiating a vision yourself? I mean, rather than waiting for it to happen?"

Campbell's entire face registered his shock. "Hadn't even thought about it."

"It was just a thought. I know it's scary, but if you're set on helping Teresa Dawson, and you believe the girl you've been seeing is her, then . . ."

"No, you're right. I just hadn't thought about it." He sat up and swung his legs off the bed. "Shadow!"

Hope reached for the light switch and turned it on. She blinked against the sudden brightness. Shadow stood up, shook himself, and came over to the bed. He sat by Campbell and looked up into his face.

God, the dog really loves him! She'd seen enough dogs look at their masters to know when the relationship was a close one. Shadow waited, patiently, earnestly. His tail wagged slowly, brushing across the carpet. Did Campbell know that Shadow had bonded to him so closely?

Maybe, maybe not. It was something you had to see. She had the feeling that Campbell thought of Shadow merely as his eyes. A tool, to be used.

"What did we do with the harness?"

"One second, I'll help."

She slid off the bed and came to Campbell's side. The harness and glasses were on the floor by Shadow's feet. She picked them up and guided them to Campbell's hands. He slid into the harness and used his right hand and teeth to fasten the clasps. Naked, with the harness, he looked sinister.

He reached for Shadow, found the coupler, and connected himself. He sat up straight, took a deep breath, then released it through puffed cheeks. After a few seconds he shuddered and took another deep breath.

"Okay, we're connected."

"So, how do you start this?"

"It was your idea. You tell me."

"I don't know, Campbell. You're the one who has the visions. Do they just happen? Or is there some sort of triggering stimulus?"

"I haven't really thought about it. It's like they . . . seep in. No, that's wrong. Fade in. I know this sounds cinematic, but that's the way it is. Or . . ."

He frowned again.

"What is it?"

"Just thinking. Maybe they're *always* there. Like peripheral vision, you know? But you don't notice unless you pay attention. It's like there's a dark edge to whatever Shadow sees. Almost like tunnel vision. And once in a while the edges suddenly become more important. They close in, and I'm there."

"But you don't know what causes it, or triggers it."

"No."

"Is the dark edge there right now?"

"Sort of, I guess."

"Try focusing on it."

"I am trying. It doesn't work. It's just dark. Maybe . . ."

"What?"

"Focusing on it is the wrong terminology. That's not the feeling I get when it happens. It's more of a widening of the view, not a narrowing. Like I'm pulling back to . . . oh."

"What is it?"

"Oh God."

He had become very stiff on the bed, sitting rigidly, hands clasped between his knees. Now he rocked forward, mouth open, as if he'd been hit in the stomach.

"Campbell?"

"That's it. It's a broadening of perception. Not a pulling closer at all. It's like going unfocused, to bring in the peripheral darkness. I'm there, Hope."

Hope felt suddenly uneasy. Despite the sheet she gripped to herself, she felt chilled. She suppressed a shiver.

She was sitting here in the hotel room with Campbell and Shadow, and yet Campbell was somewhere else. Campbell was looking into some dark place where Teresa Dawson was being held captive.

He moved his head as if looking around himself. Hope took one of his hands and squeezed tightly. He squeezed back.

"It's not like it was," he said. "I'm not in the cage. I'm . . . in a house, I think. It's dark. Not completely dark. Light is coming from somewhere. Let me . . . oh, there. A window. Moonlight, I think."

"So, this is real time," she said.

"It must be. I'm in a kitchen. No. Scratch that. I'm in a hallway, looking into a kitchen."

"Do you have any control?"

"I don't know. I've tried to look around, but it doesn't seem to work. Not that I can tell. If the view changes, I don't think it's my doing."

"Is there anybody with you?"

"Not that I . . . wait. There's something in the kitchen. Strange, it's oh. Wait."

Campbell's grip on her hand became suddenly much stronger. He squeezed so hard that it almost hurt.

"Campbell?"

"A door opened. Down the hallway. It's dark, and I can't see very clearly. Wait. Now I'm moving toward the open door. There's . . . ah. Christ!"

"Campbell, what is it?"

"Somebody is coming out of the room. Somebody big. Tall. I can't see who it is. Dark shape. It's *her*. I know it. I can feel it."

He shook his head, as if responding to something that Hope could not hear. He cocked his head, as if listening. His frown deepened. His grip on her hand lessened somewhat, then intensified again.

"Maybe you should end it."

"She's standing in the doorway. Talking to me, I think. Can't hear anything. Strange."

He inhaled deeply, leaned away from Shadow as if trying to get away from something.

"She's holding something. Looks like . . . Christ!"

He fell back on the bed, pulling her hand with him, and she leaned over beside him. He thrashed his head back and forth, half crying out, seemingly unable to get the words out.

His lips peeled back to reveal teeth clenched together. For the first time, Hope looked at Shadow. The dog, sitting on the floor, was staring at Campbell intently. More than intently. The dog's lips were peeled back in a half-growl, just like Campbell.

"Campbell, I'm going to disconnect you from Shadow."

He stiffened again, as if an electric current had passed through him. Hope reached for the coupler, twisted it between her fingers, and disconnected him.

Campbell slumped. His legs straightened, hanging over the edge of the bed. Shadow whined softly and scuttled away. He lay down by the desk, head on paws, and looked nervously at Campbell.

"Campbell, I disconnected you."

He inhaled deeply, let it out. Breathed in again.

"I'm okay," he said.

"What happened?"

"She hit me. With a bat, or something. A stick, maybe. I couldn't get away. She was holding me."

"You keep saying it's a woman. Are you certain?"

"Just an impression. I couldn't tell for certain. It's just a big, dark shape. It seems female."

He scrambled up the bed until his head was on the pillow, then rolled to his side and shuddered.

"Are you sure you're okay?"

"Just tired."

Hope got off the bed. She pulled up the sheets and the blanket to cover him. His hands hugged the coverings tightly. Hope leaned over him, stroked his sweat-soaked hair, kissed his cheek. He groaned softly.

"Get some sleep. I'll take Shadow out for his walk."

Campbell only nodded. The harness and glasses were still on. She thought about taking them off, but stopped herself. She did not want to see what lay behind his glasses. Even the sight of his scar seemed like too much to bear.

Shadow tugged at his leash, pulling Hope into an alley. She followed him a yard or two into the dark space, then stopped him with a yank on the leash. He lifted his leg against a wall and urinated, watching her intently.

"Good boy," she said.

He finished, wagged his tail, and pulled her out onto the pavement again.

The night was cool, but not uncomfortable. It was almost 11:00 P.M., and the streets, though not empty, were quiet. A few pedestrians strolled down Hennepin Avenue. Most of them, she realized, were not of the sort she would want to meet. They walked with their hands stuffed into their pockets, heads bowed. The city lights, which had looked so soft and pleasant from the sixth floor, were much harsher at street level.

Maybe Campbell was right. A nice place to visit, or to see from way up high, but not a place to live. Not for her, anyway. She felt as if anything might happen at any moment. If Shadow had not been with her, she might even have been frightened.

She walked as far as South Fifth, just past the parking lot at the northwest corner of the Plymouth Building, then turned around and started back. The Radisson towered above the other buildings, and she tried to pick out their room on the corner. Most of the windows were dark, however, and she couldn't count to exactly the sixth floor. Somewhere . . . there.

Campbell was in bed, waiting. For her.

I love you.

She shivered as she walked, smiling to herself.

Some night! A great night! She wished she had somebody to talk to about it, somebody to confide in. A girlfriend. But she had none. She never had.

Shadow squatted by a newspaper box and defecated, looking up at her guiltily.

"It's okay boy, you gotta go somewhere."

When he had finished she used the plastic bags in her pocket to pick up after him, tied a knot in the bag, and dropped it in a trash container. When she looked up a police car cruised by. The officer in the driver window smiled at her and gave her the O.K. sign. Nobody minded a dog in the city if you cleaned up after him.

After doing his business, Shadow walked more quickly, pulling her all the way back to the hotel. In the lobby, the man and woman at the desk looked up at her, smiled, and went back to their work. They had been informed of Shadow's presence.

In the elevator, Shadow stood by her side and watched the door. For a dog, he seemed very comfortable, very calm.

She reached down and petted him. "Good boy, Shadow."

He wagged his tail.

On the sixth floor he led her unfailingly to the door of the room, and waited while she dug out her key. Amazing dog. The training that must have gone into him!

She had not even touched the key to the lock when the door opened. Campbell, naked, stared at her, eyes shielded by his glasses. She was so surprised that she stepped back.

"Hope?"

"You scared me. What are you doing out of bed? Get back in before somebody sees you."

She pushed him in and closed the door. Campbell turned away from her and paced to the mirror. He must have counted the steps, because he turned without knocking into anything and paced back. He was breathing quickly, rubbing his chin.

"What is it? Did something happen?"

"I know what it is."

"What *what* is?"

"My point of view. In the visions."

Hope frowned, and reached down to unclip Shadow's leash. Campbell had stopped pacing and was staring at a point above her head, as if she were standing.

"It's a dog, Hope. She's got a dog."

TWENTY-THREE

Eleanor opened her eyes, instantly awake.

She held her breath for a few seconds, then let it out slowly. The sound of blood flowing through her veins was like the roar of a truck's engine. She breathed deeply, let it out. Another breath. Another. Deep and easy. Relaxing. Until her heart stopped pounding. Until she could hear beyond her own body.

What had awakened her?

A noise. A feeling.

She listened to the sounds of the house.

The refrigerator, humming like a distant, secret machine. The wind against the windows, rattling like wineglasses clinked together in an adjacent room. The house itself, settling, creaking, as if alive.

Something else.

But what?

She stared into the darkness beside her dresser, straining to hear.

There!

Soft, padding sounds. As of stealthy footsteps.

Somebody was in the house!

She thought immediately of Teresa, had a startling and frightening image of the girl sneaking out of the cellar, small hand curled around the lost butter knife, blade now honed to razor-sharpness.

No. Not possible.

Teresa could not get out of the cell.

When she'd gone down to see Teresa, only an hour before retiring, the girl had been sleeping, curled up on the mattress, oblivious. Max had been lying by the cell door, nose poked through the bars. She had taken the dog back up to the house with her, but Teresa had not even stirred.

Teresa wouldn't hurt her, anyway.

Teresa loved her.

She gritted her teeth, realized that her heart was pounding again.

If not Teresa, then who?

Or what?

She got out of bed, kicking the sheets to the floor. She suppressed a shiver as the cool air of the bedroom touched her skin. She was wearing a thin, white cotton nightgown. It made her look like a ghost in the mirror. The lady in white.

She picked up a bottle of hair spray from the dresser. It was almost full. Heavy enough. Holding it, she felt slightly less vulnerable.

She tiptoed to the door and listened. Silence. She could no longer even hear the wind. The house seemed to have been caught in a lull, as if time itself had stopped.

Eleanor held her breath again, and silently counted.

On three, she opened the door and stepped into the hall. A dark shape moved at her feet and she cried out in alarm, swinging the can of hair spray with all her strength. She missed, clipping herself on the thigh instead, and staggered back against the door.

The dark shape froze.

Then it whined.

"Damn it!"

Eleanor reached behind her and turned on the bedroom light. Max cowered in the nimbus of light reaching through the doorway, half covered by her shadow.

"Max! What are you doing?"

The dog sat up. His tail wagged once. He looked into her face.

Had he heard something, too?

Had he been looking around the house, seeking the source of the noise?

No. That wasn't it. It had been *him* moving around that had awakened her. The sound of *his* paws on linoleum. But without the usual clicking of his claws.

It was as if he had been trying for stealth. Trying, somehow, to sneak up on her.

His eyes were locked on her face, staring at her with what she could almost believe was intelligence. It was as if he were waiting for something, waiting for her to say something, do something. The sight of the dog made goose bumps pop on her shoulders as the cold night air could not.

"What are you looking at, dog?"

Max cocked his head. His mouth opened a fraction, revealing the white of his teeth, the tip of his tongue. Eleanor had the discomfiting impression that she was looking at a person, a person who was judging her, a person who knew everything about her, everything she had ever done, everything she had ever hoped or dreamed.

You're supposed to love me!

With a groan, she lunged at the dog, swinging the can of hair spray. This time, he could not move quickly enough, and the can smashed into his snout. He scuttled away, whining, snorting.

"Come here, Max!"

He stayed in the shadows, out of reach of the light, and went down on his belly, pawing at his face. His eyes never left her.

Eleanor felt instantly guilty about what she had done. She dropped the can of hair spray and reached for the dog. But as she went down on her knees on the linoleum, he edged backwards.

"Poor, poor, Max," she muttered, crawling toward him.

Then Max did something he had never done before.

He growled at her.

He stared right into her eyes, bared his teeth, and let loose a low rumble.

It was a sound that came from deep in his throat, hardly audible at all, like a distant rockfall. It might even have been a sigh, if not for his stance and appearance.

"Max!"

Eleanor backed away and stood up, reaching behind her for the can of hair spray. Max, too, stood up. His mane was bristling. He looked large and dangerous.

"Bad boy!"

Max whined. Once. Only once.

And then, as if it had never been there at all, the intelligence in his eyes was gone, and he was just Max again.

His tail dropped between his legs. Without looking at her, he turned and padded into the kitchen. She listened to the sound of him lapping at his water. When the sound ceased, she waited for him to return to the hallway. But he did not.

He remained in the darkness of the kitchen.

She thought about going in after him, kneeling by him, hugging him, loving him.

She thought of him growling.

She backed up a step, into the bedroom, and closed the door. She turned off the light and leaned against the door, pressing hard against the wood.

She felt unaccountably saddened. As if she had lost something very dear.

But what?

She did not know.

She felt troubled, too.

Something about Max's eyes. About his stance. His aggressiveness. His stubbornness. His *intelligence*.

He had seemed like a person. An *angry* person.

Shaking her head, she got back into bed. But it was not until sleep was almost upon her, that she realized who, exactly, he had reminded her of.

Teresa.

He had been like Teresa! Stubborn, resistant. Denying the love thrust into his face. Just like the girl!

She hoped she would remember the connection when she awoke in the morning. Maybe sleep would provide her with a clue as to what to do about it.

Campbell waited patiently in the darkness.

The inside of his head still throbbed with the after images of grids and moving points. A headache clawed at the base of his spine, not yet painful enough to make him cringe, but definitely heavy with potential.

"One more second, Campbell," Russell said.

A pinpoint of light emerged from the fog of the headache, expanded, exploded like fireworks.

Campbell was looking at himself from across the room. They'd put Shadow in a cage during the tests, and now a long cable snaked between them. The lab looked sterile and white. From this viewpoint, Russell looked like a mad scientist bending over an unfortunate victim. It was difficult to put himself in the position of the victim.

"How's that?"

"Okay."

"How are you feeling?"

"The usual. Dizzy. It will pass. I know the routine."

Russell turned away from him, looked at Shadow, and Campbell found himself studying the other man's face.

"Everything looks fine. Nothing showed up in the tests. The connection is one hundred percent. At both ends. No faults, no errors."

"Okay."

Russell turned to him, and although Campbell could not see his face, he knew the other man was confused.

"Would it make any difference if I told you it was flat out impossible for you to receive any information from Shadow other than impulses from his optic nerve?"

"Nope."

Campbell had debated telling him about last night's experi-

ence, his initiation of the vision, his conviction that the visions
were not coming from another person, but from another dog,
and had decided against it. He knew already what Russell's
reaction would be. Disbelief. Perhaps worse. And beyond that,
he was experiencing a strange urge to keep things to himself.
Or at least from Russell and Nina. This morning he'd had the
horrible thought that they might take Shadow away from him,
set him up with another dog, and if that happened. . . . He did
not know what would happen. But if the visions stopped, he'd
have no chance of helping Teresa Dawson. He could not take
that chance.

"Has there been a recurrence of the visions in the past twelve
hours?"

Russell spoke the word "visions" as if it were a slug in his
mouth, something to be expelled quickly, not looked at.

"Nothing that hasn't happened before."

"Any more information about the missing girl?"

"No."

"But you're still going to go ahead."

"Unless you've got a better idea."

"How about staying here? We could try monitoring you during one of the visions."

"I don't know when another one will happen."

Liar, he thought, and hoped he wasn't blushing.

"Still, if we keep you here, we'd have a better chance of
understanding what's going on."

"Russell, you don't even believe anything is going on. You
just want to keep me out of trouble."

"That's not true. I'm trying to help."

"I can't just hole up here until you find what you want. The
visions aren't debilitating. It's not like I can't function. And if
you're right, all this will pass once I complete the accommodation. Right? So what are you worried about?"

"Why do I get the feeling you're holding something back?"

"Because you're suspicious. That's your job."

"Are you? Holding something back?"

"No."

Russell inhaled deeply. "Are you going to go to the police?"

Campbell smiled. "Not if you help me. I did what you wanted. I let you run your tests. Now, it's your turn. Put me in touch with the others."

"Jesus, Campbell."

"What can it hurt?"

"If you influenced them in any way . . . planted the idea that they might experience . . . visions . . . it would contaminate all our results. Virtually invalidate everything we've done."

"I won't influence them."

"If Nina found out . . ."

"I'm not going to tell her. Are you?"

"Campbell . . ."

"Help me, Russell, or I'll go to the police. Which scenario is worse? Headline: TOP SECRET DOG OPERATION MAKES MAN PSYCHIC! Or I ask a few questions, quietly, discretely."

Russell shook his head and rubbed his chin. He probably wishes he never met me. Campbell felt a twinge of guilt. But not a very strong one.

"Jesus, I'm glad your sister isn't as stubborn as you."

"You haven't known her very long, have you?"

Russell didn't laugh.

Hope's car wasn't in the parking lot when Campbell emerged from Miriam Technologies. He turned his face up to the sun, smiled at the warmth. The sky was mostly clear. A light breeze came from the northwest, cool but not uncomfortable.

He led Shadow across the parking lot to a grassy area beside the fence that bordered the Miriam site. There were a few picnic tables here, empty this early in the morning. The grass would be littered with Miriam workers at lunchtime, lazing in the sun, eating, napping.

Campbell sat at one of the picnic tables. He turned Shadow to face him.

"Shadow, look."

Shadow looked up into his face. Campbell studied himself. He could see Shadow reflected in the darkness of his glasses.

Strange. We're like two mirrors lined up face to face, forming a corridor into infinity. It made him feel slightly uneasy to look at himself this way.

I never see Shadow, he thought. Ever. Unless he looks into a mirror. He is my eyes. He is part of me. We are one.

He reached out and found the dog's head. He ran his fingers gently over the angular skull, stroked the smooth, black fur.

"Shadow, front."

The dog turned around, and Campbell surveyed the parking lot. Still no sign of Hope. The brightness of the morning sun reflecting off myriad cars in the lot made his head hurt, amplified the ache that still lurked somewhere behind his eyes.

"Shadow, sleep," he commanded.

Shadow went down on his belly and closed his eyes. In the sudden darkness, Campbell relaxed. He breathed deeply, exhaled in a sigh.

It wasn't true darkness, really, with Shadow's eyes closed. He could see faint images, blobs of light, flashes and lines. The same things anybody saw when they closed their eyes and continued to pay attention. But the lack of glare eased the pain of the headache.

Campbell leaned back so that the wood of the picnic table pressed firmly into his back.

He thought about trying to initiate another vision, but immediately decided against it. Not without Hope here. Not without somebody to help him should things go wrong.

Wrong, how?

Just . . . wrong.

He thought about Teresa Dawson, and wondered what she was doing right now. If the dog, the *other* dog, was with her, he could find out. All he would have to do was . . .

The darkness in his head became almost oily. Campbell held his breath. Like last night, he suddenly felt as if a tunnel were closing in on him, as if the darkness at the edges of his vision were really walls, pushing closer.

And then the darkness was full of light. Soft light, diffuse, not like the harsh glare of the sun in the parking lot. It seemed, at first, as if he were looking at a jumble of dark lines and strange shadows. And then his perception shifted.

The lines were the legs of a table and chairs. He was *under* a table, viewpoint close to the floor. The darkness beneath him was linoleum. The light was coming from his right, somewhere high. A window. In front of him, a pair of boots. Construction boots. Scuffed, muddy. Legs rising from them, sheathed in jeans.

Campbell sat up straight.

"Shadow, front!"

The image was flooded with harsher light, and suddenly he was looking at the parking lot again. His heart was pounding. Sweat dribbled down his back, and he shuddered.

He had done it. Again. The experiment was repeatable, verifiable, which meant . . .

It was real. All of it.

He watched, feeling as if he were in a dream, as a car pulled into the lot. It drew closer, parked next to the curb. Hope leaned out the driver window toward him.

"How'd it go?"

Campbell stood and walked toward the car. His heart beat was slowly returning to normal.

"Okay," he said, and got into the car.

Shadow jumped up beside him and looked at Hope. Campbell leaned toward her and kissed her on the mouth. "Where did you go?"

"The library. I wanted to check a couple of things. Sorry I wasn't here."

"Anything interesting?"

"Want to hear something weird? There have actually been experiments conducted with dogs, to test their extrasensory abilities."

"And?"

"You don't want to hear this stuff, Campbell. It's all pretty silly. Dogs predicting the outcome of football games, dogs picking cards, dogs picking winning lottery numbers. Junk. I can see why scientists don't take parapsychology seriously."

"So, there was nothing."

"I didn't say that. There is some interesting research into dogs predicting earthquakes, weather changes, things like that. That's probably just sensitivity to environmental changes that humans can't detect."

"Predicting how?"

"By behavioral changes. Increases or decreases in aggression or tractability."

"Nothing about psychic connections, then."

"The closest I found was the tendency of siblings to react similarly. A dog is introduced to a person, reacts a certain way. A litter mate of that dog, without prior experience of the person involved, will tend to have a similar reaction. Anybody who works with dogs could tell you that. I suppose you could argue that litter mates are getting and giving some sort of feedback."

"You mean they're getting feedback from other dogs?"

"Or maybe they just have a feeling about which people mean them harm. The same as children do. Who knows. All I can tell you is that dogs are very sensitive. You'd be surprised. I've worked with them for years, and you couldn't get me to swear they don't communicate with one another."

Campbell stroked Shadow's head. The dog licked his fingers.

"So why didn't Shadow bite my hand off when he first met me? Why didn't he know that I didn't like dogs?"

"But you've got a heart of gold. Any dog could tell that on first sniff!"

She leaned across and kissed him. Shadow, looking past Campbell, gave him a full view of her breasts within her shirt, the darkness between the pale orbs. When they parted, Campbell pushed Shadow's head aside, took a deep breath.

"So, did Russell come through?" Hope asked him.

"Partly. One name. Abraham Singer. The rest aren't local, so they'd be too hard to reach, anyway."

"Address?"

"He said to check the phone book."

"Better than nothing," Hope said, and put the car in gear.

"This is what you call a bad neighborhood," Hope said.

"Definitely the wrong side of the tracks," Campbell agreed.

"Have you ever had the feeling you're about to make a big mistake?"

Looking through Shadow's eyes, colorless and starkly shadowed, he expected he was seeing a seedier and more degraded version of Abraham Singer's neighborhood than even Hope was seeing. They were in St. Paul, close to the university, in a neighborhood that provided a lot of rental accommodation for students. Cheap accommodations. Very cheap.

The houses on Weaver Street were crushed so close together that you'd probably have to stand sideways to get between them, Campbell thought. Edge along, feeling your way by touch on the walls. From the car, he couldn't even *see* between the houses. The houses themselves were a hairsbreadth from dilapidated. Most had filthy stucco siding, or wooden slats badly in need of painting, badly warped or leaning porches, rotting front wooden steps, or impossibly skewed cement steps. The lawns were, for the most part, unkempt and filthy. There were no children on the street, this in itself not unusual. Being summer, the vacancy rate was probably very high. Campbell wouldn't have been surprised to discover that more than half the houses were unoccupied.

"Twelve-thirty-six," Campbell said.

"I know, I know. Isn't that it up there?"

"Where?"

"Sorry. To your left. Shadow's left. Doesn't matter, we're here."

The car slowed to a halt at the curb. Hope turned off the

engine. Campbell studied the house. Twelve-thirty-six was a brick bungalow on an overgrown plot surrounded by a battered chain-link fence. The windows all seemed to be covered by curtains or blankets from the inside. It looked like a week's worth of flyers and newspapers were scattered on the front step.

"That's it, all right. Christ, what a mess."

"Who is this Abraham Singer person?"

"Just an earlier version of me."

"Maybe we should have phoned first."

"What if he said no? This way is better. At least we'll be in his face, have more leverage."

"I don't know if I want to be in his face."

"Chicken. Come on."

Campbell got out of the car, pulled Shadow after him, and closed the door. Without waiting for Hope he walked across the boulevard to the sidewalk, and then to the gate of Abraham Singer's yard. Hope rushed up behind him.

"How are we going to handle this?" she asked. "Is there any way to do this without giving away the whole story?"

"Play it by ear. I'll do the talking."

They walked up the path, up the front steps. The concrete wobbled as a single unit beneath their feet. Campbell looked for a doorbell but could not find one. He knocked three times, hard.

From inside the house came the sound of swearing. A man's voice, angry. The inside door swung open. Campbell found himself looking up at a pale shape beyond the screen door.

"Who's there?"

"Abraham Singer?"

"What do you want?"

"We're from Miriam Technologies."

There was a shuffling noise from inside, and then the screen door opened. A dog stuck its head out and looked up at Campbell. Shadow backed away a step. Campbell saw the harness on the dog, the cable snaking up Abraham Singer's arm. He felt suddenly very strange; excited and frightened. Because the

screen door still blocked most of Shadow's view, he had not yet
clearly seen Abraham Singer.

"Jesus Christ, they did you too, huh?" Abraham Singer said.

"Could we come in and talk to you?"

"What for? I got nothing to say."

"It won't take long. It's very important."

"That's exactly what they said when they conned me into
this. Jesus Christ. You people." He shook his head, then
shrugged. "Okay, hell, come in.

Abraham Singer backed away from the door, then disappeared into the inside of the house. Campbell turned to Hope.

"Do you want to wait in the car?"

"In this neighborhood? Are you trying to get me killed? I'm
sticking with you."

TWENTY-FOUR

Hope thought that Abraham Singer was a perfect match for his house.

His hair was long and reddish, thin and dry and void of lustre. His face was gaunt and pock-marked, the dark glasses that hid his eyes giving him the look of a junkie. His thin, pale skin, did nothing to hide the shape of his skull. He wore brown polyester pants with a belt at least three inches wide, and a decade-old blue dress shirt with two buttons open at the collar to reveal a bony, acne-spotted chest. Singer's dog was an Irish Setter, long and lean with a friendly looking face. Hope could readily see signs of neglect, if not abuse, on the animal. Its fur was matted in places, tangled hopelessly around its ears. Mucous had gathered in large clumps at the corners of its eyes. Although Setters were traditionally gaunt, this one showed far too many ribs. The dog's bowl, sitting by a garbage bag near the door, was empty of both food and water.

"What's his name?" Hope asked.

"Pointer. I call him Shithead."

The linkup between Singer and Pointer, though superficially similar to that between Campbell and Shadow, was substantially different. Most obvious of all, Singer had a black plastic coupling port embedded in the skin behind his left ear, into which the cable from Pointer's harness plugged directly. None of the sophisticated subcutaneous coupling between Campbell and Shadow.

The moment Hope stepped into the house she wished she

had taken Campbell up on his offer to wait in the car. The smell that assaulted her was a combination of old garbage, stale dog, and too many years of greasy cooking to count. The floors were tattered linoleum from front to back, with an old and ragged carpet in the living room to the right of the entrance. The walls were painted brown, but the paint was flaking everywhere, stained and mottled by substances that Hope tried hard not to think about. The ceiling was a satellite map of thin cracks and peeling plaster.

Every window was covered in a sheet, hung up by nails. The only light entering the house from the outside had a yellow, sickly tinge. Within seconds, Hope felt claustrophobic.

Singer walked into the living room, pulling Pointer roughly, and sat in an old easy chair facing the television.

Hope sat on the sofa next to Singer's chair, and Campbell sat next to her. Singer's pant legs had pulled up from his running shoes. Hope saw a black plastic circle around his ankle. On the side of the anklet was a box perhaps an inch across, and in the middle of the box a red light flashed every second or so.

"My prison," Singer said, smiling. His teeth were brown.

"Pardon?" Hope asked.

"Home confinement program. I can't leave the house. You understand? They monitor my location."

"You're a prisoner here?" Campbell asked, his voice disbelieving.

"It's better than Stillwater."

"What did you do?" Hope asked, and realized the moment she asked the question, that perhaps this was something Singer wanted to keep private.

But Singer grinned. "Armed robbery. Assault with a deadly weapon. Assault with intent to inflict grievous bodily harm. Shoplifting. Jaywalking. Name it, I've done it, and been caught doing it."

Hope turned to Campbell. Both Campbell and Shadow kept their attention on Singer and his dog. Neither of the dogs, Hope noted, showed any inclination to meet. It was unnerving seeing dogs so well behaved.

"So, what do you want? You got something new you want to try out on me?"

"Nothing like that," Campbell said. "We just want to ask you a couple of questions about you and Pointer."

"Fucking mutt," Singer said, and kicked Pointer on the rump. Pointer yelped but did not move.

"How long have you had him?" Campbell asked.

"Two years. They came to me in Stillwater. The thin broad with the phony British accent."

"Doctor Ladeceur?"

"Her. Said if I volunteered for the surgery I could get out of the hole on a home confinement basis. Wish I'd never heard of her. Second biggest mistake of my life, letting her saddle me with the mutt."

"How long have you been blind?"

"Three years."

"How did you lose your sight?" Hope asked.

Singer grinned. The expression was nothing if not malicious.

"You really want to know?"

"I'm curious."

Singer leaned forward, resting on his knees, and looked directly at her. Hope felt a tightening, crawly feeling in her crotch. She could see white lines of scar tissue reaching behind Singer's dark glasses.

"I was in medium security at the time. Three of them cornered me in the wood shop one afternoon. Two of them held me down. They shoved a rag in my mouth to keep me quiet. The other one had a shiv. He poked the shiv into each of my eyes. Did you know the eyeball itself has no nerves? It can't feel pain. So, to make it hurt, they gouged around a little. Did a pretty good job, didn't they?"

Hope's stomach lurched. She covered her mouth.

Singer grinned. "Got me into the infirmary for six months."

"Why did they do that to you?"

"I saw too much. I talked. Biggest mistake of my life."

"Were you the first to receive the surgery?" Campbell asked.

"They told me I was the third. Didn't have it perfected yet, did they? Your setup looks more comfortable. Is that what you want to talk about?"

"Not exactly. I want to know how you accommodated the linkup."

"Accommodated?"

"When you were first hooked up with the dog, were there any problems?"

"Took me a couple of days. Nothing but fog, you know? Then suddenly it tuned in. Better than nothing I guess."

"Were there any problems after that?"

"Like what?"

Campbell took a deep breath. **Hope** squeezed his hand to calm him. "Any distortions of the images from Pointer? Any bad dreams?"

"A couple of headaches. I don't remember much else. That's all you wanted?"

"There was *nothing?*"

Singer lifted his chin, a frown now ridging his forehead. "You're not from Miriam."

Campbell said nothing for a few seconds. "Dr. Graham gave me your name."

"Buttface Russell. But I don't have to talk to you."

"I just . . ."

"You're having trouble with *your* dog, right? That's what you want to talk about, isn't it?"

Campbell took another deep breath. "Partly."

Singer leaned back in his seat, smiling a little more, happy to be in control.

"What kind of trouble?"

"Nothing I can explain."

"So, what do you want from me?"

"I was hoping that . . . if you had had similar . . . it doesn't matter."

"That's it then."

Hope could feel Campbell's tension beneath her hand. The muscles of his legs twitched.

"Just one more thing."

"What?"

"Let me link with Pointer."

Hope was startled, and stared at Campbell in surprise. Campbell, that might not be a good idea. You don't know the differences between Pointer and Shadow. Maybe the technology is different. What if it causes damage?"

"I have to know."

Even Singer was shocked. "You gotta be kidding."

"I want to see what it's like. The coupling port looks the same. It shouldn't be a problem."

Singer laughed. He shook his head.

"Just for a minute," Campbell said.

"Fifty bucks for a minute," Singer said.

"I don't have that kind of money with me."

"I've got it," Hope said, and couldn't believe she had spoken.

She opened her purse and took out two twenty-dollar bills and one ten-dollar bill. She put the bills on the coffee table by the sofa.

"Fuck," Singer said. "I should'a asked for more."

"I don't have more," Hope said.

"It's your money."

Singer reached down to Pointer and uncoupled himself. Pointer did not move.

"One minute," Singer said.

Hope got up and walked to Pointer. She reached down and let him sniff her hand. His tail wagged. She picked up his harness and led the dog over to Campbell. Pointer did not resist.

"Are you sure about this?"

"I'll know if it's different. I'll know if it's Shadow or if it's me."

Campbell unclipped his connection with Shadow and held out his hand. Hope took the coupler from his fingers. The plugs on Pointer and Shadow were a match. That much of the technology was identical.

"Ready?"

Campbell nodded. His hands, she saw, were trembling.

She bit her lip and pushed Campbell's coupler into Pointer's harness.

Campbell stiffened, clasped his thighs with his hands. His lips parted slightly to reveal teeth tightly clamped.

"Pointer, left," he said hoarsely.

Pointer obediently looked to the left. Campbell trembled.

"Tell me when to unhook you," Hope said.

"Not yet."

He reached down to touch Pointer. His hands felt the dog's head, snout, ears.

"Pointer, look."

Pointer turned around and looked directly into Campbell's face. Campbell leaned momentarily toward the dog, then fell back into the sofa.

"That's enough," he said.

Hope pulled the cables apart. She plugged Campbell back into Shadow. Again, Campbell stiffened. After a few seconds he relaxed, sinking into the sofa.

Hope returned Pointer to Singer. After he was hooked up to the dog, Singer leaned forward.

"So? You like my Shithead?"

"Thanks," Campbell said.

"Easiest fifty bucks I ever made. You want to trade dogs? I'll give you a deal."

Campbell stood up. Hope stood with him, holding onto his hand.

"We'll show ourselves out," Campbell said.

Eleanor walked slowly, feet dragging on the ground, shotgun hanging over her left arm. She stumbled on a gopher hole, caught her balance, and swore. She wasn't paying attention. She could hardly think straight.

Max ran on ahead of her, skirting the trees and high grass at the sides of the rutted trail.

With the sleeve of her right arm she wiped a sheen of sweat off her brow. Sweat from exertion, not from the day itself. Although the sun was up, the sky clear, it was cool on the wooded trail. A beautiful day. A day to be walking and loving life.

But all she could think about was Teresa.

Their one meeting today had been a disaster.

When Eleanor had brought the girl her lunch, Teresa had squatted by the side of the cell, hands clasped between her thighs, staring at her blankly, unsmiling, face pale and lifeless. Eleanor had stared back, waiting for the girl to say something, but that expression of . . . had it really been disdain? It had remained unchanged.

"I brought you some lunch," Eleanor had said. "If you eat it all, and if you're good, I'll let you outside. Later."

"That's what you said yesterday."

The voice had sounded as lifeless and hollow as the face looked. It had made Eleanor's skin crawl.

"Yesterday, you . . ."

"I was good."

"Not good enough."

"What are you going to do with me?"

"Nothing. I'm just trying to help you, that's all. A girl like you . . ."

"You're sick."

"Don't say that again."

"Why not? You're going to kill me, aren't you?"

"No."

"Am I supposed to be a pet? Do you want me to beg and wag my tail?"

"Stop talking like this. It really hurts me to hear you talk like this."

"Are you really as stupid as you sound? How do you *want* me to talk? Like you're my mother? Like I'm happy to be here?"

"You don't know how lucky you are."

"My mother is dead. I wish you were dead."

"Enough!"

"When you die, you're going to go to hell. Did you know that?"

Eleanor's hands had started shaking. She had bent down quickly to put the tray of food on the floor.

"That was a cruel thing to say."

"I hate you."

"If you're going to be like this, I'm going up."

"Wait!"

For just a moment, it had seemed as if the girl's manner were changing. Still, she had continued squatting, staring.

"Where's Max?"

"Max is outside."

"Could you let him come down here?"

"He didn't want to come down. I don't think he likes you anymore. Did you do something to hurt him last night?"

In truth, she had made the dog stay in the house. The sight of Max and Teresa, so close, upset her too much.

"You're lying! You wouldn't let him come down!"

"I'm not lying, Teresa. I think that Max hates you."

The girl had sobbed, face falling toward her knees. In the beam of the flashlight she had trembled, her shadow trembling with her. Eleanor's heart went out to the girl. Now she needed love. Now, perhaps, she would accept Eleanor's approach.

Eleanor had kneeled by the girl, had reached out to touch her.

Teresa had stiffened, lifting her head.

"Don't touch me. I hate you. You're a liar. You're pathetic."

Eleanor had stood abruptly, nearly dropping the flashlight.

"Get out of here. Leave me alone. I'd rather be locked up forever than talk to you!"

Stifling her own cry of shock, Eleanor had backed away,

closed the cell, and stumbled up the stairs. Only when she had emerged from the cellar, had closed the door and locked it, had she allowed herself to sob.

It was all going wrong!

All of it!

Now, walking along the rutted road in the woodlot, her despair felt so heavy that she could hardly breathe. All she had wanted was love! To love and to be loved! And what had she received in return for her efforts! Hatred! Fury! A child who detested her! It was too much for her. Emotions erupted, tears poured.

Eleanor slumped to the ground, sitting hard on the grass at the side of the road. She could not help it. She could not stop. She started to sob. Sobbed so hard and so deep that she had to hug her knees to stop herself from keeling over, from burying her face in the dirt.

Why was this happening!

Max must have heard her outburst, for he stopped his scurrying through the high grass and bushes, and returned to her. His tail hung down between his legs. He approached her cautiously, sniffing, head cocked.

He had never seen her like this.

She wanted to reach for him, but could not make herself do it.

Why does she love *you?* Why can't she love *me?*

Max sat down on the trail and stared at her. He whined and lifted a paw.

Eleanor inhaled deeply, held the breath a few seconds, then let the breath out. She stood up, leaning on the shotgun for support. Max backed away, tail wagging slowly.

She started to reach out to him when a rustling sound came from the grass behind her. Max bolted, charging into the bushes. In seconds, the rabbit jumped clear of the grass, onto the trail. For half a second it stood frozen, staring at Eleanor, eyes wide. Then Max emerged from the grass, mane bristling.

Eleanor reacted instinctively. She pumped the shotgun, lifted it to her shoulder.

"Max, back!"

Max, despite his eagerness to seize the smaller creature in his teeth, to rend its flesh and fur and bones, scuttled backward. It was the moment the rabbit needed, and it leaped forward. Eleanor squeezed the trigger at the same moment, and the shotgun erupted fire.

The rabbit whirled in the air like a boomerang, spraying blood, and fell to the center of the road. When it hit the dirt it started to squeal, a high, warbling sound like a kettle boiling. Most of the blast had missed, but its rear legs were sodden with blood, ragged. Still, those legs seemed to move instinctively, trying to take the creature away. Instead, it spun in place like some crazy, mutilated dancer, sending droplets of blood in a wide circle.

Max growled and moved closer.

"Max, stay!"

Eleanor stepped up to the rabbit, stopped it spinning by stepping lightly on its midsection. Its rear legs continued to bat at the ground, splattering Eleanor's boots with its blood and fur. She stared down at it, fascinated by its eyes. It seemed to be staring at her. Needfully.

Its pain had pushed it to a bizarre, unnatural precipice. It *loved* her, it *needed* her.

Careful not to crush it with her boot, she bent down and touched its nose. Its eyes blinked. For a moment the squealing stopped. It trembled.

Then it started to cry again. Even louder than before. Almost ear piercing in its intensity.

Eleanor pumped another shell into the shotgun's chamber, lowered the barrel so that it hovered above the rabbit's black, needful eye.

She squeezed the trigger. The creature beneath her boot exploded in a mist of fur and blood.

Eleanor stepped away and took a deep breath.

Max edged closer, sniffing at the mess.

In that final moment, in its pain, the rabbit had loved her more than it had loved any creature in its life. Under her boot, it had no choice but to love her. She had seen it in its eye. Love.

She turned and started walking quickly back to the house. Max barked once, then ran to follow her.

Her thoughts were racing.

Perhaps all that Teresa needed was a little nudge. A little *something* to push her toward love.

When she reached the house she stopped at the woodpile, kicked through scattered bark until she found the old axe handle. It was half-rotted, useless for holding an axe head. But it was still sturdy enough for what she needed it for.

She leaned the shotgun against the back door, then went to the cellar. Max followed her, tail wagging.

"We'll see who she loves," Eleanor muttered.

She opened the door, turned on the light, and went down. The darkness below sucked at her, pulling her onward, as if she were falling.

Teresa was lying on the mattress, sleeping. As the cell door opened, she rolled over, then sat up.

Eleanor showed her the axe handle, then smiled.

Teresa started to shake.

"I know you're not looking out the window, Campbell. Shadow has been staring at me for the past five minutes."

He turned his face away from the window to look at her. Looking away from where Shadow was staring had become a habit. He wasn't quite sure what it meant. Probably a defense mechanism.

"Sorry, I was just thinking."

"You still haven't told me about your linkup with Pointer."

That, in fact, was what he had been thinking about. He slid off the windowsill and walked over to the chair by the desk. He sat down and leaned back. Shadow continued to watch Hope.

She kept packing her suitcase, but did not take her eyes away from him.

"It wasn't what I expected."

"In what way?"

"It's hard to explain. I guess I'm more closely linked to Shadow than I knew. It was just . . . different. I can't put it into words, Hope. It was like there was no . . . potential. Nothing *beyond* the image that I was seeing. No . . . magic."

"And there is with Shadow?"

"Until this afternoon I'd have said no. But that darkness at the edge of what Shadow sees, that place where the visions are, must be with me all the time, even when I'm not aware of it. It wasn't there with Pointer, and I *felt* it missing. Whatever is giving me those visions, Shadow has it, and Pointer doesn't."

Darkness squeezed the room with such suddenness that Campbell reeled, even while seated.

"Campbell, what's wrong?"

"Vision."

He gripped the arms of the chair, holding himself steady. The darkness wavered, filled with strange, jumping light. He'd found himself looking at Teresa. The girl was sitting on a mattress. Her face was dirty, her hair tangled. The changes in the girl in the last day or two were astonishing, frightening. Campbell sucked in a breath. With great effort he managed to find and control his voice.

"It's Teresa. She looks okay. I mean, she's alive. But . . . Oh, God."

"What is it?"

Hope's voice, though as loud as it had been while he had been watching her, seemed to him now to be coming through a wall.

"She's here, too. The other one. The dark one. She's got . . ."

A stick of some kind. A baseball bat. No . . . an axe?

No, just the axe handle.

The shape seemed huge to him, towering over him, dark. He

could not see a face. But it *was* a female. He was sure of that. Sensed it, though he could not say why.

She was holding a flashlight, and the beam was blinding. When it swept over him, his head was flooded with light.

She moved toward Teresa, axe handle held high.

"She's going to hurt Teresa!"

The axe handle crashed down.

Teresa opened her mouth in a silent scream, lifting an arm to protect herself. The handle glanced off Teresa's arm, the end smashing into the side of her face.

Campbell cried out as a tear opened on Teresa's cheek; blood poured out.

"No! Stop it!"

"Campbell!"

The axe handle raised again, disappearing momentarily into shadow.

"No! Stop it! Stop it!"

As the handle descended again toward the cowering girl, Campbell lunged out of the chair.

Eleanor raised the axe handle again.

Pain would bring love! Pain would bring need!

Light from the flashlight swept the room, sending shadows leaping.

"I don't want to hurt you!"

She brought the handle down, toward Teresa's terrified, screaming face, and connected with something. Hard.

Max yelped, and then growled.

Eleanor raised the handle again, and then realized what was wrong.

Max had moved between her and the girl, and had taken the last blow across his flank. Now he squared against her, teeth bared, growling.

She was so shocked that she did not swing again.

Max lunged at her, his growl erupting into a fierce bark. His paws drummed the floor of the cell, claws clicking on the cement.

"Max!"

He growled again. Edging closer.

Eleanor backed away, through the cell door. She closed it quickly, sealing both dog and child behind the bars.

Max sat down.

He stared at her, growling.

Then he whined.

Eleanor's heart pounded, her blood roared. Even through that she could hear Teresa's whimpering. Max's whining.

"Max," she whispered.

But the dog turned away from her, moved toward Teresa, head low, tail wagging slowly, to comfort the girl.

TWENTY-FIVE

Campbell came out of darkness and realized he was lying on the floor of the hotel room, left arm outstretched, fingers barely touching Shadow's harness. His view was of the bathroom door, the end of the bed, his own suitcase.

Had he passed out on the floor? He couldn't remember drinking, couldn't remember much of anything. But the position was a familiar one. Incidents like this had happened frequently when he had first lost his eyes. Binges followed by blackouts, shame, fear, self-recrimination. This time, though. . . . It came back to him suddenly, like a sucker punch to the jaw, and the room started to spin. He inhaled deeply, concentrated on anchoring himself to the floor, keeping his stomach from expelling its contents.

As he breathed, trying to reorient himself, Hope emerged from the bathroom with a glass of water and a wet towel. Campbell forced himself up on his elbows, groaning at the exertion.

"You better have a good explanation for what just happened," Hope said, kneeling by him.

She pressed the cold, damp cloth to his head, and Campbell moaned. It felt good. He breathed deeply.

Shadow had moved to a sitting position and was studying Hope. From that angle, Campbell could see both himself and Hope. She looked very nurse-like he thought, stroking his head, regarding him with concern. He liked the look on her face.

"How long have I been lying here?"

"Not long. Less than a minute. You jumped out of the chair like somebody shot you. I almost had a heart attack."

"Sorry."

"You could have warned me."

"I stopped her, Hope."

Hope halted her ministrations for a moment to frown at him. "Stopped who?"

"Her. The woman. Stopped her from hurting Teresa."

Hope's frown deepened, then she put the wet cloth at the back of Campbell's neck. Campbell shuddered.

"How did you stop her?"

"I don't know. I mean, that's a good question. I was there, with them. Teresa and the woman. She had something in her hands. An axe handle, I think. She started hitting Teresa with it."

"God, are you sure?"

"It's what I saw. Hit her on the arm. Teresa tried to protect herself, and the blow glanced off her cheek. Cut her. Then the woman raised the axe handle to hit again and I . . ."

"Leaped at her."

"Yeah. I guess. It was just a gut reaction. I mean, I was reacting as if I were really there and not just *seeing* it."

Hope dipped the cloth into the glass of water, stroked the sides of his face. Campbell leaned his head back and sighed, enjoying the attention.

"What did Shadow do when I was having the last vision?"

"He whined a lot. When you leaped out of the chair, he leaped with you. You both ended up on the floor. I thought you were both unconscious."

"Is he feeling the connection, too?"

"He must, on some level, or you wouldn't feel it, would you? If what we think is true, then you're just tapping in on *his* tele-pathic connection to this dog. Or perhaps he's not conscious of it. Perhaps it's just one of those things that are with him all the time, that he doesn't pay attention to. Maybe it's just *you* who's actually focusing on it."

Campbell heard little after Hope said "telepathic." He understood that they'd virtually accepted what was happening, but hearing the word brought an entourage of emotions, primary among them disbelief, followed closely by incredulity, with downright suspicion taking the rear. He and Hope were sitting in a Minneapolis hotel room talking about a Goddamned telepathic dog!

"God, it's too weird."

"What happened after you jumped at her?"

"She reacted. She backed away from me like she was scared of me. Went out of the cell, closed the door. Then it got dark. That's all I remember."

"You were really there?"

"Not me. The dog. *Her* dog. I got into her dog, through Shadow, and I . . . used him. Judas Priest, Hope, can that be right?"

"You tell me."

"It happened."

"Did you . . . bite her?"

"No, just scared her. I was shouting. Barking, I guess."

Hope stood up, held out a hand to him. Campbell took her hand and pulled himself up. His legs felt week. Dizziness oozed behind his eyes.

"I better sit down."

Hope led him to the bed and he sat heavily, then leaned over his knees, balancing with his elbows.

"Are you all right?"

"I think so. Just got to catch my breath."

"What happened to Teresa? Is she hurt?"

"I don't know. Like I said, it went dark."

"Could you find out?"

"I'll try."

"But not if it's going to hurt you."

"I'll be okay."

She sat down beside him on the bed and held his hand. "Just wait a second."

"What?"

"I was thinking. If you can actually manipulate the dog o the other end, could you communicate with Teresa somehow?

"By barking?"

"No, of course not. By your reactions to what she does. Something that would let her know she's not alone, that she's got an ally, a friend."

Campbell frowned. It was a good idea, but he was not sure, exactly, how he could go about doing what she suggested. His attack on the woman with the axe handle had been precipitated by extreme emotion, instinct almost. There had been nothing conscious about it. He didn't know if he'd be able to simply . . . communicate through the dog.

"I'll try."

Hope squeezed his hand tightly. Campbell lowered his head to his chest, focusing on the image he was getting from Shadow. It took a slight shift in his perceptions to become aware of the dark edge to his sight. It was like rolling his own eyes backwards, straining to see behind him, as if by . . .

The darkness in the corners of the room pushed closer, then rushed in as if the lights had been turned off. He inhaled deeply, held it. The quality of the darkness suddenly changed, became grayer, became almost *textured,* as if he could reach out and touch it. He was there.

He let his breath out in a hiss. "I'm there."

"Teresa?"

Hope's voice came from his right. He could feel the pressure of her grip on his hand, could even sense her proximity, smell her . . . and yet, it was hard to believe that she was right next to him. It *felt* as if she were in another room, talking to him on the phone.

"I can't see her yet. Let me . . ."

He seemed to be lying on the floor. The dark lines of cell bars hovered in front of him. A large square of darkness reached beyond the bars. The corridor, leading to the stairs. That was it. He was lying by the cell door. Which meant that Teresa was *behind* him, probably on her mattress. If he could just . . .

He turned his head to the left, shifted his whole body so that he was facing behind him. His view suddenly shifted. The bars swung away, the square patch of gray that was the covered window passed above him, and suddenly he was looking at a pale shape curled into a fetal ball on the floor.

"She's hurt," he said hoarsely. "She's not moving."

"How badly?"

"I don't know. I can't seem to control . . . If I could just move toward her, I could . . ."

He was suddenly approaching Teresa, moving slowly closer. He circled her, moved closer until, at one point, he seemed to be hovering only inches from her face. He saw her eyelids flicker.

"She's alive."

Then he was behind her, close enough to her hair to touch it, then down by her legs, then moving back up her front.

"He's sniffing her, I think. He keeps on moving."

"He *who?*"

"The dog. I'm at her face again. Her eyes are closed, but the lids are moving."

He tried to edge closer, to nudge her. The very act of willing such a thing involved thinking of himself as a dog, with no arms, doing everything with his face. It was like leaning closer, trying to kiss the girl.

But it worked. He nosed her, pushing her forehead.

Teresa Dawson's eyelids fluttered for a few seconds, and then her eyes opened wide.

She did not move. She stared at him.

"She's conscious. Eyes open. Now she's sitting. Easy, kid, not so fast."

Teresa Dawson sat up. She blinked a couple of times, then lifted filthy hands to rub her eyes. Campbell tried to move toward her, ended up in front of her. She stared at him, tried to smile, and suddenly burst into tears.

Campbell could hear nothing, but he clearly imagined the sound of the girl's sobs.

"It's okay, kiddo. Everything is going to be okay. Don't worry."

After a few seconds, her crying stopped. She gingerly touched her face. The cut didn't look too bad, now. It was no longer bleeding. She would have a nasty bruise, though.

She turned her attention to her left arm, poking and prodding at the point where the axe handle had struck her. She winced, but continued to test the arm. Probably not broken, Campbell thought. He had seen her use it to lift herself off the mattress. Again, though, she was going to have a nasty bruise.

"She's okay. Nothing broken. Not too badly cut."

"Have you tried . . ."

"Not yet. Give me a minute. I'm still trying to figure out what to do. Damn."

"Campbell, what is it?"

Campbell felt himself smile. Teresa had leaned toward him and put her arms around him. Although he couldn't feel it, he knew she was squeezing him with all her might.

Campbell couldn't keep the emotion from his voice, and when he spoke it was with a hoarse thickness. "I think she pretty well knows she's got a friend," he said.

Max was warmth between her arms. Max was soft fur and wet nose and safety, snuggled up against her.

Teresa breathed deeply, inhaling the smell of him. Even that reached deep inside of her and made everything seem all right.

With Max beside her, everything *was* all right.

Teresa gave the dog a final squeeze and backed away from him. He remained on his haunches, watching her.

"You saved my life, Max," she said.

He cocked his head, as if he had understood. His tail whipped across the floor once, and then was still. In the semidarkness, he seemed to glisten, as if his fur was wet. She had to be very close to him to see his eyes.

Teresa moved back to the mattress, leaned against the wall.

Her left arm was still throbbing, and where the stick had hit her it was completely numb, almost cold, as if some terrible iciness had seeped out of Ellie and into her. Her cheek, on the other hand, felt as if it was on fire, and when she touched it she could feel the raw edges of a cut. It did not seem to be bleeding too badly, however, so she kept her fingers away. Touching it could be worse than anything else.

She still was not sure what had happened, exactly. She had been sleeping when Ellie had come downstairs, but she had seen right away that the woman was mad. Mad, insane. Mad, completely gone around the bend. When she had seen the stick she had known she was going to be hurt, and hurt badly. All she could think about was her father, about how she was never going to see him again, about how she was going to die in this hole in the ground and never again see the light of day. And then Ellie had hit her, hit her hard. And then . . .

Max had saved her.

Max had moved between her and Ellie, taking one of the blows from the stick across his back, growling like some monster dog from one of those movies Aunt Elizabeth was always watching. And then he had growled some more, tail straight up, the hair on his back looking like it had exploded. Teresa had been half-unconscious, but she had seen the fear on Ellie's face.

Max was Ellie's dog, but he had turned against her.

"Max, come here," she said.

Max remained where he was, watching her.

"Max, here."

This time she held out a hand to him and he wagged his tail and waddled forward, plopping himself down right next to her. He sniffed her hand and licked her outstretched fingers.

"Thank you, Max."

He cocked his head again. As if he were waiting for her to do something. As if he wanted to *talk* to her.

"You're a strange dog, Max."

She reached out and stroked his head. He immediately lifted his right paw and waved it in front of her.

"I've got nothing to give you, boy."

He put the paw down, waiting.

Teresa shook her head. Such a strange dog. She couldn't shake the impression that he was trying hard to communicate with her.

She rubbed her arm where the stick had hit her, winced in pain despite the numbness. She held the arm up to look at it closely, but of course, in the darkness, she could see little.

Max put down his right paw and lifted up his left.

Teresa stared at him and blinked.

No, that was impossible. Dog's couldn't do that. One of their neighbors had a dog, a little Collie, and he was forever giving his paw for food, but he always gave the paw you asked for. If you stuck out your right hand, he would lift his left paw, a mirror image.

She slowly lowered her left hand to her lap, clasped her hands together. Max put his paw down. Although sitting, he had assumed an alert stance, as if waiting.

Teresa lifted her left hand.

Max lifted his left paw. His tail wagged.

"Oh, boy," Teresa said softly. Her heart had started to pound. She put down her hand. Max lowered his paw.

Coincidence. It *could* be. It *must* be.

She lifted up her right hand. Max raised his right paw. Again, his tail wagged.

Teresa laughed softly.

She lifted up both hands, held them out to the dog.

Max put down his right paw, then lowered himself to his belly. His tailed wagged, and he let out a soft growl. Nothing menacing. Just a warning. Like, *don't be so stupid, Teresa, I can't lift both paws.*

She put down her hands. Max sat up again.

"What are you trying to tell me?" she whispered.

He cocked his head, growled softly again.

"I wish you could talk, Max."

He stood up and nudged her chest with his nose. She put her

arms around him and hugged him fiercely. When he was looking directly at her she said, "I love you, Max. You're not like her, are you?"

Max whined. He lay down on his belly, snout resting on his paws. His eyes watched her.

Teresa lay down on the mattress. She stared at the dog. She smiled. His tail wagged.

"What are you trying to tell me?" she whispered again.

She closed her eyes. She breathed deeply. The numbness from her arm seemed to be spreading through her whole body. Her legs felt weak and insubstantial.

She heard Max move, but did not open her eyes. She felt him lie down right next to her, his body warm against hers. She put her arm around him, felt his hot breath on her throat.

She smiled and fell asleep.

Campbell fought out of the darkness, back into the glaring light of the hotel room. In the intensity of focusing on Teresa, he had stopped feeling Hope's proximity, her grip on his hand, but those sensations suddenly rushed back.

"What happened, Campbell?"

Campbell inhaled deeply. He reached out to touch Shadow. The dog was looking up at him. Hope was leaning close, looking worried.

"I think I managed it. I'm not sure. It's hard to tell. It was so strange. God, that's an understatement if I ever heard one! I can't explain it."

"How did you . . ."

"I tried to mimic her. When she raised her hands, I raised mine. My *paws*. Left, right, whatever she did. I couldn't think what else to do. I don't even know what I *can* do. But I think she got it. I'm not sure. I could see that she was confused, excited. She ended up going to sleep."

"She's okay, though?"

"I think so. Probably just in shock."

"Thank God."

"We've got to get her out of there, Hope. That woman is . . . she's crazy. She'll kill her. I know it. I can feel it. Teresa's not . . . doing what she wants."

Hope frowned at him. "What does she want? And how do you know what she wants?"

"I don't . . . just a feeling. Teresa's too aggressive. I don't think it's what she expected."

Hope suddenly gripped his hand. She stared at him.

"What is it?" he said.

"Something just occurred to me. About why you get visions from Shadow and not from Pointer. Remember when we were talking about how litter mates are so close? Do you think that she might have one of Shadow's litter mates?"

Campbell stared at her and felt his heart start to pound.

"Judas priest. I never even made the connection. It makes sense, doesn't it? That's got to be it!"

"What about Pointer's litter mates? Why wasn't Singer getting anything from Pointer?"

"Maybe it's the way me and Shadow are linked up. Maybe we have a *stronger* link than the one between Singer and Pointer. Maybe Shadow likes me more than Pointer likes Singer, maybe we're closer. Maybe Shadow is an oddball. Maybe his whole damned litter is oddball. I don't know, but it's something to look into. We've got to find out if Shadow had any litter mates. If he did, and she has one of them . . ."

"We can track her down. That seems too easy. Where does Miriam Technologies get their dogs?"

"I'll ask Russell."

"What if he doesn't want to tell you?"

"He'll tell me, or I'll feed him to Shadow, piece by piece."

The Oprah Winfrey show was all about kids who had turned on their parents, kids who had no respect for the people who had raised them, kids who wanted divorces from their families, and Eleanor could understand completely how the poor mothers and fathers on the show felt. She could not stop thinking about Max, about how he had turned on her. Max, in many ways, was her child. Her adopted child. She had loved him and nurtured him and given to him the deepest part of herself, and still . . . he had turned on her.

Part of her knew that Max had simply acted instinctively. It had been a mistake to allow him into the cell with Teresa and herself. The dog's natural inclination was to step into any violent situation. She knew that from when she had been a little girl. Her best friend, Tammy, had owned a cocker spaniel named Springy. Every time Eleanor and Tammy had fought, even in fun, Springy had jumped between them, barking, whining, until they had stopped. It had been the same with Max, she knew it.

And yet . . . part of her could not accept that explanation. Max had never acted that way before today. He had always been obedient. He was *her* dog, and he knew it. To turn on her like that, for whatever reason, was unacceptable. It was just one more sign that something was wrong with the dog.

Hadn't she noticed that he was acting strangely recently? He had seemed, at times, like a stranger's dog. She had felt his eyes on her, watching her, at the oddest moments, and when she turned to look at him he would quickly look away. As if he knew, understood, that he was not supposed to look at her. Not like that, anyway.

It was hard to concentrate on Oprah. Max and Teresa filled her thoughts. If Max had not interfered, Teresa might be in her arms at this moment, cuddling her, crying, needing her and loving her. She and the girl would have been brought closer. Sometimes all it took was a little push.

Or Teresa could be dead, another voice inside her said.

Teresa could be dead.

That troubled her. It was true, she had lost control in the cellar. She had meant to frighten the girl with the axe handle, had meant, at most, to whack her on the behind. Instead, she had started to beat the girl. Something inside of her had snapped, a horrible tension released, and she had wanted to . . . hurt Teresa. Yes. Admit it. She had wanted to smash the girl into smithereens.

Max had intervened. Max had saved Teresa's life. Max had stopped her from making a huge and terrible mistake. And yet . . . he had turned on her. She couldn't forget that! He had turned on her!

She made herself sit through the whole Oprah show, and only when it was over did she go back down into the cellar.

She carried the shotgun down with her, carrying it in the crook of her left arm.

Both Teresa and Max were asleep. Eleanor stood at the door of the cell and watched the pair of them. The girl was curled into a fetal position on the mattress, and Max had his back pressed into hers. Teresa's breathing was slow, deep. Max snored softly. His front paws trembled as he dreamed some dog dream.

Eleanor felt a warmth inside her for both of them. Her children.

Even with the feeble light reaching from the stairs, she could see the dark mark on Teresa's face where the axe handle had struck a glancing blow.

"I'm sorry, sweetie," she whispered.

Max heard her and raised his head. He stood slowly, moving away from Teresa. Eleanor leveled the shotgun at him.

"Come on, Max. Up. Let's go."

As quietly as she could, she slid the key into the lock and opened the door. Max stood in the middle of cell and looked at her. He looked stupid, almost confused. His tail wagged slowly.

"Come on, Max," she whispered.

He lowered his head, wagged his tail harder, and waddled toward her. At the door he halted, turned to glance back at Teresa. The girl continued to sleep, oblivious to what was transpiring. Then Max padded out of the cell and along the corridor to the stairs.

Eleanor closed the cell door, locked it.

"Sleep tight, little one," she whispered at Teresa, then followed Max.

Max was waiting for her outside, sitting in the shade at the side of the house. Eleanor walked slowly over to him. The afternoon sun was hot on her arms and neck. Max's tail wagged against the ground, making a fan shape in the dirt.

Eleanor stood over the dog. He lowered his head slightly, continuing to wag his tail.

Eleanor pumped a shell into the chamber and raised the shotgun, leveling the barrel at Max.

He whined softly. God, those eyes. They seemed so knowing, so full of intelligence.

"You turned on me," she said softly.

Max whined and went down on his belly. His front paws nearly touched her boots.

Eleanor's finger tightened on the trigger.

Max whined again.

"Oh, Max," she said.

She leaned over and crashed the stock of the gun against his head. Max yelped and scurried backward, stopping when his rump banged into the rear step. He swatted at his eyes with his paw, blinking away his pain. Flecks of blood beaded his snout.

Eleanor stood over him again, her shadow covering him, and pointed the shotgun at his face.

"Don't you ever growl at me again. Not ever. I'll kill you, Max. I'll send you to heaven. Once and for all. I will."

Max whined, pawed at his snout, smearing the beads of blood into long red streaks. Eleanor dropped the shotgun, then collapsed to the ground beside the dog. She held out her arms and surrounded him. She hugged him tightly, pressing her face into the hot fur of his throat.

His love poured into her, and hers into him.

Her tears soaked his black mane.

His blood soaked her breasts.

TWENTY-SIX

By 4:00 P.M. Campbell and Hope were headed away from the Twin Cities on I-94.

Russell had asked no questions when Campbell phoned him, did not even mention Abe Singer, or Campbell's visions. When Campbell asked where Shadow had come from, Russell told him to phone back in five minutes. When Campbell phoned back, Russell gave him a name and an address. Shadow had come from the Ajax Kennels in Marchmount, a small town near St. Cloud, three years ago. The owner's name was Grant Whitten. Hope wrote the information down, and when Campbell hung up she said, "We can be up there in a little more than an hour and a half."

Campbell hadn't argued. If worst came to worst, they could drive on to Battle Lake after Marchmount, and stay the night in their own cabins.

Half an hour out of Minneapolis, Campbell began to feel the effects of his earlier visions, the connection with the unknown dog at the other end of the line, the effort he had put into communicating with Teresa. Fatigue made his whole body ache. Hope squeezed his hand without taking her eyes from the road.

"Why don't you unhook yourself, take a nap. I'll wake you when we get there."

"Are you sure?"

"Positive."

Relieved, Campbell unhooked himself from Shadow. The dog clambered into the back seat and lay down. Campbell leaned against the door, the vibration of the engine filling him with drowsiness. Hope started to hum a tune. Her voice was smooth, melodic, beautiful. He had a clear picture of her, hands on the wheels, humming, nodding slightly. He didn't recognize the tune. Whatever it was, it reminded him of summer. He slipped into sleep to the steady thump of the wheels passing over the asphalt joints in the interstate, smooth, regular percussion behind Hope's voice.

When Campbell awoke, he was looking at the back of Hope's head. She turned to look at him, smiling, and held out a hand. It took him a moment to realize she was smiling at Shadow and not at him, but he smiled in return anyway.

"Hold that any closer and I'll bite your fingers off," he said, and growled. "How long until we get there?"

Hope jumped, startled, and stared at him. At *him* this time, not Shadow.

"Are you awake?"

"Watch the road!"

She turned back to the road, but then looked at him again, frowning. She turned to Shadow, then away again quickly. They passed a large, faded sign at the side of the road, proclaiming Marchmount the eternal home of fine food and lodging.

"They're probably talking about a burger grill and a six-room motel," Campbell said, and chuckled.

He yawned, stretching his feet out. Again, Hope was staring at him. She looked decidedly confused, almost unwell.

"Have I got something hanging out of my nose?" Campbell asked, only half joking.

"Did you just read that sign back there?"

"Sure. Now, ask me If I believed it."

Hope shook her head. "Campbell . . . you're not hooked up to Shadow."

Campbell stared at her. Stared at the back of her head through Shadow's eyes. His heart started to pound. He lifted his left hand. Saw the shock on his own face. Saw the coupler, hanging loose.

"Oh, God."

And suddenly it was as if somebody had clamped their hands over his eyes, over Shadow's eyes. His vision darkened, and the sounds of the car seemed very far away. He was suddenly dizzy, and feeling sick. He leaned over and bumped his head against the passenger window.

"Campbell, are you okay?"

"I'm going to throw up."

He heard the car slow down. The smooth hum of the blacktop suddenly changed to a clatter of gravel. Hope must have pulled onto the shoulder. When the car came to a stop, he fumbled for the door handle, opened it, and leaned out of the car. He breathed deeply, slowly. His stomach rumbled, but the imminent threat of expelling the contents of his stomach seemed to have passed.

He heard Hope's door open, footsteps coming around the car. She touched his hands, and he held on tightly.

"What are you seeing now?"

"Nothing. It's gone."

"What about before? Could it have been a dream?"

"You tell me. I woke up and you were turning around to smile at me. I mean, at Shadow. You held out your hand. I said I was going to bite off your fingers. Then we passed a sign. It said Marchmount in 15 miles, fine food and lodging."

"Incredible."

"No dream, huh?"

"I don't think so."

"Then what the hell happened?"

"Maybe the couplers were close, and you were getting some sort of, I don't know, static or something. Or maybe the seat covers were carrying the impulses from Shadow to you."

"My hand was in my lap. It wasn't that. I was connected to Shadow, but without the cable."

Hope's grip on his hand was suddenly tight, almost painful. "Like the connection between Shadow and the other dog."

"It felt just like that."

"Do you want to hook yourself up to him?"

"I don't know. This is freaking me out a bit."

"We're almost there. You could wait."

She released his hand, and then she kissed him on the mouth. Campbell pulled himself back into the car and closed the door. Hope slid into her seat, put the car in gear, and pulled back onto the road.

"Shadow," Campbell said softly.

Shadow's nose pushed over the top of the seat. Campbell gently stroked the dog's head.

"Good boy."

He found the dog's harness, then pushed the couplers together. Light flared in his head, brilliant for a moment, then subsided. He was looking at his own face. The quality of the image seemed no different than when they hadn't been connected.

He petted the dog again, pulling him close.

"What the hell are we doing to one another, huh boy?"

Shadow licked his chin, then scrambled over the back of the seat to sit beside him. The dog looked at Hope. Hope looked back, for a moment, troubled.

"You and Shadow are closer than you know," she said.

"I don't doubt it."

"I mean, way closer. Closer than Singer and Pointer, for sure. Maybe closer than any of the others who had the operation before you. That connection you've got is more than just sight. Maybe sight is part of it. But there's more. You've somehow plugged into the feedback loop between the litter mates."

"You're suddenly an expert on inter-species telepathy?"

"Maybe I'm envious."

"I guess this makes me some kind of telepathic dog freak," Campbell said, and laughed halfheartedly.

Hope's smile was cold. "I guess so," she said, but did not look at him.

On a leaning, faded, half-concealed, bullet-hole riddled sign on the way into town, Marchmount proclaimed itself the dairy capital of Minnesota. Campbell knew of at least three other towns that made the same claim, and judging by the lack of cows on all sides, and by the decrepit state of the sign, he assumed that Marchmount's claim had been overturned somewhere along the line. Like many small central Minnesota towns, Marchmount's primary reason for existence was the seasonal tourist trade, just now switching into summer gear. A nearby lake promised cool, clear water and reasonable rates at any number of waterfront cabins. Other signs promised reasonable lodging for hunters in the fall. Other signs promised great skiing come December. All in all, it was a year-round kind of place.

Campbell made himself observe the town carefully, trying to keep his thoughts away from what had happened with Shadow. If he thought about it, he was going to get frightened. Already he was asking himself, in a small, worried inner voice: *What is happening to me?* He wasn't sure he wanted to know the answer. If the same question had occurred to Shadow, the dog wasn't showing it.

Marchmount's main street was lined with small American flags on metal poles that had probably once supported parking meters. The cars now parked free. The flags were not stirring. Pedestrians walked slowly along the sidewalks. The early evening sun cast long shadows.

"Nice place," Hope said, driving slowly.

"Sure. Just like Battle Lake. I bet they have one movie theater, currently showing *National Lampoon's Vacation.*"

Hope turned her head to look for a theater, but didn't make the bet.

"You don't like these little places, do you?"

"They're fine."

"But you prefer the big city."

"Maybe, once. Not anymore."

"Because nobody knows you, out here. A great place to hide."

"*You* know me."

Of course, she had hit the nail on the head. Hiding had been his very reason for moving to Battle Lake in the first place. It had continued to be his reason for living there up until only a few weeks ago.

Hope drove all the way through the town of Marchmount and out the other side. As they left downtown, a lake appeared on their right, glimmering in the trees. Shadow was immediately drawn to it, and shoved his head out the open window beside Campbell.

Half a mile outside of town, Hope began to slow down.

"Here it is."

Campbell tugged Shadow away from the window. Hope turned off the blacktop, onto a narrow, gravel road. Great Norway Pines leaned close, blocking off the sun, and for a moment, as Shadow's eyes adjusted, all was dark for Campbell. When he could see again, they had turned off the gravel road into a clearing. Beyond a high chain-link fence stood a large white house, and beside it a long, one-story building.

"Not exactly like your place, is it?" Campbell said. "Is this the Hilton of dog kennels?"

"This is a real kennel," she said, with only a very small hint of defensiveness. "And they do breeding, too."

When the car had come to a stop, Campbell opened the door and got out. The evening was warmer than he had thought, the air still. The clear sky was like a warm blanket, resting on the tops of the trees, touching the roof of the house and the longer, lower building beside it. Although he could not actually see colors through Shadow's eyes, Campbell had begun to notice that with many objects with which he was familiar, he *perceived* color. Looking at the sky, he called it "blue," and saw it as "blue," though a few seconds of solid effort allowed him to see the washed-out white that Shadow saw.

The house and the kennel were situated at the edge of a field that rolled across the hills toward a line of trees that seemed like ominous clouds to Campbell. The field looked untended, uncultivated, but Campbell guessed that at one time this place had been a farm of some kind. Probably, like Hope, the owner had looked after dogs as a sideline. The sideline had become more profitable than the main concern, and so he had given up the one for the other.

When Hope slammed her door, a chorus of barks arose from inside the kennel. Low, gravelly shouts, and high, whining yelps, and long, eerie, keening. Shadow cocked his head, and Campbell's view was at once skewed.

"You woke the dead," he muttered.

The symphony of howls and barks continued as they passed through the gate, into the compound surrounding the long building. Shadow remained at attention just behind Campbell's left leg. He was amazed at the dog's self-control.

A sign beside the entrance warned:

WE NEED TO SEE PROOF OF YOUR
DOG'S RABIES/DISTEMPER VACCINATION.
PLEASE HAVE IT READY.

Campbell scratched Shadow behind the ear. "Guess you're out of luck, boy. You and me are both nuts."

Hope paused with her hand on the office door. "Do we have a cover story, or are we coming out with the truth?"

"I don't think I could make the truth sound convincing. Let's lie."

"Any ideas?"

"We'll wing it."

Hope shrugged and opened the door. A bell tinkled above their heads, and a buzzer sounded from somewhere deep within the building. It kept buzzing until the door had closed behind them. The office consisted of a small counter, a cash register, and a wall full of pamphlets about a variety of canine problems, from heartworm to tooth decay. Another door behind the desk had a sign that read:

DOGS PAST THIS POINT MUST BE LEASHED

The intensity of the howling from within the building had increased. It quickly grew so loud that Campbell began to feel embarrassed. Their arrival was most assuredly the cause of the disturbance. When the door behind the desk opened, the noise level jumped dramatically, and Campbell, who had been vaguely studying the wall of pamphlets, started.

When he turned around he saw that a young woman was standing behind the desk, smiling. He guessed her age at late teens, perhaps early twenties, in jeans and a white T-shirt, hair cut short and swept off her forehead. She was so slim she reminded him of Mia Farrow.

When the door finished closing the sound of the dogs dropped again, and after a few moments actually began to diminish.

"Don't mind them. They're always like this when a car arrives. They all think they're going home." She looked down at Shadow, a slight frown on her face now. "Are you dropping him off?" She looked down at an appointment register on the desk. "I don't have anyone listed."

"We're not dropping him off," Campbell said. "Just looking for a little help."

She looked a little confused. Her smile wavered, but did not disappear.

"Okay, I'll try."

"My name is Campbell Knight. This is Hope Matheson. We're from Miriam Technologies, in Minneapolis," Campbell said, reaching for the name of the Kennel owner. "I thought you might have recognized Shadow. We purchased him from you, about three years ago. You must be Grant's daughter."

Her smile brightened a little. "That's right. I'm Leslie. Mom and dad aren't here right now. Do you need to talk to them?"

"I'd hoped to. But we don't have much time to spend here, I'm afraid. I'm sure you'll be able to help us."

He tried to smile disarmingly, but wasn't sure how well he was doing. When Hope glanced at him, she looked quickly away.

"I'll try," Leslie said. "Is it about the dog?"

"Not him in particular," Hope said. "We're doing some research into Shadow's litter. We've been very impressed with his adaptability to the experiment. There have been, however, a number of developmental anomalies, nothing serious, nothing that would jeopardize the program, but we'd certainly like to track down and have a look at his siblings, to determine if they're experiencing the same abnormalities."

Campbell had to stop himself from turning to stare at her. She had rattled off her spiel as if she actually knew what she was talking about. And Leslie Whitten was looking a little distraught.

"Abnormalities?" the girl asked.

"Nothing serious, as I said. We'd just like to track down his siblings. We were hoping you'd be able to help us with that. It's possible we'll make a sizable investment in this breed, especially considering how successful Shadow has been in adapting to experimental protocol, but we'd like to be sure."

"Oh, sure. So, you want to know about the other pups from his litter. Like, where they went, you mean? Who bought them?"

"Well, that would certainly be a big help," Hope said.

Definitely a teenager, Campbell decided, judging by her body language, and the ease with which she'd been bamboozled. He still couldn't get over Hopes facility for lying. It was incredible.

"You know, my dad usually handles that sort of thing. He'll be back later, if you could wait."

Campbell turned to Hope, though he continued to look at Leslie through Shadow's eyes.

"I'm afraid this is our only window of opportunity," Hope said, voice heavy with disappointment. "Well, I guess we'll finish with our other suppliers, and, I suppose, if we get a chance at a later date, we'll look at Ajax again. Thank you, Leslie. Please let your father know I've dropped by."

Campbell turned at Hope's urging, but stopped at the door when Leslie called for their attention. She looked small, vulnerable, and easily manipulated, standing there behind the counter. Campbell felt terribly guilty.

"I suppose I could just check your file. If the sale is listed there, I should be able to trace it back to the sire and the dame. I could try, anyway."

"That would be wonderful," Hope said.

Shadow was looking up at her, and Campbell was astounded by how calm she looked. She looked down at Shadow and grinned.

"This shouldn't take too long," Leslie said.

"Take your time," Campbell said, shaking his head at Hope.

Campbell stood back with Shadow as Hope and Leslie bent over a file on the counter. Hope kept pushing a strand of hair away from her eyes as she studied the file, and Campbell felt a knot in his throat as he watched her.

"There were nine pups born to Caledonia, with Deeside as the sire. Your company took one. Were you interested in Caledonia and Deeside's other litters? I think we paired them four or five times."

"Just this litter," Campbell said.

Leslie nodded without looking up. "Okay, well, then. Three of the nine were disposed of right off the bat."

"Disposed of?" Hope asked.

"They were runts, and Caledonia was a bit sick, anyway. So that left six. Numbers four and five went to the Hanson Pharmaceutical Laboratory in St. Cloud, but I know that both of them are dead."

"How do you know that?" Campbell asked.

"We dispose of all their animal carcasses," she said matter of factly. "And it says so right here. So, that leaves four. Your company took number six. See, here? That was Shadow. The remaining three were sold to private purchasers. Do you want to know who they were?"

"That would be very helpful," Hope said, smiling encouragement.

"Number seven was purchased by Mr. David Anderson, of Melrose. Number eight was purchased by Ms. Bettie Cormier, of Morris. And number nine was purchased by Mrs. Willa Ojakan, of Deer Creek."

"Why are all of them so far afield?" Hope asked.

"We advertise in a lot of farm papers," Leslie said. "Some people will come a long way for the right breed. Would you like the addresses?"

"That would be excellent," Hope said.

"Do you know if the dogs are still alive?" Campbell asked.

Leslie shook her head, reaching for another file. "You'd have to ask the people who bought them."

Hope squeezed Campbell's hand, and he squeezed back. Three names and addresses, he thought.

Could it really be that simple?

And then he thought: it could be one of them. Any one of them. The woman from the visions.

By the time they left Ajax Kennels, Campbell's heart was pounding and his forehead was cold with sweat.

"Are you all right?"

"Just worried."

"We'll get to the bottom of this, Campbell."

Leslie stood at the gate and waved to them as they pulled away. Campbell waved back.

"We could make Melrose in an hour," Hope said. "It's only six."

"I'm bushed," Campbell said, and felt sick for the lie. He

was scared, that was all. "Let's just get a motel. We'll start tomorrow. We could do them all in one day."

"Whatever you want."

They drove toward Marchmount. Campbell let his forehead rest against the window.

"You know, Deer Creek is between Battle Lake and Godfrey," Hope said quietly.

"I know," Campbell said, but did not look at her.

TWENTY-SEVEN

Hope found a motel overlooking the lake, just outside of Marchmount. As Campbell had earlier speculated, the Bayview was comprised of six rooms, three each on either side of a dilapidated office. Campbell waited in the car while Hope went inside to register. The woman at the counter was, Hope guessed, in her early forties, tanned, slim, with long dark hair tied loosely behind her back. A cigarette burned in the ashtray beside her right hand, filling the office with gray haze. Her welcome was perfunctory, and she asked no questions when Hope signed her name in the register, though she did look past Hope to study the car outside. On the wall behind her was a sign that said, "SORRY, NO PETS."

"Uh oh, we've got a dog," Hope said, smiling nervously.

The woman pursed her lips. "So long as he does his business outside, and doesn't sleep on the bed." She handed Hope a key for room six, at the east end of the building.

"I'll make sure of it."

The place was empty. They weren't going to be turned away just because of a dog. Not yet, anyway. In August, perhaps. She turned to leave and saw the newspaper by the phone. A *Minneapolis Star/Tribune*. Today's. It looked disheveled, previously read.

"Could I buy this?"

"Just take it."

Hope smiled her thanks, picked up the paper, and went back to the car. Campbell was leaning against the window. He sat up straight as she closed the door, but said nothing. Shadow, sitting beside him, didn't even look at her. She put the car in gear and drove up to their room.

It was small, neat, dim, old-fashioned. The television worked on only two channels, and neither with particularly good reception. The bed was a double, but a small one. The walls were dark wood panel, hung every few feet with a variety of department store prints. Lake scenes, forest scenes, harbor scenes.

Campbell lay down on the bed. Shadow lay down beside him.

"God, I'm tired," he said.

"Hungry?"

"Famished."

"Sit tight. I'll be back in a few minutes."

She went back out to the car and drove slowly downtown. She found a restaurant adjacent to a Mobil station and picked up four cheeseburgers, two orders of fries, and two vanilla milk shakes. When she got back to the motel, she found Campbell asleep on the bed, Shadow unhooked and lying against the wall. She put one of the cheeseburgers, one of the fries, and one of the milk shakes on the table beside Campbell, but did not wake him.

When she sat down in the chair by the window, Shadow walked over to her, tail wagging slowly. She fed him two of the cheeseburgers. He bolted the food, then lay down at her feet with his snout on his paws. She gently stroked his flank with her toes as she ate. After she had finished, she sipped the milk shake and read the newspaper.

The Teresa Dawson story had moved to page three. Police and hundreds of volunteers continued to search the Godfrey area, but a police spokesman confirmed that they had little hope of finding the girl. New information had come out. A green, or light blue pickup truck had been seen in the area the day of Teresa's disappearance, and investigators were now looking at this as their best and only clue, but so far it had led them nowhere. Teresa Dawson had disappeared from the face of the earth.

One of the photographs showed the girl's father. His face was haunted, his eyes lost. Hope could almost feel his pain. How often had he lain awake in bed at night, thinking, half dreaming, reluctantly, of the predators who roamed the world in human skin, the monsters who lifted children out of their everyday lives and dropped them into hell, leaving, in the end, nothing but shattered, soulless bundles of broken skin. How often had he lulled himself to sleep thinking, *not my daughter, not Teresa, not here.* And yet here he was, facing it at last, the nightmare come true, his child abducted by . . . a shadow. A monster. Facing God only knew what kind of fate. She felt his pain, his despair, and she could not stop herself from trembling.

She touched the photograph gently, afraid, almost, to disturb the image of the tormented man. "We're going to bring her back," she whispered. "Don't give up."

She dropped the paper to the floor, leaned back in the chair, and closed her eyes. She must have drifted off, because when she opened her eyes again the room was completely dark. The sun had set, and rain was pattering against the window. She reached for the lamp beside her and turned it on.

Campbell was still asleep, on his back, left arm hanging off the bed, snoring softly. The cheeseburger, fries, and milk shake were untouched. Shadow had returned to his position against the wall. The dog was trembling in his sleep, dreaming, paws twitching, lips lifting spasmodically off his teeth.

Shadow, dreaming, lifted his left paw and swatted at his snout, snorting softly. On the bed, Campbell lifted his left hand and swatted at his nose, snorting softly. Shadow growled quietly, then whined, and rolled to his other side, facing the wall. On the bed, Campbell groaned, a deep, throaty sound, and rolled over. He made a small, high sound, and then started to snore again.

Hope stared at them. She felt suddenly cold, alone, and frightened. The realization hit her that she understood nothing of what was happening here, absolutely nothing. She was involved in something so far beyond her comprehension that she might as well be a child in a nuclear physics laboratory. And vulnerable. She felt very vulnerable.

Although Campbell was now silent, she could not find the strength to get into bed beside him. Instead, she turned out the light, lay her head against the back of the chair, and closed her eyes.

They checked out of the Bayview Motel at 7:00 A.M. and stopped at a coffee-shop in St. Cloud for breakfast. Afterwards, they drove toward Melrose in what, to Campbell, felt like uncomfortable silence. He felt as if, though he couldn't explain why he felt it, he and Hope had argued during the night. Argued bitterly.

Clouds now clogged the sky. The world was crushed beneath their dark weight. Campbell seemed to have lost all sense of depth of field; the freeway looked as if it disappeared into the horizon only a few yards in front of the car, the lights rushing toward them as if they had erupted from some invisible veil. The feeling of enclosure was intensified by the steady rain that had been falling since they left the motel. The world shimmered and dripped like an old black and white photograph dipped into acid.

After half an hour on the freeway he leaned his head against the window and slept. Shadow had already given in, lying on the seat between him and Hope. Campbell let the hum of the engine and the steady drum of the tires along the concrete soothe his nerves that somehow felt raw. Hope would wake him when they arrived.

In fact, Campbell awoke without help.

He awoke to silence and darkness, his stomach knotted with fear.

A vision. Another vision.

Only it wasn't.

His left hand slapped down on Shadow's back and the dog opened his eyes and sat up. He was still in the car, with Hope. She had pulled to the side of the road, and was now looking through the windshield with worried, somber eyes. He had the horrible feeling that he'd somehow unhooked himself from Shadow, and that he was seeing everything now through some bizarre, supernatural mind-connect.

He whispered hoarsely, "What happened?"

"Nothing. We're here."

Thank God. Still connected.

"Shadow, front."

Campbell peered through the windshield, but the rain was still falling, and his view was as through deep water.

"This is Melrose?"

"We passed through the town a couple of miles back. But this is the address."

"I can't see anything."

"Sorry. Hold on."

Hope turned on the wipers. The rain cleared away in two moaning swipes. He was looking at a small farmhouse, nestled on the edge of a rolling, brown field. A windbreak of ash and maple trees stretched from the road, around the house. It looked like a toy farm to Campbell, a little plastic model, minuscule and fragile beneath the sky.

"Why are we stopped?"

"I started thinking, what if this is the one?"

He heard the worry in her voice.

"I didn't think of that."

"Now might be a good time start. Do we just march right up there and knock on the door?"

Campbell took a deep breath, held it, let it out. There seemed to be a hell of a lot he hadn't considered.

"Do you have any feelings about it?" Hope asked.

"I'm probably ten times more scared than you are."

"No, I mean, does this place feel right? Are you getting any . . . whatever it is that you get? *Is* this the place?"

He studied the farm house, the trees, the fields. He continued to feel uneasy, but there was no recognition.

"I can't tell. I have a feeling that wherever Teresa is, it's a

farm. The inside of her house felt . . . small. Like our cabins.
And there were trees outside. It seemed like the country. But . . .
I just don't . . ."

"We could pretend we're lost and ask for directions. When
we get closer, you should be able to tell, right?"

"I don't know. I've never done this before. Maybe I won't
recognize anything. Unless the dog is there."

"What if you tried connecting with it?"

Campbell took another deep breath. He shook his head. "I'm
too nervous. I can't concentrate."

"Then I guess we knock on the door."

"What's she going to do, shoot us?" He had hardly spoken
the words when he flashed on the memory of the boy in the
shallow grave, shotgun pointing at him.

"It could be a start."

He didn't get a chance to respond to that. Hope put the car
in gear and pulled back onto the road. She drove a hundred
yards or so, then turned right down a gravel road. To Campbell's
left the ash windbreak became a dark wall against which Hope's
face was a pale silhouette. Shadow continued to stare out the
windshield, at the house. Campbell could feel the dog's tension,
expectancy, and the knot in his own stomach became tighter as
they approached.

"There's a truck parked at the side of the house," Hope said.

Campbell saw it. Late model GMC.

"She has a truck."

"Yes, but *that* truck?"

"I can't tell."

As they drew closer to the house, Campbell could see lights
glowing within. "Somebody is definitely home."

Hope came to a stop behind the truck. Their headlights glared
off the rain-sheen on the truck's gate. Hope turned them off, but
kept the wipers slowly moving. The glow from the house's windows looked warm and welcoming, and yet the cold in Campbell's stomach seemed to radiate throughout his whole body.

"What now?" Hope said.

"One of us should knock on the door."

"This was your idea."

"Thanks." This wasn't nearly as easy as he had anticipated. His grip on the door handle was almost painful. He inhaled deeply, held it, let it out. "We'll both go."

Hope nodded. "All right."

Without another word she opened her door and got out. She pulled up the hood of her thin jacket, held the collar closed with one hand. Campbell came around the car. The rain was a hundred cold fingers tapping on his face, sounding like a distant crowd talking, whispering, filling the world with muddled voices. Through Shadow's eyes, the rain itself was invisible. He glimpsed occasional streaks, a quick dark line traversing the space directly in front of his face.

Hope took his right hand and they started to walk toward the house. The ground beneath their feet was gravel, solid. Each step sounded crisp in the humid air.

"What if this is the place?" Hope whispered.

"We ask for directions, go back to the car, and drive the hell away and call the cops the first chance we get."

"She won't recognize you?"

"She's never seen me, Hope. I've never really seen her, either. Unless I see her dog, I doubt I'd recognize her."

But he knew that wasn't true. If he saw her, the woman, the dark shape, he'd know it. He'd feel it in his gut. His whole body and soul would react, pulling away from something hot, something dirty, something evil. But he didn't say anything.

As they passed the front window a shape moved inside the house, a shadow behind the glass. Campbell tightened his grip on Shadows harness, gritting his teeth. At the door, Hope looked at him, nodded as if to convince herself they were doing the right thing, and rapped her knuckles on the wood.

Campbell didn't breathe. He listened, through the hiss of the rain, through the pounding of his own heart, the rush of blood through his veins, waiting for the sound of the door handle turning. When the door started to open he let out his breath with a short cough. Warm air reached out to engulf him. He found himself looking up at a silhouette framed in the brilliant, open door.

"Yes?"

A female voice. Campbell's skin crawled. "We . . ."

Before he could speak, another shape filled the doorway behind the woman. Larger, darker.

"What is it, Anne?"

"I don't know yet."

"Can we help you?"

The man had now stepped in front of the woman, and though Campbell knew he probably wasn't much taller than himself, he felt himself towered over. Campbell couldn't find his voice.

"Actually," Hope said, "we're a bit lost. We were wondering if you could tell us how to get to the exit for I-94."

"You're a bit out of the way, aren't you?"

"I suppose so. In the rain and everything, I must have missed a sign."

"Coming from Petersville?"

"That's right."

"Well, you're on the right track, then. Turn right at the road, keep going about three miles, you'll come to the overpass."

"Oh, good. Thank you very much. Sorry to disturb you."

Campbell still hadn't found his voice. Although he now knew this wasn't the place he'd been dreading, his heart still felt gripped by fear. When the man lowered himself, kneeling, Campbell almost cried out.

"Nice dog. We used to have a dog like this. Doesn't this look like Blackie, Annie? What's his name?"

"Shadow."

Campbell found himself looking into a lined, weather-worn face, hard but friendly.

"Poor Blackie. Got hit by a truck on the road last year. He was a good dog. Wasn't he, Annie?"

Since her original greeting, Annie hadn't said anything. She didn't say anything now.

"I'm sorry," Campbell said.

Hope took his arm and guided him away from the door. "Thanks for the help," she said.

Once they were back in the car, Campbell started to shake. He leaned against the dashboard, wiped his face with a sleeve.

"Well, that wasn't so hard," Hope said.

"Dead," Campbell said, more for himself than for Hope. "Blackie's dead. He was a good dog."

Hope put the car in gear and started driving. When they hit the road, Campbell started to laugh. But it was a nervous reflex only, and to his own ears the sound was brittle, close to breaking.

The rain thinned and the sky cleared over the next half hour. In Alexandria, they stopped at a grocery store and picked up bread, pastrami, lettuce, tomatoes, a square of Swiss cheese, a quart of milk, and two cans of dog food, then drove another ten minutes until they hit a rest stop. The sky was a patchwork of blue and unraveling, fluffy clouds.

Hope prepared their lunch. Campbell sat at the picnic table, Shadow at his feet. When Hope handed him a sandwich, Campbell unhooked himself from Shadow and allowed the dog to eat his own meal.

"We'll be in Morris in another hour," Hope said. "We could stop at the cabins after that, clean up a bit, and then make Deer Creek sometime in the evening."

Campbell bit into his sandwich and did not respond. He hadn't realized how hungry he was. His stomach growled even as he chewed.

"Does that sound okay?" Hope asked.

"I suppose."

"You don't sound very enthusiastic."

"I'm not. I don't like this."

"Can you think of a better way?"

"No, but that doesn't mean I have to like it."

He feared for a few seconds that he had upset her, but then her hand found his and squeezed. "We're doing the right thing."

"I know."

"One down, two to go."

"Don't remind me, please."

"Are you a bit more relaxed now? Could you try connecting with the other dog?"

Campbell chewed, swallowed. He inhaled deeply. "Just let me finish my sandwich."

She squeezed his hand again. "Whenever you like. I just thought, if you could get a better idea of what we're looking for, we'd be at an advantage when we found it. At least we wouldn't be surprised."

Campbell nodded, and realized with dismay that his sandwich was finished. He brushed the crumbs off his fingers. Shadow came closer and shoved a cold snout into his hands.

"Another one?" Hope offered.

Campbell shook his head. "No, thanks." No more excuses.

He held the dog's harness and reconnected the cable. Light flared, and he found himself looking at Hope. The sun was to her left, and her face looked serene, beautiful.

"Hi, stranger," she said.

"Hi yourself."

She kissed him on the mouth. "Any time you're ready."

Campbell gripped Shadow's harness with both hands. "Shadow, look," he whispered.

The dog looked into his face, and Campbell found himself staring at his own dark glasses. So enigmatic. Anything might remain concealed behind that glass. Darkness. Deception. Betrayal. Evil. Me.

He inhaled deeply, losing himself in the dog's sight. Darkness hovered at the edge of everything Shadow saw, as if he were standing at the intersection of a number of corridors. The corridor directly ahead was the real world, normal sight. But the corridors to right or left, those tantalizing darknesses, were mysteries. Just turn a corner, Campbell thought. Turn a corner, choose a poison.

But when it happened, it wasn't like that at all. It was as if he had backed into a dark tunnel. Sight receded, and the darkness of the walls closed in, smothered him, swallowed him, blinded him. Then the darkness took on texture, like wool held next to the eyes, and then light sprang from everywhere.

Campbell exhaled slowly.

"I'm there," he said hoarsely.

"I'm right with you. Don't be frightened."

"I'm not frightened."

Liar!

He was lying on a floor. A linoleum floor, the pattern not quite checkered, but consisting of darker and lighter flowers arranged in a coiling double helix, a veritable DNA flower pattern, but probably older than the discovery of DNA itself, Campbell thought. Directly in front of him were the legs of a table, thin and spindly. Beyond the table he could see an old oven, cabinets painted a dark color. Green, he thought, but was not certain.

"I'm in the kitchen," he whispered.

"Is she nearby?"

He knew without asking that *she* meant the woman, the dark figure, the nightmare. He tried to look around, but realized that in the period between the last vision and this one, he had forgotten how to control the dog on the other end.

Be that dog, he thought.

He concentrated on the vision, the feel of it, the textures around him, the coiling flower pattern beneath him, the distant contrasting colors of oven and cupboards.

He turned his head. His view changed.

"Okay," he said softly. "It's working."

He inhaled deeply, sighed. The kitchen was empty.

He stood up. He could see some dishes on top of the table. A coffee mug. A magazine.

"She's been around, but not right now."

He walked around the kitchen, stopping at the back door. A shotgun was leaning against the wall by a coat rack. He bent close to it, then backed away, suddenly frightened.

"Is there a window you can see out of? Are there any features you could recognize as we approached?"

There was a window in the kitchen, but too high for him to see through. He walked around the table again, to the doorway that led into the hall. There was a carpet here, a dark color, probably brown. He looked to his right and saw a closed door. Her bedroom. Yes. He remembered that.

"Campbell, what's wrong?"

"Nothing. Just remembering."

"You're shaking."

"I'm okay."

He turned away from the bedroom and moved down the hall. No sign of *her* yet. He entered the living room and paused to get his bearings.

"It's old-fashioned," he said. "The layout. Crowded, you know. Old furniture, but not antiques. There's a mantle with a bunch of pictures on it, but I can't . . ."

He moved closer, but as he drew up to the mantel his angle of view was too steep, and the pictures above were merely glares of light. Even when he jumped up, leaning on the bricks with his hands . . . paws . . . he could see nothing.

"Wedding pictures, maybe. I can't tell. Shit."

He lowered himself, and padded around the room. A large window glowed behind the sofa. He moved toward it, jumped up onto the sofa.

"I'm at a window. It's got a sheer curtain. Just hold on."

He nudged the curtain, lifting it with his nose, pushing close to the glass. The sheer veil lifted, fell behind him.

"Did it. I can see outside. Its sunny here. I'm looking at a yard. I can see a wooden fence, with barbed wire I think, and beyond it a field. It's cultivated. There are trees to my right, and a road. It looks deeply rutted, like mud. I think I'm looking toward the *rear* of the property. Yeah, definitely. I can see the shape of a porch at the back. There's an entrance behind it, I remember that, to the cellar. That's where Teresa is. I can't see a truck."

He felt Hope's grip on his hand tighten. "Anything, Campbell. Anything that would help us recognize the place."

"Just hold on. Okay. Over by the trees. It looks like a foundation of some sort. Wooden planks or beams. I bet a barn stood there at one point. It has been torn down, though. Behind it, there's a steel tower. I can't tell how high, exactly. I'd say thirty feet, maybe. It looks like there's a wind generator at the top. A really old one. It doesn't look in good shape. One of the prop blades is bent. I can't see anything else. Not from this window, anyway. I'll look around."

He pulled away from the window, hopped off the sofa. As he moved around the coffee table by the sofa, he saw a newspaper on top. He stopped and his heart raced.

"Judas Priest, Hope. There's a newspaper on top of the coffee table. If I can see the name of it, it'll tell us where she is."

"Can you see it?"

"I have to hop up. I can't . . ."

A shadow passed across the table, and Campbell felt his stomach knot. He backed away from the table. She came from his left, towering over him. He saw boots, jeans, muddy stains, and then two large, raw looking hands.

Her face, he thought. Look at her face.

But when he looked up all he saw was shadow, darkness, as if she had purposely concealed herself.

"Campbell, what is it?"

"It's her!"

The hand came out of nowhere, crashed into his face. Campbell cried out.

He pulled away from the darkness, gasping in pain, reaching for the light that seemed to want to run away from him. He cried out again, then blinked against sunlight, raised a hand to shield his eyes. He heard Shadow whine, and then saw Hope reaching for him.

"Are you all right?"

"She hit me. *I felt it.*"

He lifted a hand to his nose. Pain hovered like some malignant spirit, just beneath the surface of his skin, and yet when he touched his face he felt nothing.

"It felt so real."

He shuddered. Hope held him tightly, but still he shuddered.

"Something is happening to me," he said hoarsely, not even sure what he meant.

He felt dizzy, almost dislocated. Here, right now, felt no more real than what he had been experiencing only moments earlier.

"It's okay now, Campbell. It's okay."

He felt a low rumble begin in his throat, but clamped down on it before it could emerge as a sound. A growl.

"I'm changing," he said. "It's changing me."

"Shhh," Hope said, and held him tight.

TWENTY-EIGHT

It was just after 2:00 P.M. when they passed Fergus Falls on the way to Morris, and Campbell's first instinct was to drive straight through to Battle Lake, to forget their strange, frightening search for the phantom dog of his visions, but when he looked at Hope she was staring straight ahead, chin slightly lowered, lips clasped tightly, as if she were walking into a stiff wind, implacable, determined. He pulled Shadow away from her and looked out the window instead. She made him feel inadequate. Why didn't he feel that determined, that sure?

The sky had completely cleared now. The sun was high and bright, warm against his arms and legs through the car's windows. The promise of a hot summer hung in the air. Blue skies, sunny afternoons, no cares in the world. But when he thought about Teresa Dawson in her dark prison, all thoughts of summer fled. How could he possibly enjoy summer, his new sight, his new life, with the knowledge of Teresa Dawson always before him? It wasn't fair! Shadow had given him far more than sight. Shadow had burdened him with impossible, unbearable obligations.

As they approached Morris, Campbell sat straighter in the seat, his uneasiness and discomfort growing by the minute. Morris and its surrounding countryside were enough like Battle Lake to make him feel perfectly at home. That was the trouble. He knew he was moving closer and closer to the source of the nightmare that was consuming him, and at the same time he was moving closer and closer to home. This darkness, this evil, was not somewhere far away, at the end of the rainbow, over the horizon. It was right here, right where he lived, nearby. He had been living beside it all along, and had not realized it.

"Here it is," Hope said quietly as she slowed to enter Morris. "We're looking for 22nd Street."

"This place isn't big enough to have a 22nd street."

"It will be outside of town."

It took only a minute to drive from one end of Morris to the other. The main street was quiet. They passed only one other car, driving slowly in the opposite direction. A handful of pedestrians strolled on the sidewalks, pausing to look in storefronts that seemed, to Campbell, to be almost festive. Like Battle Lake, Morris was gearing up for the flood of summer residents. Once they had passed through the town proper, Hope maintained her low speed, carefully watching for street signs. They passed a Mobil station. They passed a restaurant in a large, open parking lot, surrounded by pickup trucks, dusty cars, even a police cruiser. Then there were a lot of trees.

"Here it is," Hope said, slowing the car to a stop on the shoulder.

She looked down a gravel road, inhaled deeply, then turned to Campbell. "Are you ready?"

"No, but go ahead."

She smiled, nodded, and put the car in gear. She shoulder checked, then crossed the highway. Gravel rattled against the undercarriage, and a plume of dust rose behind them. Large fir trees crowded the road, but with the sun directly overhead there were no shadows. The homes here were a mixture of new and old, large and small, hidden in large nests of trees, widely spaced, private. Some had old cars and appliances surrounding them like sentinels, some looked as well-groomed as any upscale city property.

When Hope brought the car to a stop, Campbell immediately opened the door and stepped out. The air was far more humid than he had expected, and immediately sweat popped out on his forehead and back. He breathed deeply of the heavy air, pulled

Shadow to the front of the car. The surrounding trees towered over him. The sky looked like a mirror. From here, he could not see the house within the trees. But he *felt* it, like a magnet pulling him.

Hope came up beside him and touched his arm. "Something?"

"I don't know. Everything seems familiar. I don't know."

He suddenly felt very cold, and a tremor passed through him. Hope's grip on his arm tightened.

"Is this the place?"

"I don't know, I said."

He heard his own voice as if from a distance. He felt dizzy, close to being nauseated.

"It's not a farm," Hope said. "You said it was a farm."

"I could be wrong. I can't tell. I just know that I feel like I've been here. But I *know* I haven't. Not me, anyway. Not in this life."

Hope took a deep breath. "Well, we're here. Let's just check it out. If we see anything you recognize, we'll go back and get the police."

Campbell nodded, his mouth too dry to speak. Hope pulled him across the road, and he let her lead, his feet and legs feeling stiff, frozen, reluctant. The trees along the drive leading up to the house were mostly oak and elm, their branches entwining above, blocking the sunlight. It was cool and moist as they walked, almost cavelike. Campbell's heart pounded in his chest like a drum.

When the house appeared, Campbell froze, feet and legs stiffening.

"Is this it?"

"No, it's . . ."

The feeling of having been here intensified. His legs suddenly felt weak, and he leaned against Hope for support. Her hands gripped him tightly.

He *had* been here. But not in his visions. In dreams. Recent dreams.

"Dead," he said, voice hoarse.

"What?"

Hope twisted him around to face her. Even Shadow looked up at her, and Campbell could see that she was terrified.

"What did you mean?"

"I'm sorry."

A cry came from the house.

Hope pulled him sharply. "Campbell, let's go!"

"No."

The cry came again. A child's voice. And suddenly a shape was running toward them along the driveway. A boy. Maybe 12 years old. Behind the boy, a woman was kneeling in a patch of dirt by the corner of the house, working with a potted plant. Immediately she stopped what she was doing, picked up a small bundle beside her, and ran after the boy.

"Campbell?" Hope whispered, voice urgent.

"It's not her," he said.

"Then what were you talking about?"

The boy reached them, and fell immediately to his knees before Shadow, reaching out hands to hold the dog.

"Hi, boy!"

Campbell stopped himself from pulling back as the boy's face pushed close to Shadow's. The joy in the child's face was clearly evident. He could feel Shadow's tail wagging against his leg. The dog leaned closer to the boy, licking at his face.

The woman came up quickly behind the boy. The bundle in her arms was a baby. The woman was dressed in jeans and T-shirt, her hair cut very short, dark. Her hands were in gardening gloves, covered in dirt.

"Jack, leave the dog alone!"

"But look, mom, he's just like Sandy, except he's a boy!"

The woman, Campbell saw, recognized that Shadow was a guide dog, and with a free hand she tried to pull the boy away.

"It's okay," Campbell said. "Let him pet the dog."

"I'm sorry. We had a dog just like that."

Up to now, Hope's grip on Campbell's arm had been tight to the point of being painful, but it suddenly relaxed.

"Yes, that's why we're here," Campbell said.

The woman frowned. "Sandy?"

"We were directed to you by the Ajax Kennels. Your dog is from the same litter as Shadow, and we're trying to track down all of the pups from the litter."

"Is there something wrong?"

"No, nothing like that. We're interested in seeing how they've developed. We've had success with this type of dog in our program, and we were considering using another litter from the same sire and dame, and we wanted to find out how the other pups had done."

"I'm so sorry. I wish you had phoned before driving up here. Sandy died back in April. It was an accident. My husband . . . it was right about here, actually. The dog was so excited, and she never seemed to realize the danger of cars, and . . . Dennis felt so bad."

Jack was hugging Shadow now, face pressed tightly to the dog's mane.

"I'm sorry to hear that," Campbell said.

"Sandy was a very good dog, though, if that's what you're wondering. She was so good with Jack, and with Terry. We were worried at first, with the baby, but Sandy just took right to her. She loved children. Older kids, too, even when they were rough. Your dog looks just like Sandy. It's amazing."

Jack released Shadow and looked up at his mother. "Can we get another one, Mom? Just like Sandy?"

She smiled at Hope, then turned curious eyes back to Campbell, fascinated and repelled at the same time by his blindness.

"If there's going to be another litter, we'd certainly be interested," she said.

"You'd have to talk to the kennel," Campbell said. "Thanks for talking to us. We won't take any more of your time."

The woman smiled wistfully. Jack followed them as they

walked back along the drive to the car, then stood on the road and waved as they drove away.

When they were back on the highway, Hope asked, "What was that all about?"

"I think Shadow must have had some sort of connection with Sandy. I felt like I'd been there. I must have dreamed about it. Even recently. I didn't know when it was. But when I saw the place . . . God, it was so strange."

He reached out and petted Shadow gently. The dog looked at him, licked his hand.

"This is one bad luck litter," Hope said. "They all died."

"Which leaves just one," Campbell said, feeling hollow.

"Just one," Hope said softly, not looking at him, her voice echoing his fear.

She started the car, backed up a little, then made a tight U-turn. They started back along the road toward the highway.

The morning of hard work, cutting wood, loading it onto the truck, hauling it back to the house and stacking it in back, had brought Eleanor close to a resolve she had not felt in some time. Her confrontation with Max when she had broken for lunch had been the impetus to make the final decision.

She had returned to the house, tired, aching, to find the dog poking around in the living room as if he were actually looking for something. She had stood in the hallway, out of sight, watching as he had jumped up on the sofa, lifted the curtains with his nose to peer outside. She had held her breath as he had hopped down, walked around the coffee table, eyeing the newspaper on top.

She had never seen Max act so strangely. At least, not until recently. All of his behavior this past couple of weeks had been of the strange variety. His quiet padding around the house at night; the way he stared at her with his big black eyes, as if he were trying to tell her something; and now this, this skulking, sneaking around behind her back, as if he were . . . what?

She did not know *what,* exactly.

But she knew the feeling she had. She felt as if he were spying on her. As if he were looking through her things, seeking something very private.

She had flown into a rage and had beaten him badly, and afterwards, as he lay whining on the floor by the sofa, she had cradled his head in her arms and held him tightly.

It was all going wrong.

She had never imagined it could go so wrong.

Life was not fair. It had treated her very badly. First, it had taken Frank from her, leaving her alone with their son. And then, pushing its cruelty to new heights, it had taken Luke from her.

Since then it had promised much, so much. First, in Max, who had filled the place in her life that Luke had left so empty, at least for a little while. Until she had come to realize that there were children, real children, who needed love, who were deserving of love, and who were capable of loving her back. Ruth Burns had been the first. Ruth, so pretty, so frail, so frightened. Her fear had kept her from love, and in the end Eleanor had no choice but to send her to God's arms, the bosom of the one true love. And then Jesse Hampton, sweet Jesse, who had been so much like Luke in so many ways, but who had built a wall around himself and had refused to accept her love. For him, too, had come the final comfort of God's embrace, the only place in the universe where love might reach him.

But with Teresa, she had felt it would be different. Teresa had seemed like a gift from God. As if Love itself had been sent to earth.

How could she have been so wrong? In scant days, Teresa had revealed herself to be so far removed from love that she might even be its enemy. How could she have been so deceived?

And now Max, who had been the one constant in her life since Frank and Luke, Max who gave his love unconditionally, who accepted her love gratefully, was turning on her, drawn by Teresa, poisoned by the girl.

It was almost too much to bear.

As she sat by the sofa, stroking Max's angular head, feeling the pulse of his heart beneath his coat, she had prayed to God for guidance.

What was she doing wrong?

What should she do next?

She had so much love to give!

If only Luke had lived, he would have been the recipient of her love for all his life. But he had left her, left her full to bursting with love.

Max whimpered under her fingers.

Was it possible she had been wrong from the start? Was it possible that God wanted her to seek a *worthy* receptacle for her love? Was that what he was trying to tell her?

It could be, she thought. It might be.

Neither Ruth, nor Jesse, nor Teresa had it in them to receive, or to return her love. God had not given them that gift. But somewhere, surely, there was a child in need. A child for her.

It would be best, perhaps, to send Teresa where true love awaited her, love stronger than even Eleanor's, love strong enough to reach through the girl's cruel armor.

She pushed Max gently out of her lap and stood slowly, legs slightly numb from the dog's weight. Max raised himself stiffly, looking old. He followed her into the kitchen, sat by the table, and watched her as she prepared a peanut butter and strawberry jam sandwich for Teresa. She poured a glass of milk and placed it on the tray with the sandwich. Max's tail wagged slowly, and Eleanor felt the loss of him again.

He knows, she realized. He knows we're going downstairs. He wants to be with Teresa.

He followed her out of the house, through sunshine, into shadow, down into the cellar. With each downward step he grunted, an almost human sound, as if the impact of descending was painful. She wondered, for a moment, if she had seriously hurt him this time. He seemed almost to be limping, and yet to be hiding that hurt from her. This, too, pained her.

Teresa was sitting on the mattress, legs crossed, elbows to knees, fists under chin. She did not look up as the flashlight beam passed across her, but Eleanor could see that the girl was attentive, waiting.

"Are you hungry?"

"Yes."

"I have something for you."

"Are you going to hit me again?"

"No. I'm sorry that happened. You made me angry, that's all."

Teresa's mouth pursed, and her eyes finally looked up to Eleanor. She inhaled deeply, let it out with a sigh.

"I'm sorry I made you angry."

The words caught Eleanor by surprise, and she fought back a feeling of elation that rose within her. The girl's words meant nothing. Words were empty things, devoid of meaning without actions to prove them.

"I brought Max," she said.

Teresa raised her eyes again, smiled at the dog. Max pressed against the bars, sat down, looked at her, and wagged his tail.

"Hi, Max," Teresa said.

Eleanor opened the cell door and went in. She placed the tray in front of Teresa. Teresa looked up at her and smiled. It was a such a sweet, honest expression, that Eleanor had to fight tears that threatened to spring to her eyes.

"Thank you," Teresa said, almost shyly.

The girl picked up the sandwich and bit into it. Eleanor, for the first time feeling no animosity from the girl, crouched down and watched her. As she chewed, Teresa looked down at the tray. When she had swallowed the first bite she looked up at Eleanor and smiled.

"It's good."

"I'm glad you like it."

The girl said nothing more as she ate. When she had finished the sandwich she picked up the glass of milk and drained it in one long gulp. The action was so much like Luke, the thirst that needed to be quenched, that Eleanor felt her stomach churn. When the glass was empty, Teresa put it back on the tray and pushed the tray toward her.

Eleanor picked up the tray and stood. Teresa looked up at her.

"I'm sorry I've been bad."

"That's okay. I'll be down later."

"Could I come up? Outside, I mean?"

Eleanor looked down at her, not quite knowing what to make of this sudden change in behavior. Part of her could not quite believe it, could not quite comprehend such a sudden shift, and yet another part of her was thrilled, elated. It was with great difficulty that she controlled herself, stopped herself from reaching out to hold the girl. She had been hurt too many times.

"I'll think about it," Eleanor said carefully. "I'll tell you later."

"Okay," Teresa said.

Eleanor turned to leave.

"Ellie?"

She turned to the girl. Teresa was holding something toward her. The blade of the butter knife glittered in the flashlight beam. Eleanor's breath caught in her throat.

"I found this," Teresa said.

She shifted her hold on the knife so that the blade was between her fingers, the white handle turned out toward Eleanor. The girl rose, approached slowly, knife held out. Eleanor tentatively took it from her, put it on the tray.

"Thank you, Teresa," she said.

Teresa smiled, then went to the bars of the cell where Max was sitting. The dog's tail wagged. He licked the fingers she thrust toward him.

"Can Max stay with me for a while?"

Eleanor smiled, holding her jubilation in check with great difficulty.

"I don't see why not. You've been good. I'll be down later."

She closed the cell and locked it. Before leaving, she waved at Teresa. The girl smiled sweetly and waved back.

Upstairs, Eleanor left the light on for Teresa and Max. She was feeling magnanimous, generous, loving. Outside, she leaned against the door, face upturned to the warm sun.

Oh, God, could it be true? Was the girl really returning her love?

She wiped tears from her eyes, and rushed toward the house. She needed to pray. She must pray. Now.

She must ask God's forgiveness. She had tried to rush things. God worked in his own sweet time. Love demanded sacrifices, and hard work. She of all people should have understood that!

She would ask God to wait. To allow Teresa to stay with her a little longer.

Just to be sure.

Surely, surely, heaven could delay the arrival of its angel for a little while longer.

Deer Ridge was north of Battle Lake, an hour's drive from Morris. It was after 4:00 P.M. as they neared the town, the sun now a white blur through Campbell's window, hot against his neck and cheek. Shadow kept his attention on the road ahead. When they passed the turnoff for Battle Lake, Campbell looked wistfully down the road, but again, Hope was determined to finish what they had started. The tension in the car was palpable, a taut sheet ready to tear.

Both of them knew that in Deer Creek they were coming up on the only answer they were likely to find, the final pup of Shadow's litter. One way or another, this was their only lead, and whether it turned out to be real or fantasy, everything was going to change in the next half hour.

They were still ten miles out of Deer Creek when Campbell felt it, and he straightened up in the seat and put both hands on the dashboard.

"What is it?" Hope asked, voice hushed.

"I felt something. Something strong." Campbell could hardly speak. His voice sounded like a dry desert wind.

"This is it?"

"I'm not sure, but it's all . . . familiar. I don't even know if that's the right word. I'm just getting a really creepy feeling, like I'm drawing closer to something I don't really want to get close to."

"Just hold tight."

"I'm not going anywhere."

Shadow, too, seemed to have sensed something. He became agitated, and would not sit still, raising his rump repeatedly, pushing his wet nose into Campbell's face, hardly able to obey the order to look straight ahead.

The address they were looking for was this side of Deer Creek. Hope paused at the county road exit and looked down the long, dusty avenue of trees. The land here was hilly, poor for farming, but everywhere you looked there were cultivated fields. They sat on the sides of hills, between outcroppings of rocks, bordered by small, mysterious woods. On either side of the county road was a field. Both were uncultivated, looking almost barren. The fields were short, climbing a low hill, ending at a wall of trees.

"Well?"

"I don't know. I still have that feeling."

It was more than just a feeling now. He was on the verge of throwing up. His heart was pounding, his palms sweating.

"Then let's go take a look," Hope said softly.

Let's not, Campbell thought, but said nothing.

TWENTY-NINE

Hope turned onto the road, and they drove slowly down the long line of trees. After half a mile they came to another sign, and Hope stopped the car. To their right was a narrow road, gravel, leading through a small stretch of wood, and beyond it a cleared area. Campbell could see the corner of a building. A house, or a utility shed.

He felt cold now. His hands were shaking.

"Anything?"

He nodded sharply. "Yes."

"Maybe we should just drive into Deer Creek and tell the police. We don't have to get any closer."

"And what if I'm wrong? What if all this is just some weird psychosis, or even one of Russell's accommodation symptoms, what then? We bring the police down on some poor farmer for no reason, and make ourselves look like idiots, or worse."

"You think you're wrong? You think we're on some wild goose chase? You *still* think that? I don't. I wouldn't be sitting here with you right now if I thought that, so damn it, Campbell, don't you start thinking that. If you think this is the place, then let's go to the damned police and stop second-guessing yourself!"

"I want to be certain."

"All right."

She turned off the car and got out. Campbell opened his door, and nearly had to pull Shadow out by the scruff of his neck.

"What's wrong with him?" Hope asked.

"Maybe he feels it, too."

They began to walk up the drive. The sun, lower now, cast long shadows across the road, turning Campbell's vision into a checkerboard of white and dark squares, each square blinding with too much or too little light. Shadow put some resistance into his harness, and Campbell was forced to pull the dog along. When the house came fully into view, Campbell stopped in his tracks. The farmhouse was typical of those built fifty years ago, small, sturdy, more like cabins than homes. This one was surrounded by a low wooden fence, inside the fence a neatly trimmed lawn. There was no sign of a barn. In the trees behind the house, visible above the shingled roof, rose a metal tower. At the top of the tower sat a rusting old wind generator.

Campbell realized he'd been holding his breath, and released it now in a shudder.

"Is this the place?"

"It feels like it. I feel like I've been here a hundred times, but some things aren't right."

"Like what?"

"The fence, for one. I don't remember a fence. And the wind tower is behind the house. For some reason I think it should be out front. And you can't see the field from here. I should be able to see the field, through the trees. It's right, but it's not right enough."

"You're shaking."

"I'm shaking because I could be wrong and this really could be it."

"Let's knock on the door."

"Do we have to?"

"You tell me."

Campbell gritted his teeth, nodded. "Okay."

He was glad Hope was holding his arm, because he needed her support as they moved to the gate. His legs felt like rubber. He leaned on her heavily as they walked up the stone path to the front door. Campbell's mouth was so dry it hurt to breathe.

On the front step, Hope looked at him. Campbell said nothing. Hope rapped her knuckles on the door.

For a handful of heartbeats, Campbell thought nobody was going to answer, and a feeling of giddy relief overcame him. He was about to smile when the front door opened.

The woman who stood there was in her mid-forties, he guessed. Plump, gray-haired, wearing overalls and a plaid shirt. Her face was sheened with sweat. Campbell couldn't breathe. Everything was right, so right, and yet . . . he had never seen the face of the woman in his visions.

"Can I help you?"

Her voice was pleasant, smooth, rounded by that midwest accent that seems to come from nowhere and everywhere. Campbell tried to speak, but couldn't.

"We're looking for a dog," Hope said, and Campbell could hear the tension in her voice.

"Did you lose one?"

"We were directed here by Ajax Kennels. They said you bought one of a litter that we're interested in for breeding purposes. A black lab."

"Thompson," the woman said, and smiled.

"Thompson?"

"That was his name. Beautiful dog."

"Is he here?"

She started to smile, a strange sort of wistful, sad smile. Before she could speak, an engine coughed behind Campbell, and he turned to see an old, battered pickup truck pull up to the gate. A man stepped out of the truck, as lean and unpleasant looking as the woman was plump and happy. From the other side of the truck a boy appeared, perhaps thirteen, in jeans and T-shirt, hands stuffed into his pockets, baseball cap on his head. And then, behind the boy, tail wagging furiously, came the dog.

Campbell saw immediately that it wasn't a labrador. It appeared to be some sort of spaniel, younger than Shadow, much smaller, lighter in color. When it saw Shadow, it leaped over the small gate and rushed toward the step.

Campbell involuntarily backed up, but the spaniel skidded to a stop a foot away, lowered its head, and started to wag its tail furiously.

"She won't bite," the woman said.

Shadow imperiously ignored the other dog, looking up at Campbell.

"This is Thompson?" Campbell asked, his voice now back.

"No, no. Thompson is . . . well, I don't suppose we know, exactly. He disappeared about a year and a half ago. Wandered off one day and never came back."

Campbell turned to her, yanking Shadow around.

"He ran away? He's not dead?"

"Couldn't say, really. Haven't heard anything. He just disappeared."

"He's dead," the man said, coming up behind Campbell. "Dog was a pup. Wouldn't stand much of a chance. Ran off just before Christmas. Damned cold that year. He's dead."

"Now, Graf, we don't know that. Thompson might have found a happy home. He looked just like your dog there, almost. Thompson had a white diamond patch on his rump. I'd recognize him in a second if he came around."

The boy had come up beside Campbell, and had dropped to his knees beside Shadow. Shadow sniffed at him.

"Nice dog, mister."

"Thanks," Campbell said.

"Does he guide you?"

"In a way, yes."

"Cool."

Hope squeezed Campbell's hand. She stepped away from the door, tugging Campbell with her.

"Sorry to have bothered you. Thanks for your help."

"Y'know, Shakey'd make a good breeder. Make some nice pups with your dog," the woman said.

Campbell shook his head. "No. Thanks anyway, but no."

They were beyond the fence, walking quickly back to the car, when Hope spoke again.

"Something's wrong. We went about this the wrong way. Maybe Shadow's not connecting to one of his litter mates. It must be something else. We have to think about it."

Campbell didn't answer. His mouth was dry again, and his legs shook as he walked. At the car, he leaned on the roof and caught his breath. He wiped his face and inhaled deeply.

"We'll figure it out, Campbell," Hope said softly.

"He was here. It was him. I can feel him everywhere. Like I've been here. But not like the other place. This place is directly connected. Thompson is the dog."

Hope stared at him quietly. "She took the dog, too?"

"Yes."

"Just picked him up?"

"Like Teresa."

"God, what is she? What's wrong with her?"

"I don't know. But she's got him. It's Thompson. And he was our last lead. We've got nothing else. Teresa is going to die."

Hope said nothing. She got back into the car. Campbell opened his door and got in, pushing Shadow ahead of him. Once he was seated and buckled in, he leaned his head against the window, exhausted by his despair.

The sun was moving toward the horizon now, a large orange ball, dipping into a line of clouds. Hope started the car.

"I'm bushed. I'm hungry. I need a shower. I don't feel like driving back to Battle Lake. Let's find a motel. Maybe if we sit down and think about this, something will come to us."

Campbell shrugged. It was hopeless. It was over. They were never going to find Teresa. They might as well just go home. But he said nothing.

Hope put the car in gear and started driving.

The motel in Deer Creek was attached to a noisy service station on one side, and to a busy coffee shop on the other. After they checked into their room, Campbell collapsed onto the bed. His whole body seemed to be groaning and begging for sleep. Hope leaned over him and kissed him on the mouth, at first gently, then insistently. He felt himself getting aroused, but didn't have the energy to push her away. After a minute she lay down beside him.

"How do you feel?"

"Like crap."

"We did everything we could."

"We wasted our time. We can't find Teresa. That last pup was our only chance."

"Don't feel bad. There's nothing to feel bad about."

"You're not the one who sees her face, who has to watch what happens to her."

She said nothing, sat up, swung her legs off the bed.

"I'm sorry," he said softly. "That was uncalled for."

"But it's also true."

"No. Stop listening to me when I talk like that."

She stood and looked down at him. "You need some sleep. Maybe afterwards, everything will look different. We're not thinking clearly."

He didn't tell her what he really thought, but shrugged instead.

"I'll take Shadow for a walk. You relax. I'll be back soon."

He had no energy to disagree. He stretched out his arm to let her unhook the dog. Darkness wrapped him up. It felt as if a huge weight had been lifted from him. He felt almost weightless. He couldn't remember why he had hated this so much. Now it seemed so damned comforting.

"Later," Hope said.

He listened to her remove Shadow's harness, clip on a leash. He listened to the door open, close. He listened to the silence.

A month ago, life had been simplicity itself, and he had fought to escape it. Darkness, like this. No obligations, no fears. No knowledge of Teresa Dawson, or Jesse Hampton.

Part of him wanted to return to that time so badly he almost groaned thinking about it. And then the anger came, fury at himself, his weakness. Nobody had said it was going to be easy!

In fact, he'd known from the start that it would be the opposite of easy.

And besides, there was Hope.

He smiled as he thought about her. He remembered her touch. Her voice. The feel of her breath on his cheek. He'd regained a lot more than just sight. In fact, sight might be the least of the benefits he had reaped. He rolled over, pressing his face into the pillow. His darkness, of course, remained the same.

He let himself drift, breathing slowly, deeply. He cleared his mind, thinking of nothing, sinking into the darkness, into sleep.

But it was not sleep he found at the bottom of this dark pit. He knew immediately what had happened, but by then it was too late. He did not fight, did not deny, did not question. Deeper, inkier darkness, surrounded him. Within moments it had dissolved into a pale, golden light.

Teresa looked at him through the bars. Her face was slightly swollen, streaked with dirt and tears, and yet she seemed not so much sad as resigned. There was no hope in her eyes, and yet no fear either. It was as if she knew that Campbell had given up on her, as if she knew that no rescue was forthcoming. Understood, accepted, forgave.

If Campbell had eyes, he would have wept. As it was, the emotion remained inside of him, filled him, scoured him. He could only look into Teresa's eyes.

"I'm sorry," he whispered.

Hope walked Shadow around the end of the motel, across the parking lot, and into an area of brush surrounded by a field of trees. The evening sun was warm, the shadows long. It was a time of year she usually loved, but this evening it did not hold the promise of new growth, warm summer, soft air . . . it felt so bloody hopeless she could hardly keep herself from crying.

She was reacting to what Campbell had said of course. It was *Campbell's* hopelessness that had touched her.

A day ago he had been eager to begin their search for Teresa

Dawson, but now he had given up. Whatever well of strength he had been drawing upon to keep him going had dried up. And Campbell had dried up with it.

She could understand how he felt, of course. The last pup had been their best hope, and now that was shattered. They had returned to square one. Terrible visions, and no answers. And not *just* terrible visions. For these had a definite cause. There was a child at the center of them.

Shaking her head in dismay, she unhooked Shadow's leash. He looked up at her, wagged his tail.

"Go on. Run."

He needed no further urging, but bolted into the knee-high brush, tail wagging furiously. Hope skirted the clearing, sticking to gravel, watching the dog.

She had believed Campbell. Believed him now. His visions were real. Teresa Dawson was real. But she had also believed that she and Campbell could use the visions to help the girl. Now . . . that belief, that hope, seemed hollow. They could do nothing but watch. They were voyeurs, peeping at something horrible, powerless to intervene.

In the brush, Shadow did his business. Hope watched him. When he stopped moving, she knew what was happening. She could see his back, his tail suddenly erect. She knew the signs. Either a cat, or a rabbit.

A low growl emerged from the clearing, and suddenly Shadow bolted. He lunged forward, then to his right, then to his left. He barked. For a second or two all movement stopped in the brush. Then Shadow barked again. The bark quickly changed to a growl, low and deep. And then the rabbit appeared. It hopped into view, saw Hope, and froze. It was all the time that Shadow needed. She saw his back, then his snout, then his tail, a blur of black rushing through the brush. She almost shouted out for him to stop, feeling at the last instant a pang of pity for the rabbit. But no sound emerged from her mouth.

Shadow pounced. The rabbit cowered. And suddenly the small animal was in the dog's jaws, shaken violently. A tiny squeal erupted from the creature, and then silence. In moments it was over. Shadow dropped the bloody bag of fur to the ground. He sniffed at it, pawed at it. When it did not move, he stood erect and padded out of the clearing, tongue lolling, happy as only a dog can be who has just caught a rabbit.

When he padded up to her, Hope tut-tutted him. His snout was covered in blood and fur. She looked around and found a piece of old newspaper, picked it up, and bent over the dog. He stood still as she wiped the blood from his fur.

"Happy now?"

He wagged his tail and seemed to grin up at her. She shook her head. Campbell could use a similar kind of catharsis, she thought. With Shadow leashed, his business done, she led him to the front of the motel, and then along Deer Creek's main street.

A few cars moved slowly along, their occupants peering out the windows at the pedestrians walking. There were more than a few pedestrians around, Hope saw, and she kept Shadow tightly reigned. Some people were nervous with dogs.

She walked half a block; past a movie theater showing, apparently, nothing; past a used-book store; past a grocery store; past a general store. Then she came to the realty office. It was the map in the window that caught her attention, and she led Shadow over to it.

The map showed only a handful of counties, including Otter Tail and its neighbors. Hope found Battle Lake with her finger. There were points on the map where the office had property for sale. She noticed a couple of lots around Battle Lake. She wondered how much they were worth these days. Probably at least twice what she had paid.

She had turned to move away when, from the corner of her eye, she picked out Godfrey, and immediately thought of Teresa. She touched a finger to the town. Not so very far away, she thought. She ran her finger across the map until she found Glenwood, the town from which Jesse Hampton had disappeared. In the news reports she had read, the police had not connected the

two disappearances. Only Campbell had done that. Campbell
and his strange, dark visions.

Again she moved her finger, this time to Deer Creek.

She pulled her finger away and stared at the map.

Her heart suddenly pounded furiously, and she suppressed a
shudder.

"Oh, God," she said softly.

Shadow whined up at her. Hope turned away and started back
toward the motel, yanking the dog. He immediately moved to
her heel, keeping up with her.

She had to tell Campbell. He had to know.

It seemed incredible that it could be so simple! Why hadn't
the police come to the same conclusion?

Because the police aren't connected by supernatural means
to the kidnapper's dog, she thought.

Only Campbell is. And I know what Campbell knows.

At the motel she opened the door to their room and ushered
Shadow inside. Campbell was lying on the bed, but he sat up
abruptly, a cry erupting from his mouth.

"Campbell?"

His face was pale and soaked in sweat. He was shaking, his
teeth chattering.

"Campbell, what's wrong?"

She dropped the leash and rushed to him, putting her arms
around him. He was trembling so violently that even when she
squeezed him he would not stop. She saw with dismay that there
was blood on his lips. Something had frightened him so badly
that he had bitten his tongue.

"Campbell, tell me! What happened?"

He pulled away from her, still shaking. His teeth chattered
again when he tried to speak.

"Rabbit," he forced out. "I felt it. I . . . tasted it. Hope, it
was . . ."

Hope covered her mouth. "Oh, God, Campbell. I'm sorry! I
never thought! I just let him . . ."

He shook his head, chin up, trembling still. His mouth was twitching, as if trying to smile.

"No. You don't understand. It was . . . I loved it. I can't explain it. The blood. I could taste it. It was alive in my mouth. I've never felt anything so . . ."

He started to shake again, and then he started to sob. No tears. Just a convulsive rocking, heaving forward across his knees. She put her arms around him, tried to hold him, comfort him.

"It's okay," she whispered. "Everything is going to be okay."

"What's happening to me?" His voice was muffled against her shoulder.

She started to answer him, but kept her mouth closed. Instead, she stroked his hair. She had no answers.

THIRTY

Campbell had stopped questioning his connection to Shadow. Since the incident in the car, he had accepted that the bond between he and the dog went far beyond mere wires. The vision of Teresa, while Hope and Shadow had been out of the motel, had been part of that bond. He had come to accept that.

But the rabbit had been different.

Campbell had experienced the killing of the animal as if he had done it himself; worse, it had been a self stripped of everything, *nearly* everything, that made him who he was. A self pared down to pure blood lust and fury, and yet, a self he recognized, for all its ferocity, as part of him. At the time, he had been withdrawing from his vision of Teresa, unable to look at the girl without feeling terrible guilt. He had felt the tone of the vision change, the darkness leaking away to be replaced by something else, something more familiar. He was with Shadow again, walking with Hope.

He looked up at Hope as she unleashed him, and felt a thrill as he realized he was free. That was when he felt the first flush of fear. For he *did* feel the thrill, as if he himself had been freed. And he was suddenly rushing into the high grass, leaping and jumping.

In the motel room, Campbell had felt the bed beneath him, and smelled the mustiness of the little-used bed sheets, and yet all of that had seemed pale and unreal next to the clarity of the grass surrounding him, the darkening sky overhead, the rush of air across his face.

He sensed the rabbit before he saw it. A feeling at the back of his neck, hairs rising, and he had frozen. And there, there, just visible behind a small bush, trembling . . .

Part of him wanted to back away then, to flee back to the room, to the reality and darkness he knew, and yet another part of him wanted the opposite, wanted to leap at the small animal, catch it and . . . and what?

There hadn't been time to think about that, for no sooner had he become aware of the desire, than he was lunging toward the petrified rabbit. The rabbit leaped away and Campbell's teeth slashed down on the air where the fluffy white tail had raised itself only a moment earlier. He felt as if he no longer had hands to manipulate, only teeth, only his snout. He was at once conscious of himself, the Campbell, he knew, receding into a red mist that had somehow entered his head, and at the same time of a new Campbell comprised entirely of his hunger for the rabbit. His entire existence narrowed to a dark tunnel at the end of which the rabbit bounced and leaped and pulled him forward.

For barely a second, Campbell felt fear again, and during that second, time compressed into a blur of grass and sky and trees. And then suddenly the rabbit was in front of him again, and he was leaping, growling, and this time he wasn't fooled by the flash of white tail, but reached ahead of it, jaws clamping shut on warm fur. Tearing. And blood pouring over him, into his mouth, and the fury was so great, so deep, that all he could do was shake, shake, until the thing that fell from his mouth wasn't a rabbit anymore, but only a bundle of bloody, rended fur.

The hunger pulled away, the sky bent over him, and he was looking up at Hope again.

Campbell had managed to pull away then. With a cry of horror he sat up in bed, gripping the sheets. His mouth tasted of blood. He had bitten his tongue. But he remembered the taste of the rabbit's blood exploding down his throat, and he groaned with pleasure. He fell back onto the bed, shuddering.

When Hope had returned with Shadow, he still hadn't regained his composure, or his old self. He felt lost within his own skin, the desire to leap and to tear with his jaws so strong that he had to squeeze his fingers into tight, painful fists to control himself.

He lay cradled in Hope's arms for nearly half an hour before he felt well enough to sit up without support. Hope immediately put a hand to his forehead, stroked the skin of his face.

"How do you feel?"

"Like I just broke a fever."

He sat still while she put Shadow in his harness and then reconnected him. He held tight to the edge of the bed as light returned. Hope was looking at him with grave concern.

"Do you feel well enough to listen to something crazy?"

"Sure."

"Sit still for a second. I'll be right back."

She went outside. He heard the car door open, and then close again. When she came back she was holding a road map. She came to the bed and spread it out beside him.

"I think I know where Teresa is," she said.

Campbell slid off the bed and ushered Shadow up to take his place. He directed the dog to look down at the map.

"This is Godfrey, where Teresa was abducted," Hope said, and circled a small black point on the map. "Now, this is Glenwood, where Jesse Hampton was taken."

She circled another point only inches from Godfrey. Both towns were well off the interstate, one on highway 210, the other on a county road fifty miles away.

"So?"

"The police haven't connected Jesse Hampton with Teresa. I mean, they've talked about it, but they don't have anything to connect them with."

"So, they're both from roughly the same area. That doesn't mean Teresa is around there now. She could have taken her miles away."

"I know that. But look." She circled another point on the map. "This is Deer Creek. Where Thompson went missing. The police don't know about that. How could they? And even if they did, why would they connect it to Teresa Dawson and Jesse Hampton? Only you and I know that this pup is important."

"Okay," Campbell said, more slowly now. "That still . . ."

"You need at least three points to triangulate, Campbell. When you fit Deer Creek into the picture, you have something."

Hope joined the three points with a rough circle, and then drew a line from the circumference of the circle to a larger point in the center.

"Judas Priest," Campbell said.

"Hollyfield. Population, roughly six thousand. I bet you anything that's where she's from."

"We can't be sure."

"We can't be sure about anything. But it's a lead. And I bet if we search the records, we'll find other children that have gone missing in the area, and all of them in a circle around Hollyfield."

Campbell pulled Shadow off the bed, sat down, then lay back with his head on the pillow.

"It makes sense, doesn't it?" Hope asked.

"Nothing makes sense anymore."

Suddenly Hope was towering over him. "Campbell, what's wrong?"

"I can't do this."

"Hollyfield is only a few hours drive away. We can be there before lunchtime tomorrow."

"It's too much for me. This thing with Shadow is scaring the crap out of me, Hope."

"I shouldn't have let him kill the rabbit. I'm sorry. But that doesn't mean . . ."

"No, no, you don't get it. I liked it, Hope. I liked killing that rabbit. The taste of the blood, the fur . . . God . . . it's like nothing I've ever felt. If I could do it again right now, I would."

Hope inhaled deeply, sat down on the edge of the bed.

"We're so close."

"Let's just call the police and tell them what we know."

"You know what will happen then. They'll think we're crazy.

They won't listen. And even if they don't think we're crazy, and somehow believe everything we tell them, it might take forever to get things moving. How long does Teresa have before she ends up with Jesse? We have to do this ourselves."

"Take me back to Minneapolis. If you can't do that, then back to Battle Lake."

Campbell reached his right hand over his body and disconnected Shadow. Darkness took the room away.

"I'm not going to abandon Teresa," Hope said quietly. "Not now."

Campbell did not respond.

It was dark when Eleanor left the house. Max was still in the cellar with Teresa. Both of them would be hungry now, but they could wait. She got into the truck, started it, and sat there, window open, thinking.

Her prayers had not been answered. She had kneeled in the living room for hours, head bowed, hands clasped, eyes squeezed so tightly shut her head had pounded with the darkness of it, and yet still God had not answered her.

She had prayed that Teresa's departure for heaven might be delayed, if even only for a day or two, enough time for Eleanor to experience the love the girl now seemed willing to give. But God had not answered. He had been in an answering mood only a day ago, when he had agreed that it was time for Teresa to join him, but now he was silent.

Eleanor knew what that meant, of course. God did things in his own sweet time, and she had tried to rush. First she'd found Teresa too quickly, and then she'd grown impatient with Teresa. God was teaching her a lesson. If she had waited another day, then she would have had the child she had so often dreamed about. Teresa was changing, expressing her love. But Eleanor had not waited. Eleanor had wanted to be rid of Teresa. And God, in his wisdom, had granted her request.

She swallowed the bitter taste in her mouth and backed the

truck up, then drove through the gate, and along the road by
the field she leased to Len Tate. Even in twilight she could see
his big tractor out there, where he had left it this morning. In
another month the field would be green with new growth, the
way it used to be when Frank had been alive. She felt a passing
anger at the way life had forced her to give up the field, most
of the farm, as it had taken from her both Frank and Luke, Ruth
and Jesse, and now Teresa. But that was life. There was no point
in complaining about it. Life was life, and whatever happened
was the way God wanted it to happen.

The truck bounced along the road into the woodlot, headlights spearing into the trees, sending shadows swinging
through the night like banshees. When she reached the clearing
at the end of the road she stopped. The headlights cast an eerie,
white mist. She turned off the engine, then the lights. It took
her eyes a few minutes to adapt to the darkness, and then she
got out.

The moon was up, spreading a silver carpet through the
woods. The night was cool, but no breeze. Eleanor wore a thin
jacket over her overalls. She got the shovel from the back of
the truck, then entered the path that took her to God's special
place.

Jesse Hampton's grave still looked fresh, despite two weeks
of rain and spring growth. A couple of green shoots were pushing out of the mound. In the moonlight, the other mounds appeared more visible than during the day, but they were slowly
disappearing. Soon, the earth would swallow them, the sky and
wind would erase them, and their occupants would be forgotten.

"God's peace," she whispered to them all.

Then she found an open space and started digging. She
worked slowly, lost in thought, and it took her a good half hour
of easy labor to dig the shallow grave. Sweating, she leaned on
the shovel and regarded her work. The slow erosion of the other
graves gave her a strange feeling, a deep sense of loss. To her
right, a light suddenly appeared, flashing through the trees, then

suddenly disappeared. A car on the highway. Its driver would never know of this place. That made her sad.

On impulse she walked through the trees and found a number of grapefruit sized rocks she had dug up from the other graves. She walked around each site and placed a rock on top of it, whispering her love to the children and animals beneath her feet. She never wanted to forget them. Ever.

She was halfway back along the rutted trail, the house just coming into view, when she decided that she did not want to be alone. Not now. Not tonight.

She turned away from the fence, onto the road that led down to the highway. It was still early. Not even eight. Plenty of time.

In five minutes she was in Hollyfield, driving along the main street. The lights of the town were bright, garish, but tonight she wanted that, wanted signs of people, of life. A few people were out strolling, enjoying the spring evening. She drove by the movie theater, noting with dismay that its marquee was empty. Most of the cars were parked outside the tavern, but she did not stop there. She drove straight on to Banning's Ice Cream Parlor, and parked a half block away.

Banning's was not empty. A few couples sat at tables, spaced widely. A man and a woman with two children sat at the counter, drinking milk shakes. Eleanor walked up to the counter, and when Mrs. Banning, a dour-faced, gray-haired Scottish woman came up to her, Eleanor ordered a small cone. Pralines and cream.

Eleanor took the cone and sat down at a table alone. She ate the ice cream slowly, feeling conspicuous and foolish. It would be so nice to have Teresa with her right now. A child. Her own child to love and to pamper. It would seem just right, to anybody watching, to see her with a little girl in here.

She grew so depressed thinking about Teresa that she did not finish the cone, but dropped it in the trash on the way out. She walked along the pavement, hands pushed into her pockets, feeling lonely.

It wasn't right.

Nobody should feel like this. And tomorrow, after Teresa returned to God, it was going to feel a lot worse. She fought back the tears that wanted to come. She had no right to cry. She had brought this upon herself. Pushing God to his limits. Silly woman.

At the pharmacy she stopped to read a newspaper in the dispenser. The story of Teresa's disappearance, and the search for the girl, had moved off the front page. Gone and forgotten. Her father had probably given up on her by now. Probably he was thinking about having another child. A man like that, who could forget Teresa so quickly, did not deserve any more children. Perhaps, sometime soon, she would write him a letter and tell him so.

She would never forget Teresa. Never.

She walked slowly back to the truck, feeling tired now, aching from her earlier exertion. A good night's sleep would make her feel better, help her to see clearly.

She was halfway through town, just passing by a small restaurant by the theater, when she saw the boy. She pulled the truck to the side of the road and stopped, craning over the seat to see him more clearly. Eight years old she guessed. Maybe nine. Blond hair, thin face. Oh, so perfect! So sweet! Just like Luke!

He was standing on the sidewalk outside the restaurant, shoulders hunched, small hands pushed into his pockets.

"Oh, God," Eleanor whispered hoarsely.

He looked so lonely. So sad. So unloved.

Some instinct nearly made her open the truck and get out, but she held herself back, unsure why. The restaurant door opened and a woman came out, followed by a man, and then by a teenage girl. They came to the boy. The woman put her arm around his shoulder, ruffled his hair. He smiled.

But not a happy smile. That much was obvious. Clear to anyone who cared to see. This boy was not a happy child.

Eleanor watched the family as they crossed the road and got into their car. When the car started, pulled out into the street,

Eleanor made a U-turn and followed them. The car drove to the east end of Hollyfield, then turned on Adelaide Street. Eleanor turned too, following the car as closely as she dared. When the car slowed again, then turned onto a driveway, Eleanor pulled to the side of the road. She waited a few minutes, heart pounding, and then put the truck in gear again. She drove slowly past the parked car. The house it belonged to was small, but neat. Lights blazed inside, illuminating nearly every window. She saw shadows move behind curtains. At one window she saw a dark shape appear, then recede, and she knew it was him.

"Please, God," she whispered.

She had never found a child so close to home. She was not even sure it was a good idea.

She kept driving, went back to the main road, and then drove out of town.

She knew where he lived. She knew that he needed love. Would it be right to ignore him? Could she, in all conscience, leave him to his loveless existence?

She would pray when she got home. She would ask God if he was the one.

In her heart of hearts, though, she knew the answer already.

She and that poor, lonely boy, were meant for each other.

Hope woke with a start, bursting free of a horrible nightmare that had kept her twisting and turning for hours. Campbell slept on beside her, snoring softly, oblivious. She got out of bed, shuddering, and went to the motel window. It was not yet 6:00 A.M., but the sky was brightening to the east, dark blue leaching into a shallow lake of light. In her nightmares, Hope had been searching For Teresa Dawson, running after the girl through a maze of dark corridors, slimy caves, and the wet, neon-bright streets of a decrepit Minneapolis. The girl had remained forever out of reach, looking back at her with pleading eyes, begging for help. But Hope had never been able to reach her. Every time she drew close she was blocked by a dark, menacing figure that she could not properly see.

She showered slowly, feeling as if she needed to be thoroughly cleaned after her dreams. The spray of piping hot water turned her skin red, filled the bathroom with steam, and when she emerged she felt fully awake.

When she came out of the bathroom, Campbell was up and dressed, sitting by the television, Shadow by his side. He looked tired.

"Good morning," she said.

"Morning," he answered.

He watched her as she dressed. Or, rather, Shadow watched her. As she sat at the dresser and brushed her hair, he came up behind her and put his hands on her shoulders.

"I'm sorry," he said.

"About what?"

"The way I feel. About not wanting to go on."

"You don't have to explain it to me, Campbell. I know how tough it has been."

Campbell turned away and went back to his chair. "So, we're heading back this morning?"

"In a roundabout way. I want to go to Hollyfield."

"Hope . . ."

"I can't just forget about her. And you can't, either. I'll take you back to Minneapolis, if that's what you want, but we're going to Hollyfield first."

Campbell said nothing. After a few seconds he sighed, then shrugged.

They breakfasted in the coffee shop next to the motel. Campbell poked at his eggs and bacon, but hardly ate anything. He was pale, and his hands shook when he put them on the table. He said nothing through the meal, and Hope felt guilty at pushing him. Really, she had no idea what he was going through. He told her of his visions, but she had not experienced one, could not guess at their toll on him.

But she could not stop now. Not now. He had asked for her

help, and she had given it, willingly. But in helping she had involved herself. She could not give up on Teresa so easily.

After breakfast they got in the car and started driving. Campbell unhooked himself from Shadow and put the dog in the back seat. He leaned against the window, hands clasped in his lap. Hope did not know if he was asleep or merely thinking. Whichever one it was, he was uncommunicative.

Half an hour out of Deer Creak they passed through a wetlands conservatory, the swamp on either side of the raised road glittering in the midmorning sun. She nudged Campbell with her elbow. He sat up straight.

"You should see this, Campbell. It's beautiful."

"I've seen enough," he said, and his voice was flat, without emotion.

Hope bit her lower lip and fought back the wetness that flooded her eyes. She felt as if she were losing him, losing everything they had between them. Campbell put his head back against the window. In the rear seat, Shadow whined softly. Hope kept her grip tightly on the wheel, and did not bother him again until they were approaching Hollyfield.

She pulled the car into the rest area and parked. Campbell was indeed awake. He sat up and cocked his head as if listening.

"Are we there?"

"Almost. Fifteen more minutes. I want you to hook up with Shadow while we drive into town. I want you to see the area. Maybe something will strike you as familiar."

"I doubt it."

"Please, Campbell."

For a couple of seconds she thought he was going to refuse, but finally he shrugged, sighed, and patted the seat for Shadow to come forward. The dog scrambled over the back of the seat and landed between them. Campbell connected himself. He stiffened, then relaxed.

"Thank you," she said quietly.

She left the rest area, but kept her speed below 50 as they continued the journey toward Hollyfield. She tried to keep her attention on the road, but every time Campbell moved his head, she turned to watch him, hoping for some sort of reaction. But he said nothing. Shadow watched the countryside move by, head moving from left to right, left to right, as if following food on a conveyer belt.

"Does it seem familiar?"

"It's all the same around here, Battle Lake, Deer Creek, I can't tell the difference."

"You know what I mean."

He shook his head. "Nothing. Not really."

They were only a couple of miles from Hollyfield when Campbell made a small sound. They were passing a cemetery. From the road, Hope could see gently rolling fields, many headstones and markers. Campbell was sitting stiffly, hands gripping the dashboard.

"What is it?"

He shook his head. "I get that feeling again, but . . . I don't know. It's just a cemetery."

"Maybe she was here. If I stop, we could have a look."

"No, just keep going. Please."

She pursed her lips and kept driving. Campbell said nothing more. When they entered Hollyfield, he gave no sign of recognition, and Hope felt sudden despair.

"How long are we going to be?"

"I don't know," she said.

She stopped the car in front of a restaurant. Campbell immediately got out of the car. They went into the restaurant and sat at a table. Campbell clasped his hands in front of him, waiting. It was too much for Hope. She started to cry and turned away from him.

"What's the matter?"

"You. The way you're giving up like this. I can't bear it."

Campbell sighed. "I'm sorry."

At his feet, Shadow whined. The waitress approached their table, smiling. "Can I help you?"

Hope rose abruptly. "I'm going to take Shadow for a walk, Campbell. Have a coffee and I'll be back soon."

Campbell shrugged. "Okay. Coffee then."

The waitress walked away. Hope unhooked Campbell from Shadow, then removed the dog's harness.

"Hope, I really am sorry."

She said nothing. She walked to the door, Shadow following silently.

THIRTY-ONE

The coffee was very good. Campbell made a sound of appreciation as he tasted it. A hand touched his shoulder.

"Let me know if you want anything else. I can see you from the counter. Just wave and I'll come."

It was the waitress, her voice soft with pity. Her perfume smelled more expensive than he would have expected, but he could not place it. He remembered that she was a woman only slightly older than Hope, not unattractive, leaning toward plumpness. He tried to smile warmly.

"I will. Thanks."

He continued to drink the coffee, this time silently. The restaurant sounded empty, and he was sure it had been empty when he and Hope had entered, but the suspicion began to bother him that there were actually a number of people sitting around him, all watching him, all very quiet. His cheeks began to glow.

He wished Hope had not left him alone, but could not blame her, and he certainly had no right to be angry about it. He knew, that to her, he must be acting selfishly, possibly inexplicably so. It was very hard to explain to her how he felt, the fear that he was being changed by his connection to Shadow, the even greater fear that that change would uncover a part of him that should not be uncovered. Something inside of him was echoing something inside of Shadow, something very animalistic, basic. Something beastly. Something that could take pleasure in ripping a helpless rabbit to shreds. And not only that. There was the connection itself, that inexplicable *joining* with Shadow, and with his litter mate, at a level far beyond mere sight.

Mere sight. Now, wasn't *that* ironic. That he should even think such a thing!

He thought back with longing to the time when he had been blind. It was the same longing he had felt, back then, for the time when he had been sighted. God, what a change! If someone had told him a month ago that he would soon pine for darkness he would have laughed in that person's face. He had been desperate to see. Life had seemed meaningless and empty without sight.

But now he saw too much. Far too much.

He must have made a small sound, for the waitress was suddenly at his side again, touching him.

"Need a warm-up, honey?"

"No, I'm . . ."

"Here, it's okay. On the house."

He heard the coffee being poured and tried to smile. "Thank you."

"And here's a little something on the table. Right next to the coffee. Can you feel it? Here, let me help you."

He almost started when her hand picked up his and moved it. He felt something soft beneath his fingers.

"That's a sweet roll. I toasted it for you."

Campbell inhaled deeply. "Thank you."

"Oh, you're very welcome."

When she was gone, he could feel her eyes on him, watching, waiting. His cheeks became even warmer. If he didn't touch the bun, she would wonder what was wrong. She might even come over and try to talk to him again. He didn't think he could bear that.

He reached out and found the bun, picked it up and took a bite. Slightly warm, heavily buttered, but even the toasting couldn't hide the staleness. He chewed and swallowed stoically, smiling for whomever was watching.

God, Hope, come back. Get me out of here.

But Hope was out looking for Teresa. Hope wasn't ready to give up. Hope had no terror of becoming something that she wasn't. She didn't have to worry about finding herself inside some damned dog's body, facing the business end of a shotgun, tasting the blood of another living creature.

He heard the door open, the tinkle of a bell. Voices. The waitress's voice. Good. Give her somebody else to worry about. No sign of Hope, though.

Where was she?

Impulsively, Campbell reached for the darkness inside his head, the black ring that now surrounded even his inner imagery. In seconds it had surrounded him, and he was looking up at tall trees, clear sky. A shape moved in front of him and he recognized the overalls, the muddy boots.

"Christ!"

He was following close behind her. She was walking along a poorly defined trail. Branches of low bushes slid off her shins and slashed back at his face. He wanted to pull back, protect himself.

"Everything all right?"

At the sound of the waitress's voice, Campbell started. "Yes! Fine!"

"Well . . ."

"I'm fine! Just leave me alone!"

He heard a sniffle of protest, of hurt, then her receding footsteps. The legs in front of him stopped walking, and Campbell realized he was in a small clearing. Something was horribly familiar about it all. He had been here before.

He looked around himself. The wall of trees seemed within arms reach. To his left was a small, open hole in the ground. Freshly dug.

"Judas Priest," he muttered softly, consciously keeping his voice low.

He *did* recognize this place. This is where she had brought Jesse Hampton. But here was a fresh grave. He looked around frantically, but there was no sign of Teresa. Only the large shape of the woman, who even now, in broad daylight, he could see only as a shadow, as if, somehow his mind did not *want* to see her.

He moved past the open trench, looking at the remaining three. One for Jesse Hampton, but what of the others?

He turned again, and she was standing directly in front of him, only now the shotgun was in her arms and pointing right at him. He backed up slowly, never taking his eyes away from the barrel of the weapon.

It's my turn, he thought.

But the shotgun lowered. Campbell let his breath out in a hiss. If the waitress heard, she had apparently decided not to respond. Campbell gripped the edges of the table.

Draw away, he commanded himself. Pull back.

Instead, he followed the woman again, coming up close behind her legs. He was so close he could see speckles of mud on her jeans, dried dabs of it on her leather boots. She passed through the clearing, into deeper, thicker tree growth. The impression came to Campbell that she was taking him somewhere, but he did not know where. Somewhere he had not been before.

The fear began as a flutter in his stomach, but soon reached out to encompass his limbs. His hands trembled. Wherever she was taking him, he did not want to go. Whatever she was going to show him, he did not want to see. The trees thinned again, and they entered another clearing.

Something glinted in the trees to Campbell's left, and he turned to look. A sliver of light rushed through the trees, disappeared.

A car, he realized. Sunlight reflecting off chrome or glass. Wherever she was, it was close to a road.

He turned back to look at her, and caught his breath again. She had lowered herself to sit on a white rock, and she was staring at him. He knew this, because for the first time he could see her face. He stared back at her, unable to look away, convinced she was looking at *him,* not at some unknown, unnamed dog, but at *him,* and knowing him. She was in her forties, he guessed. Big, but not fat. Round-faced, dark-haired. A vague, unremarkable sort of woman. He could hardly believe that this was the nightmare that had terrorized him. If he had harbored any hatred for her, he lost it then, completely. She was nothing. If he turned away from her, he realized, he might forget what she looked like.

But he would never forget her eyes. Small and dark, but brimming with sadness, despair, pain. He could hardly stand to look at her. And this feeling was made worse, because she would not stop looking at him. And she was a woman, he realized suddenly, who was contemplating doing something that she very much did not want to do.

Walking with Shadow, but without Campbell, Hope realized very quickly that she was on a fool's errand. Campbell was the one who could help Teresa Dawson, not her. All she could do was walk Shadow and pick up after him!

Hollyfield was a quiet town, and as she walked down its main street with Shadow on his leash, she attracted a number of friendly, curious looks. A little girl came out of a grocery store, licking a frozen treat of some kind, and grinned when she saw Shadow. She walked over, still smiling, and held out her hand to the dog.

Shadow wagged his tail and sniffed her fingers. The girl giggled, looked up at Hope. Hope felt suddenly sick.

It was *this* easy for the woman who had abducted Teresa Dawson. Dogs attract children. To a child a woman with a dog would look particularly harmless.

"Oh, you bitch," Hope muttered softly.

The girl looked up at her again, and Hope smiled. "His name, is Shadow," she said.

"Hi, Shadow," the girl said, and then smiling up at Hope, "I have a dog, too. His name is Winslow."

"That's nice. Is he a dog like Shadow?"

The girl shook her head. "He's small."

The girl's mother came out of the store and, seeing her daughter petting Shadow, slapped her thigh as if the girl were a dog that needed leashing. Hope walked on, Shadow at her heel. The incident with the girl had given her an idea. Across the street, sitting in front of what looked like a video parlor, was a police car. She quickly crossed, noting the Hollyfield Police crest on the car's door, the Sheriff's Deputy insignia below that.

A man was sitting in the car, eating a sandwich, drinking from a paper cup of coffee, reading a paperback book. Hope took Shadow onto the sidewalk behind the car, then walked up to the passenger door. The window was down, and she leaned in.

The deputy glanced up, eyebrows rising, and put down the book.

"Hi," Hope said.

"Hello there," he said.

He was a big man, tall and lean, bony looking, with a tanned face and very blue eyes widely set under straight-cut blond hair. His teeth were square and even when he smiled.

"I'm looking for a dog," Hope said.

"Looks like you found one!"

Shadow had jumped up to lean on the door. Hope laughed.

"Actually, I'm looking for a dog just like this one."

"Lost one?"

"Not exactly. The kennel where we got this one told us that one of the other pups from the litter was sold to somebody around here, and we were trying to find it."

"Well, that's interesting. What for?"

"Breeding, of course."

"Of course. Well, that's nice."

Hope smiled nervously. "Well . . . are there?"

"What?"

"Any dogs like this around here."

He frowned, large eyebrows crawling down his face like hairy caterpillars. "That a black lab?"

"Yes."

"You know, I've seen a dog like that."

"Do you remember where? Do you know who owns it? It would really help if I could find that dog."

He shook his head. "I can't remember, off the top of my head. So many people with dogs around here."

"Damn," Hope said softly.

"Where are you from?"

"Battle Lake."

"Staying in town?"

"Just passing through."

"That's a long way to come for a dog you've never met."

"Getting the right sire for breeding can be worth a lot of money. Getting the wrong sire can cost even more."

"I suppose so. Haven't really thought about. Sorry I can't help you."

"Thanks anyway," Hope said, and gave him a bright smile.

It had been worth a try, anyway. She pulled Shadow away and walked along, looking disinterestedly through store windows, eyes open for even a glimpse of other dogs. She had walked perhaps fifty feet when the police car pulled up beside her.

"Maybe there is something," the deputy said out the window.

Hope looked at him expectantly.

"You could try the animal hospital. You can just see the sign over there. Doctor Brand might be able to help. He sees a lot of dogs."

"Thanks!" Hope said.

"Give you a lift?"

"I'll walk."

He tipped his hat and pulled away, then turned a corner up ahead. Hope crossed the street again, into the shade on the other side. It took her only two minutes to walk the few blocks to the sign that the deputy had indicated, which turned out, when she drew close enough to read it, to say "HOLLYFIELD ANIMAL HOSPITAL," and beneath that, "DR. GEORGE BRAND, VETERINARIAN."

Holding tightly to Shadow's leash, she opened the door and

went inside. She found herself in a long, narrow waiting room. One wall was lined with shelves on which sat a variety of dog, cat, bird, and fish foods of the expensive variety. Next to that were a couple of racks of cat and dog toys, birds on strings, wind-up mechanical mice, leather and rubber bones. Other than the displays, Shadow, and herself, the waiting room was empty.

Hope walked up to the counter. There was no receptionist. Just a typewriter and a bell. The door behind the counter had a window in it and she could see through to a hallway with a number of cages stacked one upon the other, all of them empty.

She rang the bell. The single clang sounded like a heavy glass being dropped to the floor. Seconds later a bearded face appeared in the door window, looking somewhat surprised. When he came through the door he wiped his hands on a white smock that hung down to his knees. The smock was stained with something bright red, and Hope swallowed hard. He saw her dismay and immediately turned.

"Oh, Jesus, I'm sorry. I was cutting around with one of Herb King's chickens. This must look pretty disgusting."

He dropped the smock into a can behind the counter, and when he turned to her again he was smiling, wearing jeans and a plaid shirt, sleeves rolled up, tanned and hairy forearms revealed.

"Doctor Brand?"

"Can I help you?"

"I was talking to the deputy outside, and he sent me here."

"Problem with the dog?"

He came around the counter and kneeled beside Shadow. Before Hope could protest he had turned Shadow's head and was looking at the connection port for the harness cable. He frowned, looked up at Hope.

"Is he a working dog?"

"Yes."

"I've never seen a guide dog quite like this. What's this for?" He tapped the coupler.

Hope inhaled deeply. "It's the way he works. It's hard to explain."

"I read an article about something like this. New guide dogs hooked up to portable computers to aide them with predefined traffic routes and such. Is he one of those?"

"Something like that."

"Amazing. What's wrong with him?"

"Nothing. That's not why I'm here. Actually, I'm looking for a dog. Another dog."

"What for?"

Brand stood, frowning again. He was full of questions, not easily put off. Hope had the horrible feeling she was going to give away too much.

"Well, it has to do with the breeding program Shadow is from. We're checking on the other dogs from his litter, that's all."

He didn't look like he bought it, but he nodded. "Okay."

"The kennel people said that one of the dogs went to an owner around here, but they couldn't tell us exactly who."

"You came here from . . ."

"Battle Lake."

"Just to find a dog?"

Hope shrugged. It was obvious that Brand suspected there was more to it than that, but he had nothing to go on.

"It's important. That's all I can tell you."

Brand kneeled by Shadow again, this time petting him gently, lifting his snout and lips to look at his teeth.

"There aren't many black labs around here," he said. "I actually don't see too many dogs. Country people are very pragmatic when it comes to animals. If they get sick, and there's no investment of money involved, they tend to handle it themselves."

"You mean kill them?"

He shrugged. "There *was* a dog."

"Like Shadow?"

"A woman. Brought him a couple of times. Looked to me

like he'd been severely beaten, but she said something about some kids. The dog was okay. I couldn't do much. I certainly couldn't take him away from her, though I felt like it."

"I know what you mean," Hope said. Her mouth was suddenly very dry, and she could hardly speak. "Do you know her name?"

"She didn't give it. She paid cash both times. The dog looked a lot like yours."

"It would really help if you could tell me something about her."

He shrugged. "I think she lives west of town. I don't know exactly where. I could even be wrong. Definitely a farm dog. I don't think I can help you more than that."

"Thanks anyway," she said.

"His name was Max. I remember that, because my dad's name was Max. Oh. One more thing. He had a mark. A white diamond on his rump."

Hope's heart started pounding so hard she was sure he could hear it.

Max was staring at her, and his eyes were not his own.

Eleanor held the shotgun tightly in her hands. Her skin was crawling. The way Max was staring made her feel dirty, ashamed. As if he knew everything she had done and despised her for it, judged her, judged her as only God was to judge.

A warm breeze blew through the trees, rustling grass and leaves. Max sat still, a black statue, staring at her with those eyes.

Devil dog, she thought.

She had brought him out here for a reason, but the strength had fled her. If Teresa was to rest in Gods arms, then Max should be with the girl. They'd proved that, the two of them. A love she could not share.

"Come here, Max."

He cocked his head, stood as if uncertain.

"Come here!"

His tail wagged and he walked over. After a few steps he stopped, as if something inside of him had overridden her command.

"Oh, Max," she whispered.

He had been with her so long, since that day she had found him wandering, lost, at the side of the road. He had taken to her right away, accepting her love without question, returning his own love, unconditional, pure. There had been times when their relationship had grown strained, but nothing like the past week or two. He had changed. He was not the same dog. Teresa had changed him.

"Sit, Max," she whispered.

He sat. He looked at her. He looked expectant now, pensive, as if he understood that something was going to happen.

Eleanor drew a deep breath. Max stood up, tail rigid, hackles now exploding around his shoulders.

He knew. He knew what was about to happen.

And then he growled. A low, wet thing, coming from deep inside of him, and full not of love, but of hatred.

Shocked, Eleanor could only stare, feeling the upcoming loss far more deeply than she would have thought possible. Max was only a dog! She was wiping the slate clean for God!

"Max," she warned.

He backed up a step, still growling, teeth exposed now. Eleanor felt suddenly afraid. Max was a big dog. A very big dog, broad-shouldered, all muscle. If he should . . .

She pulled up the shotgun, pointed, and fired. The blast nearly knocked her off the rock on which she was sitting, but she caught her balance and stood quickly. She heard a loud whine, then a rustle of grass.

"Max!"

Something black flashed through the trees to her right, and she swung that way and fired again. The forest swallowed the blast as if nothing had happened. Max was gone.

"Demon dog! I hate you!"

She walked over to where he had last been standing. Dark droplets of blood covered the grass. She had hit him. But how badly? She followed the droplets until they disappeared into the trees.

"Max! Come back!"

The forest remained silent, but she could feel his eyes on her. Still watching. She shuddered, and began to walk quickly back to the clearing. At the truck she leaned against the door and surveyed the trees. She had hit him. She knew that. A good hit, judging by the amount of blood on the ground. He would die quickly.

She climbed into the truck, started the engine, and started driving. She drove far too quickly, and the truck bounced violently through the ruts. As she approached the house, she slowed. Another truck was parked in the drive. Len Tate's red Ford. She drove up behind it, turned off her engine. For thirty seconds she sat there, heart pounding, watching the house.

Len came from the back of the house, frowning, rubbing his chin. Eleanor got out, shotgun over her arm, and walked around his truck. When he saw her he smiled, raised his hand, and came toward her.

"Eleanor! I wondered where you'd gotten to."

He blocked her path to the house, glanced down at the shotgun, up at her face.

"Shooting rabbits?"

She nodded.

"Get one?"

She shook her head.

"Listen, I came because I was thinking, you've got that old Windcharger up on that tower. Don't suppose it works anymore. But I thought I might buy it from you, fix it up. What is that, 6 volts, 80 watts?"

Eleanor glanced over at the tower, at the beaten, rusted wind generator on top. Frank had talked of fixing it and using it to charge batteries. She shook her head and stepped past him, but he put a hand on her arm.

"You got an injured animal in your cellar, Eleanor? I heard some crying when I walked back there. Sounded like a cat in heat."

She turned to him. He looked down at her feet, then up at her face, and his eyes were a little wider. Eleanor looked down at her feet. Her boots were speckled with Max's blood. She looked up at Len.

His face was paler than it had been. The line of his jaw trembled. "I better be heading back. You think about that Windcharger. I'll pay a decent price."

He turned to walk back to his truck. Eleanor lifted the shotgun, pumped it once, and fired. Len Tate leaped forward about four feet and fell flat on his face. His blood and intestine splattered his truck's windshield. Eleanor walked over to him and looked down at him. His eyes were glazed, his mouth opening and closing like a fish. She could see the gravel of the drive through the hole in his body.

With a satisfied nod, she turned back to the house.

THIRTY-TWO

"His name is not Thompson anymore," Hope said. "It's Max."

Campbell put down his coffee. The corners of his mouth twitched. He looked, Hope thought, like a man who has just discovered that he has only six months to live.

"Who told you that?"

"The vet. Doctor Brand. He said he knows of only one dog around here like Shadow. He described him down to the patch on his butt!"

Campbell licked his lips. His hands were on the table, the fingers curved like claws. She could feel his tension, his fear, his dread. A black mood emanated from him like a cloud. Although his glasses concealed the greater part of his expression, she knew he was deep in thought. Shadow sat beside him, looking up at her earnestly. Although Campbell's face was turned away from her, he was looking directly at her. This did not disconcert her as it had once done.

"This is what we've been looking for, Campbell. The last pup."

"We can't be sure of that. The trail ended at Deer Creek. This is all just . . . speculation."

"Yes, but logical speculation. It is to me, anyway."

"Then go to the police. Make an anonymous phone call."

She stared at him, confused and angry. The entire burden of Teresa Dawson's life had been placed on her shoulders. Campbell had abandoned her, if not physically, then spiritually.

"I know you're frightened, Campbell. I am, too. But we've come this far. I think we're close to finding Teresa. And once we do, this will all be over."

"Will it?"

He turned to face her now. His mouth was still trembling. If anything, he looked even more frightened than he had when she had left him here.

He knows something, she thought. Something happened.

"Did you connect with Max?"

He inhaled deeply, licked his lips. "It's all over, Hope."

It felt as if cold, dead fingers had suddenly speared into Hope's abdomen.

"What did you see?"

"I think she killed Max."

"You're wrong."

He leaned across the table, voice hoarse, intense. "I saw it! She had a damned shotgun. She fired it at me!"

"What about Teresa?"

"She must be dead. I haven't seen her."

"No. You're wrong.

"I know what I saw."

Hope leaned away from him. Her legs trembled.

"Are you all right?"

"No, I'm not all right."

Teresa couldn't be dead. She couldn't. Not after all they'd been through.

"We did everything we could," Campbell said.

"Did we?"

"We can't start feeling guilty because we couldn't find her, couldn't save her, couldn't do whatever. It's not our fault."

"Something has happened to you, Campbell. You're not the same man you were. You've changed."

"I can't help that."

"You made me believe we could help her. You were the one who convinced me. I believed you. I came on this journey because of you."

"I thought we could. I believed it, too."

"Something frightened you. I can understand that. But . . . you can't let your fear stop you."

"Hope . . ."

"No. Listen to me. Teresa is not dead. Just because you haven't seen her doesn't mean she's dead. All that means is that Max hasn't seen her. Maybe Max is dead. Okay, I can accept that. She killed the dog. You saw it. But Teresa is still alive."

Campbell shook his head, then lowered his chin. He looked as if he might weep. "Hope, I can't do any more. Something is happening to me that I don't understand. I'm scared."

"I'm scared, too. But I won't let Teresa Dawson die just because of my fear. Or yours."

"Take me home."

"No."

"I won't help. Just take me home."

The weight around her shoulders felt as if it had doubled. There was no standing up beneath it. It was crushing her, and there was nothing she could do about it.

"Campbell, when I first met you down on the beach, there was something about you that I liked, right away. You were blind. You were helpless. But you wouldn't give in. You wanted to stay in control. I respected that. I respected that a lot."

Campbell looked away from her, but Shadows eyes did not move. "I hated it."

"Being helpless is the worst thing in the world. I've been helpless, too. I think it was your helplessness that attracted me to begin with."

He turned to her, surprised.

"It's true," she said. "Two of a kind. I thought we could be helpless together. Or maybe I thought you would be more helpless than me, being blind, and I could feel better about myself."

Campbell shook his head but said nothing.

"Whatever it was, you showed me I was wrong. When you got your sight back, with Shadow, I was scared of you at first. I didn't know how to deal with you, how to relate to you. But you showed me how. You showed me that you weren't helpless, and you showed me that I didn't have to be helpless either. Without you, I never could have faced my mother, or Warren. That was *your* strength, in me. And it turned into my strength. After that, I didn't want to be helpless anymore. Not alone, and not with you. I wanted to be strong, together."

He looked at her again. "I'm not strong."

"You *are* strong. When you started having the visions, I knew we couldn't just let it sit. I knew we had to do something. When you decided to look for Teresa, I wanted to come with you. You were doing the right thing. You were being strong. You weren't helpless. I mean, one week you were blind, stuck in that cabin alone, and the next week you were about to do something that even sighted people couldn't do."

"Don't make me into a hero. I was just trying to heal myself."

"Bullshit, Campbell! You were doing it for Teresa, not for yourself. And so was I. You put yourself second. You were willing to suffer with the visions, because you knew you could help."

Campbell did not deny it. His hands had turned into fists on the table. Hope glanced around and realized that a few of the other restaurant patrons were looking at them, drawn to the intensity of the conversation. At the counter, the waitress was frowning, concerned. When Hope looked at her she held up a coffeepot and raised her eyebrows. Hope shook her head.

She leaned closer to Campbell and lowered her voice. "We can still help. *You* can still help. We're close. Let's finish what we started."

Campbell pulled away from her. His shoulders were slumped. "Just take me home."

The defeat, the self-pity, the self-loathing in his voice, made her want to cry out. She couldn't stand to look at him. Not like this. She stood quickly, knocking the table with her thighs in her hurry to flee, spilling the remains of her coffee.

"Then, let's go," she said, and walked away from him.

* * *

Teresa opened her eyes and sat up straight. Her stomach let loose a howl, a long, winding growl of hunger. She rubbed her eyes and yawned. There was still light coming from the window, pale and gray. It must be sunny outside, she thought. She wondered what day it was, then stopped. It didn't really matter.

Even thinking about sunshine made her eyes sting and water. Not tears, just water. From thinking about the brightness. It had been a long time since she had seen the sun. She leaned forward and rested on her knees and tried to remember if it had been sunny the day that Ellie and Max had found her. She couldn't remember. It had all been darkness since then, and for some reason, in her memory, that darkness was extending farther and farther backwards, as if it were a disease infecting every moment she had ever lived.

Her stomach growled again. She rubbed it and urged it to keep quiet. Ellie would probably come down soon, with Max.

Thinking about Max, she smiled. When Ellie had left him down here yesterday, they had sat together for hours, staring at each other, looking into each other's eyes, touching. He was no ordinary dog, she knew that now. His eyes told her that. She'd known all along that he was trying to communicate with her, trying to tell her something, but yesterday, when he'd stared into her eyes, she'd felt it in her heart. He was intelligent. And he was good.

"Don't worry, Max," she had whispered to him, stroking his head. "We'll both get out of here someday. I know it."

She had fallen asleep, arms pushed through the bars of the cell, linked with his paws. It was only Ellie descending to take Max up that had woken her again. Max had looked into her eyes one more time before he left, and it was as if he were apologizing to her. As if he were begging her forgiveness for something.

She had reached out and gently touched his nose. "Bye, Max," she had said.

Ellie had smiled and followed the dog upstairs. This time she had turned off the light, and Teresa was again plunged into absolute darkness until her eyes adapted.

That had been this morning. She was sure of it. Max had stayed with her through the night. Since then, she had mostly slept. She seemed to do a lot of sleeping now.

Once, shortly after Max had left, she had woken up, crying. She had been dreaming about her father, about how sad he would be. When she woke, her cheeks were wet, and the tears wouldn't stop coming. She had given in, then, and fallen to the mattress, and had let the sobs erupt. She had stopped only when she had glanced up and seen the shadow blocking the window.

Ellie, she had thought, was standing there. She did not want Ellie to hear her crying, so she had covered her mouth, buried her face in the mattress. She had been nearly asleep, minutes later, when she had heard the explosion. She had sat up straight, alert, terrified, but after that there had been only silence, and she thought she must have dreamed the noise.

After that, she had slept again. And again, something had wakened her.

What?

She sat now, on the mattress, leaning on her knees, staring at the gray square of the covered window. Had there been footsteps outside? Had she heard the door up above, opening?

She had the sudden suspicion that Ellie had sneaked down here in the darkness, and was watching her. She looked into the darkness where the corridor lay, but only deeper darkness swam before her eyes. She listened intently, so intently that she could hear nothing beyond her own heartbeat and breathing.

No. Ellie was not down here. She was alone.

She sighed and lay back down on the mattress. No sooner had she made herself comfortable than the door up above opened, and light flooded the cell. Teresa sat up, covered her eyes, and waited. Footsteps descended, shuffled along the corridor. Then Ellie was standing at the door of the cell, looking at her, smiling in a strange, sad sort of way that Teresa had never seen before.

She knew what Ellie wanted. She had known for some time.

Ellie wanted to be loved, to be liked. At first she had thought that refusing to give Ellie what she wanted might buy her freedom, but that wasn't going to happen. Ellie was never going to let her go. Ever. If she wanted to stay alive, she had to give Ellie what she wanted. Even if it made her sick, even if she really wanted to shout and scream and cry and rant, she couldn't. Ellie would get angry. And she didn't want Ellie to get angry.

Teresa smiled. She positively beamed. She was smiling so brightly she thought she could feel her own teeth reflecting the light.

Ellie watched her, expression unchanging. She was standing next to the cell door. A shotgun was cradled over her arm, pointing at the floor.

Teresa remembered the explosion she had heard, and felt a chill grip her neck.

"Where's Max?"

"Around somewhere," Ellie said.

"Is he coming down?"

"Actually, I was thinking of bringing you up."

"Really?"

"Would you like to?"

"Oh, yes!"

"Will you behave?"

"I will."

"I don't want to hurt you, but I will if you don't behave. I wouldn't have a choice, you know."

"I'll be good. I promise."

"You won't try to run away?"

"No."

"If you do, I'll shoot you."

Teresa nodded, swallowed hard. Her heart was pounding. She had to slow her breathing because she was becoming dizzy.

Ellie opened the cell door and stepped back. The shotgun was raised slightly now, held with both hands. Teresa stood and walked to the door. She paused for a moment, and then stepped through. The moment she left the cell she grinned, and this time it was an honest grin, even though Ellie was there to see it. Ellie smiled back at her.

"Up the stairs. Very slowly."

Teresa stepped to the stairs and started up.

"Slowly!"

The voice was right behind her. The skin between her shoulders crawled. She waited for the sound of the explosion, but it did not come. She moved very slowly up the stairs, but when she got to the last step she did not open the door. Ellie came up beside her.

"Open the door and step outside."

Teresa held her breath. Tears were springing to her eyes. Her hand shook as she reached for the handle. She turned it and pushed.

Light slid into her eyes like shards of glass and she cried out, covering her face with her hands. The cry that came from her mouth quickly turned into a laugh. She could not help it, could not stop it. Even when Ellie's hand touched her shoulder. She could only grin, and laugh.

The sky was blue. The sun was beaming down. She guessed, by the angle of the light hitting her face, that it must be mid-afternoon. When she looked down she could see well-trod grass, weeds, gravel. She shielded her eyes again and looked up. Trees, a field. She was in the country somewhere.

"Go around to the front," Ellie said, and gave her a nudge.

Teresa walked forward, nearly tripping on her own feet, around the corner of the building in which she'd been held. It was attached, she saw, to a small house, painted red. She walked past a red truck, behind which sat a green truck. The red truck was a mess. Something had been poured on the windshield. She saw a shape lying on the ground beside the truck, saw the dark glistening patches beside the shape, saw arms and legs bent at strange angles.

A man. A man covered in blood.

She froze in her tracks, staring at the shattered body, seeing blood everywhere. She knew she should be reacting in some way, horrified, frightened, sickened. But she felt none of that. She felt curiosity more than anything else. A dead body. She was seeing a dead body. Writers were supposed to see things like dead bodies.

She thought: I'll put a dead body in my next story, and it will look just like this.

And then she did feel sick, did feel frightened, all in one, dizzying moment. She turned away, hand over her mouth, squeezing her eyes shut.

"Keep moving," Eleanor said, and pushed her toward the house.

"Who . . . was . . . that?" Teresa managed to say.

"A bad man."

"Is he dead?"

"Yes, he is. Open the door and go inside."

Her skin suddenly felt hot, clammy. She did not want to be inside. Enclosed.

"Can't we stay outside?"

"No. Go inside."

Still fighting dizziness, Teresa opened the door. She stepped into a narrow, dark hallway. She smelled fish and antiseptic and dog. She looked around, but could not see Max. She felt immediately better. There were walls between her and the body outside.

"Move forward. To the first door on your left. Open it and go into the room."

Teresa moved forward. She passed the doorway to the living room and glanced in. It was very old fashioned, like Grandma Taylor's house, with furniture pushed close together, and old photographs filling open spaces on the walls. When she came to the first door on the left she opened it and stepped into a small bedroom.

It was, she saw, a child's bedroom. The curtains were drawn, the room dim. Not as dark as the cellar, but still dark. The room was very tidy, the bed neatly made. A small desk in one corner was piled with crayon drawings. She wondered how old the child was who lived here. It felt, she thought, like a boy's room. Hanging over the closet handle was a red plastic holster and a silver six-shooter.

"Whose room is this?"

"It doesn't matter," Ellie said. "Lie on the bed."

Ellie's voice was trembling. She sounded as if she were going to be sick. Teresa did as she was told. She moved to the bed. As she did so, she passed a dresser with a small mirror, and saw her reflection. She froze, staring. Her face was dark, filthy, streaked. Her hair was matted, tangled. Her shirt and jeans looked as if she'd rolled down a hill of dung.

"Go on, lie down."

She turned away and lay down on the bed. She put her arms at her sides, legs straight. Ellie kneeled by the bed, leaned the shotgun against the dresser. Teresa wondered, for a moment, if she could reach it, but Ellie was suddenly draped across her. The woman's head pressed into Teresa's chest. Large arms held her tightly. Ellie wept. Teresa could feel the tears through her shirt, soaking her stomach.

"What's wrong?"

"Nothing," Ellie choked, and continued to cry.

Ellie lifted one of Teresa's hands and placed it on her head. The feel of the stiff, frizzy hair made Teresa's stomach churn. But she knew what was expected of her. She stroked the big head, slowly, lovingly.

"Luke," Ellie whispered into her belly. "Luke."

Teresa squeezed her eyes shut.

"Where's Max?"

"Max isn't here anymore," Ellie said, and sobbed.

"Where is he?"

"He's gone."

Teresa fought back her tears, but they squeezed out of her eyelids nonetheless, rolling down her cheeks. She continued to stroke Ellie's hair.

I hate you, she thought. *I hate you.*

"Can I see him again?" she said.

"You'll see him soon," Ellie whispered hoarsely. "You'll both be together soon."

"Stop the car," Campbell said.

They had driven out of Hollyfield, and were passing the cemetery again. Hope pulled the car to the side of the road. Campbell surveyed the headstones, visible through an avenue of evenly spaced ash trees.

"This isn't the way home," he said.

"I wanted you to look around. Maybe you'll see something familiar. What is it about this cemetery?"

Campbell sighed. She wasn't going to let him escape.

"It's familiar."

"Were you here before?"

"Maybe. I think it was one of the early visions. At Miriam."

"Details, Campbell. Anything?"

He shook his head. Nothing. It seemed incredibly distant, as if it had happened years ago. He remembered running between the gravestones. The shape of the woman ahead of him. He remembered . . .

"Luke," he whispered.

"What?"

"She stopped at a marker. The name on it was Luke."

"Luke was the last name?"

"I don't think so. I can't see the last name. It's gone."

Hope turned to look at the markers. She shook her head. "There must be thousands of them. It would take us forever."

"That's all I've got."

"Doctor Brand said he thought she lived west of Hollyfield. If I double back, do you think . . ."

"I don't know." He sighed again. "Hope . . ."

"Please, Campbell. We'll never be able to live with ourselves if we don't try. I know I won't. I know you well enough to know that you won't, either. Please."

Campbell wished he could lie down. Lie down and sleep. Lose himself in darkness.

But there was no escaping Hope.

He nodded.

Hope turned the car around, and they started back for Hollyfield. Five minutes later they were past the town, driving through a countryside of rolling hills and clumps of forest. Every so often Campbell glimpsed a farmhouse, or a leaning barn, or abandoned farm machinery. At one point the road sank into the hills and the land rose on either side of the car in sheer, rocky faces. Then they were entering another forest area, rising on a hill on Campbell's side of the car, rolling away more gently on Hope's side.

Time had slipped away. The sun was still up, but lower now. The trees and hills cast shadows across the road.

Cars passed them, heading for Hollyfield. To Campbell, the faces behind the windshields were pale smudges, ghostly.

They drove for ten miles, and then Hope turned the car around.

"She can't be that far. Doctor Brand said he thought she was fairly close. You didn't recognize anything?"

"Nothing."

With a sigh, Hope started driving back to Hollyfield. Campbell leaned back in the seat. Shadow crawled onto his lap and nudged the window with his nose. Campbell opened it a slit and let the dog get some fresh air. The wind thundered around his ears, through the car.

They were passing through the wooded area again when Campbell felt his insides turn to mush. The trees now rose on Hopes side of the car, eased away on his.

"Judas Priest," he muttered.

Hope slammed on the brakes. The car skidded to a halt. Shadow banged into the dashboard, then sank to the seat between Campbell and Hope.

"Shadow, right," Campbell said.

Shadow stared out the passenger window. Campbell found himself looking into the trees.

"Something?" Hope asked eagerly.

For a second or two, Campbell could not speak. His heart pounded crazily in his chest. Then he managed to find his voice.

"I know where we are," he said.

THIRTY-THREE

Despite the afternoon sun, the breeze felt cold to Campbell as he got out of the car. Hope opened the trunk and found a jacket for him. He unhooked himself from Shadow while he slipped into it, then connected himself again while Hope held onto one of his arms.

"It's just trees, Campbell. There's nothing here. Are you sure?"

"No, I'm not sure. That's what I've been trying to tell you. But I have a feeling. That's all I've ever had. I've been here. In there."

"Doing what?"

"Walking. With her. I remember seeing something glittering in the trees. It was a car. I was seeing this road from in there."

Hope pursed her lips. "How do we get in there?"

They were standing next to a shallow ditch overgrown with tall grass. Campbell couldn't see if there was water beneath the grass, but thought there might be. Beyond the ditch was a gradual rise, ending in a wire fence, old and rusted. Beyond the fence, trees. Some saplings, but mostly older growth.

Still holding Hope's hand, Campbell edged down into the ditch. At the bottom, with grass up around his waist, he released her and jumped, hauling Shadow with him. His feet hit soft grass on the other side, but no water, and he scrambled up the embankment.

Hope followed without question, then helped him up to the fence. Campbell leaned against a wooden post. Shadow stuck his head between two strands of wire. The trees seemed to loom over Campbell, a conglomeration of dark shapes. He shuddered, and the memory of the morning's vision came to him like a thump on the back.

"Are you all right?"

"Yeah. Let's go."

And quickly, he thought, before I lose my nerve. He lifted up the two strands of wire for Shadow to slip through, then bent over and followed the dog. Hope scrambled nimbly over the fence and landed beside him solidly.

"Show off," he said.

She squeezed his hand. "Thanks for doing this, Campbell."

Campbell grunted, then started walking. The trees surrounded them quickly, and within minutes it would have been easy to imagine that they were in the far north, far from any sign of civilization.

"Do we know where we're going?"

"Not exactly. Let's just walk."

Hope did not argue, but kept her grip on his hand. They moved on, slowly, working their way around trees and bushes. The ground was a carpet of brown needles and fallen trunks, springy underfoot, but firm. The air was permeated with the odor of life, strong and earthy. For the most part, Campbell let Shadow pick the route, following where the dog led. Although this was not Shadow's normal method of operation, he seemed agreeable, and tended to take the path of least resistance. Sunlight beamed down through spaces in the canopy overhead, illuminating patches of brown earth with beams as from a spotlight.

Although Campbell saw nothing he judged as familiar, the feeling persisted that he was in the right place. He *had* been here. It felt right.

They walked for nearly half an hour before Hope finally pulled him to a stop. She brushed a stray curl of hair from her forehead, inhaled deeply, and puffed her cheeks.

"Campbell, maybe you were wrong."

"No."

"There's nothing here but trees. We might even be lost."

"A few minutes more. Come on. You're the one who convinced me not to give up. Don't make me turn the tables."

She gave him a pained grin, then nodded. They moved on again. It looked all the same to Campbell. Tree melted into tree, brush into brush.

And then Shadow lunged forward, as if he'd caught the scent of some elusive prey. For a moment Campbell had the horrible feeling he was about to crunch his jaws into some rabbit. Then Shadow came to a stop, sniffing furiously at the ground.

"What has he found?" Campbell asked.

Hope kneeled down. She touched the ground and brought up her hand.

"I think it's blood," she whispered, as if whispering might make the discovery less awful.

Campbell's heart raced. He pulled Shadow up and moved into the trees, leaving Hope behind. She came after him quickly.

"Hey!"

Campbell did not stop. Now he was pulling Shadow, bumping into the trunks of trees, tripping over his own feet. And then, abruptly, his headlong rush ended. He stepped into a small clearing. Hope came immediately behind, caught him, gripped his shoulder.

"Oh, wow," she exclaimed softly.

The trees leaned together overhead, forming a cathedral over the small open area. Sunlight bathed the ground in soft light. Three small mounds were clearly visible, each one marked with a softball-sized stone. Beside them, a small pile of earth sat beside a newly dug trench.

Hope stood over the hole and looked down into it. She frowned, looked up at Campbell. Campbell, breathless, leaned against a tree and wiped sweat from his face.

"This is it," he said, his voice a mere whisper.

Hope stumbled away from the open grave, grabbed onto his arm.

"The blood? Teresa?"

"Max, I think."

"He's dead?"

For the first time since this morning, Campbell reached for the dark band in his head. It was there, still waiting. He pulled back and did not enter it.

"I think he got away."

"Then, the grave?"

"Is for Teresa."

Hope sat heavily on the ground and covered her face. Shadow sniffed at her. She put out her arms and hugged him.

"It's all real, Campbell. I believed you, from the start, but I guess I must somewhere have still doubted you."

"Come on, get up."

He held out a hand for her. She took it and he pulled her to her feet.

"What are we going to do?"

"First, we get out of here. This way."

He led her along a narrow, barely discernible path that led away from the graves. In another minute they emerged onto a rutted, muddy road. The road ended in a broad clearing surrounded by trees. The ground had been recently torn up by tires.

Campbell recognized everything now. He knew that barely a mile along this road he would come to a field, and beside the field, hidden by a windbreak of trees, the farmhouse.

"Go back to the car," he said.

"I'm not leaving you."

"Yes, you are."

"Campbell . . ."

"There's no point in arguing about this. What I have to do, you *can't* do. And what you have to do, *I* can't do. If you want to save Teresa Dawson's life, then you'll do what I say. Please, Hope."

She took a deep breath, closed her eyes, then nodded. He held her shoulders tightly.

"Okay. Good. Now look through the trees there. That's where the highway is. If you look carefully, you'll see sun reflecting off your car. Can you see it?"

"I think so. Wait. Yes."

"Go to the car. Drive into town. Get the police."

"What about you?"

"I'm going to find Teresa."

"You can't go alone!"

"I won't be alone. I'll have Shadow with me. And Max, too."

"Oh, Campbell!"

"Don't worry about me. I'll be fine. You go. Now. Bring help."

She leaned toward him and kissed him, then held him tightly and kissed him more. When they finally parted, her eyes were moist.

"Keep safe, or I'll kill you," she said.

Then she turned and jogged into the trees. He watched her until she disappeared, a shadow among shadows, swallowed by the woods. Then he turned around and started walking back along the road.

For the longest time, Ellie was silent, and Teresa thought she must have gone to sleep. The woman's head was a weight on her chest, making it difficult to breathe. Under her hand, the skin of Ellie's forehead felt cool and dry.

Was she dead? Had she had a heart attack while she knelt here by the bed? The thought of it gave Teresa a chill, and she squeezed her eyes tightly shut. She did not even know how long she had been in the room. It seemed like hours, but it couldn't have been that long. The sun, which she could see as a bright blob through the curtains, was lower, but not very much lower. It was probably late afternoon, early evening.

Maybe she should try to move Ellie. If she shifted her head, just a little, then she could slide her legs off the bed, and once her legs were off the bed then . . .

"What are you doing?"

Ellie's voice was low, hoarse, dry, as if it had not been used in a very long time. It was the voice, Teresa imagined, of a long dead vampire, suddenly revived.

"Nothing," she said.

Ellie lifted her head and looked at her. The woman's eyes were red, tired looking. Her face seemed to sag from her bones, as if her flesh were slipping away. Her hair looked like a badly made wig.

Ellie stood and picked up the shotgun. She towered over the bed. Teresa lifted her head to look at her.

"Are you tired, Teresa?"

"Not really. Maybe a little."

"Would you like to go and see Max now?"

"Yes!"

"I'll take you. Wait here for a minute. Don't move, Teresa. If you leave this room, I'll know it. This is a test. I have to know if I can trust you."

Teresa nodded. "I won't move."

Ellie stared at her a few seconds more, silent, then turned and left the room. She closed the door behind her.

Teresa inhaled deeply, let the breath out. Somewhere in the house she heard heavy footsteps, a door opening, closing. Then there was silence.

She waited ten more seconds, then slid off the bed. She moved to the door and put her ear to it. Nothing. Not a creak. Not a peep.

She opened the bedroom door. She had watched Ellie leave, had seen how the door had not squeaked when it was opened quickly. She did the same thing, pulling the door open in one smooth motion.

She stepped into the hallway. To her right was the door through which she had entered the house. She stared at it, frozen, unsure what to do.

Then she heard it. The noise came from behind her. Muffled. But she recognized it for what it was. Crying.

Ellie was behind a closed door. Teresa listened, astonished, to the sound. Ellie was sobbing her eyes out.

She heard a squeaking sound, and water running. Ellie was in the bathroom.

Teresa squeezed her eyes shut, took a deep breath, then moved for the front door. She moved carefully, but quickly, lifting her feet up for every step. She turned the handle and pulled the door toward her. Fresh air tugged at her hair. She shuddered.

Part of her wanted to fall to the floor, to curl into a ball, to start crying, to forget, to take herself home, if only in her mind. But part of her knew that this would be death, that any such escape world be purely imaginary, that the only way she was going to stay alive, to see her dad again, was to run. Right now. To close the door behind her and run.

She stepped outside. Behind her, she heard the flush of a toilet. She closed the front door, jumped off the step, and ran for the trees.

The wind break was perhaps fifty yards from the house, but it seemed like a hundred miles. Every step seemed to take her farther and farther away from the safety of the trees, and with every step she knew that Ellie was coming out of the bathroom, returning to the bedroom, shotgun slung over her arm.

How far could Ellie's gun shoot, she wondered?

What would happen to her if she were hit?

She knew exactly what would happen. She'd look like the man beside the red truck, the bad man who probably wasn't a bad man at all, arms all bent the wrong way, bleeding everywhere.

And suddenly she was at the trees, curving around the end of them, over a clump of bushes. Ahead of her was a field, plowed but bare. To her left a narrow, muddy road stretched to a grove of trees perhaps a couple of hundred yards away. Would she have time to run that far?

She looked back at the house. No sign of Ellie yet.

No time to think. Time only to *do* something.

She turned toward the trees and started running. She had run less than twenty yards when the shape stepped out of the brush at the side of the road and grabbed her.

Teresa tried to scream, but a hand was crushed over her mouth. She looked up into a pale face with huge, dark, evil eyes. She tried to scream again, but the face was bending close to her.

"Shhh," it said. "Don't scream. She'll hear."

And then the face pulled away and she saw that the evil eyes were actually dark glasses, and it was a man, not Eleanor, and he was smiling at her. From behind him stepped a dog.

"Max!"

He looked at her and wagged his tail, and she saw right away that it wasn't Max at all. It was another dog. Like Max, but not Max.

Then she looked up at the man again. He was bending down to her, and something in the way he turned his head made her think of Max, made her think of the way Max had tried to talk to her in the cell, and she knew, knew in her heart, that it had been this man all along. What she was thinking was impossible, crazy even, and yet the idea would not leave her. Her thoughts started racing so quickly that she couldn't grab onto any of them.

"We've been looking all over the place for you, Teresa," he said.

"It's you!" she cried, and threw herself into his arms.

"It's me," he said, as if he didn't believe it himself. He squeezed her tightly, then pushed her away, still looking into her face. "Teresa, where is she?"

"Ellie? Back at the house. But she'll be coming soon."

He held a finger to his lips. "Be calm. I want you to keep going the way you were going. This road leads into that woodlot. When you come to the end of the road, just walk into the trees. If you walk far enough, you'll come to a road, and help will come soon. Do you understand?"

She nodded.

He squeezed her again. "Go on, now. Keep to the side of the road, close to the trees."

"But you . . . Ellie . . ."

"Shadow and I will take care of Ellie," he said, and there was something about his voice that frightened her.

She nodded, and when he urged her onward she moved, and soon began to run.

The road unwound before Hope like an endless ribbon and she was sure, as she rounded yet another bend to a vista of rolling hills, that she was never going to reach Hollyfield. Like some hapless Twilight Zone victim she'd entered an infinite loop of road, and her fate was to travel forever over the same stretch of highway. The speedometer read 90, and once or twice she saw the needle pass over 100. She slowed down because of the high-pitched scream of the engine, the buffeting of the car in the wind, as if it might, at any moment, lift off and sail into the trees.

But Hollyfield did, eventually, come into view, and she was still going over 80 when she roared down Main Street. Pedestrians turned their head in shock to look at her. The drivers of other cars raised their eyebrows and steered for safety.

She was halfway through town when the police car passed her going in the opposite direction, and before she had managed to skid to a halt she saw in her rearview mirror that his flashers had come on and that he had turned around to follow her.

She met him in the middle of the street. The police car parked at an angle blocking her. Hope was out of her car before the driver had a chance to react. She saw as she approached that it was the same deputy who had directed her toward the animal clinic.

He leaned out of his window as she approached. "Jesus Christ, lady, is that how they drive in Battle Lake?"

"Listen to me . . ."

"No! You listen to me! I clocked you running through town going on eighty miles per hour! This is a thirty zone!"

"Shut up! Just listen!"

Something in her tone, or the desperation that must have been in her eyes, reached him, and he lapsed into silence.

"There's a girl missing. Teresa Dawson. From Godfrey."

Something happened to his face. A pall descended on his features, and his mouth hardened. Everybody had heard about Teresa Dawson, and everybody had taken it to heart in one way or another.

"Yeah?"

"I know where she is."

He took a deep breath. "Lady, if you're . . ."

"It's a farm. About three miles from here. There's a forest or something, a wooded area, just past where the road cuts through all the rocks."

His brows lowered and his eyes brightened. "That's Eleanor Dueck's woodlot," he said. And then something else happened to his eyes, and he looked up at her in surprise. "Eleanor's got a dog," he said, as if he had just remembered.

"I know."

"Do these dogs have something to do with this?"

"Please. Teresa Dawson is going to die unless you come with me right now."

He did not need more convincing. He nodded to her car. "Pull that to the side of the road and get in here."

While she parked the car, he turned the police cruiser around. The cherry bar was already flashing, and by the time Hope was slipping into the passenger seat, the siren was going. He hit 90 miles per hour before they reached the end of the street.

When they turned onto the highway and started heading east, Hope said, "Call for backup."

"I think I can handle this."

"Think anything you want. But call for backup right now. If we don't make it, I want somebody to know where Teresa Dawson is."

He looked at her, frowned, and then nodded. "Okay."

The speedometer needle was pushing 100 when he picked up the radio microphone and pressed it to his mouth.

Teresa was gone.

Eleanor stared at the empty bed, eyes wide, disbelieving. Teresa had promised her. Teresa had been glowing with love for her, and Teresa had promised that she would not run.

She heard a cry emerging from her own mouth, a tortured animal scream than fled the house, reaching every corner, bouncing off walls and ceilings, returning to her amplified, intensified. She fell to her knees and sobbed.

"Teresa!"

She bowed her head in prayer, but the words that slipped from her mouth were full of hate and anger and betrayal, not meant for God. After a few moments she stopped herself.

How had she been so easily duped! The girl's love had seemed so real, so honest! For the first time in years Eleanor had basked in the love glow from a child. It had been wonderful. It had been the essence she had sought since Luke's passing. She had believed in it!

But she had been tricked!

She bowed her head again, this time begging God for his forgiveness. He had taught her a lesson. A painful lesson indeed. She would find the love she needed in His good time, not hers. The only love Teresa was meant to know, was His pure love. Eleanor should not have delayed. The angel must be returned. Now.

Furious at herself, at how easily she had been swayed from the path of righteousness, she rose. She picked up the shotgun, pumped a shell into the chamber, and barged through the front door. The yard was empty.

"Teresa!"

There were small footprints in the soft mud by the gravel drive, leading toward the wind break, but beyond the trees no sign of the girl. How far could she get? Not far. If she took the road to the woodlot, she would reach a dead-end. It wouldn't take long to catch her.

Still, her fury was uncontrollable. She raised the shotgun and fired a shot through Len Tate's windshield. Then, anger unabated, she pumped another shell into the chamber and fired it into Len's corpse. Len leaped into the air with a scream, and fell down twitching.

He had not yet been dead. She crossed the drive to where he lay. His mouth was still moving. The eyes had lost their glazed look and were staring up at her in terror.

"You . . ." he began.

"Shut up, Len," she said. "I told you it wasn't for sale."

She pressed the barrel into the back of his neck and fired again. This time, his head rolled away, underneath his truck.

Eleanor took a deep breath. She pumped another shell into the chamber, and walked briskly toward the wind break.

She was coming. What had Teresa called her? Ellie? All fury and hatred and darkness. Coming toward him. Campbell felt fear as he'd never felt it before.

He tugged Shadow's harness. "Shadow, left."

Shadow looked back along the road. Teresa was a small figure, just now disappearing beyond the curve in the road. In a minute she'd be invisible. But Ellie would be here before then. Unless . . .

Campbell turned the dog around. Ellie was almost at the windbreak. In another few seconds she'd be on the road, and shortly she'd be on top of Campbell. Against the shotgun, he did not like his odds.

But he had to give Teresa a chance. That's all he had to do.

He reached for the coupler and unhooked himself from Shadow. In darkness, he fumbled with the dog's harness and pulled it off. He tossed it aside, then put his arms around Shadow.

"It's up to you, boy," he whispered. "Give her something to think about."

He slapped the dog on the rump. "Run, Shadow! Run!"

Shadow slipped out of his arms as if he had expressly understood the command. For a moment Campbell heard the thump of the dog's paws on grass, then gravel. And then, splitting the afternoon air, a loud bark.

Campbell held his breath.

The bark came again, from toward the house.

"Max!"

Ellie's voice roared, followed immediately by a shotgun blast. Campbell hunched his shoulders.

Good boy, Shadow, he thought.

Another bark.

"Max!"

Campbell crawled into deeper grass, pulling himself off the road. The sounds around him, the wind, the whisper of the branches above him, his own breathing, formed no picture in his head. It was static. He was lost in darkness.

He bumped into a tree, leaned back. Inside his head, darkness swirled, chaotic. He reached for the edges of it, looking for Shadow.

He heard a snap. He sat up straight.

"Shadow?"

And then something cold was pressing beneath his chin, pushing him so hard that he had to stand up. He felt warm, sweet breath in his face. He smelled blood. Ellie.

"Where is she, you bastard? Tell me now, or I'll send you to God without a prayer."

THIRTY-FOUR

Teresa's legs were stones. Each step felt as if she were dragging a terrible weight. The air in front of her had become, she imagined, thick, syrupy water. Even the sun, which was on her back, hot and prickly, felt as if it were throwing rays with tiny hooks to catch her clothes and reel her in. The road was soft, covered in grass, almost muddy. She tried to stick to the area between the tire ruts, but sometimes her feet slipped and slid and she stumbled.

The days of sitting, crouching, lying in the clammy cellar, in the dark, had taken their toll. But the man with the dark glasses had said to run. He had said to keep running until the road came to an end. And then to run farther, into the trees. And she was going to do exactly what that man had told her to do, no matter how much it hurt, no matter how scared she got, no matter how much she wanted to do otherwise, because she knew who the man was.

He was Max.

It was crazy. It was impossible. But she had seen it in the way the man had held his head, in the way he had looked at her, in the way he had calmed her. Just as Max had done in the cellar. Max's eyes had looked upon her and given her strength. When she had curled up beside him, ready to give up, he had touched her with his paws, gently nudging her with his snout. He had tried to let her know, from that very first day, that everything was going to be all right.

She remembered how he had protected her. Tears sprang to

her eyes as she thought of it. How he had thrown himself at
Ellie, taking the brunt of a beating meant for her. He had saved
her life.

And it had been that man all the time. That man, somehow
inside of Max, moving him.

She had felt, at times, during the long days in the cellar, that
a guardian angel was watching over her. Well, she had been
right. An angel in the form of a black dog, and a tall, strange
man.

She kept running until the road curved into the trees, and the
line of sight to the farmhouse was blocked, then stopped and
leaned against a tree trunk at the side of the road to catch her
breath. The sun, low now, blinded her, heated her face. She
squeezed her eyes shut. The afternoon was silent. Her own
breathing filled the air, as loud as an idling engine. She breathed
deeply, exhaled slowly.

She was out. She was free. Everything was going to be all
right.

When the blast split the air like a crack of thunder, Teresa
cried out and leaped away from the tree and into the middle of
the road. She stared back along the way she had come, but there
was no sign of Ellie. Moments later, another blast. But she was
ready for this one, and merely started, then wrapped her arms
around herself.

Would the man and his dog be okay? What had he called the
dog? Shadow. A strange name for a dog.

A voice carried over the breeze, faint, wavering, then suddenly stronger, as if the caller had drawn closer. Ellie. She had
called out Max's name.

Teresa shuddered, and then froze.

Could Max be alive?

Since Ellie had brought her up from the cellar, she'd lived
with the fear, a hard knot in her throat, that Max was dead, that
Ellie had shot him. Everything Ellie had said, her evasiveness,
her cryptic comments about Teresa being with Max soon, had

told Teresa that her fear was well-founded. But if Ellie were calling for Max . . .

But there was no time now. The man had said to run. And she was going to run.

She turned away from the sun and started moving again. The short rest seemed to have revitalized her, and the weights slipped from her legs after a few yards. It felt good to run again, to be outside, in the sun.

Silence surrounded her, followed her. She did not know how far she ran, but the road continued to curve away from her, disappearing into the wall of trees. The man had said it would end soon, but it showed no sign of that yet. She slowed to a halt again, catching her breath.

The silence seemed almost solid, a blanket laid over the trees. She looked up at the blue sky. Glimpsed through the trees, it looked like a river, flowing above her. Its immensity, its emptiness made her shudder. The sky, the trees, the grass, the sun . . . all of them had been there, unchanged, every day she had spent in the cellar. The thought made her feel small and cold. The world had gone on as usual, its course uninterrupted by her disappearance. She was *that* small. What did the Bible say? Not a single sparrow should fall? Was she, then, smaller, less important than a sparrow? The world had not noticed her when she was here, and it had not noticed her when she was gone.

She shuddered and hugged herself, trying to shake free of the strange thoughts. She stared back along the bend of the road. No sign of Ellie. No sign of the man.

But the suspicion suddenly assailed her that Ellie was, at this moment, about to round the bend. The man was dead. Ellie was coming after her. She knew where she was going, and she wasn't going to stop.

Panic prodded her, sharp as a needle, and she started to run again. She had taken only ten steps when she heard the footsteps behind her.

Her heart exploded in her chest and she cried out as her feet slipped into one of the muddy ruts. She stumbled forward and lost her balance, barely managed to bring her arms up to break her fall. She crashed into the grass at the side of the road. For a moment, the trees were reaching over her like impossibly long arms, rolling her like a barrel, and then she was still.

Her breath was caught in her throat like a barb, unable to emerge. She stared up at the sky between the trees, waiting. Waiting.

And then the face loomed over her.

Teresa cried out.

Max licked her face. She threw her arms around, tears flooding her eyes.

"Max!"

But she had barely managed to embrace him when he faltered, then collapsed to the ground. Terrified, Teresa scrambled to her knees.

The dog whined and licked at her hand. He was covered in blood. She saw in horror that her own arms were swathed in red. It soaked her T-shirt, the tops of her jeans.

"Oh, Max," she whispered, and lay down beside him.

His tail wagged slowly. His mouth was open, as if he were smiling. When he looked at her, she could see the man, the movements of his head. She touched him gently.

The wound was on his flank, a huge gouge, above his tail, like a bite from some terrible predator. She could see bone, and tattered flesh. He had suffered this for her.

"Max," she whispered, and put her face next to his.

His breath was warm. She petted his neck and shoulders, gentle, barely applying pressure.

"Everything is going to be okay," she whispered. "Everything is going to be just fine."

But it wasn't. Because Ellie's voice came to her again on the breeze, full of fury and hatred. It wasn't going to be all right at all. Because she couldn't leave Max. Not like this.

And Ellie was coming.

* * *

"What's your name?" Hope asked.

He didn't take his eyes off the road. "Bill Kelly."

"Deputy Bill Kelly?"

"That's right."

"My name is Hope Matheson."

"Nice to meet you."

"Sorry to ruin your day like this."

Now he looked at her, though the speedometer needle didn't waver from its perch at 100, and he smiled. All teeth.

"If you're telling the truth, you haven't ruined my day."

"I'm telling the truth."

"I believe you."

What had seemed to take hours to drive with Campbell, and even longer when she was racing back to town, now flashed by in seconds. Before she realized it, they were racing past the high faces of rock before Eleanor Dueck's woodlot. Hope put a hand on Bill Kelly's arm.

"Let me off here."

"What?"

"Stop the car. This is where Campbell went. I'll go back the way I came."

He slowed the car quickly, but when he turned to looked at her he was skeptical.

"We're only a few minutes from the house this way."

"Well then, you go to the house. I'll cut through the wood lot again. One of us should go this way, and since it's your car, it should probably be me."

He thought about it for less then five seconds, brought the car to a shuddering stop on the shoulder. "Okay. But be careful."

Hope got out of the car, but before she closed the door she leaned down and looked at him. "You be careful, too."

He nodded. Hope slammed the door. The car rolled away and picked up speed, and before Hope had crossed the road, Bill Kelly was receding quickly, turning a wide bend. She hopped down into the ditch, leaped over it, and scrambled quickly up the other side. Once she was through the fence she paused to catch her bearings. If she moved directly toward the sun, it should only take a few minutes to reach the rutted access road where she had left Campbell.

She lowered her head and squeezed her eyes shut. It had been a long time since she had prayed to God, a long time since she had even thought of God, but she did so now. She muttered a prayer, and sent it with all the faith and hope she could muster.

Then she took a deep breath and started running.

The man was blind. She could see that much.

But there was something else about him that she could not quite pinpoint, something that was at once familiar, terrible, and strange.

Eleanor kept the shotgun pressed to his chin as she studied him.

"Where is she?"

"I don't know," he said.

When he spoke he moved his head, as if listening for her response. She frowned at him and wondered why she hadn't pulled the trigger already. Teresa was gone! She needed to be looking for Teresa.

"I know you, don't I?"

"No."

"You're lying. We've met. Where?"

"We've never met."

He wasn't a big man, certainly not as big as Frank had been, but he was slim, well-muscled. Not work muscle, of course, but play muscle. A man like this would never have work muscle.

She yanked him hard, pulling him away from the tree, and pushed him down onto the rutted track. He fell unceremoniously to his behind. His hands came out for balance, and he planted them on the ground beside him.

Eleanor looked around for Max. The dog had disappeared again, flashing past the house. He had not look injured at all.

"Max!"

He did not respond to her call. She took a deep breath and closed her eyes. Think. Think. What did it mean that this man was here? What could it possibly mean? He could not know of Teresa, not fully. Had he been with Len?

"You're trespassing on my property."

He looked up at her, attracted by her voice. "I'm sorry. I was lost, that's all. I was walking."

"Walking? You?"

He shrugged. "It's a nice day."

She crouched beside him. "Listen, mister. I'm looking for my little girl, that's all. I'm sorry if I got angry with you. She's run off, and I have to find her."

"I didn't see her."

He smiled, as if this were funny, but she did not smile back.

"My dog's gone, too. It has been a bad day. I'll tell you what. Are you with anybody?"

"I'm alone."

He was lying. It was so obvious it wasn't even funny. He was lying to her for some reason, and she did not know why. He could not possibly know about Teresa, and yet . . . he *did* know about Teresa. She could feel it. The girl was the only reason he was here. And if *he* was here, then who else might be coming?

"Were you with Len? He's gone back, if you're looking for him."

He shrugged. "I don't know any Len."

"Mister, I'm getting impatient."

"I've lost my dog."

"Your dog?"

She looked back toward the house, frowning. His dog? *His* dog? Not Max. A guide dog.

She looked back down at him. His head was angled, looking up at her. Eleanor felt her heart skip a beat. He was looking at her just like Max had looked at her, full of judgment, full of knowing.

She felt suddenly cold.

Len Tate was lying dead beside his truck. Teresa had escaped.

And this man was sitting beside her, knowing everything. But, more than that, he had been here before. Had been here in a way she could not understand. Could not comprehend. Could hardly believe.

She kneeled beside him and nudged him with the barrel of the shotgun.

"Who are you?"

"No one."

"Max," she whispered, horrified to hear the name on her lips.

He smiled then. His teeth were very white. It was not a pleasant smile. It was a gloating, hateful smile.

"Ruff, ruff," he said.

Eleanor shuddered, could not speak.

"She's gone, Ellie. And she's never coming back."

"What are you?"

"Exactly what you think I am. Somebody who knows everything about you. You sick, evil bitch."

She slammed the shotgun into his face. His glasses shattered, flew into the grass, and blood sprayed out of his nose. He collapsed, hands over his face. She lifted him by his jacket to a sitting position.

"Who are you? How do you know me?"

Blood seeped between his fingers. His eyes were missing. A fiery line slashed across his face, ear to ear, where his eyes should have been. Eleanor's groin crawled at the sight. His nose had split, and she could see cartilage and torn flesh. When he spoke again, his voice was thick, pained.

"I've lived with you, Ellie. I've seen everything you've done. I know about Jesse Hampton. I know what you did to him. I know about Teresa. I know where you found Max. And I'm not the only one who knows. A lot of people know about you, Ellie. And they're coming to get you. I'm just the first."

She could see that he was lying again. He wasn't very good at it. Yes, he knew about her. He knew far more than he could possibly know. But there were no others. Just him. This strange, blind man.

When Max had padded silently around her house at night, it had been him. When Max had put his head down beside Teresa, loving her, it had been him. When Max had turned on her, it had been him. It had been him all along. She did not know how it was possible, but she knew that it was so.

And now it was over. He had destroyed everything. Taken everything from her.

There would be no more children. No more love to be shared.

All that remained to be done, was to settle up with God. God was waiting for Teresa.

She stood and raised the shotgun to his head. He turned his face up to her as if he could see her, and he looked frightened, helpless. Some part of her reached out to him, in his helplessness, and she lowered the gun.

She kneeled by him again and stroked his head. He leaned into her hand, seeking her caress.

"I'm sorry I hurt you. You made me angry."

She put her arms around him and pulled him to his feet. He was shaky, but managed to find his balance. Keeping the shotgun trained on him, she nudged him toward the house, toward her truck.

He moved slowly, unsteady on his feet, head turning this way and that, as if seeking something. At the truck, she opened the door and poked him with the gun. He climbed in. She closed the door behind him and went around to the other side.

Once she was inside, she reached over and touched him. He was leaning against the passenger door, streaking the glass with his blood. He lifted his head a little, but did not turn to her. He looked very frightened. More frightened than he had only moments ago.

"I'm glad you came. It's right. It's all over now. But we have to find Teresa. God is waiting for Teresa. God is waiting for all of us. We'll go together. It will be beautiful. The angels will sing this day."

Back along the drive, beyond the house, toward the highway, she glimpsed something flashing between the trees. It looked like the lights of a police car.

She watched the light, undisturbed. It would take a minute for the car to clear the trees. The driver would not see them, or where they had gone. Plenty of time. She knew where Teresa had gone.

She turned the ignition, revved the engine, backed up a few yards, then started down the road toward the woodlot.

After what seemed like an eternity, Hope emerged from the trees into the clearing where she had left Campbell. The sun was a brilliant, fiery heart, beating within the ribs of the trees. Shadows reached out for her.

How long since she had left the police car? Not too long. Knowing where she was going, she had run quickly. It had only taken a minute or two to reach the clearing from the road. Her face stung from the lashes of branches, but this pain was nothing to the empty ache in her chest.

She leaned over her knees and breathed deeply, trying to catch her breath. She allowed herself ten breaths, then started running again.

The road was no easier than the woods had been. The ground was soft, and her feet could find no purchase on slippery grass or muddy rut.

No sign of Campbell yet. Where was he?

She repeated her prayer and kept moving, keeping her balance as best she could along the edge of the road.

She had turned a bend in the road, had entered a long straight stretch, when she saw the dark shapes huddled at the edge of the trees. One, she saw was a dog. The other might be a man, or it might be a child. The way they were huddled together, she could not tell.

Her heart caught in her throat, and a sob erupted. She stumbled to a halt, staring, unable to go on.

"Please, God, let them be okay. Let them be okay."

Fighting back tears, she ran on.

Max was shaking. The tremors started in his chest and radiated from there. His paws twitched in the dirt, as if he were dreaming.

Teresa kept her arms around him, holding him tightly.

"It's going to be okay, boy," she whispered.

But it wasn't going to be okay. She knew that. No, it wasn't going to be okay. Because Max was going to die. Max wasn't going to make it.

She started to cry, and her tears dripped onto his face, he licked at her cheeks. His tail wagged feebly.

The man had said to run, and to keep running, but she couldn't leave Max. She couldn't. Not like this, not to die.

Max growled.

Teresa felt it as a low rumble. And at the same tide she heard ragged breathing, the approach of footsteps. She squeezed her eyes shut, pressed her face to Max's throat.

The footsteps drew closer.

I'm sorry, I'm sorry, I couldn't run, I couldn't leave him.

"Oh, God."

The voice was directly above her. Teresa opened her eyes and looked up. A face was staring down at her. A woman's face, streaked with tears, red from welts. But not Ellie.

"Teresa?"

Teresa nodded.

The woman dropped to her knees beside her, threw her arms around her, and squeezed her so tightly that Teresa thought she might break in half.

"You're real," Hope whispered into Teresa's hair, even now not quite believing it was true.

Teresa pushed herself away. The girl was crying copiously. Hope's own tears continued to flow.

"M-M-Max is h-h-hurt," Teresa stuttered.

"Max?"

Hope looked down at the dog. Not Shadow. She saw that now. The white triangle on his rump, right next to a terrible wound. She touched him gently on the throat. Max shuddered, lifted his head, looked at her. His tail wagged.

"There was a man," Hope said, hardly able to make herself speak. "And a dog."

"They helped me. The man. And Shadow."

"Where are they?"

"Back there. With her."

"Are they . . ."

Teresa looked back along the road. "I don't know. Ellie is coming."

Hope's heart hammered. "We have to go."

"But Max is hurt."

"Max is going to be all right," she lied. "But we have to go. Right now."

"I can't leave him."

"We must, Teresa."

And then Max stood up. The hair around his shoulders rose, and he growled deeply. Hope felt goose bumps explode on her neck, and she leaned away from the dog. He glanced at Teresa once, barked, and then he bolted.

Teresa jumped to her feet. "Max!"

"Let him go."

Teresa stared at her in horror, shook her head. "No!"

And before Hope could move, the girl was running.

"Teresa!"

Somewhere along the road, an engine roared. A car, or a truck, was coming toward them.

Hope ran after the girl and the dog.

THIRTY-FIVE

Campbell kept has hands clasped between his legs as the truck jostled and jounced along the road. His head bounced against the passenger door glass, sending shards of icy pain shooting to the back of his skull. His face throbbed, a firestorm of pain, so hot and deep that it reminded him of the aftermath of the explosion that had destroyed his eyes.

But he had to fight the pain. He had to remain calm.

They were headed toward the woodlot. And that's where Teresa was. It wasn't likely that the girl had made it to the woods, and even if she had, he didn't doubt that Eleanor was capable of running the girl down.

And that would be that.

We'll all go to God together.

Just one great big happy fucking family.

But he couldn't let that happen. No matter what, he wasn't going to let that happen.

Ellie was humming a song as she drove, a hymn he guessed, by the sound of it. A strange sort of calm had descended upon her, apparently. The calm before the end. Whatever was going to happen, whatever she had ordained should happen, she had come to terms with it.

Campbell inhaled deeply, let the breath out, inhaled again. The pain was a fog inside his head, but it was a fog he needed to clear. Fast.

He sought the darkness that had crowded his vision for so long, the dark ring in which, he now knew, a terrible kind of madness lay. It was there, beyond the fog. Waiting for him. And even now, even as he knew he must act quickly, he hesitated, unsure, more frightened of where the darkness might take him than of whatever end Ellie had planned for him.

A strong hand gripped his thigh, and Campbell started, pulled out of the fog.

"You can stop calling me Ellie, by the way. Never did like that. I'm Eleanor."

Campbell grunted. Her hand did not leave his thigh. She's waiting for an answer.

"Campbell," he said softly.

"Campbell," she said. "That's a nice name.

The weight left his leg. She started to hum again. It sounded like *Onward Christian Soldiers,* a hymn Campbell hadn't heard since childhood. To her low, humming voice, he rushed into the fog of pain, through it, beyond it, hesitating no longer. The darkness circled him and he reached into it. The roar of the truck's engine became terribly clear for a moment, and then receded.

Trees rushed by his face, and he found himself running along the road. He could see the truck ahead of him, perhaps only fifty yards.

Run, Shadow, he urged.

And then, as he watched, another darkness ringed his vision, pulling closer, blocking out the sight of the truck, and he was again running along the road, this time into the sun.

Max?

It had to be. Max was alive!

Get off the road, Max! She's coming! And as if the dog had heard the command, understood, he was suddenly veering away from the deep ruts, across grass, into low brush and thick trunks, but running still, the sun glittering in the trees above.

Campbell could feel the window against his face, could still hear Eleanor humming her hymn, but that was in another place, another world, not his world. Max's vision began to shrink, squeezed by a dark band, but Campbell fought it, pushing back the darkness. He needed to be with Max now. Needed to see the truck coming so that he would know when . . .

But the darkness did not recede. Instead, it pulled closer. And then something happened that made Campbell gasp.

The visions merged. He was running through the trees and bushes at the side of the road, the sun glittering between the branches ahead of him, and at the same time he was racing along the road itself, away from the sun, toward the rear of the truck. It felt, to Campbell, as if he had suddenly drawn back from the scene, jumped into the air a hundred feet and was looking down. He did not perceive each vision separately, but as one broad, encompassing vista. He had become a third party, apart from the dogs, yet seeing and aware of what both of them experienced.

At once he knew that the truck was approaching him from the front, rushing closer, closer, and also that it was moving away from him, inexorably, widening the gap between them.

Now, Max! Now! He urged the dog back onto the road, watched brush and grass clear as he lunged onto the muddy track, saw the truck rush closer, bouncing like some incredible beast through a tunnel of trees. Beside him, Eleanor gasped.

"Max!"

The truck shuddered as Eleanor applied pressure to the brakes.

Campbell lunged across the cab, flailing his fists madly, and connected with something soft. Eleanor screamed, and the truck careened wildly.

From Max's eyes he saw the truck veer across the road to the right, bouncing over the ruts like a toy. From Shadow's eyes he saw the truck's brake lights flash, and suddenly turn to the left. And then Eleanor screamed again, her voice joining the sudden roar of the engine. The air was filled with the thunderous explosion of breaking branches. The truck came to a sudden, jarring stop.

Campbell smashed into the dash board. He continued to flail his fists, striking Eleanor repeatedly. She was screaming incoherently now. Campbell pulled away from her, fumbled for the door handle behind him. He found it, pulled it, and pushed hard against the door. It opened, and he fell out of the truck, banging his shoulder against the rider panel.

He did not stop to think, but started to crawl. Branches scratched at his face, and his hands sank into mud, but he kept moving.

He was both dogs now, moving in on the truck, one from the rear, one from the front. Close now, so close.

He saw himself, crawling desperately through the high grass at the side of the road, and saw, behind him, the shape of Eleanor. She had the shotgun. Blood was pouring down her face.

Campbell stopped and rolled onto his back.

Eleanor was standing over him, lifting the shotgun to her shoulder.

He was too late. And he could not even turn away from the blast. He was going to see it all, from the point of view of the dogs. His own death, from a distance.

And then the dogs barked. Both of them, simultaneously.

Eleanor lifted her head and looked at Shadow. Through Shadow's eyes, Campbell found himself staring into Eleanor's face, only a handful of yards a way.

"You mutt," Eleanor said calmly.

The shotgun rose. Shadow rushed toward her and leaped. Campbell heard the blast and saw the muzzle flash at the same instant. Trees arched overhead, a kaleidoscope of broken sky and twisted branches. And then Shadow's vision shrank to a pinpoint.

"No!"

But even as he cried out, even as the vision faded, something dark moved in to replace it, and he was looking at Eleanor now through Max's eyes.

But it was more than simply looking. He could feel something in his gut, a deep, searing pain. An urge so powerful, that he could not resist it. And he knew what it was.

It was the feeling he'd experienced when Shadow had attacked the rabbit in Deer Creek, but intensified a thousandfold now, and mingled with his own rage and outrage.

Blood lust.

He tried to pull back from the vision, but he could not do it. The darkness had him, and it would not let go. What he had feared the most, was coming to pass.

Inside of Max, he leaped at Eleanor, the souls of both man and dog screaming for her blood.

Eleanor screamed when Max leaped at her. Her attention had been drawn by the other dog, the guide dog, and she had managed get off a shot that had sent the dog spinning, harmless, across the ground. But when she turned around, Max was there.

For a moment she had stared at him, stunned, shocked to see him alive, even more shocked at his condition. His hind quarters were soaked with blood, and his rump was a ragged mess where her earlier shot had hit him.

She thought: *He can't be alive.*

And then he leaped.

She tried to swing the gun around, managed to pump a shell into the chamber as she did so, but he crashed into her as she brought the barrel up. His chest hit her arms, his teeth flashed in her face.

She cried out again, and the shotgun fell from her hands and skittered into the grass. The force of the collision knocked her to her behind, but she scrambled quickly to her knees.

He was standing right in front of her, less than a yard away, staring at her, lips pulled back from teeth she had not realized were so big. He growled from some place far inside of himself, some deep, dark, terrible hole.

"Max," she whispered, and held out her hands to keep him at bay.

Behind the dog, the man who said his name was Campbell was moaning, one arm flung across his face as if he were trying to avoid a very painful sight. From the corner of her eye, Eleanor saw the shotgun. Too far to reach. If she moved, Max would be upon her.

"Now, Max," she calmed. "Be good. Good boy, Max."

He stepped forward, teeth slashing together with a loud clack that sent saliva spraying. Eleanor pulled back her hands in horror. She had never seen him like this. Ever. Not since the day she had found him. He had always been a timid dog, loving, kind.

But the look in his eyes now was not love. It was as far from love as it is possible to get. His eyes were black pools of hatred, so deep that she thought she might drown in them. And yet, she could not look away from them. She was captured by them. He hated her. *Her!* Who had given him only love!

A cry came from down the road. A child's voice.

"Max!"

The dog shifted his weight when he heard Teresa, and Eleanor knew her only opportunity was at hand. She lunged for the shotgun, throwing herself horizontal to the ground.

But Max was ready. It was as if, she realized, he had tricked her. He had wanted her to move, to give himself the opportunity *he* needed.

Her hand closed around the stock of the gun, but it was too late. She felt the weight of his paws on her shoulders. She threw herself onto her back, hoping to dislodge him, but instead found herself staring up into his face, into his eyes.

All the strength left her. Her hand released the shotgun. She could only stare, horrified, into the pools of utter hatred that were looking down upon her.

"Max . . ."

Then his jaws lunged forward, smashing her chin upward. The force of the blow caused her to cleanly bite off the tip of her tongue, and blood spurted out of her mouth. When she tried to speak again she could not because searing heat was burning into her throat. She felt herself twisted and torn. She heard his low, throaty growl. She felt blood explode at the back of her throat and realized in horror that it was not from her severed tongue, but from her lungs. She was drowning! Her arms gripped the monster who now straddled her, but he could not be moved. His grip on her was unbreakable.

Blood sprayed from her lips and fell back into her eyes like hot summer rain. But she had no will now to wipe it away, no will to do anything. She let her hands drop to her sides. Above her, the wells of hatred seemed to drink of her soul. There was no escaping them.

And then, beyond the dog's head, the face of the angel. The angel looking down upon her. Teresa.

But in those eyes, too, no pity. No love.

"Please," Eleanor tried to say, but heard only a gurgle.

And then the darkness that was her dog's hatred seemed to encompass her, shrinking around her, pulling her in, and she had the terrible thought that this was it. The end. This terrible darkness.

Then she was gone.

There were no angels singing this day, after all.

Hope ran with all her might. She had heard the crash of the truck, and now as she rounded the bend in the road, she heard Teresa's cry.

Ahead of her, the scene of the crash was a tableau of horror that burned itself into her mind.

She saw Campbell, lying on his back, arm thrown over his face, covered in blood. He was not moving, and her heart, for half a second, seemed gripped in a tight fist.

She saw Teresa, standing over a lump on the ground. The girl's hand was around her own mouth, and she was shaking.

The lump on the ground was Eleanor Dueck. Max was on top of her. Neither of them were moving.

The only thing she could see that *was* moving was a dark shape in the grass that seemed to be crawling toward Campbell. The fist gripping her heart loosened and she stumbled forward.

Teresa turned to her as she approached and threw herself into Hope's arms. Hope held the girl, unable to comprehend exactly what she was looking at.

They were dead. They were *all* dead. Campbell. Eleanor. Max.

Her eyes were drawn to the dark bundle moving on the ground, and she realized it was Shadow. Half his face was gone, and blood glistened on the rest of him. But he moved on, pulling himself forward with his paws, until his nose pushed into Campbell's side.

And then Campbell's arm fell away from his face, on top of the dog. Shadow whined, and his tail wagged once.

"Oh, God," Hope said, and put more of her weight on Teresa, until she and the girl were standing only because they were holding each other up.

Campbell groaned, and Hope managed to disengage from Teresa. She kneeled by man and dog and picked up his right hand. He squeezed her fingers, lightly. He raised his head an inch.

"Teresa?"

"She's okay."

"Eleanor?"

"Dead."

"Max?"

"Dead. I think. Oh, God, Campbell."

He started to shake. His whole body trembled, and he released her hand.

"I couldn't stop myself," he said. "It was like the rabbit."

She leaned over him. Bent down and kissed his lips. Tasted his blood. "Shush."

Teresa came up beside her then. Tears rolled down the girl's cheeks. She leaned on Hope, and then fell to her knees by Campbell and threw herself across his chest, one arm over Shadow, now weeping uncontrollably. Campbell put a hand across her shoulders. Hope put her arms around all three of them, her head on top of Teresa's trembling back.

Down the road, she glimpsed flashing lights, approaching quickly. From beyond the trees, toward the highway, sirens.

"It's over," she whispered. "It's all over now."

EPILOGUE

Hope closely followed the aftermath of Teresa's rescue, still unable to fully comprehend that she had been a part of it.

Eleanor Dueck was pronounced dead at the scene by the Hollyfield Coroner. Cause of death, other than heart failure, was listed as massive trauma to the trachea caused by animal attack. With Hope's help, the police located the small graveyard that Eleanor had dug at the back of her woodlot.

They found four graves in all, and exhumed three bodies. Two were of children, identified by their dental records as Ruth Burns, an eight-year-old girl who had disappeared two years ago, and Jesse Hampton, who had been missing since May. The third body was a dog, an old dog, and by the state of the remains, had been dead and buried a good six years. Probably it had been Eleanor Dueck's own dog, and this had been where her husband Frank had buried it. She had continued to use the site for her own ends. The fourth grave, of course, was empty, and had been intended, it was generally considered, for Teresa Dawson.

Campbell's and Hope's involvement in the case was never mentioned in the newspapers. Although Deputy Bill Kelly testified that Hope had come to him with the information about Eleanor Dueck, the true core of the matter was never revealed. Hope told reporters that while she and Campbell were driving, she had seen something in the woods that caught her attention, and had gone to investigate. This claim stood the assault of all questions.

In the weeks following the recovery of Teresa, Jesse Hampton and Ruth Burns received burial services. Hope attended both, alone, and although great sadness filled the hearts of all who were there, she sensed, on some level, a terrible, liberating relief. For the first time since their ordeals had begun, the parents of both children wept tears of true grief. Soon, one way or another, lives would resume, and children would be properly mourned.

Campbell's physical injuries were, for the most part, minor. The worst of all was a broken nose. His psychological injuries were another matter, and for weeks afterward, he would not talk of the incident. Sometimes, at night, he would wake, shaking, and it would be hours before he managed to sleep again. But in time, Hope knew, he would be healed.

Shadow's injuries were of a more permanent nature. The shotgun blast that Eleanor Deck had unleashed upon him in her final moments had blinded him. Campbell refused to allow the dog to be put down, and for many weeks Shadow lay around either Campbell's or Hope's cabin, his head swathed in bandages, a protective funnel around his throat to stop him scratching the wound. He looked, Hope imagined, as Campbell must have looked when he lost his eyes. It was a very long time before she saw his tail wag.

The people at Miriam Technologies offered to replace Shadow with another dog. Part of the circuitry embedded beneath Campbell's skin had been damaged, but repairing it should be relatively easy. They could have him up and seeing again within a month. Campbell refused the offer, and Hope was not surprised. He had changed in many unanticipated ways.

Although neither Russell Graham nor Nina Ladeceur officially acknowledged Campbell's story of canine telepathy, Hope learned from Claire that Miriam Technologies had established a program to test a variety of dog sibling groups. Campbell refused all invitations to come to Miriam to talk about his experiences. As far as he was concerned, the party line on which he'd so briefly snooped, had been disconnected for good.

* * *

It was in August, almost a month and a half after Hope had last seen her, that the letter came from Teresa Dawson. Hope read it first, and then read it aloud to Campbell. He sat in the easy chair in her living room, head cocked in that intent, listening way he had, and said nothing. When she had finished, he stood and walked to the living room window. He stood there, facing the lake, for a long time, the sun warming his face.

Hope sat down and read the letter again.

Dear Campbell, Hope, and Shadow,

I'm sorry I didn't write to you all before now, but I have been very busy. My dad took me on a trip to see my Uncle Fred in Chicago. and then, because we did that, we had to visit every other relative I have, even the ones I haven't seen in years! But it was fun. School starts in about three weeks and I'm looking forward to that.

The real reason I'm writing, though, is to thank you for what you did for me. My dad knows all about what happened with Max, but he doesn't want me to tell anybody. He says that some things are better left unsaid. He says that if Campbell ever wants to talk about it, then that will be fine, but that I'm not to do it before then. I guess he's right. He's right about a lot of stuff.

I wanted to tell Campbell that when I was in Ellie's prison, I was very sad and frightened. I didn't know what was going to happen to me, and I didn't know if I was ever going to see my dad again. Max became my friend. He helped me to be strong and helped me to keep hoping. I know it was Campbell, inside of Max. Campbell and Shadow. I guess that makes you guys my guardian angels or something. I don't know why you picked me, but I'm glad.

This part is for Shadow. Hope, could you please read this to him? I know he'll understand. Shadow, I'm sorry you got hurt trying to help me. I know that because of you and Campbell and Hope I managed to see my dad again. I wish you hadn't got hurt, though. I wish it was me instead of you. I hope you're not too sad about it, and I hope you aren't angry at me. I know we would be friends if we met again, because I love dogs and dogs love me. My dad says a blind dog is a pretty weird thing, but not that weird. He says blind people have been living perfectly useful and productive lives for years and that there's no reason a blind dog shouldn't do the same thing. I know that Campbell will be a good example for you. I hope we can meet sometime soon, and I promise that when we do I will be your "guide person!"

I know you're probably wondering how I'm doing. Sometimes I have nightmares, but not every night. My dad says this is okay, and that they will stop soon. Until they do, I'm allowed to go through to his bedroom and sleep in his bed if I wake up in the middle of the night, but I'm not supposed to take advantage of the situation. As if there's enough room in there anyway, the way he sleeps like a big human X.

I don't think Ellie was an evil person. I think she was sick. My dad thinks so, too. He says she went through a lot of bad things, and took a wrong turn along the way. He says I shouldn't start distrusting people just because of what happened. He didn't have to tell me that. I knew that.

Sometimes I think of Max. I miss him a lot, even though I only knew him for a short while. Dad says he doesn't know if there's a heaven for animals, but that he doesn't see why not. He says if anybody deserves a heaven, it's dogs. I think so too. I think Max is in heaven. I think he's feeling pretty good right now. Maybe I'll find out someday. My dad says I shouldn't be in a hurry. Yeah, right, no kidding! Sometimes he can be dense.

Anyway, I have to go now. I hope you are happy. I am.
Love,
Teresa Dawson, Age 9. (My birthday was last week!)

Hope put the letter away. She approached Campbell from behind and put a hand on his shoulder.

"I think you did something pretty special. The world is a better place with Teresa in it."

He smiled and squeezed her hand.

In the first week of September, the bandages were cut from Shadow's eyes. No sooner had the protective funnel been removed from his throat, than he began to wag his tail.

In the car, on the way home from the vet, he lay with his head in Campbell's lap. His tail wagged unceasingly all the way back from Fergus Falls. By the time she pulled into the drive behind the cabin, Hope thought she might have a bruise from that damned tail.

Campbell and Shadow got out of the car. Campbell immediately clipped a leash to Shadow's collar.

"Where do you think you're going?"

"I'm going to take him for a walk."

Hope held her breath, then let it out. It was late afternoon. The sun was high, but the temperature was cool. She had goose bumps on her neck and shoulders.

With great difficulty, she made herself say, "Okay. But not for long. I'm getting dinner ready."

Campbell grinned. Shadow's tail wagged.

She watched them walk slowly down the trail, to the beach. Up at the cabin, she stood at the living room window, arms crossed over her breasts, and watched them on the beach.

They walked slowly, but without hesitation. They picked their way among rocks and sandy potholes as if they knew exactly where they were.

The blind leading the blind, she thought.

When Campbell suddenly laughed, she could hear it even from up here, and her eyes became moist.

Blind they might be. But sometimes, the only light you need

is the light that's on the inside, and both Shadow and Campbell had enough of that to last a lifetime.

She watched them a while longer, smiling to herself, and realized that she was the happiest she had been in her entire life.

Completely, supremely happy.

HORROR FROM PINNACLE . . .